*lover*

POPULAR

# TORN&
# BOUND
### DUET

*outsider*

*friend*

*antisocial*

STRAIGHT

USA TODAY BESTSELLING AUTHORS

# K WEBSTER
# NIKKI ASH

POPULAR

outsider

lover

antisocial

friend

STRAIGHT

# TORN APART

LABELS ARE FOR FILING. LABELS ARE FOR CLOTHING.
LABELS ARE NOT FOR PEOPLE.
-MARTINA NAVRATILOVA

# ONE

*Ashton*

"**I** can't believe you're making me play this."

Her cackle makes me smirk, even if she's forcing me to play the game with the worst graphics in history. Minecraft is the babysitter for grade school kids who are all jacked up on Mountain Dew when mommies and daddies around the world need a break.

It's not for people like us.

Real gamers.

"I'm going to build a cute pen here to house my sheep," she tells me. "If you're a good boy, I'll make you one too."

"I don't want sheep."

"Pigs?"

"I could lock *you* in my pen."

"You sayin' I'm a pig?"

We tear our attention from the train wreck graphics to look at each other. Mia's dark, sculpted eyebrow is popped up, trying and failing to give me hella attitude. She's anything but a pig. Guys practically trip all over their damn feet when she's around.

Straight guys.

I'm a little fucking crooked.

"Did you see the way you annihilated that pizza, MiMi?"

She groans, jerking her dark brown eyes back to the screen. "Pineapple is my weakness."

"Oink, oink," I tease.

A loud, unladylike snort escapes her, sending us both into a fit of laughter. For the fun of it, I start wrecking her dumbass pig pen because it's in the spot where I'm going to build a pool. She screeches, all kinds of pissed at me, and starts kicking me.

"What the fuck?" I groan, dodging her small but deadly socked feet. "Keep those weapons on your side of the couch, dickhead."

"You owe me a new pen!"

"Stay here with me tonight and I'll let you build ten pens."

She grows silent, darting her eyes over to me. "I already promised Sasha I'd go."

"I'm sure there are fifteen other girls just waiting to do Sasha's bidding. You don't even like them," I grumble.

"I do too," she argues. "Sasha is in my Humanities class. I know you think she's a snob, but I like her. She's been inviting me to a lot of stuff lately. She's just trying to be nice."

But we both know that's not true.

Sasha is the president for Delta Delta Delta. A gorgeous senior with a trust fund. The girl's family runs in the same circles as mine. Where our dads may associate, Sasha and I do not.

I'm not cool enough for her.

Which means Mia's not either.

But pledges are pledges, I guess, and Sasha is on a hunt for them.

We're too normal, Mia and me. Or unrefined. Maybe even a bit rebellious. We're certainly not the types who fit perfectly into a mold. It's what brought Mia and me together in the first place this past summer. She's my best friend, albeit by accident, but still my best friend.

"You're mad," Mia says, frowning. "Why are you mad?"

"I'm not mad." I'm so mad. Mad that she can't let this whole "I want to fit in" bullshit go. Of course she'll never admit that's why she's doing it. Her excuse is that she wants to make friends.

She has a friend.

Me.

The best one.

The only one.

I'm not a possessive bestie or anything.

"You're pouting," she says, her lips quirking up on one side. "For someone who claims to never pout, you sure do it a lot."

"I do not."

"Ask your dad. He'll agree with me."

"That's unfair. My dad loves you more than me. We're not asking him."

"Because it's true," she sings and then laughs. "Seriously. It's just a club. And if you weren't such an antisocial asshole, you could go with us. Sasha likes you."

Sasha tolerates me because my dad is the dean.

"Hmph."

"Come on," she chirps. "Enough pouting. Let's go next door and you can watch me get ready. Help me pick out something sexy. I might meet someone hot."

At this, I laugh. "You're asking me for outfit ideas?"

She skims over my worn Nirvana T-shirt and holey jeans. My face is sporting scruff because I can't be bothered to shave unless Dad rides my ass about it. And my mop of messy brown hair… Yeah, my style is a little too fucking grungy to be giving advice to others.

"Gay men know style," she tells me, grinning as she stands.

"That's some stereotypical shit right there. Sit your ass back down. I'm about to build that pig pen back up for you and stick you in it."

"Dick."

"Vagina."

We both laugh.

"Just come next door with me," she pleads. "I'll let you eat gummy bears."

Wicked woman taunting me with my favorite candy.

"I can't. Duty calls."

"You're going to go whack off to gay porn?"

"You're such a bitch," I say with a laugh. "No, asshole, I'm meeting some brainless hockey player. Needs answers for a test. Bad grades in a class and if he doesn't get them up, they won't let him play."

"Why is he coming to you and not the tutoring center?" she asks, her eyes narrowed in question. "You're not exactly the star student of Atlantic Pointe."

"I'm smart," I argue.

"Undeniably so." She grins. "But you skim by on your classes because you can. Not exactly tutor material."

My smile twists up into a devious one. "It's answers. Not tutoring."

"Again?" she asks in exasperation. "Your dad will kill you if he ever finds out."

"He won't." I shrug. "Besides, someone's gotta pay for your sugar habit around here."

A rap on the door has me hopping off my sofa and sauntering over to it. Mia grumbles from nearby as she slides on her shoes. Ignoring her, I open the door.

Fuck.

I hate athletes.

With a goddamn passion.

That's something I'll psychoanalyze one day, but for now, I chalk it up to the fact most are ridiculously hot but total assholes. This dude's no different. He got my name through the grapevine. Being the dean's son and pretty proficient with computers, I can get access to just about anything at this university I want to. He texted his coded request and I told him the price.

A hundred bucks and the test answers are his.

"Hey," he grunts out, not looking up from his phone.

He might be a dick, but I can appreciate when someone is fucking hot. This guy with raven-black hair styled in one of those obnoxious just-fucked ways stands at least a couple inches above my six-foot frame. But where I'm lean with muscle tone that comes from good genes and swimming, he's built from sheer hard work and frequent lifting. His shoulders are broad and sculpted, his fitted olive-colored Henley showcasing each curve of his form nicely. I sweep my gaze along his arms to his hand that grips his phone. Strong. Veiny.

Fuck.

Maybe I do need to watch some gay porn.

No sports shit either.

Just regular guys with regular hands jacking each other off.

I bet his hand is strong and those veins would pop with each move of his fist around my—

"You Ashton?" he grits out, a sneer on his perfectly carved face.

"Yup."

"Brayden."

I shrug. "Cool. Got my money?"

His dark eyes drift past me into my apartment. I've got a nice place. So what? It's all paid for by my generous daddy anyway. Insert huge fucking eye roll.

"You should give me a discount." His deep brown, almost black eyes lock on mine. "You don't seem to be hurting for money."

"And you must be pretty fucking dumb to jeopardize your hockey career over buying test answers from the dean's son but here we are." I don't back down when he steps forward, hostility rolling off him in waves. "Give me the money or leave. No sweat off my back."

Mia creeps up behind me. I know she's there because Brayden's gaze turns molten, greedily drinking in my beautiful friend. I'm used to it by now. Mia downplays her looks with her silly braids, sexy librarian glasses, and gamer shirts, but my girl cleans up well. I know for a fact when she goes out later, she'll be the hottest chick at that club. Fuckers like Brayden will buy her drinks and try to woo her into their beds. Unlucky for them, my girl is smart.

Guys like Brayden don't stand a chance.

"Hi," Mia greets, injecting friendliness into her tone. "I'm Mia."

"Brayden."

"You know there's a legitimate way to passing," she sasses. "It's a novel idea…"

"Oh yeah?" Brayden says, smirking. "What's that?"

"It's called studying."

He chuckles. "Right. So, you got my shit or what, bro?" His hard eyes land back on mine. "I have places to be."

Like starring in my fucking fantasies…

"I'm not your bro, *dude*." I turn on my heel, pushing past Mia, and saunter over to my bag. After yanking out the answers, I make my way back over to them.

Brayden has stepped over the threshold of my door and is peering down at her, wearing one of those confident grins guys like him so easily slap on when they're making a move on a chick.

Mia lifts her chin and gives him her nasty-ass attitude I love so much. "Sorry. Can't."

"I didn't even ask yet," Brayden says, his lips curling into a wolfish grin.

I try not to think about that same ravenous stare seconds before those lips wrap around my dick.

"The answer is no."

"But you want to say yes," Brayden tells her, undeterred. "They always eventually say yes."

"In English that translates to something really fucking rapey, man," I tell him, slapping the answer key against his ridiculously hard chest.

His features darken. "Rapey? Fuck you, bro."

"I'm not your bro."

He lifts his chin just so he can look down his nose at me. All that arrogance dripping off him is suffocating. I can be a bit of a masochist, though, because I willingly step closer just so I can have a little sniff of the way he smells. Asshole or not, he calls to the baser parts of me.

"I was flirting," Brayden explains. "That's what people like me do. Not sure what it is people like *you* do."

What the hell is that supposed to mean?

"Gay people can't flirt too?" I challenge, anger surging through me at his gall.

His dark lashes blink fast at my words. "What? No, man. I'm not a homophobe. I mean… forget it." He digs out a hundred-dollar bill and tosses it at me. It flutters to the ground and I make no move to pick it up.

"No, *dude*, please explain. My girl Mia here would like to know as well."

At least my bestie and I stand side by side as a solid force against this jock.

"A loser." Brayden curls his lip up in disdain. "A loser in desperate need of a haircut who lives off Daddy's money and sells test keys in order to stay relevant to his peers."

Fuck this guy.

I stalk up to him until our chests bump. Mia wisely stays back, but I feel the tension rippling from her. We're not confrontational people, she and I. There's just something about this guy that amps me up.

"You gonna hit me, *bro*?" He laughs.

I run my tongue across my bottom lip, loving how uncomfortable it makes him. He tenses, but the stubborn ass refuses to step back. "Do you *want* me to hit you?" I drop my voice a few octaves, letting the words roll through the air like tires on gravel. "I'm more of a lover than a fighter, though."

His dark eyes flash with fury and then the fucker storms away, sucking the air from my lungs with him.

"Don't come back," I call out. "I've met my asshole quota for the year."

With his test key clutched in one hand as he stalks away, he raises his muscular arm to flip me off.

Once he's gone, I step back into my apartment. "Sorry," I tell Mia. "He pissed me off."

She pats my chest and stands on her toes to press a kiss to my cheek. "That was completely warranted. If you weren't going to put him in his place, I absolutely was."

"All one hundred and twenty pounds of you?" I tease.

"I'm feisty," she sasses, cocking that hip of hers out to the side.

I'm annoyed some asshole is going to be all up on her tonight at the club. One day, she'll like one of those said assholes and then he'll have to start hanging out with us. Can't say I'm looking forward to that day.

"Bye, MiMi. Don't get roofied by dude bro Brayden."

She laughs all the way to her apartment next door. I've barely gotten my door closed when my phone starts ringing.

Britney Spears' "Oops!...I Did It Again" is blasting over and over, which only means Dad needs to have a word. And it's urgent.

Ignoring the incessant calling of my overbearing father, I walk into the kitchen and grab a Cherry Coke. After popping the tab, I make my way back over to the sofa. I kill the stupid game, hoping Mia's house doesn't save so we won't be forced to play again, and finally answer Dad.

"Yo," I grunt out and sip my sweet soda.

Annoyed silence screams through the line.

One.

Two.

Three.

"Ashton Elliot Carter."

"Yeah, Dad?"

He sighs heavily, already exhausted over our inevitable argument. Tonight, though, he bypasses the usual lecture and cuts to the chase. "You'll have a new roommate soon."

I bark out a laugh. "What?"

"Don't start," he grits out. "This is important. With it being well into the semester, the housing is limited and—"

"No," I snap, cutting him off. "I don't like people."

"Oh, please. I'm not in the mood for this today. Besides, you don't get a say in this. The new coach is starting and I don't have a place for him to stay."

"Wait a minute…"

"I know it's not ideal."

"Ideal? Dad, I don't want to share a space with a freaking old-ass coach. I don't even like sports."

"You like swimming," he counters.

"Not the same thing," I grumble. "This is lame."

"Maybe it is lame, and I agree. I don't want to subject him to this, but it's my only option."

*This* being me.

All my gayness that might be catching.

"When?"

"I'll let you know."

"I use that spare room for an office," I lie. "This is going to make studying harder."

"Ashton, we both know you don't study."

I smirk. "I hope he's okay with me walking around in my boxers. Is he hot? Does he like guys?"

"Just clean out the spare room and stop being a brat."

He hangs up on me. I laugh, knowing I hit a nerve. Dad hates when I throw it in his face that I'm gay. Before I came out to my family and friends at age fifteen, Dad had high hopes of me marrying some sweet rich girl. I sure ruined that dream he had for his only son.

I shoot out a text to Mia.

**Me: Dad just dropped a bomb on me.**

**Mia: Need me to cancel tonight and hang out?**

It'd be easy to play the needy best friend card. Unfortunately, I love Mia and I'm not some possessive friend who'll isolate her from her friends— even if they are prissy sorority princesses—just to keep her for myself.

**Me: Nah, just bring me chocolate donuts for breakfast.**

**Mia: How do you not weigh five hundred pounds?**

**Me: Cardio.**

**Mia: You do NOT do cardio.**

**Me: Sure I do. Naked cardio. It's a thing.**

**Mia: Getting ready now. Go do your naked cardio alone. See you in the morning.**

She sends some eye roll emojis but then ends it with a black heart.

I send her back some eggplant emojis and one of two guys kissing.

If only I really were getting some naked cardio in, that'd be great. But no. While Mia is off grinding on jocks with big dicks and tiny IQs, I'll be cleaning out my barely used office to please my father.

I can't wait to get the fuck out of college.

At least then, I won't be squirming under Dad's thumb twenty-four-fucking-seven.

# TWO

*Mia*

"**W**ow, Mia, don't you clean up well," Sasha says, her nasally voice hitting my ears like nails to a chalkboard. Cliché, I know. But then again, so is Sasha. Dressed in her black BCBG halter neck cut out dress and Saint Laurent heels, with her Tory Burch clutch, she screams affluence and class and unoriginality.

And I cringe at the fact that I even know who she's wearing, or that my outfit—a black Dolce & Gabbana minidress and Louboutin red sole pumps—costs triple what hers does. Sasha might come from a wealthy family, but in comparison to my movie star mother and award-winning surgeon father, her family are peasants, whereas my family is Hollywood royalty.

And again, the thought makes me internally recoil.

"Thanks," I say, plastering on a fake smile while wishing I were cuddled up with Ashton in his apartment playing video games, instead of at The Lodge, an upscale nightclub in Hawk's Landing, trying to fit in—something I've been trying and failing to do my entire life.

I'm matte in a glossy world.

Much to my mother's horror.

"I did the honor of ordering for everyone," Sasha announces, handing out pretentious looking drinks to everyone in our party. "Blackberry gin and tonic," she says. "Only the best for my girls."

Melina, Tori, and Jade, Sasha's resident ass-kissers, beam in delight, while I do my best not to roll my eyes. She ordered us drinks. She didn't cure world hunger. And really, gin and tonic? Can she be any more cliché?

I'm miserable already. Just like Ashton predicted. Sometimes I really hate how well he knows me. It's hard to hide from yourself when someone can always find you.

"To being us," Sasha yells over the music, raising her glass.

The cliché Sasha moments are plentiful tonight.

"To being us," the other girls echo, raising their glasses and then taking dainty sips of their drinks.

It takes all of my restraint not to throw back my entire drink, especially when it feels like the only way I'll ever make it through tonight is by being drunk.

The entire reason why I moved to Hawk's Landing was to get away from women like the ones I'm with, yet here I am, making friends with them and planning to join the sorority they belong to. Why? Because it doesn't matter how far I move to get out from under my parents' shadow, I can't help but want to make them proud. In this case, it means joining the elite sorority at Atlantic Pointe to impress them, especially Mom, but unlike her, I don't seem to fit in anywhere.

"Should we dance?" Jade suggests, glancing out onto the dance floor. Most of the people dancing appear to be at least ten years my senior, which makes sense since this club is an over twenty-one club, and the only reason I got in is because Sasha knows someone who knows someone.

"Jade," Sasha chides. "Please remember why we're here." She takes another delicate sip of her drink and sets it down, glaring her green eyes at her friend. "No respectable man is going to want to marry a woman who shakes her ass on the dance floor."

Inwardly, I sigh. Then I down my drink because as much as I'd like to be ladylike like my mom taught me to be, I need the alcohol more.

Sasha, of course, catches me in the act. "Respectable men don't like lushes either," she scolds.

Good thing I'm not looking for a respectable man, then—or really any man—I think but don't voice. The only man who has my attention is probably at home, either destroying my Minecraft house and killing all my pigs, or jacking off to gay porn—because he's gay. Yep, it would figure that the only man who really sees me and understands me swings the other way.

"Ma'am, the gentleman over there saw your glass is empty and ordered you another," a waitress says, handing me a new drink.

"Oh, Mia, it looks like you have an admirer." Jade giggles, nodding to her left. I follow her line of vision, landing on a guy leaning against the bar sipping on his whiskey.

His eyes meet mine, and the corners of his lips curl into a sexy smirk. It's not smarmy like that douche Brayden, but instead playful. Even from across the room, he exudes confidence, but it's clear he isn't cocky. He knows he's good-looking, but he isn't arrogant.

"He's cute," Sasha muses, envy and jealousy in her tone. Sasha's entire purpose in life, and her reason for going to college at the prestigious Atlantic Pointe University, one of the most elite and expensive colleges in Michigan, is to find a rich man who will take care of her, just like her daddy does. "And, if I'm not mistaken, wearing Ralph Lauren," she adds.

It's actually Tom Ford. I noticed the distinctive cut immediately, but I don't point that out. It would only raise questions I have no desire to answer. What Sasha sees is what she gets. I don't give any more than what it takes to fit in. I save the real me for Ashton.

The good-looking man raises his glass, silently letting me know the ball is in my court. I can raise mine back, thanking him for the drink, or—

"Mia," Tori hisses. "You better go over there before another woman claims him."

Without giving myself time to overthink this, I allow my feet to take me over to him. When I get closer, I notice his hair is dirty-blond, trimmed neatly on the sides and slightly longer on top. His eyes are a shockingly bright blue. And his watch that's peeking out from under his suit jacket is Vacheron Constantin, priced at twenty-five thousand dollars. I know that because my mother bought one for my father after he caught her cheating on him with her co-star and she needed to smooth things over. My heart squeezes at the thought of my dad. I haven't seen him in several months and I miss him like crazy.

"Thank you for the drink," I tell him, stepping into his space. I'm so out of my element here, but maybe this is just what I need—not a husband like Sasha and her posse are looking for, but a distraction, someone to make me stop thinking about my openly gay best friend who views me like he would his cute little sister, if he weren't an only child.

"It's my pleasure," he purrs, his smirk shifting into a breathtakingly beautiful smile. "I'm Drew." He extends his empty hand, and I give him mine.

"I'm Mia," I tell him as he raises our hands and stands, interlocking our fingers. His grip is firm and strong, his fingers long and thick, which makes me wonder if the saying is true about hands and feet and—

"Dance with me, Mia," he croons, stepping so close our bodies are flush against each other. My eyes glide up his tall frame. I'm five-foot-four with a few added inches thanks to my heels, and he's still a good head taller than me.

His eyes dance with lust, and I find myself nodding in agreement. He reaches for my still full drink, but before he can take it, I down it in one gulp, the burn of the alcohol giving me a false sense of confidence.

I set my drink on the bar top and then he guides us to a somewhat empty part of the dance floor. His arms wrap around my waist, and he grinds his body against mine to the music.

For the next couple hours Drew and I dance and drink and laugh. We don't talk about anything of consequence, and I'm okay with that. We simply have a good time.

And when we find our way to a darkened corner of the club and his mouth crashes against mine, his tongue delving between my parted lips, I push aside my need to fit in, my messed up family, and my attraction to my best friend, and allow myself to get lost in the moment, in the here and now.

I stay lost in the moment when he breaks the kiss and murmurs against my lips, "I have a room upstairs…" He leaves the statement hanging, but I know what he's trying to say.

"Let's go," I say in response, refusing to second-guess myself.

He entwines his hand in mine and pulls me down the hallway and up the stairs. There's a single door at the top and, after unlocking it, we enter. It's a small room, with only a single dresser on one side, a kitchenette on the other, and a queen-sized bed in the center.

"I just moved here," he says. "This is just temp—"

Before he can finish his sentence, I crash my mouth against his. I should probably care why he's staying here, or where he came from. But I know if I don't get us back to where we were a few minutes ago, I'm going to overthink things and chicken out.

His hands find my butt and he lifts me, carrying me over to his bed. When the backs of my knees hit the side of the mattress, he sets me back down and drags the straps of my dress halfway down my arms.

His eyes meet mine, silently asking for permission to continue. Instead of answering him with words, since I'm so nervous, I would probably squeak, I pull my cell phone and credit card out of the top of my bra and set them on the bedside table. Then, I reach behind me and, with trembling hands, unzip my dress slightly, so the straps fall the rest of the way down, exposing my lacy bra.

Drew must see the way my hands are trembling because he takes them both and brings them to his lips, softly kissing my knuckles. The act allows me to take a deep breath, telling myself I can do this. I can be with a man… It's what women my age do. They hook up, have one-night stands.

After kicking off my heels, I turn around and crawl up the middle of his bed. I should probably remove my dress, but I'm not ready yet. I've never been this brazen before, and I almost question if I'm making a fool out of myself, but when I glance back and see the smoldering look in Drew's eyes, it gives me the courage to keep going. He clearly likes what he sees.

I flip over onto my back and Drew is on me, spreading my thighs and kneeling between them. He palms the side of my face with his strong hand and our lips reunite, his body sinking against mine. He tastes like whiskey and bad decisions, and nothing has ever tasted better.

His lips leave my own and he trails kisses down my jawline and across my collarbone. When he gets to my breasts, he plucks them both out of their cups and wraps his warm lips around one of my hardened nipples. He sucks on it, and it feels as though an electrical current is zapping through my body, straight to my center. I had no idea it could feel this good. I lift my chest slightly, wanting him to continue, and he chuckles against my flesh.

While he laps and licks at my breasts, his hand slides down my body, landing at the apex of my thighs. His fingers trail along the seam of my panties and then dip in between my legs. I spread my thighs farther, assuming he's going to finger me, but instead he pulls them out and breaks our kiss. He brings his glistening wet fingers to his mouth and parts his lips. "Fuck, you taste good," he says, making a show of licking my arousal off his digits. "I think I'm going to need a better taste."

In response, my thighs clench in need. Grabbing the lapels of his jacket, I pull it off his shoulders. He understands my intentions and quickly strips out of his jacket and button-down shirt. His upper body is beautiful. All toned and muscular. He's got a perfect set of six-pack abs, and that delicious V women always talk about.

He drops his hands to either side of my face, and our mouths mold against each other. I dart my tongue out, moaning when I taste myself on him. He deepens our kiss as I find the button of his pants and undo them. My hands are shaky as I pull his dick out of the hole in his briefs and wrap my palm around his thick shaft. I've never felt a dick before. Eighteen years old and I've never been with a man like this. It's smooth and hard, and when my thumb runs along the top of it, it wets it with a sticky substance—pre-cum. I briefly wonder what it would taste like…

Drew drops to the side of me, kissing me and exploring my body, while I gently stroke his dick. I don't question where this is going, simply living in the moment, until my phone goes off with the theme song from Super Mario World, indicating that Ashton's calling.

And just like that, the wall I had built to separate myself from my reality crumbles. Standing on the other side is Ashton, my best friend. The man I have feelings for. My heart clenches behind my ribcage, making it hard to breathe. I can't do this. I can't have a one-night stand to try to rid myself of my feelings for Ashton. This isn't me. It's not who I am.

I'm not my mother, who's screwed every director, producer, and co-star straight to the top because she views sex as nothing more than a tool or a weapon to get what she wants. I might not have the same intentions, but it's still the same thing—I'm using him to bury my feelings for Ashton, and that's not okay.

Because I'm in love with my best friend, who doesn't feel the same way.

I push Drew away and shuffle off the bed, tucking my breasts back into my bra and quickly zipping up my dress. All the while Super Mario World sings from my phone.

"What's wrong?" Drew asks, sounding genuinely concerned and not pissed that I pulled the brakes on what we were about to do.

I slide my heels back on and then grab my phone and credit card, stuffing them back into my bra.

"I'm sorry," I say over the incessant ringing that won't stop. "I can't do this."

Before Drew can argue, I'm running out of the room and down the stairs. I don't bother to look for any of the girls, instead finding my way to the exit, where I call for an Uber. One is nearby and picks me up, bringing me back to my apartment.

The entire drive, my mind is running. I was attracted to Drew. We hit it off. He was sexy and sweet and had I not had the feelings for Ashton I have, we could've explored the chemistry that was apparent between us. But I do, and having sex with Drew isn't going to change that.

I get back to my apartment and am changing out of my dress when my phone rings again, the same ringtone as before.

"Hey, what's up?" I say, trying to sound casual. Between all the drinking

I did tonight and almost having sex, my heart is beating erratically and I'm slightly shaking.

"I heard you slam your door," Ashton says.

"Stalker much?" I joke, throwing on my vintage Zelda shirt Ashton bought me at a flea market over the summer and cotton shorts.

"You wish," he quips. "I was calling in case you needed an out."

"An out?" I step into the bathroom and start removing my contacts.

"Yeah, an excuse to ditch the mean girls and come home. I was fake emergency calling you. You're welcome."

I force out a laugh at the irony of his statement. "Thanks," I say dryly. Then, just to see how he'll react, and because the alcohol is still flowing through me and giving me false bravado, I add, "But you weren't saving me from the mean girls. I was with a guy." I grab a wet wipe and clean the makeup off my face.

Ashton clears his throat and I wish I were in front of him so I could see his facial expression.

"Were?" he questions.

"Yeah, you called and it ruined the moment." *And I realized how much I want my first time to be with someone I love and not someone I'm only physically attracted to and using to push you out of my thoughts.*

"Well, damn." He laughs. "Didn't mean to cockblock anyone. Who was the lucky… or in his case… unlucky guy?"

"No one you know." I slide my glasses onto my freshly-cleaned face and look in the mirror. It's as if I'm Cinderella and it's struck midnight, transforming me from a princess back into… well, me.

"Did you get his number?"

"What's with the twenty questions?" I ask, exasperated, ready to change the subject.

"Just doing my duty as your BFF."

I roll my eyes. "Your duty doesn't include girl talk." *And the last person I want to talk to about my non-existent sex life is you.*

"Does it include helping you build pig pens in Minecraft?"

"Thought you hated that game," I taunt.

"I fucking hate it, but I love you, MiMi, and you need cheering up."

My heart does a stupid little flutter that I ignore because he most definitely doesn't mean it in the way I want him to. "Fine."

"Fine," he mimics and then laughs. "Don't forget the goods."

"Sometimes I think you use me for my gummy bears."

"Oops. My bad. You weren't supposed to find out," he jokes. "Guess I'll have to find some other poor sap to mooch candy from."

"Be there in five, asshole."

"Door's always open, brat."

# THREE

*Brayden*

"Humor me," I grit out, glowering at Derek Holden, my backup center. "Just do it."

"Not our coach," he mutters as he stomps across the ice like a petulant toddler.

My right wing, Aaron Wexler, snorts. "Who pissed in your Cheerios, Holden? Was it Tiff? Did you two break up again?"

Holden ignores his taunting. "Fuck off, Wex."

I glide over to where our left wing, Nolan Finn, is waiting quietly. "Pretend he's me."

Holden makes a crude gesture of jacking off. "Am I doing it right?"

"When's Coach coming back?" Finn asks, worry lacing his tone.

Like a lot of us here, Finn is riding on a full athletic scholarship. It means he fought tooth and nail for a place on this team. Coach getting ball cancer really fucked up our senior year. Most of us were hoping to go pro, but without a coach after the season's already started, we're fucking doomed—especially since our assistant coach isn't worth a damn. In bigger colleges, they have several assistant coaches, but Atlantic Pointe is known for their academics not athletics.

Which is why I've stepped up in the interim. I'm team captain and that's my job. Well, they certainly don't pay me to, and no one sanctioned it, but I know these guys still need structure and guidance if we have any hope of taking home the championship.

"Soon," I lie. I don't fucking know if he's coming back. Last I heard from Coach's wife, Jessica, they were gearing up to remove one of his balls. I'm sure as fuck not passing that on to these guys. Talk about dampening someone's spirit. Talking about cutting off balls will do that to any guy.

"From the top," I bark out. "I'm going to drive down the center hard and with everything I've got. Try and stop me."

The guys are ready, and our goalie, Cordell Boswell, moves into position. Finn and Wex look at Holden, who's still being a bitch about following my orders today. He's always wanted to be team captain, but that shit won't ever happen as long as I'm around.

"Don't be lazy," I call out. "I want to see direct passes. No one rimming the puck. It's fucking amateur."

Wex snorts. "Like your mom, Holden."

Boswell hollers. "Hey, Holdy, I know better. Your mom wasn't lazy last night when she was moaning out my name!"

We all laugh because Boswell is a thick, black guy with no game whatsoever. Sure, he can guard the goal like no other and flirts with anyone with a vagina, but he never gets laid. Poor fucking guy.

"Make smart plays," I remind them. "Stop fucking around."

Everyone grows serious as I tap the puck with my Bauer Nexus ADV leftie stick. It cost almost four hundred dollars. I love this stick, but hated that Mom and Dad spent so much on it. My thoughts start to drift to my family, but I quickly push them back into their compartment. Feelings and shit have no place on the ice. If they did, I'd play like shit.

And I don't play like shit.

I eat fuckers like Holden for lunch. When he sees the vicious glint in my eyes, he groans. The next several minutes, I make my teammates work for it. Truth is, I carry this team. We all know it. They all talk a lot of crap, but at the end of the day, the Ice Hawks rely on me to help them win.

Boswell is on his game today. I can't get shit past that fucker. Makes me glad we're on the same team. Holden grows more and more aggressive. With each play, he gets more pissy until we're smashed against the boards, him snarling at me.

I'm about to lay his ass out when someone whistles.

"That's enough, Murphy."

My blood runs cold with unfiltered rage.

What the fuck is *he* doing here?

"Is that—" Wex starts, awe in his tone.

I cut him off as I push Holden away. "Why are you here, Thompson?"

The smug asshole is sitting in the box, a St. Louis Blues baseball cap on his head, watching us like he has every right to be here. He leans forward and nods at us.

"Looks like you're without a coach."

Unfuckingbelievable.

"He'll be back soon," I lie. "Leave."

Finn skates up beside me, nudging me. He's the calm to my fury, my closest friend on the team. "Chill, man."

They don't understand. No one does. To them, Thompson is a local hero—the one who got to go pro. To me, I see my ex-teammate from high school. The fucker who left me high and dry while I stayed back, forever known as second best. He went on to play for the Blues and was fucking good at it. Not sure why he's slumming it with us college kids.

I refuse to look him in the eyes. His puppy dog looks won't work. They haven't worked over the past four years, and they're not going to now.

"Brayden," he grinds out. "I can't leave. I'm here now."

This time, when I lift my gaze in confusion, I don't find his sad eyes. He's tilted his head down, letting the cap on his hat hide whatever storm is brewing. And there's a storm brewing. I've known him since we were kids. There was a time, before high school, I thought of him like a brother.

Those thoughts make me think of *my* brother, which really puts me in a bitchy mood.

"Couldn't hack it in the NHL?" I sneer, skating right up to the box.

My teammates are quiet. I know I can be a dick on the ice, but it's usually to the other team. Since most of these guys worship Thompson, they're probably feeling pretty awkward at my blatant disrespect.

"I left," he says, shrugging. "Now I'm here."

As much as I want to dig into him and demand to know why he'd up and leave to come coach these delinquents, I bite my tongue.

I don't care.

I don't care.

I don't fucking care.

"Whatever, man," I grumble. "We have this shit handled. You can crawl back to your fancy-ass house in St. Louis and leave us the fuck alone."

His jaw clenches, one of his familiar tells when he's pissed. In high school, I used to taunt the fuck out of him until I'd see that muscle tick. It's how I knew I'd pushed him over the edge. He's not a hothead like me. A master of controlling his anger. But once he loses it...

It proves pretty brutal on the ice.

It's why his nickname from high school—Destroyer—always seemed funny on the perfect golden boy with his one-dimpled grin. That was until he Hulked out and literally destroyed your ass. We've been known to throw down a time or two in our past, both of us bearing scars to prove it.

He stands and clears his throat. "Coach Garrison isn't coming back. I'm your coach now whether you like it or not. If you have a problem, you can ride your whiny ass on the bench for the next game."

Holden cackles like it's the funniest shit he's heard in his entire life. All it takes is a death glare from me to have him swallowing down his laughter.

Shoving past Holden, I storm across the ice toward the locker room. Thompson can fuck right off if he thinks I'll ever listen to him. I want to know why the hell he's here. There's a story behind his abrupt arrival, and I'll dig until I find out what it is.

I strip out of my skates and gear, beating everyone to the showers.

They're probably out there fangirling over our new ex-pro coach because when I finish my scalding hot shower, they're just making their way into the locker room.

Like a fucking douchebag, Thompson saunters over to Coach's old office and uses a key to let himself in. I quickly dry off before throwing on some sweats and a hoodie. Once I've stuffed my feet in some socks and my tennis shoes, I pull on a Hawks ball cap, flipping it backward to cover my messy wet hair. After my shit is put away, I tug my backpack on over my shoulders and make my way into his office.

A derisive snort leaves me when I see him sitting in Coach's chair, looking very much like a kid who's not supposed to be in Daddy's office. I cringe inwardly because even my inner joke isn't funny considering he lost his dad a few years ago.

"Why'd you leave?" I demand.

His lips press together and his nostrils flare. "Can we not do this right now?"

"That sounds familiar."

Hard eyes snap to mine. "What's that supposed to mean?"

"It means, you said the same fucking thing to me back then."

We have a silent, heated standoff. He remembers as well as I do. When I confronted him about him taking the offer to go pro. In high school, we weren't as close as we used to be, but it was always unspoken. We were supposed to go off to college, most likely separate ones so we could get the most play out of our positions, and then work our asses until we got drafted by the NHL. I always had these visions of us on the ice, him playing for the St. Louis Blues maybe, and me with the Michigan Wolves, the two of us showing the world how badass we were until one of us led our team to the top. Imagine my shock when he skipped ahead on our dream without me.

"Because you always do this," he grits out, keeping his tone low so the other teammates don't hear us arguing. "You fly off the fucking handle and don't let me reason with you."

"Abandoning your best friend is not reasoning. It's cruel." Familiar emotions from the past—back when everything was horrible—begin to resurface. No matter how hard I try to stuff the lid on them, they bubble over like boiling water in a pot.

He pinches the bridge of his nose. "We weren't best friends."

Even though his words are the truth, they still sting. Sure, we weren't close like we were, but our pact was an unspoken one. Our friendship was in a phase, because of me, but it would have eventually dug its way back out.

Only he didn't give it time.

He left me in that hole to go skate off into the motherfucking sunset without me.

"I'm sorry," he mutters. "That was mean."

I shake my head. "Nope. You're right. We were nothing. Not since…" My chest aches when I think about my brother Ben. "Whatever." Turning on my heel, I start for the door, eager to get the fuck out of here.

"Bray, wait."

I freeze, hating how young his voice sounds. Like when we were in middle school and he tried to comfort me when my heart was shredded to pieces.

"I just… this is my only place right now." He sighs. "I need this. I know you don't understand that, but I do. Please just let me do my job."

A sardonic chuckle lets loose. "You always thought you were better than me. Just skipped ahead of me with no warning. We were supposed to wait until after college and do that shit together. Instead, while you were playing for the NHL and getting adored on by your fucking groupies, I was here."

Heavy silence fills the air. He won't deny it because he knows I'm right. How in the hell am I supposed to respect him as a coach when I fucking hate him?

"It is what it is," I mutter. "Just stay out of my way. This is my team. You can pretend all you want that you're some badass coach because you played pro for a fucking minute, but we all know you're a washed-up has-been who couldn't cut it. Maybe if you'd waited until after college, you would've been better prepared."

I swallow down the bitter pill with his name on it and walk out the door.

He doesn't try to stop me because I'm right.

Finn is already dressing by the time I emerge from the office. His eyes assess me, worry shining in them. I flash him an arrogant grin and wait for him to gather his shit. Once he's ready, we head outside. Cold wind rushes around us, and I note as always Finn's underdressed. I yank out one of my many beanies and toss it at him.

"Keep that big head warm," I grunt out, shoving my hands into my hoodie pocket. "You hungry for tacos? I'm craving tacos."

Finn pulls the beanie down over his wet hair and grins. "When am I not hungry for tacos?"

We leave this bullshit day behind us, and my friend doesn't mention my pissy-ass attitude.

Unfortunately, tomorrow it starts all over again.

I'll be forced to face reality.

He's back.

# FOUR

*Ashton*

*S*hut up, Britney.

Her song plays over and over. Like a warning that the storm is coming. That storm comes in the form of size thirteen black Berluti calf leather loafers, a gray Emporio Armani wool suit, and a hazel-eyed glare fiery enough to melt glaciers.

Otherwise known as Dad.

He doesn't knock. Nope. Why would he? He owns not only my apartment, but the entire complex. This one and about three other complexes in Hawk's Landing, along with several lodges and entertainment venues. Dad may be the dean of Atlantic Pointe University, but that's not where he made his money. Between Mom's oil royalties and Dad's commercial real estate business, I was born with the silver spoon shoved up my ass.

"Oh, hey," I say, adopting a bored expression as Dad pushes through the front door with his phone pressed to his ear.

Britney stops singing from the coffee table the moment he cancels the call and shoves his phone in his pants pocket.

"Ashton," Dad rumbles, infecting the air with his overpoweringly expensive scent. "You should answer when I call."

"I was about to," I lie, "but then you walked in. What's up?"

I can't help but rile my father. It's a favorite pastime of mine. Mia says I'm an asshole, because for some lame ass reason, she likes the guy. I say I learned from the best.

Dad's nostrils flare, a clear indication of how pissed he is at me, but takes a calming breath. Our therapist—yeah, we're that fucked up in the Carter family—taught him that move. The only thing our therapist taught me was how to pretend everything is just fine so you can get the hell out of your situation quicker.

Which is exactly why I'm going to school for psychology, rather than business, much to Dad's horror. I want to actually help people like myself, not fail at it like so many have done for me.

"Andrew will be here soon and I'd like it if you'd at least pretend you respect me. This guy is going through a lot, and I want to be there for him." His dark brows furrow and his lips press together. "I don't ask much from you, son, but I need you to behave."

Wait…

He's serious.

"Why?" I ask, trying to contain my laugh of disbelief. "Since when are you the good Samaritan of Hawk's Landing? I thought everything revolved around money with you?"

Dad rolls his eyes, reminding me of myself. "Just don't make it weird for him."

"Weird…" I shrug. "Can't promise anything there. I mean, have you met me?"

As if he's just been reminded, he sweeps his gaze over my clothes. Earlier today, after a swim, I changed into a pair of old, holey jeans and a black vintage long-sleeved Led Zeppelin shirt. It's a usual outfit for me, but Dad hates when I'm slummin' it.

"I'd prefer it if you just stay out of his way and let him do what he came here to do," Dad grumbles. "And, you know… don't hit on him." His face burns crimson.

A snort escapes me. "Now I'm interested. How hot is he that you'd be worried I'd embarrass you by—"

Soft rapping on the open door has my words disappearing from my mouth.

Fuck.

I get it now.

Dad knows I have a type and this guy is absolutely it.

Tall, muscular, a fucking dimple.

I'm stunned stupid as I stare at Andrew's crooked grin, focusing for far too long on how nice and pink his lips are. Lips like those would taste pretty damn good, I can guarantee it.

Dad sighs upon seeing the look on my face. "Ashton, this is Andrew Thompson. He was the starting center for the St. Louis Blues. That's hockey in case you weren't familiar."

Andrew's eyebrow arches and a smirk plays at those sinful lips of his.

"Anyway," Dad continues. "He's been so gracious as to agree to fill Coach Garrison's place since he'll be out for the foreseeable future. I don't feel right about him staying in some cheap, filthy apartment above his friend's bar the whole semester until some housing opens up, so I've offered your spare room. He'll be within walking distance to the ice rink, which will be nice as well."

"Why'd you leave your hockey gig?" I blurt out.

The color drains from Andrew's tanned face and he drops his gaze to the floor, the bill of his Blues cap hiding his striking blue eyes from me. "I'm not at liberty to discuss." His gravelly voice has a hint of shame threading in his statement.

Interesting.

"Ashton," Dad hisses. "I've assured him, and even wrote it into his employment contract, that he's not required to discuss his reasons for leaving the NHL. The point is, we're incredibly happy to have him. It's an opportunity our hockey team has never had before."

Ahhh.

Now I get Dad's play with this guy.

Ex-hockey player to coach our university's hockey team means championships won and a potential way to recruit new players to go to school here. There's always an angle with my dad—one that has him smelling like a fucking rose.

"The room's all yours. It's technically a guest room, but I was using it to study," I tell Andrew. "I guess I'll have to work in my room until you leave."

Dad shakes his head at me. We both know I don't study, but he's not going to correct me on it in front of this guy. Dad has become the master of choosing his battles with me.

"Great. I appreciate it," Andrew says, tipping his head up to look at me. Goddamn, he's hot.

Blue eyes that are nearly electric with intensity. Lips that pout out just a bit but seem to be inclined to tip up in a smile. A neck corded with muscle and a lickable Adam's apple. His shoulders are broad like Brayden's—*the fact that I whacked off last night in the shower to that prick's image was regrettable*—so it must be a hockey player thing.

Maybe I *do* have a thing for athletes.

His navy-blue hoodie is stretched across his biceps, which makes me a little excited to see him take it off later. I'd been joking about me walking around in my boxers to fuck with Dad, but the truth is, I'd give my left nut just to see Andrew walk around with his shirt off.

I wonder if he's tatted.

I wonder if he has those sexy V muscles that point right to his dick.

I wonder what his naked ass looks like.

Turning my back, I walk down the hall, gesturing for him to follow me. With each step, heat burns down my spine. My dick is half hard in my jeans. I'm so fucked if this guy is going to live here with me. There's nothing worse than wanting someone who will never want you in return. Typically,

I can tell when a guy bats for the other team, or might even swing both ways, but this guy screams chick magnet to me.

"Here you go," I grunt as I stand in the doorway to the guest room, waving inside.

"Nice view." His deep voice rumbles its way right to my dick.

Since he's so solid, he has to turn slightly to get past me in the doorway. His arm brushes against my chest as he passes, and I get a lungful of his scent.

Soap.

He smells like soap.

Since when does soap smell like sinful happy endings?

As he inspects the small space, I try not to wonder if he showered before he came over. Did he jerk off in the shower? I bet he's fucking hung. Now that I'm thinking of his dick, I can't unthink it. Things grow more awkward when Dad walks over to me and clutches my shoulder.

"Thanks for doing this, Son."

Not like I had a choice.

"No problem," I mutter, unable to make my tongue work properly.

Andrew sets a bag down on the bed and then peeks out the window that does, in fact, have a good view of the pond. When it gets cold as shit, as it always does in Michigan, people ice skate on it.

Dad launches into some formalities with Andrew, and I bail. I'm headed for my kitchen, eager for some sort of distraction, when my favorite one peeks her head in.

"Hey, Ashy C."

"Hey, MiMi."

"The old dude here yet?" She waltzes in like she owns the place, nosily looking around for my new guest. "Does he smell like Bengay? I feel like all coaches smell like Bengay and disappointment."

My mood lifts at seeing her. She's cute today in two dark brown braids and no makeup on. A black baseball cap she stole out of my closet sits flipped backward on her head, and she's sporting her librarian black-rimmed glasses. She has the whole Super Mario look going on with her dark-wash overalls and a long-sleeved red thermal on. The black Doc Martens on her feet complete the look.

"He smells like soap," I reveal. "And he's fucking hot."

Her brown eyes widen. "Really? Where is he? I want to see. Is he gay?"

"No." I scrub my palm down over my face. "I fucking wish."

She frowns and walks over to me. "Are you okay? I don't ever see you frazzled. You're definitely frazzled over this guy. He's so hot he made you stupid?"

Laughing, I poke at her stomach. "So stupid I got a fucking boner in front of my dad."

"No way," she shrieks, and then giggles. "How mortifying! Still hard up?" She waggles her brows at me.

"Nope." I pop the P in the word. "Dad has always been great for being a buzzkill."

"Is your new roomie a gamer or like a total sports jock like Brayden?"

We both share a guilty look. Last night, after that dickhead left and she bailed on the sorority witches, she came over. For at least an hour, we discussed what a monster Brayden was. Then, we discussed how hot he was, both of us laughing over our fantasies of what we'd do to him if he weren't such a dick.

"Looks like a jock. Not sure about the rest. Don't ask him about why he left the NHL."

Her perfectly plucked brow hikes up her forehead. "Ohhh. Dirty little secret?"

"Something bad enough he wrote it into his contract here that he wouldn't discuss it."

"Wow," she says, emphasizing the word dramatically.

I can't help but notice she has on shiny lip gloss today. I mean, her lips are rounded, drawing my attention to them when normally I wouldn't even look. Thoughts of last night when she described how she would blow Brayden the Brat if he were cool come flooding to the front of my mind. It'd been funny when she mentioned it. Now, I can't stop thinking about her blowing Brayden.

Laughter has me tearing my gaze from her mouth. Andrew's laughter echoes through the apartment, waking my dick back up. Fuck. This guy is going to stress me the hell out.

Mia's eyes are wide when she glances down to the front of my jeans. Her cheeks turn crimson, which has me rubbing the back of my neck in embarrassment. For as much as we joked around last night with our dumb fantasies, I know better. Mia is a virgin, so seeing her best friend get a chub in the kitchen is probably mortifying to her.

"Sorry," I grumble.

She walks up to me and stands on her toes to kiss my cheek. "It's okay. I'll stand in front of you. Pretend to be your girl or something so he doesn't notice."

Chuckling, I pull her into my arms, her back against my chest, and rest my chin on her head. Dad walks out of the hallway and into the living room. When he sees Mia, he smiles genuinely.

"Hello, Mia. How are classes going?"

"Great, Curtis. *Hard*, but great." Her ass presses slightly up against me, and I refrain from tickling her for being a brat.

"This school is a challenging one, but the reward your degree will bring will be worth all the hard work. Keep my boy in line. See you soon, sweetheart." Then to me, he nods. "Thank you, Son."

We wave to him as he leaves. Andrew decides to come from his room to… I don't fucking know what. But he's walking our way, a one-dimpled grin on his stupidly gorgeous face.

"Don't look at his lips," I tease, bent to whisper against her ear. "You'll get the girl version of a boner."

She laughs but then it dies off as her body tenses. Andrew saunters into the kitchen, glancing over at the way we're hugging, before he blanches.

What the hell?

"Drew?" she croaks out.

By the look of horror on his face and the strange way Mia's behaving, I quickly connect the dots.

My call last night cockblocked my bestie from losing her virginity to my new roommate. The same roommate I have the world's most painful hard-on for.

Well, this is fucking lovely.

Andrew, *or Drew*, clears his throat as he pinches the bridge of his nose, clearly freaking the fuck out. Mia is still panicked it would seem based on her unusual silence. I remain quiet as I imagine them together. She'd told me about how she made out with him. They were alone in some room he was staying in, and things were getting heated. My call pulled the brakes on the whole event. She said she was glad because she wasn't ready to have sex with some stranger, though I sensed there was more to it.

What if he's a douchebag like Brayden?

Did he hurt her?

Is that what she's not telling me?

Possessiveness curls around my heart, and I hug Mia tighter to me. I'll find out what the fuck this guy did to have her bail and then to send her into a state of panic. Mia's my best friend and I'll be damned if I let some jock make her feel uncomfortable.

"Your dad gave me a key," Drew mutters, unable to look at us. "I need to drop by my office. See you later, man."

He doesn't acknowledge Mia.

Just fucking bails.

As soon as the door closes, I whirl Mia around and glower at her.

"Tell me everything and don't leave out a thing."

She frowns, looking down, but I capture her chin with my thumb and finger, lifting it back up so I can see her soft brown eyes.

"Mia," I rumble. "Did he hurt you?"

Her dark lashes blink several times in confusion. "W-What? No."

"Why are you being so weird?"

"I'm not," she murmurs. "Can we talk about this later? I just… let's go to my place and order dinner. I'm hungry."

I let it slide.

For now.

# FIVE

## *Drew*

Fuck. Fuck. Shit. Fuuuuuck.

Mia, the hot fucking chick I almost hooked up with last night at The Lodge, is a student. The same woman who was dressed in a skimpy little number with fuck-me heels, today is wearing goddamn pigtails, glasses, and overalls like she's a teenager, fresh out of high school.

Fuck, what if she's a freshman? What would that make her, eighteen?

Jesus. I had my fingers in her pussy last night. Tasted her sweet essence on my tongue. I had my lips wrapped around her perfect little pink nipples. And after she bolted, I jerked off in the shower, imagining that instead of her leaving, we finished what we started. I came all over the wall, pretending that my cock in my hand was in her warm, tight pussy.

Damn it, I can't fucking believe I almost hooked up with a student at the university I just got a job at. The university I have no doubt has a rule regarding employees not hooking up with the students.

That's what I get for trying to have one last night of fun before I'm forced to buckle down and behave like a grownup. I'm not a college student attending this university. I'm not here to party and get laid. I'm a coach. A respectable employee at a prestigious university, brought on to bring the team to a championship, so it can bring in more revenue. More revenue means more money in the university's pocket. Atlantic Pointe is known for its academic programs, but what they're lacking is their sports programs. Michigan is the hockey capital of the US, yet Atlantic Pointe has never even won regionals.

But that's about to change.

*As long as I don't almost dick down any more college students…*

After losing myself this last year, I'm so close to finally having hockey back in my life, and with a single, poor decision I could've destroyed it all. I need to be more careful, make better decisions. I can't risk losing hockey again. I need it in my life like one needs air to breathe. I've missed it this past year. The coldness of the rink, the smell of the ice, the crowd cheering, the teams battling it out. I miss waking up at 5:00 a.m. for practices, the adrenaline that comes with game days, and since playing is out of the question, the next best thing is coaching. And I'll be damned if I lose it over a hot brunette with a banging body.

Not happening. Ever.

Besides, if I'm not mistaken, it seemed like there was something going on between her and my new roommate, which in itself is confusing as fuck, since his dad—my new boss—told me his son is gay, before he assured me he would be on his best behavior and wouldn't hit on me.

I need to get this shit out of my head. Mia and I didn't hook up. Sure, she had her hand wrapped around my dick, and my mouth was feasting on her tits. But she stopped it, and while I was disappointed last night, now I feel like I should be thanking her.

Technically my contract didn't even begin until today, so I'm good. What I need to do is focus on my job, this team. And the first order of business is to get to know my players.

I make the trek across campus and over to the athletic department where my office is located. I saw it briefly this morning when I showed up to introduce myself to the guys, which didn't exactly go as planned.

I knew Brayden would be there. I've been following his college career the last three years and knew when I took this job he was the starting center. Deep down, I think it was part of why I took the job. A way to make shit right after it went so wrong. I had a hunch Brayden wouldn't welcome me with open arms, but I wasn't prepared for the outright hate and resentment he's clearly been holding onto all these years.

The shitty part is he's acting like what happened between us is all my fault. When the truth is, it takes two, and he's just as much to blame for what went down as I am, if not more so. I might've reacted badly, but it was in response to the shit he pulled.

Well, he's just going to have to get over it, because I'm here to win this fucking season and if he can't get on board with that, then he can sit his ass on the bench. I don't care how damn good he is.

I drop onto my chair and grab the stack of folders. Each player has a file that includes everything I need to know about them, from their physical and emotional health, to their academic history.

As a coach, my job is to not only lead the team to the championship, but to be their leader in all things.

"Good afternoon, Mr. Thompson," Denise, my new secretary, says from the doorway. She's a short, fit, brunette woman in her early fifties, whose husband is the athletic director here. According to what she told me this morning when I met her, she, her husband, and their children all went to school here.

"Please, call me Drew."

"Drew," she says sweetly. "Because Coach Garrison was having health problems he was a little behind on things." She walks over to my desk and hands me a stack of papers. "Before the first game, we have to confirm all the players have had their physicals and their grades meet the minimum requirements."

She flips through the pages from across my desk. "I've wrangled all the players and had them go to the team doctor to have their physicals updated. I've flagged any possible issues that need to be addressed."

"Thank you," I tell her, making a mental note to find out what kind of coffee and pastries she likes, so I can bring her some tomorrow as a thank you for going above and beyond.

"Of course," she says with a soft smile. "This stack here"—she points to the second packet of papers—"are the players' grades. We run bi-weekly progress reports and the top three are those who are at risk of becoming ineligible to play."

The top name gets my attention. I'm shocked he's failing two of his classes: English and American History. In high school his answer was to have all the girls who were drooling all over him to do his work for him. Guess he couldn't find any puck bunnies here to handle it for him.

Well, looks like I'm going to have to handle it for him.

I glance at the other two players. Both are struggling in their math classes.

"Can you call these gentleman in, please?" I glance at the clock. "Tell them I want to see them as soon as they're done with their classes for the day."

"Sure," Denise says.

I spend the next couple hours going through file after file, getting to know each player the best I can, so when we have our first official practice tomorrow, I'll be prepared.

Zack Ryan, one of the guys failing math, stops by and we discuss what he needs to bring his grade up. His girlfriend is a math major and is helping him. He assures me next progress report his grade will be up.

Jeffrey Franks, the other guy failing math, must know why he was called in, because when he walks through my office door, he hands me a tutoring appointment.

"Miss me already?" Brayden says dryly, when he steps halfway into my office. He's dressed casually in a royal blue collared shirt and jeans with an Ice Hawks ball cap on his head.

When I linger too long on his hat, memories of our past trying to push their way out from where I long ago buried them, he crosses his arms over his chest and glares his dark eyes at me. "Feel free to get to the point any time."

"Have a seat, please." I gesture toward the chair on the other side of my desk.

"I think I'll stand," he says, leaning against the doorframe.

I could play the coach card, threaten him to comply, but I know the way Brayden works and his stubbornness would have him quitting the team before he would bow down to me. So instead I go with a different approach.

"I'm concerned about your grades."

"Me and my grades aren't your concern." He juts his chin out and sucks his teeth. Something he always did when he wanted to appear like he didn't give a shit, but was really nervous.

"They are when they can mean you riding the bench instead of helping the team get our first win." I lock eyes with him, hoping he'll take what I'm saying seriously. This isn't about our past. This is about the game, and at the end of the day, here, we're on the same team.

"I'm not getting benched," he scoffs. "I am the damn team."

"Oh, yeah. Is that what your old coach led you to believe?" I counter. "Well, you better get that shit out of your head because I'm not him, and I'm not about to kiss your ass because you can hit a puck into a goal. For every one of you, there are ten more who can do the same thing you do, if not better."

I lean forward in my chair, keeping my gaze on his. "If your grades don't meet the minimum requirements, your ass will be warming that bench, and that's a promise."

Brayden shrugs like he doesn't give it shit, and even though I know better than to let him get me, it does.

"That's it? A fucking shrug? You're going to shrug on the bench when the scouts are watching Holden play instead of you? This is your last shot at getting drafted and you're going to fuck it up because you're too stubborn to admit you need help."

"Fuck you," he barks, losing his temper. "I'm handling it." He pushes off the doorjamb. "And if I did need help, you'd be the last person I would turn to. Learned that shit the hard way. Never fucking again."

"Bray—"

"No, don't you fuckin 'Bray' me." He stalks toward me, stopping directly in front of the desk. "You want to come up in here and play coach? Fine. But don't you dare call me *Bray* like we're still friends. We're not. We're nothing. And it's best you understand that now."

He slaps his palms onto my desk and leans in, so we're eye level. "I said I'll handle my shit and I will. Just like I've been handling it for the last three years while you were busy wasting a spot in the pros."

As he stalks out of my office, slamming my door behind him, I wonder if maybe coming here was a bad idea. But then I remember why I'm here—to make shit right and be able to have a piece of hockey in my life. Brayden might be pissed, but he's not going to do anything to fuck up his chances at being drafted, and he knows damn well the only way to get drafted is to play.

After telling Denise I'm going to take the files home, and that I'll see her in the morning, I grab takeout from the cafeteria and then head to my temporary home. After selling my house in St. Louis, I put all my stuff in storage, so all I have with me are some clothes and necessities. I want to make sure this gig will work out before I place roots. It's weird being back home, like I've come full circle, only this time around it's without everyone I love.

When I walk through the door, the living room is empty. I have no clue what Ashton's schedule is like, but my plan is to stay out of his way as much as possible. Hopefully an apartment will open up soon and then I can get out of here.

Grabbing a plate and silverware, I take my food to my new room and shut the door. I have a long night ahead of me. On top of still having the players' files to go through before tomorrow, I need to email Lou, the assistant coach, to ask him for the tapes and plays he was planning to go over. His wife went into early labor, so he'll be out until the end of the month. Which means, until then, I'm on own.

I'm not sure how long I'm at the desk working, but when I finally look up, it's dark outside. Needing a cup of coffee to get me through the rest of what I need to do, I head out to the kitchen to see if Ashton has any coffee, while making a mental note to pick up some groceries tomorrow.

I'm halfway down the hallway, when I hear two voices. One is Ashton's. I've only spoken to the guy once, but I can already recognize his sarcasm from a mile away. And the other voice is one I would recognize in my sleep. Curious as to why these guys, who seem like they'd never run in the same circles, would be conversing, I halt in place and listen.

"It's always been a hundred," Brayden barks. "Now you're fucking doubling it?"

"I'm calling it asshole inflation," Ashton says, humor in his voice. "You want the goods or not?"

There's a moment of silence and then Brayden grunts out, "Yeah, give me the fucking key."

Jesus fucking Christ, that's his way of *handling* it… buying the answers from the dean's son? What the hell have I gotten myself into?

"Now, now," Ashton taunts. "That's no way to speak to the man who holds your future in his hands. Didn't your mommy ever teach you that you catch more bees with honey than vinegar?"

I peek my head around the corner and see Brayden towering over Ashton, the veins on his neck busting at the seams. "Stop being a little bitch," Brayden says, handing Ashton two bills.

"You know, I think the price just went up to three hundred."

Brayden stalks up to Ashton until their chests bump, getting in his face. "And I think you're about to get your ass beat."

Before a fight between my roommate and my player breaks out in the living room, I step forward and clear my throat, making my presence known.

Brayden's gaze leaves Ashton and lands on me, at the same time Ashton swivels around.

"What do we have here?" I say, snatching the papers out of Ashton's hands. I thumb through the packet and sure enough, it's the answers to a quiz.

"None of your fucking business," Brayden barks.

"I'm making it my business." I smirk. "This isn't happening." I hold up the packet and rip it into two. "You want to pass, you do it the right way."

I turn to Ashton. "How will your dad feel to learn his son is selling answer keys?"

Ashton snorts, shrugging his fucking shoulders. The action reminds me of Brayden. They're about to throw down in the living room because they're surprisingly similar. But where Bray deflects with anger, Ashton acts as though he doesn't care—like consequences mean nothing.

But, unlucky for Ashton, I know Brayden.

Which means I got a pretty quick read on Ashton yesterday.

He hates his dad, but riles him up for attention. The guy would probably never in a million years admit that shit, but I see it for what it is. Rather than taunting him with what his dad might think, I switch gears.

"This shit you two are doing won't just hurt each other if found out," I say slowly. "It might hurt those around you. Dean Carter doesn't deserve that and neither do I."

They both come to the same understanding at the same time, which would be comical if I weren't annoyed as fuck with both of them. Before they can argue anymore, I tip my head at Ashton.

"You want to help Bray? Tutor him. He's failing in two subjects."

Brayden is already shaking his head. "Fuck no."

"Yeah… I should probably mention the fact that I'm not doing so hot either."

"Your dad said—" I start, but Ashton cuts me off.

"That I'm his incredibly smart and also handsome gay son?" Ashton offers, a bitter bite in his tone.

"He left out the handsome part," I deadpan.

Brayden laughs. "There you go. I'm fucked. Guess I'll have to figure it out on my own. Just like always."

I shake my head, pinning Brayden with a glare. "No, Ashton knows people. He'll hook you up with someone good. Right?"

"As long as she's hot," Brayden sneers.

Ashton's eyes gleam with wickedness. It's probably a good thing these two hate each other, because on the same team, they'd cause all sorts of shit for those around them.

"Mia. She's super smart."

"Mean hot girl Mia?" Brayden asks at the same time I say, "Student Mia?"

Ashton's hazel eyes sharpen as he smirks. "She's smarter than the three of us combined. Plus, she already knows what an asshole Brayden is. You won't have to worry about any funny business."

I'm not sure how I feel about that, but I'm backed into a corner.

"Fine," I grunt out. "Make it happen. And, Bray, if I catch you cheating again, I won't be so understanding next time."

"Good morning. As most of you already know, my name is Andrew Thompson, and since your coach had to take an unexpected leave for health reasons, I'll be taking over."

My gaze skates across the twenty-two players on the team who I'm now responsible for. Several of which I'm the same age as. But unlike me, who was drafted into the NHL at eighteen years old, most of these guys will never play anything past college hockey. Some are here on a scholarship so they can get an education. But for a few, like Brayden, hockey is their life, and this season is do or die for them. Their last chance to prove they have what it takes to make into the pros.

"From the tapes I've seen, you guys are good. Last year you made it to the Frozen Four. I've gone through and noted who has what strengths, but now I want to see it for myself. We need to get ready for our first game against Western Michigan. And every game counts. So we're going to work some drills, see what you're capable of, and then we'll go from there. I want you here every morning at five a.m. for workout and practice, and back in the gym every afternoon for another workout."

My eyes meet Brayden's, who's making it a point to keep his emotions in check. "Make sure you keep your grades up. I know Coach Garrison was letting shit slide because he was sick, but that won't happen with me. I'm doing everything by the book. If you aren't academically eligible to play, you won't play. If it becomes a thing, you'll be off the team. If you're here on scholarship, you'll lose it."

Brayden rolls his eyes, but I ignore him, continuing with my speech. "I've played hockey my entire life, including three years in the pros. I need you to trust me. Every decision I make may not be the popular one, but it's being done with one goal in mind. To get you guys to the end."

Brayden lets out a sarcastic snort that has all the guys looking at him.

"You have something you want to add?" I ask him.

He sneers. "I just think it's funny that we're being led by a guy who couldn't even make it three *full* seasons in the NHL. We're supposed to trust you to get us to a championship, yet when shit got tough, you bailed." He glares at me with what looks like resentment. "Trust is earned, Drew, and until you prove yourself, you can't expect any of us to trust you."

The guys murmur at his words, shocked that a player would blatantly disrespect a coach the way he is. I could accuse him of such, force him to skate laps, but I don't because it will only prove what he's trying to imply. So instead, I step closer to him and say to the team, "In case you didn't know, Bray and I have a history. Go way back. That was until he came here and I went to the pros, where I won two rings."

"And then quit halfway through the third season," Brayden adds. "How do we know you're not going to quit on us?"

His eyes are now filled with raw emotion and my heart cracks in my chest. I hurt the man in front of me. We had plans and I walked away. No, I ran. I ran from Brayden, from our friendship. He's right. Shit got rough and I quit, and now it looks like I quit the NHL, even though that's not completely true.

"You're right," I tell him. "I have to prove myself, and I'll work every day to do that. To earn your trust, but you're going to have to meet me halfway."

Brayden's and my eyes stay locked on each other for several seconds, and I think maybe he's going to come around and give me a chance. But then he breaks our stare.

"Whatever," he mutters. "Are we going to stand around here having a heart-to-heart like little girls, or are we going to actually practice?"

And with his words, it feels like we just took one step forward and two back.

# SIX

*Mia*

I glare down at my phone.

He's being weird. Ashton is a lot of things, but not usually weird. Something's up and the next time I see him face to face, I'm going to find out. I reread his text for the third time before replying.

Ashy C: I need you to tutor someone today. I owe you.

Me: Who? Why? Since when?

Ashy C: Are you studying to be a lawyer?

Me: No, dumbass. You know that.

Ashy C: Then stop cross-examining me.

I roll my eyes and huff.

Me: Come by and see me.

**Ashy C: Can't.**

**Me: Too busy ogling Drew?**

**Ashy C: Something like that. Dude bro will be by in twenty.**

My phone nearly drops out of my hand.

**Me: Twenty minutes? What the hell? Who is it? What subjects
am I helping with?**

**Ashy C: An athlete on academic probation. I REALLY owe you.
I'll rub your stinky feet next time I come over.**

**Me: You're in trouble.**

**Ashy C: You have no idea.**

I set my phone down and go back to typing my paper that's due at the
end of the week, when Sasha sits down in front of me. "Haven't seen you
since the other night at The Lodge."

"That's because you skipped class." I drop my gaze back to my work,
hoping she'll get the hint and go away.

"It's a waste of my time," she says. "I can pass that class in my sleep."

I make a noncommittal noise, focusing on my work.

"So, that guy from the other night…" she starts, and I hold my breath,
waiting for her to out me. "What happened?"

I release a harsh sigh of relief, thankful she's just being nosy and doesn't
actually know the guy I left with the other night is the same guy who's now
employed at Atlantic Pointe.

"Nothing." I shrug a shoulder, still refusing to give her my full attention. "We didn't really click… went our separate ways."

"Hmm…" she says, making me glance up at her. "Maybe *you* weren't
his type." She raises a single brow, and I mentally roll my eyes at her subtle
dig. Based on the way he was all over me, I would say I was *definitely* his type.

"Maybe not… Either way, nothing happened." *Lie.*

She eyes me curiously for a long moment. "We're throwing a party at
the house this weekend. Invite only…"

"We'll see," I tell her. "I have a lot of schoolwork to do." Her eyes widen in shock that I would dare turn her down, and I immediately regret my words, remembering why I'm doing this: so my parents won't be as disappointed in me as they already are.

"Okay," she says, standing. "Just keep in mind, invites like these don't come around often…" In other words, *if you don't show up, consider yourself out.*

"I know," I tell her, attempting to backtrack. "I'll try."

She huffs and then disappears, and I bring my attention back to my paper. I'm lost in concentration when Brayden drops into the seat next to me.

"Table's taken," I say, quickly glancing at him long enough to glare, so if he doesn't get my point—to go somewhere else—he'll understand by my facial expression.

"I know, by us."

"No, by me," I say slowly, continuing to type. "There are fifty tables in here. Find another one."

"Would be hard for you to tutor me if I'm sitting at another table," he quips.

It takes a second for his words to sink in, but once they do, my fingers freeze in place.

Athlete on academic probation.

Freaking Ashton.

I grab my phone and shoot him a quick text.

**Me: Foot rub? More like a full body massage! And not just one, several.**

I wait a second for him to respond, but of course he doesn't. Damn wuss. He's probably hiding out in his room playing his video games and eating the Sour Patch Kids I gave him. I make a mental note to hide all his candy from him.

**Me: Next time we hang out the only thing you're getting from me is fruit.**

"Did your bestie not tell you?" Brayden smirks, leaning closer to me. "He was a little busy eye-fucking his new roommate."

"Let's just get this over with," I say with a sigh, slamming my laptop closed a little too hard. "What subjects do you need help with?"

"English II and American History."

"Aren't you a senior?" I snort. "Those are lower level classes."

"Yeah, I suck at school," he says dryly. "But you already knew that since you've been there when I buy answers from Ashton."

"So, why aren't you buying them now?" Not that I agree with him cheating, but he clearly doesn't mind doing it. Why change up his plays this late in the game?

"The new meddling dick of a coach caught me buying and threatened to rat me out, leaving me no choice but to get help. Ashton volunteered you."

Of. Fucking. Course. He. Did.

I type out another text, even though I know he's not going to respond.

**Me: Forget fruit, your ass is getting vegetables from now on!**

"Look," Brayden says, encroaching on my personal space. "I was supposed to give Ashton two hundred bucks for the answers. How about I slide it your way instead, you can pull up the answers off the main server I know the tutors have access to, and I'll throw in dinner."

He shoots me a wink, and I fake gag, making him roll his eyes.

"One," I tell him slowly so he hears me. "Don't ever wink like that again. You look even more like a douche than you already do. Two, I would rather starve to death than go to dinner with you. And three, if you don't take back everything you just said about asking me to help you cheat, I'm going to get up and walk away, and you're going to fail. Then, you can kiss your NHL dreams goodbye because they won't even know you exist when you're sitting on the bench because you can't play."

My phone vibrates against the desk and I quickly snatch it up and hit answer, ready to bitch Ashton out for this shit. But when the feminine, whiny voice comes through, I do a double take at the caller ID.

Damn it! I just answered my mom's call. I'm completely blaming this on Ashton.

"Mia Lynn, are you there?" she says. "Hello? Mia, I'm a busy woman and—"

"Yes, Mom," I say, cutting her off. "Give me a second."

She huffs over the phone, mumbling something I block out.

"I need to take this," I say to Brayden. "When I get back, either be ready to work or be gone."

Without waiting for him to respond, I walk to the back of the tutoring center and out the back door, so I can talk above a whisper.

"Mother," I say once I'm outside. "To what do I owe the pleasure of this phone call?"

"Mia, how many times do I have to tell you that sarcasm is not a positive quality?"

"Hello, Mother," I say again, my voice extra peppy. "How are you?"

"Slightly better," she says. "I'm calling because you still haven't responded to any of my invites and I need to make proper arrangements. The deal was you could go to school where you wanted as long as you understood that when we need you here you come. You've been in Michigan since June and haven't come home once. You missed several charity galas, an awards show, and my birthday. If this is the way it's going to be, we're going to have to rethink you going to school out of state. I can't have my only daughter refusing to come home. It looks bad."

I chew the side of my cheek to stop myself from saying what I want to say. Like the fact that maybe if she actually wanted me home, I would be there. But the only reason she's making a big deal out of it is because me not attending those events makes her look bad—and God forbid Claire Voss-Lexington look bad. Or how about the fact that I'm eighteen years old, which means she has no say in where I go to school, especially since I'm here on an academic scholarship.

"I just paid your rent for the month," she says, making sure to throw the only thing she can in my face. My apartment. The only part that's not covered by my scholarship. "It would be a shame if it didn't get paid next month."

I bite back a dark laugh. How twisted is it that my mother has to threaten me in order to get me to come home? If only she would realize that I would give anything for her to actually *want* me there. I begged for her attention for years.

She wanted me to model, I modeled.

She wanted me to act, I acted.

I dressed how she wanted.

Behaved how she wanted.

Dated who she wanted.

But no matter what I did, I never came any closer to her actually loving me or wanting me. The only person she loves is herself. Which is why, when I turned eighteen, I ran. So I could start over, out from under her clutches, away from her coldness, and try to find somewhere I could call home. Too bad, no matter how far I run, she's still able to get to me, because deep down, all I want is for my mom to accept me and love me, and like the idiot I am, I keep hoping she'll one day do just that.

I should put a stop to it all right now, tell her I'm done. Cut her out of my life. I can take out a loan to pay for my apartment and necessities. But then I remember what would happen if I did that: I would lose my dad, and unlike my mom, he has a big heart—one that's too big. And the only way to keep him in my life is to deal with my mom. Because, for some crazy reason, my father is in love with my mother, and my biggest fear is that if I cut her out of my life, she would force him to choose between us, and he would choose her.

"Send me the invites again, please," I tell her, "and I'll make sure I'm there."

"Perfect," she coos. "I must be going now. I'm on set. Talk soon."

She hangs up, and I squeeze my fingers around my phone, wishing there was a punching bag nearby I could take my frustration out on. This week I might need more than my usual yoga classes. I might need to sign up for Krav Maga so I can let out some steam.

Pushing through the door, I head back inside, hoping Brayden will have taken the hint and left. Only, I not only find him sitting where I left him, but with him is Drew. Could this day get any worse?

Based on the matching scowls they're both sporting, they appear to be arguing. Then it hits me. Brayden's new coach caught him buying answers. Drew is the new coach. Ugh! Seriously? I must've done something horrible in a previous life to have the shitty karma I have.

As I walk over to them, I dart my eyes around to make sure Sasha isn't around. The last thing I need is for her to see Drew here with me.

"So, you decided to stay," I say, dropping back into my seat and doing my best to ignore the way Drew is eyeing me. He really is good-looking. And my God, the way he made my body hum by just simply touching me and kissing me… It's a shame he's a coach here… and I'm in love with someone else.

"Do I have a choice?" Brayden barks.

"You always have a choice," I snap back. "And if you aren't going to choose to be here, then I can't help you. You're obviously failing at least one of your damn classes, and it's going to take more than a quick mini study session to get you back to passing. So, make your choice."

"He's staying," Drew says for him, making me look his way. His tongue darts out and swipes along his bottom lip and thoughts of the other night come flooding back: the way our bodies fit against each other so perfectly, the scent of his body wash, the taste of his tongue when it was plunging into my mouth and then working its way down every inch of my flesh…

"Hol-y shit." Brayden laughs. "And here I thought you were a lesbian. You're totally crushing on this asshole."

"What?" I sputter.

"A lesbian," Brayden repeats. "I haven't seen you around with any guys. You hang out with Ashton, who's gay. You turned me down. It's not off base to assume you like girls."

I release a loud, unladylike snort at his twisted logic. "Let me get this straight. You thought because I didn't want to date an asshole jock and I choose to spend time with a man who's gay, I must be a lesbian?"

"And I haven't seen you around with any guys," he repeats.

"So, because I'm not a whore, I'm a lesbian?" I bark out a laugh that has the people around us glaring my way.

"I didn't say that," Brayden says. "I'm just shocked this guy is who you're attracted to."

"Trust me, she's not a lesbian," Drew says with a devilish smirk to Brayden, who's glaring daggers at Drew. "And it shouldn't surprise you. Women *always* choose me over you."

"One woman," Brayden argues. "And that was only because of your money."

"If that's what helps you sleep at night." Drew chuckles, crossing his muscular arms over his chest. I try and fail to ignore the veins popping out of his forearms. They did that the night we were together, when he climbed up my body and… Oh my God! I have to stop thinking about him!

"Who ended up with her after prom?" Brayden says.

"Only because I told her it wasn't happening. I left with Missy Jenkins. You were nothing more than her fallback guy." Drew's lips curl into a wicked smile, making his single dimple pop out. Mmm, what I wouldn't give to lick that dimple… Damn it, why does he have to be so freaking sexy? *Focus, Mia. Focus on the fact that he's the coach and is just as obnoxiously cocky as Brayden is.*

Wait a second… "Did you guys go to school together?" I ask, putting the pieces together from their verbal sparring match.

"Yeah," they both say at the same time.

Then Drew adds, "Brayden spent all four years chasing my leftovers. Looks like nothing has changed."

Leftovers. Like me? My blood boils at his insinuation.

The smug look on Drew's face says all Brayden needs to know to confirm this.

"You and Mia?" Brayden asks incredulously. "Seriously?"

Drew doesn't deny his words, just flashes Brayden a smirk that maddens me to no end.

I whip my head around to look at him. "We did *not* hook up, therefore I am not *leftovers*."

"Of course not." His blue eyes flash with heat from the memory.

I stand and start packing up my stuff so I don't do something like smack them both in the heads with my book.

"Where are you going?" Brayden says.

"To shower," I hiss, glowering at Drew, who now has the sense to look ashamed.

"Wait, Mia," Brayden calls out. "What about studying?"

"We'll have to reschedule. There's piss all over my leg and it stinks." I side-eye Drew before looking at Brayden. "If you want help, make an appointment at the front desk."

On the way out, I text Ashton.

**Me: You were on my shit list, but now I need my bestie so I can talk shit about the new shitheads on my shit list.**

**Ashy C: Bring Twizzlers and I'll dig out the Fireball. I talk better shit when I'm white-girl wasted.**

**Me: I'll be there in twenty.**

# SEVEN

I hear her bitching from the living room all the way in my shower. Chuckling to myself, I rinse the chlorine off and then hop out. I throw on some of my old swim team sweats and forgo a shirt. My hair is wet and messy, so I half-ass comb through it before heading into the living room to find Mia.

"MiMi's mad," I say, observing the way she slams packages of snacks onto the bar.

"Understatement, buddy. Big one."

"To my defense, Drew cornered me into it," I explain, holding up my hands.

She pulls a giant package of Twizzlers from her sack and then skims her gaze over to me. The anger bleeds from her. Surprise washes over her features, confusing me.

"What?"

"Nothing." She drops her head and fishes around in the bag. "Explain how he cornered you."

Shrugging, I saunter up to her, stealing the package of Twizzlers. "Threw out threats. Ultimatums. Guilt trips. I thought he'd be cool since he's my age and all, but turns out, he's better suited to be friends with Dad."

At this, she scoffs. "As if. If Curtis knew Drew was a manwhore, cocky asshole, he wouldn't have a job!"

"Ready to talk about what happened?"

"No."

"You're not leaving until you tell me," I explain as I walk past her into the kitchen.

"Guess I live here forever now," she grumbles.

"I'm sure Drew would love that." I flash her a deviant grin that earns me the middle finger.

"Fine. I'll tell you, but it's stupid. He's stupid. Brayden's stupid. Boys are stupid."

I lift a brow as I find two glass tumblers. "That's a lot of stupid for someone so smart."

"Tell me about it."

Ripping open the package of Twizzlers, I pull one out and tear it in two. Mia calls it crazy, I call it garnish. I drop one half into each glass before filling each glass up with an unhealthy amount of Fireball. Normally, she'd be all in my business, micromanaging my work, but this evening, she keeps her distance, which is weird as fuck.

"Call of Duty. Fireball. And you better start talking."

She shifts on her feet, her dark ponytail bouncing. When in public, she dresses like any other college girl, but when she comes here, she dresses like Mia. I smile as I take in her black Adidas slides over her white knee-high Five Nights at Freddy's socks. She's wearing a cheesy red hoodie that swallows her tiny self that reads, "Level 18 Complete." I'm sure she has booty shorts under there, but all I see are skinny legs and a whole bunch of attitude.

Her gaze is once again on my chest, which makes me feel uneasy. I know I eat a lot of junk, but I'm nowhere near getting a gut. Swimming daily ensures that.

Ignoring her weirdness, I grab our drinks, the bottle of Fireball, and nod at the bag of snacks. We make our way into the living room. As I set up the game, she huffs and puffs. I'm dying to know what has her so riled. By the time I head back to the sofa, she's already downed her drink and is pouring more.

Oh, fuck.

It reminds me of the night we met.

I start laughing, which makes her giggle.

"You're an idiot," she says, unable to stop smiling.

"Says the idiot who told a group of my guys that I was your boyfriend so they'd stop hitting on you at that party." I shrug. "Pretty idiotic if we're comparing notes."

Her brown eyes twinkle. "You went along with it. How was I supposed to know you were into guys?"

"MiMi, baby, I had my tongue down some guy's throat not five minutes before that."

She blushes and cackles. "I wasn't paying attention."

"Because you were fighting off the wolves."

"You were the closest guy who wasn't hitting on me. I just blurted it out without looking or thinking." She kicks off her slides and turns on the couch to shove her feet into my lap. "Rub. You owe me."

I laugh as I take her foot in my hand. "Aaron was so confused when I nodded in agreement. Fucking priceless. I made out with his *guy* cousin last year, so I'm sure he didn't know what to think."

"You have to admit, we were flawless," she says with pride in her tone. "Held hands and gazed lovingly into each other's eyes. It was a total soul mate moment."

"You did save me," I agree. "My date smelled like beef jerky. I'm not a fan of that shit."

"Which is why I didn't kiss you," she sasses, wiggling her toes in my grip. "I don't like beef jerky either."

"We sold those dudes, though," I marvel. "Thought I'd given up my crooked ways and went straight for the hottie freshman."

A strange look passes over her face. She tugs her foot out of my lap and grabs her controller. I catch up to her, gulping down the fiery Fireball, and then proceed to whip ass with her on Call of Duty. We play for an hour straight, drinking Fireball and talking shit to the people we're destroying on the game.

"You should play pissed more often," I tell her, my eyes glued to the screen. "You're like a thousand times better than usual. Who are you imagining you're killing?"

"Brayden and Drew."

"Brayden I get. I almost killed him before I sent him your way. But Drew? He has nice guy written all over his stupidly sexy face."

She huffs, pausing the game, and tosses her controller on the table. At some point during the game, she pulled off her corny hoodie and is now in a white cami that shows her black bra underneath. She is, in fact, wearing a pair of black bootie shorts like I figured.

"He was the guy as you probably guessed. I was reckless. Made out with him. Let him, um, touch me." Her face burns crimson. "I even tasted myself on him when we kissed after."

I blink at her, shocked at the sudden confession. Now that I know this guy, I imagine the whole scene. Mia dressed to kill as usual when she goes out, with fucking Drew between her thighs. I'm not entirely sure it's appropriate that blood rushes to my dick at that image.

"Oh."

Her dark brows furrow. "Oh?"

"What happened next?" My voice is raspy.

"I… I stroked his dick."

Holy. Fucking. Shit. The visual of Mia's hand wrapped around Drew's shaft is enough to make my dick hard as stone.

"And then what happened?" I croak out.

"You called, remember?"

"Yeah. I did that."

"It ended. It was a mistake. Then I saw him, he was a coach, blah, blah, blah."

"You saw him again today?" I ask, hating how my body heats just thinking about that sexy ass man.

"Showed up when I was dealing with your buddy Brayden."

"He's not my buddy."

"You'd be his fuck buddy if he swung that way," she argues.

"Irrelevant to this conversation."

"Admit it."

"I'd suck him so hard he'd forget how to play stupid-ass hockey. Fuck yeah, I'd be his fuck buddy. But get to the point, MiMi."

Her bottom lip juts out and for a second I think she might cry. They both might be hot as hell, but I'm not opposed to beating their asses if they hurt my girl.

"They know each other. Like, they have history. Used to be friends. I don't know… It was like they were trying to outdo each other. Over me." She gnaws on her bottom lip. "It pissed me off and embarrassed me."

Yep, I'm going to have to punch them both in the dicks.

"Come here," I grumble, pulling her to me for a hug. "Let's think about all the ways we can kill them."

She laughs, her breath hot against my bare chest. "I'd break all four kneecaps first of all."

"You don't even need a second of all after that horrifying first of all."

We both chuckle and then she tilts her head up to look at me. It makes me mad that they'd act like douchebags toward Mia. She's too sweet for people like them.

"Mom called."

"Ew. Mommy Dearest."

"Yep."

"What did the Queen of the Cunts want?"

"For me to attend some events."

"Need a stunningly gorgeous gay wingman to pretend to be your handsome boyfriend? I'm really good at that shit apparently. Just ask my best friend."

She grins and then her mouth is on mine. I'm surprised by the unexpected kiss. Her lips are pillow soft and she smells like candy Fireball deliciousness. When her hand creeps up my chest, her thumb brushing over my pierced nipple, I let out a groan. That small action gains her access. The moment her sweet tongue swipes across mine, I grab onto her ass, pulling her closer to taste more.

The alcohol is blurring reality for the moment.

Everything is confusing but feels really good.

How she's straddling me now, her fingers gripping my hair as she tries to dominate me with a kiss. I'm mesmerized by her round ass, squeezing it and pulling her across my dick. I've only ever kissed one girl. Eva Finch in the eighth grade. I'd been so grossed out, I swore off chicks for eternity.

Mia doesn't kiss like Eva.

Mia kisses with heat and need and purpose.

She dizzies me because this is not fucking normal for me.

Since I'm feeling drunk and curious, I skate my palm up her ribs, amused by the full-bodied shiver that runs through her. My palm roams over her breast and she gasps. I'm about to pull down the front of her cami to feel up my first female breast, when I hear keys at the door.

"Oh shit," she squeaks out, falling back to the other side of the couch.

I blink at her, embarrassed by the way my dick is tenting my sweats. What the fuck just happened? I kissed Mia. I fucking kissed Mia. She must see the shock, bordering on horror, because she buries her face in her palms. I'm still staring at her when I feel a presence looming over the back of the couch.

"Did I interrupt something?"

Drew's deep, husky voice does absolutely fucking nothing for my unruly dick, making it thump, drawing his attention and now Mia's.

"Yeah," I grit out, ignoring the fact that I'm hard as fuck and confused as hell. "Mia was telling me how you were being a fucking asshole to her. She's not some whore you can brag about."

His face pales. "I… It wasn't… Fuck, I'm sorry. It was stupid."

I snort as I grab the Twizzler out of my glass and start chomping on it. "Agreed. You know what you have to do." I shoot him a warning glare that has him dropping his head in shame.

"I'm sorry, Mia. Brayden just…" he trails off. "He pushes my buttons. I should have never used you as a weapon."

She sits primly, her chin lifted in the air.

"Not good enough," I say for her. "My girl here thinks you need to grovel some more. We're hungry. If you can't cook, I suggest you find us food. Stat. Mia hates green onions and I won't touch sushi with a ten-foot pole. Other than that, we're easy to please."

He remains there, quiet, until I restart the game. Mia joins in. Together we ignore him until he disappears to hopefully get us some fucking food.

As much as I want to shut off the game and ask Mia what the fuck just happened between us, I don't. Instead, I play the game with my best friend, pretending that we didn't just screw up and do something royally stupid.

Avoidance is my favorite game.

# EIGHT

## Drew

I can't get the scene I walked into out of my head. Mia's pouty pink lips, swollen like she'd been kissed good. I recognized the look because they were the same way the night we almost fucked. Her nipples were poking out of her tank top. A clear indication she was turned on.

Ashton's face and neck had a little pink hue to them, like he was flushed. He was sporting a tent under his pants that couldn't be explained by anything other than a hard-on.

All signs point to these two going at it before I walked in, which is really fucking weird since Ashton is gay. Maybe he plays for both teams. But if that's the case, and he and Mia have something going on, why did she allow my mouth on her and my fingers in her the other night? And why does it seem like Ashton might be fully aware and okay with that?

I should be in my room studying plays, but instead I'm going to get food. It was like Ashton tricked me into that shit. His mouth was moving and words were coming out and the next thing I knew, I was jumping into my truck to get them food as he demanded.

I stop at Olympia, my favorite Greek restaurant, and pick us each up a gyro with fries, making sure Mia's doesn't include any green onions, and then head back to the apartment.

This time when I walk in, they're on opposite ends of the couch, silently playing a video game I immediately recognize as Call of Duty.

"Got the food," I say, dropping the bag onto the center of the coffee table, knowing full well I'm blocking their view of playing.

"Damn it, I was killed," Ashton whines. "You better have included dessert in there," he says, dropping his controller next to him.

He rifles through the bag and nods. "Good job. We love Greek." He throws Mia a foil-wrapped gyro. "Don't we, MiMi?"

"Yeah," she says softly, catching it.

"I aim to please," I say sarcastically, grabbing my own, so I can take it to my room to work.

"Hey, man," Ashton calls out, "don't be like that. You bought, so the least we can do is repay you with our wildly entertaining personalities."

Since I've made an ass of myself where Mia's concerned, it's probably not a bad idea. Plus, they both seem eager for the distraction of whatever it is I interrupted.

"Do you guys do this often?" I ask as I sit down in the recliner beside the sofa. I motion with my gyro to the candy and alcohol stockpile on the coffee table.

"Pretty much." Ashton shrugs and inhales his gyro.

"How are you so…" I gesture at his body—cut abs, muscular shoulders, and solid biceps. "That."

Ashton grins, wide and infectious. "Thank you for noticing," he jokes. "Genetics. I'm naturally this hot. Have you seen my dad? My mom's the better looking of the two if you can imagine it. I think Marilyn Manson calls us the beautiful people."

"Oh God," Mia groans. "Look what you started."

I smirk as I unwrap my gyro. "Genetics, huh? Keep eating that shit and it'll catch up to you."

"He swims every day," Mia tattles, shooting him a look of exasperation. "He's on the swim team but…"

"But I'm on probation," Ashton finishes, polishing off his gyro and crumpling up the foil before tossing it at Mia.

It certainly explains his physique.

"Probation, huh? What happened?" I lift a brow at him in question before taking a bite.

His eyes drop to my mouth and I suddenly become self-conscious, hurrying to devour my food in a few short bites. Ashton watches me with blatant interest. This guy has to be bi to switch gears so quickly between the hottie beside him and now me.

"I got caught with weed in my bag. This dick licker, Travis, framed me." He shrugs, but I can see the anger that flashes in his eyes. "Since Mia takes fucking forever to eat, you can play with me."

He tosses me the controller. While I'm okay at this game, Ashton destroys at it.

"For a big boy, you sure do run like a girl," Ashton taunts. "Dude, where the fuck are you going? Follow me."

I grumble, trying to keep up with his hyper ass on the game. He just blows shit up left and right. Mia laughs every time I get shot, which I deserve. When I finally get killed, Mia leaps up, leans over Ashton, and snags the controller out of my hand. The hoodie she's now wearing slides up and exposes tiny black shorts that show off her pert ass, reminding me of the way she crawled across my bed in that tiny dress. It rode up her hips, showing just a hint of her ass cheeks. She was like a different woman at The Lodge: face full of makeup, no glasses… Here, she's just as sexy, but she's different, and it makes me wonder which Mia is the real Mia.

"You suck, Coach," she sasses. "Watch a girl kick ass."

I watch in amusement as the two trash talk each other hard. When Mia ends up getting Ashton killed because she wasn't covering him like he wanted, he tosses the controller and tackles her. She squeals as he tickles her ribs.

"Help! Drew! Help!"

I stand, earning a devilish grin from Ashton over his shoulder. As I approach—to do what? I don't fucking know—he turns on me. I grunt when he tackles me down into the recliner. The fucker is strong and pins me in the chair. Problem for him is I'm not ticklish. His fingers dig into me like he'd been doing to Mia, and when I laugh at his efforts, he stops to stare at my mouth.

My eyes drag down his bare chest, noting his red claw marks Mia gave him. It's awkward with him sitting on my lap, yet I don't push him away.

"His thighs," Mia chirps. "Get him, Drew."

Ashton starts to bail, but she's already tattled on what his weakness is. I grab onto his thighs, cracking up when he howls out obscenities at me. He busts his ass on the floor, scrambling to get away from me. When he's safe, Mia and I laugh at the way he breathes heavily from his back on the floor next to the coffee table.

"Anyone ever tell you that you suck at Call of Duty," Ashton says, his words breathless.

"Put on some hockey. I'll kick your ass then."

"Pass," Ashton says. "Hockey is boring."

Mia nods, agreeing with him.

"Are you for real?" My gaze darts between them both. "Have you ever even watched a game?"

When they both shake their heads, I scoff.

"Unbelievable. If I'm going to live here, you better believe your asses are getting schooled in the best sport in existence. Come to the game on Saturday night."

Ashton rolls his eyes. "The only hockey I'm interested in is naked hockey."

Mia giggles. "I mean, I'm interested in that too."

"Okay, horndogs," I grumble. "Hockey isn't played naked, but you get to see hot, sweaty guys fighting on the ice. Tell me that doesn't entice you a little."

"Maybe a little." Ashton flashes me a deviant grin. "You buying dinner afterward?"

Mia's brow is lifted, waiting on my answer.

"Uh, I guess," I mutter. "Again."

"We're in," Ashton says. "Under one condition."

"I can't wait to hear this," I deadpan.

Ashton's eyes glimmer with wickedness. "We get to cheer for the other team."

Oh give me a fucking break.

"I'm not cheering for Bratty Brayden," Mia agrees. "Take the deal, Coach."

"Nope. No deal."

Ashton's brows fly up. "What? Really?"

Mia frowns, her brown eyes darting between Ashton and me.

"Dinner after, but you have to cheer Bray on."

"Nah," Ashton grunts out. "We're busy."

"Whatever," I say as I stand. "I'm headed to bed."

They whisper as I walk away. I'm annoyed that they want to cheer against their own school. Not that Brayden deserves their cheering, but he certainly doesn't need someone actively rooting against him. He already does that enough to himself as it is.

"Fine. We'll take the deal."

Ashton's words soothe whatever burn that ignited only moments before. Brayden might be an asshole a lot of the time, but there'll always be a part of me that wants to protect him.

"Good answer," I grunt out and wave over my shoulder. "Night, kids."

"Seal the wall, Murphy! Seal the wall! Seal the damn wall!"

Brayden stops in his place and chucks his stick across the ice. He removes his helmet and then skates over to me, getting in my face. "I'm sealing the fucking wall!"

"You need to use your body more. Focus on blocking the pass coming up the boards."

"What the fuck does it look like I'm doing?" he argues, his face contorted in rage.

"It looks like you're having trouble trapping the puck with your stick," I explain, trying to keep my cool. I'm the coach. It's my job to guide. But right now Brayden isn't welcoming my guidance. "Try blocking with both feet."

"How about you try focusing on another fucking player instead of riding my ass."

The entire teams goes quiet, their attention moving to our argument. It's been like this for the last two hours of practice. Me, trying to run drills, and Brayden arguing every step of the way.

"Fine," I quip. "Holden, you're in. Murphy, sit down."

"You've got to be kidding me," Brayden barks, throwing his helmet and stepping closer to me, until our noses are almost touching. This close, I can smell his sweat mixed with his signature cologne he's been wearing for years. It reminds me of happier days, before shit got messed up and I lost everyone close to me, starting with Brayden.

"If you aren't going to be a team player, then your ass isn't going to play on this team," I tell him, needing to make it clear to the other guys this shit isn't going to fly. "Hit the shower. Practice is over for you."

"Fuck this," he says, skating away.

"Either come back tomorrow ready to play, or be prepared to watch from the bench."

He doesn't say a word, just skates off the ice and disappears.

The rest of the practice runs smoothly, but you can feel the tension in the air. Brayden and I can't continue like this. If something doesn't change, we can consider this season over before it even begins.

Figuring it's best to talk to him without the other guys there, I pull up his schedule and see he has classes in the morning and then his afternoon is free. The guys usually use that time to get a workout in. Maybe I can pull him aside so we can talk.

When I get to the rink, he's skating the ice with a couple other guys. Not wanting to interrupt, I have a seat and watch. Much like every time I've seen him practicing this week, he doesn't laugh or joke with the guys. He doesn't smile or say anything positive. He focuses on what he needs to do and keeps to himself. He's nothing like the guy I used to play hockey with before—

"Andrew Thompson, is that you?"

I glance up and find Brayden's dad standing over me. "Mr. Murphy." I stand and extend my hand. Growing up, I practically lived at the Murphys'. Even after everything went down with Brayden and me, they would still insist I come over for the holidays. After my dad passed away in high school, they went to the funeral. Mr. Murphy helped me handle everything legally, and Mrs. Murphy made sure I was situated at my grandmother's.

"Please, Son, it might've been a minute, but you're still family. Call me Tim."

"Tim, how are you?" We both have a seat, facing the ice.

"Okay," he says. "Keeping busy with the firm." Tim is a lawyer with a small law firm in town. He dedicates most of his time to helping those who can't afford representation. Brayden always complained his dad was a waste of a law degree. He could easily make more money, but he chose to use his license for good.

"How's Molly?"

"Still teaching at the preschool." He smiles lovingly at the mention of his wife. "Loves it."

"You come here to watch Brayden often?"

When we were younger, it was always Brayden's parents who were at our practices and games. Brayden's mom who would organize the end of the season parties. My dad would call from the road asking how it was going, fund whatever our team needed, but he was never hands-on, and because of that, I always envied Brayden and his family, wishing I had a piece of what they had.

"Not enough," Tim admits sadly. "It's been a while since he's come home, though. Isn't answering our calls. So I thought I would drop by, that way he couldn't ignore me. His mother is worried and asked me to drag him home for dinner." He sighs. "She misses him. We both do."

I nod, suddenly pissed at Brayden for the way he's acting toward his parents. Here he is with two parents who are alive and want to be a part of his life, and he's pushing them both away. Not that my dad wasn't a good dad. He was, but he was a young, single father in the NHL, which meant I was raised more by nannies than my own dad.

"I heard you were the new coach," Tim says, cutting me from the thoughts. "How's it going?"

"It's been… challenging." I scrub my hand over my scruffy face.

"I bet Brayden isn't making it any easier."

"Oh, uh, well… He's…"

Tim glances my way and smirks. "You don't have to try to cover for my son. I know how much of a pain in the ass he can be."

"Let's just say he isn't thrilled I'm here."

Tim nods in understanding. "Come to dinner tonight."

"Oh, I'm not sure—"

"Six o'clock," he adds, cutting me off. "Molly will be thrilled to see you again. It's been too long." Then he stands and exits before I can argue.

Well, okay then. I guess I'll be having dinner with the Murphys tonight.

# NINE

## Brayden

This is not happening.

Unbelievable.

"Your mother is going to be thrilled," Dad says, grinning. "See you at six."

After saying goodbye to my dad, I head for the showers. The guys joke around with me, but I'm not interested. I quickly shower and then dress. When I finish, I see Drew talking to Holden and one of the other guys. I want to ask him how the hell he managed to weasel his way into having dinner at my house, but I don't bother. It won't change anything, and I'm not about to give him the satisfaction of seeing me riled up.

I've got a few hours to kill until dinner, so I head over to the tutoring center. My grades aren't going to raise themselves.

I push into the building on a mission.

Mia.

These other nerds aren't going to be able to teach me shit. At least she's hot to look at. I find her helping a guy I recognize. He spends the entire half hour session eye-fucking her tits while I wait impatiently. It annoys me to the point I'm ready to drag him out of his chair, putting an end to his titty tutor time.

"Can I help you?" a girl with blond hair and a big nose asks. "You wanting to make an appointment?"

"I have one with Mia," I lie.

She scrunches her nose and taps away on her computer. "You're Brayden Murphy, right?"

"Yep." I flash her a smug grin. "You know me from hockey?"

"Yeah. Big fan here."

I glance at her to see if there's any interest there, but she does nothing for me. I just want to see Mia.

"Oh, shoot," the girl says. "There must be a mistake. She has Jordan Renshaw next."

"Emergency session. Coach said." I shrug. "I don't make the rules, I just follow them."

She frowns hard. "I guess I could move Jordan to later or I could help him."

"You're a doll," I say, flashing her a grin that gets me out of trouble often.

Her cheeks turn pink. "There. All done. You're next."

"Thanks, sweetheart." I wink at her and then saunter over to where Mia sits alone now. "Hey, gorgeous. Miss me?" I toss my bag on the ground.

"Yuck. No. Go away. I have an appointment right now."

I yank out the chair, flip it around backward, and straddle it. "Me."

She darts her eyes over to the big-nosed blonde and frowns. "Leighanne? Did Jordan cancel?"

"Coach said this session was urgent," Leighanne calls back. "Sorry to switch up on you like that. Is it okay?"

Mia starts to open her mouth, but I stop her with my words.

"Please, Mia," I mutter. "I'll behave."

Her brown eyes tear my way, locking on me in an oddly invasive way. I squirm a little under her intense stare. "You're serious?"

"I need to pass. I have to play."

"Okay." She chews on her glossy bottom lip and nods toward Leighanne. "Fine."

"I'm sorry for being an asshole. Drew brings out the best in me," I say, my tone dripping in sarcasm.

"Apology accepted."

"That easy?" I grin at her. "Usually I have to take a girl to dinner to get in her good graces again."

"This isn't a date, dummy."

"Isn't it against tutoring protocol to call your student a dummy?" I reach over and grab her phone. "But outside of tutor time, you could totally call me whatever the hell you want."

She rolls her eyes when I type my number into her phone. "Are you always this obnoxious?"

"Always."

"How do you even have friends?" she scoffs.

Her words sting, causing me to frown. "I have fans. That's better than friends."

Rather than coming off as a joke, it sounds bitter and defensive. Mia, unlike the dumb girls I associate with, narrows her eyes, studying me.

"If you tone the obnoxiousness down a few levels, I guess we can be friends, being that you already gave me your number and all."

"Friends with benefits?" I tease with a crooked grin.

She laughs, rather than getting pissed. "If the benefit is you bringing me Starbucks next time we meet for tutoring, then sure."

I think she might be flirting with me, but it's hard to tell with this girl. I'm not going to push her away now that she's tolerating me, so I simply smile at her.

"Teach me your ways, oh wise one."

"This is going to take a while."

"Are you saying I'm a dummy... again?"

Her smirk is saucy and cute as fuck. "Nope. I'm saying I'm smart as hell. Hope you're fast because you'll have a lot of work to do to catch up to me."

"Sounds like a challenge," I say, lifting a brow.

"If that's what it takes to get you to pay attention and work, then it was. Now stop flirting and focus."

"Yes, ma'am."

"And don't say that. Makes you sound pervy."

"But I *am* pervy."

"Brayden!" She giggles, earning annoyed glares from several people around us.

"Sorry. On my best behavior starting now."

And, for once, I actually try to be good.

I need hockey.

It's the only thing I have. I'll be damned if I let a couple of bad grades stand in the way of that.

Seeing Drew's brand-new black Chevy Silverado parked in my parents' driveway makes my stomach twist into a knot. Why the hell did he agree to come to dinner when he knows we can't stand the sight of each other? Now, I'll have to pretend to be amicable for Mom and Dad.

It's all I do for them.

Pretend.

Which is why I avoid them so much. When I'm not around them, I can be a prick and no one cares. If I'm a prick at home, Mom gets worried. Dad gets disappointed. They try to fix me.

I'm unfixable.

I park my old-ass Tahoe behind his truck and climb out. He's sitting on the open bed of his truck, waiting for me. Instead of wearing a hat, like usual, he's dressed nicely for dinner. It would've been better if he'd just gone inside, rather than sat out here waiting.

"Hey," he greets, shuddering against the chilly wind that's messing up his gelled hair.

It's too cold out here to be wearing a fucking Henley and no jacket. I yank out a beanie from my hoodie pocket and toss it at him. Like old times. Fuck. He frowns at the beanie, but then pulls it on over his head.

I have to look away.

Too many painful memories claw at me.

"Why are you out here?" I growl.

"I just wanted to talk before we go inside. Are you okay with me being here?"

I snap my glare to pin him with it. "Peachy."

"Bray—"

"Next time, just go the fuck inside. Don't wait on me."

His footsteps thud heavily behind me as I stalk across the lawn. Before I reach the door, I suck in a calming breath. I'm not prepared to be here tonight. Everything is too brittle.

Drew clutches my shoulder, the heat of his hand warming me, making me forget for a moment what I'm stressed about. But the second I come to my senses, realizing who the hand belongs to, I shake it away and walk inside.

Lasagna.

Yum.

I may not be emotionally prepared to see my parents tonight, but my stomach whines happily. Mom's cooking is better than anything in this world. For as close as they live to the university, I could have home-cooked meals every night.

Instead, I'm a surly asshole who'd rather eat microwavable ramen than face his parents on a frequent basis.

"Bray, baby, is that you?" Mom calls out.

She peeks her head out of the kitchen into the living room. When she sees us, she cries out happily, rushing over to me for a hug. I inhale my mom's familiar scent and reluctantly release her so she can hug Drew. He hugs her tight, closing his eyes with unmasked joy. It annoys me I have to share her with him.

Guilt knocks me in the gut.

I'm such an asshole.

Drew and I may hate each other, but he has no one when it comes to family. Not anymore. My parents are the closest thing he has.

He had me, too, at one time.

Not anymore.

"Lasagna smells good," I praise. "Where's Dad?"

"We got a chimenea," she says. "He's getting it ready so later we can sit on the back patio. It's a nice way to unwind."

Drew follows Mom into the kitchen. I head out to see Dad. He's squatted in front of the chimenea, his ass crack showing out of the back of his pants.

"Full moon tonight, Dad," I tease, nudging his ass with my foot.

He snorts. "Don't pick on old men."

"You're not old," I grumble.

"I feel it," he says, huffing as he stands.

Pride warms me to see him wearing the Ice Hawks beanie I gave him the last time I saw him. It's pulled down over his ears, keeping him warm.

"You okay?" he asks. "With Drew being here?"

I freeze. "Yeah. Why?"

His lips press together in a firm line. I shift my gaze to the ground, avoiding his unpeeling of my outer layers I've wrapped myself up in.

"I know you and Drew aren't on the best terms. But you know life's too short to stay mad at your friends," he says softly.

Each word is a blow to my fucking heart.

Life's short, all right.

For some, nine years is all they get.

"I'm gonna take a walk," I grit out.

"No," Dad blurts out, panic in his tone. "Stay. I'm sorry. I'm prying. Just come inside. Mom misses ya, Son."

Guilt wins this round. Rather than running away like I crave to, I nod at Dad and follow him inside. Mom has already put Drew to work, making him set the table. He smiles at her as he moves around the dining table as though he lives here.

At one time, he practically did.

He catches my stare and his gaze softens. I stiffen, dragging my eyes to the bubbling lasagna. Ben's favorite. Fuck. Emotion is clawing up my chest, shredding my heart to pieces. A lump sits heavy in my throat. I'm unable to shake this feeling away. Having Drew here makes it worse.

I manage to plant myself in my chair. Mom says grace and I close my eyes, hating how my eyes burn when she mentions my brother. My teeth hurt from clenching them so hard. She finishes the prayer and I reluctantly open my lids.

Of course Drew's eyes are locked on mine, darting back and forth as he takes in my now wet lashes. He starts talking about his new job and how some of the players need a swift kick to the ass. It does wonders to drag me away from the pain, right into the fiery zone of anger.

I let him guide the conversation, thankful to have my parents' attention on him, rather than myself.

"I don't think we ever heard the story as to why you left the NHL," Mom pries. "Everything okay, honey?"

This time, Drew freezes.

Instead of saving him, I dissect his emotions.

Regret. Sadness. Despair.

Not shame.

What the hell happened?

"I, uh, I…" Drew darts his eyes my way, begging for help.

"Did you make brownies?" I ask Mom, saving the bastard at the last second. "Coach said I need to put on some weight."

She blinks a few times, realizing she's been sidelined, and then moves along to the next topic of conversation. "Brownies for my boys. Of course. Your dad even picked up some vanilla bean ice cream to put on top."

From there, we talk about their jobs and how Dad has been busier than usual lately. The conversation stays in a safe area. By the time dessert rolls around, and I'm officially stuffed, I realize we've dodged the hardest topic. Thank fuck.

"I'll clean up," I tell Mom. "Enjoy your fire and wine."

Dad waggles his eyebrows at Mom and they escape to the back with a bottle. Drew, unfortunately, follows me into the kitchen. We work silently to clean up dinner. I've barely tossed the last dish into the dishwasher and started it when he clears his throat.

"Bray…"

"Don't start."

He crowds me from behind, forcing me to turn around. "Are you okay?"

I hate the way he looks at me.

Like he fucking cares.

"I said don't start," I snap, shoving his massive chest.

He doesn't budge much, which really pisses me off. "You're upset—"

"You don't know what I am." I bump his chest with mine, snarling in his face. "Stop trying to act like you do."

"You've always been like a brother to me," he utters.

My rage bubbles over. I fist his Henley and charge him back, slamming him against the bar. His face twists into a furious scowl, and he tries to shake me away to no avail.

"We are *not* fucking family," I hiss.

"Try telling your parents that."

The smug bastard grins at me.

This is what we do. I rage and he pushes my fucking buttons.

But tonight, I'm tired.

Emotionally drained.

Releasing him, I turn and walk out of the kitchen.

"Bray!"

Ignoring him, I make my way outside and give my parents a hug goodbye. I head back inside, pretending he doesn't exist, and take off toward my Tahoe. He calls out for me the whole time. I've barely made it to my vehicle before he's on me.

With a growl, he grabs hold of me, spinning me and pushing me against my vehicle.

"Let go of me," I seethe.

"Not until you calm the fuck down and talk to me." His voice drops and he licks his lips. "Please."

I hate that my eyes track the movement of his tongue.

Hate that I'm staring at his stupid lips.

His lips are part of his goddamn problem.

"See you at practice, Coach." I clench my jaw, leveling him with a bored look.

Defeat—something I'm unfamiliar with when it comes to Drew—shines in his blue eyes. "Yeah, man. See you tomorrow."

He steps back, yanking my beanie off his head, offering it to me.

I don't take it, just glare at it as though he's trying to hand me a snake.

"Bray," he murmurs. "Take it."

"It's cold."

We share a pained look.

And then I leave his annoying ass.

# TEN

*Mia*

**Me: We need to talk about what happened the other night.**

Ugh, too formal.
Delete.

**Me: I really enjoyed what happened the other night. Did you?**

I cringe at my words. What am I, five? *Do you like me, Ashton? Check yes or no.*
Delete.

It's going on two days since Ashton and I made out on the couch in his living room and I can't get what happened between us off my mind. The way his strong lips felt curved around mine, how masculine yet gentle his hands were as they roamed over my body. The intoxicating taste of the Fireball and Twizzlers on his tongue. My body heats at just the thought of where things would've gone had Drew not walked in and interrupted. I always thought my feelings for Ashton were one-sided, but that night, the way he was all over me felt anything but one-sided. It felt right. Like we fit perfectly together.

I know there's a good chance it was the alcohol making the decisions for him, and he most likely regrets the kiss ever happened, but a part of me is hoping he'll want to do it again. Not that I'm going to get my hopes up. Everyone knows how this type of story plays out: straight girl falls for gay best friend, thinking she'll be the one to get him to switch teams, only to be let down when he makes it clear he's gay and not even his best friend can change that.

Which is probably why Ashton hasn't called or texted me since. He's trying to figure out how to let me down gently. I should just text him now and get this over with. Tell him it was a mistake before he beats me to the punch.

I start to type out another text when my phone rings in my hand. I jump at the sound, almost dropping it. Not Ashton. My dad. Great.

"Hello."

"There's my Mama Mia," Dad says, laughter in his voice. My heart clenches at his nickname for me. My dad's side of the family is Italian and growing up I loved to cook pizza with my grandmother. Every time we could make it, my dad would yell out, "Mama Mia, bring me my pizzeria."

It drove Mom nuts, which is probably why I loved it even more.

"How are you?" he asks. "How's school?"

"I'm good. School's keeping me busy. I love my English class, and I'm taking History of Film, which is really cool. I'm also working at the tutoring center."

"So, you're still set on becoming a screenwriter?" he asks, trying not to sound disappointed.

"I am. You know it's my passion."

Dad sighs in frustration. He hates the film industry, and I can't blame him. But I refuse to let my mother ruin what I want for my future. I want to write screenplays—be the person who turns books into movies. Dad wants me to stay as far away from the film industry as possible, which is why the one and only time he stood up to my mom was to side with me wanting to go to Atlantic Pointe in Michigan. I think he was hoping if he could get me far enough away from Hollywood, I would change my mind. It's not happening.

"Why couldn't your passion be to save lives?" he half-jokes. I know a part of him was hoping I would follow in his footsteps, and many days I wish I could, but I love writing and I can't imagine doing anything else. When I was in high school, in film class, I wrote a script and the students had to turn it into a mini-film. There's no greater feeling than when your words come to life on the big screen.

"I'll leave the lifesaving to you."

There's a pause of silence, and I take a deep breath, mentally preparing myself for what's about to come next.

"I heard your mother called you," he says, his tone turning apologetic. And there it is. The real reason for his call. "I'm so sorry, sweetie."

A lump of emotion fills my throat. I hate that Dad feels he has to apologize for the way Mom acts. He's been doing it for years. Cleaning up after her messes.

"She threatened to not pay my rent."

Dad sighs. "Only if you don't come home."

Of course he defends her. Justifies her actions. God forbid he stand up for his own daughter. Tell his wife the way she's acting is wrong. He has his own money. He doesn't need my mom, yet he stays with her and lets her make all the decisions. When he offered to pay for my apartment, after I found out the dorms were full and I would have to be put on a waitlist, I was so grateful. The last thing I want is to graduate in debt, and apartments aren't cheap. I should've known that nothing in life is free. Everything comes at a cost, one way or another. And my parents paying for my apartment means, even though I'm over twenty-two hundred miles away from them, I'm indebted to them, and in my mother's eyes, that means she still owns me.

"I shouldn't have to be threatened to come home," I argue. "I have school and tutoring. I'm taking a writing workshop. I don't have time to fly back and forth to attend some stupid charity functions and award shows, just to put on a fake front."

Tears prick my eyes at the thought of having to go home and deal with my mom. I thought maybe with the distance between us, it would make her miss me, accept me the way I am. Maybe even love me. What's that saying? Absence makes the heart grow fonder? Not in her case. I swear the distance has made her even meaner and nastier. The only difference is I can ignore her calls from here.

"Mia, please," Dad pleads. "She's very upset and has a movie she needs to finish. She can't be stressed right now. I've booked your flight and will email you the itinerary. All you have to do is get on the plane."

"What if I don't want to?" I blurt out, shocking myself. I never go against my parents. I've managed to avoid going home these last few months, but I haven't outright refused.

"You don't have a choice," Dad says matter-of-factly. "Not if you want to keep attending Atlantic Pointe."

"I could take out a loan," I boldly threaten.

"The apartment alone would cost you twenty-five thousand a year," Dad says. "Plus electric and water and cable. And that's if you get approved. Do you really hate your home that much?"

"Not my home," I murmur. "*Her.*"

I close my eyes and fight the tears that are threatening to spill. He knows the way she's treated me over the years, the effects her treatment has had on me. He knows why I ran and why the last thing I want to do is come home. Yet here he is, trying to guilt me into coming home for her.

"Mia, she doesn't mean—"

"No!" I bark out. "Don't you dare tell me she doesn't mean to do the shit she does. That's a lie and you know it. You want to stay with her, fine, but don't ever try to defend everything she's done to me. You offered to pay for my apartment and now she's threatening to take it away. This always happens."

"I'm sorry." He sighs.

"Yeah, you're always sorry." The tears escape and race down my cheeks. "I need to go."

"Mia, please."

"Don't worry, Dad. I'll be there," I say, then hang up the phone. It immediately rings, and I switch it to silent, done with this conversation.

Needing to momentarily forget everything, I grab a bottle of liquor from my kitchen cabinet Ashton left here one night, and without bothering to grab a glass, twist the lid off and take a large gulp. I relish the burn of the alcohol as it slides down my throat, coating my belly and mind at the same time.

"Alexa, play my music," I yell, needing to escape for a little while. A second later, the music begins to play over the speaker. Song after song, I dance around my apartment, drinking and getting lost in the lyrics. When the bottle is empty, I find another one in the freezer and get started on that one.

I have no idea how long I'm drinking and dancing for, but when there's a knock on my door, I assume it's Ashton—since he's pretty much my only real friend—and swing it open, ready to welcome him to my drunken pity party.

Only standing on the other side of the door isn't Ashton…

"Well, if it isn't dude bro Brayden," I say, then snort at my own joke.

Brayden's brows shoot up to his forehead. "Are you drunk?"

"Why?" I purr. "You planning to take advantage of me?" I grab his hand and pull him inside.

"No." He extends his hand that's holding a cup of Starbucks coffee. "I thought you bailed on our tutoring session, so I came here to bribe you not to."

Shit, our tutoring session.

"Nope, didn't bail. Just drunk." I pluck the coffee cup out of his hand and drop it onto the counter. "Dance with me."

I wrap my arms around Brayden's muscular shoulders and sway my body against his. When he stays frozen in place, I use him like a stripper pole, grinding my body against his. When I twirl around, my ass rubbing against his crotch, he grips the curves of my hips and pulls me close to him until my back is flush against his front.

"I really think you should drink that coffee," he murmurs into my ear.

"And I really think you should pull that stick out of your ass and dance with me."

He chuckles. "Fine."

His hands land on my hips and then glide up my sides, causing a shiver to race up my spine. He twists me back to face him and holds me close. Our eyes lock, and our faces come together, so close… too close. The music is fast-paced, but our bodies are swaying to their own beat. His gaze drops to my mouth and instinctually, I lick my lips, assuming we're going to kiss. But instead he shakes his head. "When we kiss, it won't be when you're drunk and can blame it on the alcohol."

My thoughts go back to my drunken kiss with Ashton the other night. Is that what he's going to do? Blame it on the alcohol? My stomach tightens at the thought. I don't care how drunk we were, I could never regret that kiss.

"When we kiss, you'll be sober," Brayden states, bringing me back to the here and now.

"Who says I would want to kiss you when I'm sober?" I jibe. "The last time I checked I didn't even like you when I'm sober."

"We'll see about that," Brayden challenges.

He twirls me around and suddenly everything around me is spinning like a tilt-a-whirl at the fair. The floor feels like it's going to swallow me up. I trip over my feet, prepared to hit the ground. But before that happens, Brayden tightens his hold on me.

"I got you," he says, walking me over to the couch.

Once I'm seated, he grabs the coffee he brought over and hands it to me. "Drink this."

He turns down the music, then disappears into my kitchen. A minute later, he returns and sits next to me. "Take these." He hands me two pain relievers, and I swallow them both, chasing them with the iced coffee. It feels good in my belly, as if it's extinguishing the burn left by the alcohol.

"Wanna tell me what has you drunk in the early afternoon?" he asks, his voice filled with concern.

The room is still slightly spinning, so I close my eyes and drop my head to Brayden's shoulder, needing it to stop so I don't throw up.

"I don't want to talk about it," I mumble, nuzzling my face into him.

"Okay, but at least drink the coffee. It will help sober you up."

I do as he says, drinking every last drop. When the cup is empty, he takes it from me and sets it on the coffee table. His arm comes around me and I close my eyes, my last thought being how warm and comfortable he is.

When I open my eyes, for a split second, I wonder if getting drunk and Brayden taking care of me was a dream. Until I sit up and glance over and find him sitting on the couch, typing away on his phone.

"Good morning," he says, looking up. "Or should I say good evening since it's already six clock?"

"Ugh," I groan, covering my face with my hands in embarrassment. *Kill me now.*

Brayden laughs. "No dying until you've helped me bring up my grades."

Great, now I'm speaking my thoughts out loud.

Having drunk a ton of alcohol and then slept it off, I suddenly need to pee. "I'll be right back," I say, standing slowly to make sure I'm no longer drunk. When the room stays still, I sigh in relief that I'm safe to walk on my own.

After going to the bathroom, I wash my hands and brush my teeth, then run a brush through my hair, so I'm not a complete hot mess.

As I'm walking back out to my living room, there's a knock on my door. I swing my gaze over to him, as if he would know who's on the other side.

"I'll get it," he says. "It's for me." He shrugs and stands, and I wonder if maybe *this* is a dream.

He speaks briefly to someone and then closes the door, walking back inside with a bag of food. The smell wafts through the air and my stomach grumbles.

"Figured you might be hungry," he says, setting the bag on the table and opening it.

I stare at him in shock, because really, who is this guy?

"You do like Chinese, don't you?" he asks, sitting back on the couch and looking at me. "You had like fifty of their takeout menus on your counter."

"I love Chinese."

"Good. Let's eat." He takes the containers out of the bag and spreads them out, then hands me a pair of chopsticks.

I sit next to him and open up the container closest to me. "Mmm, chicken lo mien. My favorite." I dip my chopsticks in and pull out some chicken and noodles, shoving them into my mouth. It's so delicious I can't help the moan that escapes. He watches with amusement as I pick out any green onions hiding in there.

"You okay over there?" he finally asks, raising a brow.

"Oh yeah." I take another bite. "So good. Thank you for this."

He nods. "No problem."

We eat in silence for a few minutes, when I remember why he came over in the first place.

"Do you have your school stuff? I can help you study."

"You sure?"

"Yeah. Sorry about missing our session. I wasn't bailing. Just having a bad moment."

"I know all about those," he mutters around a forkful of food.

"Want to talk about it?"

"Do you?" he volleys.

"Not really."

"Same," he agrees. "So, you and Drew…"

"Really? That's your conversation changer? Most people ask about the weather." I take one last bite of my noodles and drop my chopsticks, full.

"I'm not most people." He closes the containers and places them into the bag.

"And I'm not kissing and telling." I stand and grab the bag. "Grab your school stuff so we can get started."

Brayden wasn't lying. He really is serious about getting his grades up. It seems as though he hangs on my every word, soaking up the information as we study. I'm used to the other students I tutor behaving this way, but not him.

"What?" he asks after a solid hour of working. "You keep looking at me weird."

Heat floods across my cheeks. "I am not."

"Okay." He laughs, shaking his head. "I believe you."

"Stop," I mutter, poking him with my bare foot.

His massive, calloused hand grips my foot, pulling it toward him. A tingle of awareness shoots up my leg. "You started it," he teases.

"You can't take my foot hostage to get information out of me," I grumble, cocking my eyebrow at him, insinuating he better let go.

"So there *is* information to get?" He gently rubs his thumb across the bottom of my foot, flashing me his maddening smirk.

"If there was, you wouldn't get that information by tickling my foot," I sass.

"I'm just rubbing on you, Mia. Nothing more."

The husky, heated way he says those words has my brain jumbled and my heart galloping in my chest.

"Your feet are soft," he muses. "Have you ever played any sports?"

"Nope. I'm a video-game type of girl. I do yoga occasionally, but that's it. You ever play any sports besides hockey?"

"No. Hockey is the only sport worth playing. Ever skated before?"

"No way." The one time I begged to do gymnastics, my mom got one look at how uncoordinated I was, told me I was an embarrassment, and pulled me out. "I'd probably fall and kill myself," I say, half joking.

"I could teach you, and I wouldn't let you fall."

"I'll take your word for it." I try to pull my foot away, but he tightens his hold on it.

"Go out with me," he murmurs, his intense brown eyes locking on mine.

"No."

"Please?"

I laugh. "No."

"Why not?"

"Because you're a brat."

"I can behave sometimes."

We both laugh because it's not true.

"It wouldn't be wise to date someone I'm tutoring."

His eyes twinkle with mischief. "Technically you already broke the rules, Mia."

"What? How?"

"Not only did we dance and have dinner, we also slept together."

"Brayden!"

He laughs. "Well, you slept and I watched you, but close enough."

"Creep."

"I've been called worse." He shrugs, continuing his massage on my foot, and I ignore the way it reminds me of Ashton and how much I miss him. "Say yes. It's just dinner and we've already done that once."

I open my mouth to answer, when the front door flings open, effectively making me choke on my words.

"You can only avoid me so long, MiMi," Ashton booms from the doorway. "Did you get your period? I've seen you in bitch mode, but we always still hang—what the fuck?"

# ELEVEN

*Ashton*

Her face blushes bright red, a guilty look marring her features, as she jerks her foot from Brayden's grip. The way he tips his head up at me in greeting, a smug grin tugging at his lips, infuriates me.

Why?

Because Mia is mine.

*My* best friend.

Not his.

Yet she's cozied up with him getting foot massages and can't return a goddamn text.

Granted, said text was sent two minutes ago when I headed this way, but still.

Mia launches to her feet, rushing over to me. I'm not jealous, but I'm… something. Irrationally pissed. Hurt. Confused as to why I want to rip off Brayden's head. Mostly perturbed she's fraternizing with the enemy.

"I had a tutoring session," she squeaks out.

I take in her disheveled state, the lingering scent of alcohol, and the food cartons everywhere.

"Yeah," Brayden agrees as he stands. "She taught me lots and lots of *things.*"

Mia stands between us, sensing the storm brewing. I stare at him right over her head as he comes to stand behind her.

"She's not interested in douchebags," I grit out. "You're wasting your time."

"Apparently she is, because we're going on a date Saturday night."

Her head shakes. "He's just riling you up, Ashton."

"I asked. She hasn't had a chance to say yes yet," Brayden argues.

I narrow my eyes at this guy. Yes, he's hot, but he's also a major dick. With him towering over her with his soulless eyes and villain smile, he looks every bit the boogeyman who snuck into my girl's apartment.

Not my girl.

I'm fucking gay.

Ignoring him, I bank on the fact that she and I have more history. That she'll choose me over him. Turning my stare back on her, I say, "I thought we could talk. About the other night."

It's the last goddamn thing I want to talk about, but it's my winning hand against Brayden and all his superiority.

I chance a look at him, pleased as fuck to find his brows furrowed. I flash him a triumphant look. I might be gay, but I'll be damned if I let him steal my best friend away to do whatever it is douchebags like him do.

*You know what they do…*

The thought hits me hard in the gut.

Makes me think of another douchebag who I happened to run into at the pool earlier today.

"I, uh," Mia stammers, stepping away from us to run her fingers through her messy hair. "We can't be rude and make him leave just because we need to talk."

"Fine," I grumble. "Call me whenever you're done entertaining assholes."

I start to walk away, but she grabs my hand. "Ashton, wait."

I'm pissed that she doesn't send this guy packing. Just a few days ago, she hated the ground he walked on. Hell, it's part of the reason we kissed in the first place. Now, he's all chummy with her in her apartment. Makes no fucking sense.

"I'll call you later," Brayden says, walking over to her and hugging her.

"We'll see you at the game," Mia chirps cheerfully. "Drew asked us to come."

Brayden straightens, his eyes widening in surprise. "Oh yeah? Then you really can't get out of that date now."

She laughs. "Go away."

He gathers his stuff and then waves at her, ignoring me altogether. Soon, he's gone and his suffocating presence is no longer choking me.

But with his absence brings the reality of my statement.

*I thought we could talk. About the other night.*

"Want something to drink?" Mia asks, her voice shaky.

"Since when do we do formal?" I grumble. I pull her over to me, hugging her. "Sorry for being a dick and avoiding you. I just… I don't know what to think about what happened. Pretending it didn't happen doesn't make it go away."

She stiffens in my arms, telling me everything I need to know.

She liked it.

Even after she messed around with Drew. Even after God knows what the fuck happened with Brayden.

What happened with us is plaguing her.

It's plaguing me too.

She starts to pull away from our embrace, but I can't let her go. There are a million things I want to say to her. To tell her it was confusing, but I can't stop thinking about it. How I would try it again—without alcohol to blame—if I didn't think it might further fracture our friendship. I'd like to tell her that seeing her with Brayden made me crazy fucking jealous, which makes me mad at myself.

I can't tell her any of these things because my tongue won't work.

"I'm sorry I pounced on you," she murmurs, her breath hot through my T-shirt. "I didn't mean to put you in that position."

I close my eyes, remembering how spicy and sweet she tasted. How we desperately kissed as though we'd been starved for it. The way my dick was stone in my sweats. I've never once been turned on by a girl. Girls don't do it for me. So why the fuck was I about to nut in my pants when I had my tongue down her throat?

"I don't like this divide between us," I rumble out, finally finding my voice again. "You're my best friend. I can't lose you."

She tilts her head up, her brows furrowed. "I'm not going anywhere."

My eyes, against their will, drift down to her lips. I have a burning desire to taste her again. Alcohol isn't calling the shots here. No, my heart is.

"Me neither," I murmur.

I press a kiss to her cheek, near her mouth, not able to understand the way my heart stammers in my chest. Before I do something stupid like stick my tongue down her throat again, I pull away before it's too late.

Her hand touches where I've kissed her, making me stand a little straighter with pride. Brayden can pursue her all he wants, but at the end of the day she likes me. As complicated as that may be.

"Let's go fuck with Drew," I state, trying to chase away the weird vibe between us. "He's going over some hockey footage on his laptop, prepping for the game tomorrow night. Want to go terrorize him with me?" I waggle my brows at her, grinning.

Seemingly relieved at my playfulness, she laughs. "Duh. Let me get changed into something more comfortable and then we can go."

Before she walks away, I grab her hand, squeezing it.

"We're going to be okay," I assure her.

"I know."

With those words, she pulls away, tugging at my heart in the process.

A college hockey game reminds me of a college swim meet. And because of that, I'm immediately on edge. People are everywhere. Seems like the whole damn school is here to cheer on our hockey players. Mia senses my distress and loops her arm with mine, resting her head against my shoulder as we walk to the area Drew told us to go to.

Rooming with the coach has perks, including free tickets to get into the game. We make our way over to the area he had someone reserve for us and sit down. I'm not eager to watch Brayden play, but Drew kind of sold me on the whole "hot hockey dudes fighting on the ice" spiel he gave us.

A few girls nearby squeal when some of the players spill out onto the ice, all thick with their heavy gear on. I know which one Brayden is right away because he's the only one who skates like an asshole.

One hundred percent swagger, confidence, and overall arrogance.

The other guys may as well be shadows and he knows it too.

Drew makes it into the box with some of the other players, his head craned to look our way. When he sees us, he waves. His movement alerts Brayden to us. While the other guys warm up, he skates right up to the glass where we're sitting.

"Date, Mia, baby," he calls out, grinning like the guy who already got the girl. "Tonight."

Just to piss him off, I sling an arm over Mia's shoulders. "Mia has plans."

She elbows me, making me grunt, but doesn't wiggle out of my hold. Brayden seems amused by my blatant challenge.

"All the goals tonight are for you, beautiful," he says to her.

"Can you get your ass kicked a few times for me?" I ask.

He laughs, skates backward, and then swivels around, his body tensed and ready to play. I hate that the entire move turns me the fuck on.

"It's cold in here," Mia whines.

"I'll keep you warm." I kiss the top of her head, keeping her tucked against me.

It's strange how different a hockey game and a swim meet are. At the swim meets, the moist air is warm and thick with a chlorinated smell. Here it's sharp and crisp.

"He's a beast and they're just warming up," Mia mutters, pointing at Brayden. "I can't wait until the game starts to see him in action."

I hate to admit it, but he's a natural on the ice. The other guys are good, but there's just an inborn ability Brayden seems to have. We're both mesmerized and focused on him when someone comes to stand right in front of us, blocking our view. I lift my gaze and cringe. Mia, snuggled into my side, immediately notices.

"Ashton," Travis says. "How's it going? I tried to talk to you this morning at the pool, but you ran out of there like your ass was on fire."

I grind my teeth together. "I'm just fucking dandy."

"Still a grumpy asshole, I see," Travis sneers. "And no longer gay." He nods at Mia.

"You're still the same annoying motherfucker," I spit back at him.

"You didn't think I was so annoying when I sucked your dick." He shoots Mia a nasty glare.

"Get lost, freak," Mia snaps. "You're in the way."

"Nah," I grind out, unable to ignore his barb. "You weren't annoying when you were slobbin' my fuckin' knob, but you got annoying real quick when you turned me in to Coach Summers."

"Drugs are bad," Travis says, grinning. "I thought you knew."

"So are bitter assholes with fragile egos."

What did I ever see in this guy? It only took a few dates to learn he was a whiny prick and it was a bad idea to see someone from my swim team. Travis and I were cool until he realized he was second best on the team, and instead of working his ass off to beat me fair and square, he did me dirty by planting shit in my bag that wasn't mine.

"Does your girlfriend know you're a pothead?" Travis taunts, knowing damn well I don't do drugs.

"I know you're about to get your ass kicked," Mia warns.

Travis scowls at her and then nearly jumps out of his skin when something slams into the glass behind him. He swivels around, coming eye to eye with Brayden. Travis is safe behind the glass, but when Brayden taps it with his stick in a threatening way, he steps back.

"Run along, fuck boy," Brayden says, his menacing stare locked on Travis.

Travis shoots us the bird before stalking off. The tension leaves my body the moment he's gone. I hate that Brayden notices. I also hate that it wins him points in my book. The arrogant prick knows it too because he winks at me before heading back to his team.

That stupid wink from the enemy has me sweating in this stupid ice rink.

"You okay?" Mia asks.

"Yep."

"I know what will make you feel better."

"All the hockey players stripping for us?"

She giggles. "Next best thing." She reaches into her pocket and pulls out a package of M&Ms. "Candy."

"This is why you're my favorite person in the world."

"I know."

# TWELVE

## *Drew*

"Eyes," I announce, walking into the locker room. I've only been coaching these guys for less than a week, but they already know when I say that single word it means I need their attention. They all stop talking and look my way. "Nothing in this world comes easy. When we think we have it all figured out, life throws us a curveball. Coach Garrison should've been here for this game, but life's a bitch and dealt him a shitty hand. But I guarantee he's at home watching. I know I'm not Coach Garrison, but I'm here and I'll be with you guys every step of the way."

The guys nod in understanding. To say it's been a rough week would be an understatement. Some of these guys have been with Coach Garrison for the last three years. They didn't want him to go and he didn't want to leave. But it is what it is and now we need to focus on what we're here for. To win.

"Tonight, we're going to be playing Western Michigan." The team boos and grumbles. Western Michigan is our rival school, and one of the hardest teams to beat. "They're good," I admit. "But you guys are better. You're stronger. You lost your coach unexpectedly, and for some, that would mean the end of the season before it even began, but each and every one of you still came to play, and every day at practice you've busted your ass."

My eyes land on Brayden, whose head is down, refusing to look at me. After I sent him home Monday, he returned Tuesday with a vengeance. His attitude didn't get any better, but he kept his mouth shut and practiced hard. The problem is, I know Brayden leads this team and I need him to do just that today: lead.

"Today, when you go out there, you're in control of what happens. Every play, every move, is on you. Whether you win or lose is in your control. This first game is going to set the precedence for the rest of the season. Other teams are going to watch this game, study it, and when they do, we want them to watch in fear. We know the other team is going to come out hard, but I know you guys will come at them even harder. Because who are we?"

The team stays quiet, and I worry they aren't going to participate in their pregame ritual. Coach Garrison told me about it and I'm hoping if I can get them to do it, it will pump them up.

Brayden's head pops up and we make eye contact. Right here, right now, will determine if he's the true leader of the team. If he can put our shit aside for the sake of the game.

"Because who are we?" I repeat, my eyes never leaving Brayden's.

"We're the Ice Hawks," he barks.

Everyone looks up, shocked that he's speaking.

"And what do Ice Hawks do?" I prompt.

This time all the guys answer. "We fly, we soar, we hunt our prey, and then we tear them apart, limb by limb," they chant in unison.

"Damn right!" I yell. "Now, who's ready to play some hockey?"

The team whoops and hollers, and when Brayden's eyes meet mine, I nod subtly, thanking him. He didn't have to do what he did, he could've stayed stubborn, holding his grudge, but he did what a true leader does and put his team first.

After going over the positions and who's starting, the guys make their way onto the ice. The arena is full of fans chanting their names. I'm watching Brayden warm up, when he skates over to the glass where Mia and Ashton are sitting. I don't know what is said, but when he skates away Ashton looks pissed and Mia looked worried. About ten minutes later, he's back over there. This time when he skates back, I call him over.

"You need to be focusing on your upcoming game, not girls."

Brayden smirks. "How about I do both? The game now, and Mia afterward when I take her out on a date."

I scoff, letting Brayden get to me when I know better. "Will be hard to do since we're going to dinner afterward." I don't mention Ashton will also be going.

Brayden's nostrils flare with challenge. "We'll see about that."

The buzzer goes off, indicating the game is about to start, and Brayden skates away.

The first two periods of the game fly by, and at the end of the second period, we're tied at zero. Both teams are playing aggressively, giving it all they've got. I can see Brayden is getting frustrated. He's playing a perfect game, but their goalie is blocking everything he shoots, just like ours is.

At five minutes left of the third period, the score is still zero for both teams. The last thing we want is to go into overtime. I can tell Brayden is fuming. He's getting blocked left and right. I'm about to call a time-out, when Brayden and a guy from the opposing team get into each other's faces. Unlike the NHL, in college hockey, if you fight, you're automatically disqualified from the game as well as the next.

Brayden's teammates grab him, pulling him away from the guy as the coach from the other team calls a time-out.

"Murphy, you're out," I yell. "Holden, you're in."

"What?" Brayden shouts.

"You heard me. Sit down."

If looks could kill, I'd be dying nine different ways right now.

"Fuck this," he barks, falling onto the bench.

"Keep it up and you won't have to worry about being disqualified from the next game, because I won't play you."

He tears his helmet off and drops it next to him, glaring my way.

The clock starts back up and the game continues. Derek Holden is good, but he's definitely no Brayden. With less than a minute left and still tied at zero, I have a choice to make. The stubborn part of me wants to keep Brayden on the bench, but if we have any shot at winning, he's going to be it.

"Murphy," I bark. "You're in."

Brayden smirks like the cocky bastard he is before he pushes his helmet over his face and skates off, determined.

The clock ticks down as the two teams scramble to take control. Wexler gets control of the puck, but before he can get near the net, he's taken down.

The crowd boos as I try to find where the puck is. There are only five seconds left… four… three… we're going to be going into overtime.

And then… Fuck! Brayden has the puck and… Holy shit! The crowd screams as he reaches around and flips the puck into the net from behind just before the buzzer goes off, signaling the end of the period and the game.

The scoreboard changes: 1-0 and the arena goes crazy as the team piles out and attacks Brayden for scoring the winning shot in the last second. He lifts his stick toward the ceiling, and his eyes momentarily close. For a split second, my feet move forward, heading straight for Bray. But then I remember that's not who we are anymore, and I freeze in my spot, watching as Nolan Finn, Brayden's closest friend on the team, envelops him in a hug. They pat each other's backs and my heart constricts as memories from our past rush forward, damn near knocking me off my feet.

Our years of friendship—on and off the ice. The way we practiced together every damn day. We were inseparable. He knew everything about me, every flaw, every secret, and I knew him. It was us against the world… until it wasn't.

After he's done hugging the guys, he skates over to the side where his parents are waiting. Molly jumps up and down and wraps her arms around her son, while Tim pats him on the shoulder, no doubt telling him how proud he is of him.

I should avert my eyes, focus on something else, but I can't stop watching, remembering what it was like to have them all in my corner. To be part of their family. It didn't matter that I played better than Brayden and he spent more time on the bench while I ate up all the minutes. At the end of the day, we were a team—the dynamic duo, as his parents called us when we were little—and we had each other's backs.

Until I fucked it all up.

Brayden hugs his parents once more and then skates back toward the benches, a mesmerizingly beautiful smile on his face. Our eyes lock for a brief moment, and a lump the size of a damn puck fills my throat, making it almost impossible to breathe. With Bray, he's either high or he's low. There's no in between. Like the other night at dinner when he was breaking apart right before my eyes and all I wanted to do was wrap my arms around him and comfort him. I knew he was beating himself up over shit he can't change. And for the rest of the night, after we parted ways, I worried where he was, how he was handling his feelings. But right now, he's high, on top of the world, as he should be. He kicked ass tonight, came through in the clutch, and I'm so damn proud of him.

His smile falters slightly, and I instantly miss it, wishing it would come back. Because when Bray is high, on top of the world, it's the most magical sight to behold. I expect him to sneer or glare, so I'm shocked when his eyes stay trained on mine and he juts out his chin, and then, with a tiny pull of his lips, he grants me the smallest smile. If you weren't looking at him as close as I am, you wouldn't even know it happened, but I am, and I know. And it damn near makes my heart burst.

All too quickly, he diverts his gaze to a couple other teammates, ending the moment, leaving me standing here, for the first time, thinking maybe there's hope for us yet.

After celebrating the victory of our first win as a team, and reminding them they have tomorrow off, but I'll see them Monday morning at 5:00 a.m., everyone showers and then heads out. I'm walking down the hall, when I see Dean Carter walking my way.

"Congratulations." He shakes my hand. "I knew you were the right man for the job."

"Only one down, thirty-three more to go," I joke.

"Any plans for the night?" he asks as my eyes land on Mia and Ashton walking over. We made plans to go to dinner after the game, but I'm not about to mention that to him.

"Just going to go over the tapes."

"Dedicated." Curtis claps me on my shoulder. "I like it. Keep up the good work."

He's about to walk away, when Ashton and Mia approach.

"Dad," Ashton says, making his presence known. "Good game, Coach Thompson," he adds with a sly smirk. I swear the guy lives for fucking with people.

Curtis does a double take, probably shocked as shit that his son is actually here. He clasps Ashton on the shoulder and says to me, "Are you responsible for this? Getting my son to attend a college event?"

"I just extended the invite," I tell him.

"Well, thank you," Curtis says. "Maybe him living with a responsible role model will be good for him." Ashton rolls his eyes, but his dad doesn't notice. "I need to get home to my wife. Enjoy the rest of your weekend. Mia, as always, it's lovely to see you. Keep my boy in line." To Ashton, he says, "Remember to come by and see your mother. She misses you."

Once he's gone, Ashton points an accusing finger at me. "You lied. There were no hot, sweaty dudes fighting on the ice." He crosses his arms over his chest and glares.

"You must've misunderstood," I say with a laugh. "When I said fighting, I meant fighting for the puck."

"Not cool," Ashton grumbles.

"Hey," Mia says, looking past me. "Good game."

I glance back and see Brayden, freshly showered and dressed in a pair of jeans and an Ice Hawk's shirt that stretches across his muscular frame.

"Thanks," Brayden replies, raising his hand to adjust the beanie on his head. His shirt rises with the action, exposing the thick happy trail leading down to… As if he can sense me checking him out, his eyes quickly dart over to me, before he gives Mia his full attention. "So, what do you say? Have dinner with me?"

What the hell? When did they get close enough he would think he could ask her out and not get slapped? The last time I was with them together, Mia was telling us off and then stomping away from us at the tutoring center.

"I can't," Mia says, almost sounding like she's upset about that fact. "But you could join us."

My gaze darts over to Ashton, who is intently watching the exchange. I expect him to jump in, but he remains quiet.

Brayden glances at me briefly, before he says, "Nah, I'm good." A wave of emotion passes through me at his words. I prefer asshole Brayden over the one who looks like his puppy has just been run over.

"Dude, you're going," Ashton says, shocking the hell out of me. "The girl gets what the girl wants. You'll learn. It's best to give her her way or she'll attack you with those mean ass feet of hers."

Brayden's brows furrow in contemplation, as if he's actually considering joining the three of us for dinner. And then Mia places her hand on his shoulder and says, "Please, it will be fun," and his face completely softens, reminding me of what he looked like before life got rough and hardened him.

Brayden takes her hand in his and entwines their fingers together, and my stomach twists into a knot at the sight. The worst part is I'm not sure if it's because she's touching *him*. Or if it's because he's being touched by *her*. Either way, I swallow down the raw emotion I shouldn't have toward either of them touching each other. I'm the coach, and Mia is a student, and Brayden is my player *and* a student.

Fuck, this is all so fucked up.

"All right," Brayden says, giving in. "But this doesn't count as our date." The corner of his top lip tugs into a half-smile and he shoots Mia a flirty wink, making her giggle.

"Fine," she retorts. "Let's go."

"Where *are* we going?" Brayden asks, throwing his arm around Mia's shoulders. I hate how good they look together. Smart, gorgeous Mia with the good-looking jock Brayden.

"Somewhere expensive," Ashton remarks. "Mr. NHL is buying, and he owes me for not coming through with what he promised."

Mia snorts out a laugh. "Don't be such a whiny baby. That's what porn is for. Plus, you totally enjoyed the game." She glances up at Brayden. "He even cheered when you scored."

"Mia, you're riding with me," Ashton states, ignoring her comment and pulling her out of Brayden's hold. "Where are we eating?"

"How about Kuboki?" I suggest, loving their Pad Thai.

"Fine. Meet you guys there," Ashton says, wrapping his arm around the back of Mia's shoulders and guiding her away.

I stare after the two of them, as they walk back down the hallway toward the exit. Ashton says something, and Mia throws her head back in a laugh. I find myself smiling, wishing I were a part of their conversation. The last year has been hard, and I haven't had much reason to laugh or smile, but when I'm around the two of them I find myself doing both, and I have to admit, it feels damn good. Like a little bit of the weight I'm carrying on my shoulders has been removed.

When I glance over at Brayden, I notice he's watching them as well, only his one brow is cocked up and his lips are formed in a flat line.

"You're not worried about Ashton, are you?" I taunt, unable to help myself.

Brayden scoffs. "In case you missed the memo, he's gay."

I laugh to myself, because he didn't walk in on what I did the other night. Ashton might be gay, but I know he's got a hard-on for Mia.

"Well, I imagine if anyone can make a guy flip his switch, it'd be her."

Brayden glares my way but doesn't comment.

"Need a ride to the restaurant?" I ask, changing the subject.

"Nope," he says, then stalks down the hall, leaving me standing here by myself, feeling as though everything is about to change, and unsure if that's a good or a bad thing.

# THIRTEEN



**O**ne goal.

One fucking goal.

It was infuriating that I played like shit. I blame Drew. He always has this suffocating presence that seeps into my pores, reminding me I'm second best. I wonder if he was disappointed in my playing. I hate that I even care.

At practice on Monday, I'll have to go harder and more aggressive. There's no way in hell I'll make it to the NHL playing like I did today. I dread to think of the NHL scouts watching that game.

Fuck.

I'm stressed to fuck as I pull in behind Ashton's expensive-ass silver Audi at the restaurant. In my rearview mirror, Drew is right behind me. Even from his truck, his intense blues are burning holes into me. Rather than parking, Mia jumps out. Her tits bounce in her tight black T-shirt, making me grin. She makes her way over to my window, so I roll it down. The wind blows, sending her hair flying into my Tahoe, tickling my face.

"Ashton hates sushi and he says this place is prissy as fuck. His words, not mine. You care if we grab pizza instead?" She pushes her dark hair from her face, tugging at her bottom lip with her teeth.

"I'm good with pizza. Sure you don't want to ride with me?" I tease, letting my gaze drop to my lap.

She snorts out a goofy laugh that warms my heart. "Maybe later."

It wasn't a no.

The wind whips her hair again and she shivers. She starts to walk away, but I stop her.

"Mia, wait." I reach onto the floorboard behind the passenger seat and grab a red beanie. "Put this on. Your head is getting cold."

She frowns in confusion when I hand her the beanie, but nods, taking it from me. When she slides it over her head, covering the tops of her eyebrows, my heart skips a few beats.

"Beautiful."

Her cheeks turn as red as the beanie and she backs away. "Let me tell Drew and then you guys can follow us."

My mood has lightened since talking to her and I think about where I'll take her on a date as I follow them to the pizza place. I've got it narrowed down to a couple of places, as I climb out of the Tahoe. All of my good mood is sucked away when Drew gets out of his truck. He saunters my way, his blue eyes homing in on me, concern flashing in them.

I should be pissed he benched me toward the end, but I'm grateful he put me back in just in time for me to at least grab us one goal before the end of the game. With Ashton and Mia here, I can use them as a distraction from having to talk to him.

The thing with Drew is, he sees me right down to the marrow. Every single time he looks at me. At one time, it was pretty fucking cool to be that close to someone. Now, it feels invasive. Like he doesn't get that right. If I could erect walls around me, I would. Drew would just find a way to walk right through them, though.

"MiMi and I don't eat fish that still breathes," Ashton reveals, hyper as fuck tonight. "We're allergic."

They both laugh and Drew rolls his eyes at them. I can't help but smirk.

"Coach Daddy is still buying, though," Ashton says, his lips curling up into a devious grin that he flashes Drew's way.

And. Just. Like. That.

I'm pissy again.

Ashton is gay. No big deal. But flirting with Drew? It annoys the hell out of me. As though he's trying to do it to make me mad. The fucker has been pushing my buttons since I met him. At least I know his button now.

Mia.

I walk over to her, grabbing her hand and tugging her into the restaurant. "I've been thinking about our date," I tell her as the garlicky aromas hit my nostrils, making my stomach clench eagerly for some food.

"Our non-existent, never gonna happen, totally hypothetical date?" she teases.

"Yep. That one. The one where you let me kiss you and tell you how pretty you are."

She gapes at me, her brown eyes softening. "You're a real Casanova, huh?"

The hostess interrupts our flirting and motions for us to follow her. She brings us to a booth near some skee-ball machines. I catch Ashton's annoyed glare when I usher Mia into the booth and then scoot in beside her. It makes me think of Drew's earlier comment about Mia turning a gay man straight.

Ashton slides in first and Drew sits beside him across from us. Where Ashton glowers at me, Drew is watching me, analyzing my every move not unlike how he studies the way his players play.

"A pitcher of beer for the table," Drew says to the waitress. "Maybe some fried mushrooms to get us started."

No one flinches that he orders for everyone, not even me. That's Drew for you. Taking charge like fucking usual.

"You look super familiar," the woman says, angling her body so she looks at Drew. "You come here a lot?"

"First time," he says.

"He used to play for the NHL but then…" I let my words die off, leaving him hanging because I'm a prick.

His blue eyes turn icy, though his smile for her is warm. "I coach the Ice Hawks now."

"That's awesome!" she praises. "I'll grab your beer and put in your appetizer order. Be right back."

As soon as she's gone, Ashton zeroes in on me.

"So your asshole-ness isn't just directed at me. Drew gets it too? Good to know you're an equal opportunity dickhead."

"Not to Mia," I remind them both, playfully poking at her ribs.

She lets out a laugh because she's ticklish it would seem. "Stop."

"Your smile says go," I tease.

"And Rapey Dude Bro Bray has graced us with his presence," Ashton deadpans.

Drew snorts. "Bray doesn't have to rape to get what he wants."

It irks me that he's sticking up for me.

"I'm wearing Mia down," I explain. "Nothing bad about a guy who pursues what he wants."

Mia, obviously overwhelmed by the stares of three men, snatches up the menu. "What are you guys getting? We can share."

"She likes pineapple on her pizza," Ashton reveals. "Better get her a small, because no one wants to share that shit."

She scoffs, but Drew and I are both in agreeance.

"I'll get sausage," I state, knowing Drew likes it too.

"Will you now?" Ashton jokes, smirking at me.

It takes a minute for my brain to catch up. For a split second, I feel exposed by him. Jerking my glare to Drew, I accuse him with just my eyes. But he's not looking at me. His gaze is soft as he watches Mia.

"Order for me. I'm going to take a piss," I grumble, sliding out of the booth.

I spend too much time looking at myself in the mirror, wondering what Drew sees. Does he remember the times I bawled my eyes out, begging for the pain to stop? Does he see me as weak? Does he see me as someone who can't keep their grades up and who deserves to ride the bench because of shitty playing?

Or does he see something else?

I have so much shit bottled up inside me, I feel like a Coke bottle someone's been shaking over and over. One of these days, the lid is going to come off, and I'm going to explode.

After washing my hands, I exit the bathroom to find Mia waiting there. Her worried expression has me wanting to touch her. Walking right up to her, I do just that. She's still wearing the beanie, and fuck if it doesn't do something for my male pride seeing it on her. I toy with a strand of her dark brown hair.

"You okay?" she asks. "You seemed upset."

"Just off my game today." I'm surprised at my confession, but seeing as she steps closer, it feels like the right thing to say to her. Something about Mia doesn't make me feel so… defensive.

"I thought your game was perfect," she says. "Don't let that go to your head."

"Already did," I tease. "Both of them."

She laughs and playfully shoves me. Of course she's about as powerful as a kitten. I grip her wrists, grinning at her.

"How many non-dates are we going to have before our first date?"

"Hmm, maybe three," she volleys back.

"So a real date is imminent?"

"If you're a good boy."

I don't know the definition of good, but I'll pull out the Webster's dictionary and take a fucking look to find out for her.

My hand finds her hip and she doesn't push me away. "Can a good boy kiss a good girl on the second non-date? Asking for a friend."

Hesitation wars in her dark eyes. "I, uh…"

Leaning forward, I kiss her forehead. "My friend's an idiot. I'll settle for some good ol' ass whipping on skee-ball instead. Come on, beautiful."

Relief flashes in her eyes, and she happily takes my hand. Once again, I realize I made the right move. With Mia, she's different than other girls I've been with. Not a fan girl. A real girl. I didn't realize how much I craved realness until I met her this week.

We head back out to the dining room where Drew and Ashton are already in a heated skee-ball competition. I can't help but steal a glance at Drew. In his ball cap and fitted black Henley, he seems younger than when he was coaching our team with such ease earlier. In this moment, he wears his youth well, reminding me that he's our age and not some old-ass dude.

Mia takes the machine next to Ashton and they fist bump. I take the one next to her. Ashton passes two cups of quarters to us. For the next twenty minutes, while we wait for our pizza to arrive, we play skee-ball. Mia is good, but so are the rest of us. Turns out, we're all competitive as fuck. It isn't until the waitress whistles at us that I realize I've been laughing and having a good time.

Ben loved skee-ball.

The thought hits me out of nowhere, piling on bricks of guilt faster than I can fling them off. I'm in a cloud as I stumble toward our table, bile rising in my gut. Drew senses my mood immediately. He nods to Ashton and then to Mia.

I don't even have it in me to argue when Ashton takes my place beside Mia. With my teeth gritted against the pain, I push into the booth, hating how Drew's concern warms me like a familiar blanket. Ashton watches me for a long moment, and then dives into razzing Mia about her pineapple pizza.

"You okay?" Drew rumbles, his voice low so they don't hear.

"Yep," I snap.

He doesn't flinch at my harsh delivery, but I do. I hate how raw I feel. Rather than facing off with me, his hand covers my thigh and squeezes, providing comfort I didn't know I needed.

"Breathe," Drew murmurs. "You're okay."

I close my eyes, inhaling through my nose and then exhaling heavily. The chatter across the table continues, and I'm thankful for the reprieve.

"Ben loved skee-ball." My words come out pained and nothing more than a whisper, but Drew hears them.

"I know, man, I know."

I go to grab his hand, so I can shove it away, but the moment I touch it, I can't let go. He twists his hand, capturing mine in his.

"You're allowed to have fun," he says gently, squeezing my hand. "You're allowed to be happy."

His words have me recoiling. I tug my hand free to grab the glass of beer in front of me. With my eyes closed, I gulp it down. By the time I finish my beer, I've locked away my emotions.

Nudging Mia's foot with mine, I grin at her, though it feels forced this time. I just need to talk about something else. To think about anything other than Ben right now.

"After you eat that weird-ass pizza, we'll play best of three on skee-ball. Whoever wins chooses where we'll go for our first real date," I tell her, ignoring Ashton's scowl. "And if you win, beautiful, better make it someplace good, because that'll be where we have our first kiss too."

# FOURTEEN

*Mia*

**Brayden: Be ready in an hour.**

I stare at the screen, confused as to how the hell Brayden got my number. I mean, I knew he gave me his number, but I know damn well I haven't used it.

Just to fuck with him…

**Me: New phone, who dis?**

**Brayden: The guy who's picking you up for our first official date. You know, the one that'll end with a kiss that will blow your mind. Now, be ready in an hour, and dress warm.**

My heart pitter-patters in my chest at the thought of going on a real date with Brayden. A few days ago, I would've rather moved back home to live with my parents than go on a date with him. But then, when he showed up at my place, I saw another side of him, and like fungus he kind of grew on me. Those feelings only deepened when we hung out last night. Surprisingly, there's more to him than just the smack-talking conceited Brayden he lets everyone see. He's sweet and funny, and if I'm honest, I'm curious to see how we click when it's just the two of us, and I'm not drunk or hungover.

When I don't reply right away, he sends another message.

**Brayden: Please, Mia.**

That one message says more about him than anything he's said up until now. It tells me that despite his pushiness, and Ashton's running joke about his comments sounding rapey, he respects me and wouldn't do anything I don't want to do. It's his way of asking, and if I tell him no, he'll whine, but in the end, he'll respect my decision.

I start to type out that I'll go, when I remember it's Sunday morning and I'm supposed to have breakfast with Ashton. We have breakfast together every Sunday morning. He didn't mention it, though, last night when we got home from dinner and went our separate ways. I expected him to ask me to hang out and was bummed when he didn't. Ever since our kiss we haven't hung out alone. Ashton was all over me in front of Drew and Brayden, but the second we got in the car, it was as if I had the plague. And we've yet to actually discuss our kiss.

**Brayden: Just one date.**

A part of me wants to go on this date with Brayden. Push what happened with Ashton to the side. But the other part of me, the part that's in love with my best friend, needs to know where we stand first. I mean, I know where I stand. I left a club where I was about to hook up with a hot guy just because he called me, and that was before he kissed me. It was obviously a blessing in disguise since Drew ended up being the hockey coach and Ashton's roomie, and that would've been awkward as hell—well, *more* awkward than knowing Drew's dick is the only dick I've ever touched… and stroked… And then there's the fact that no guy besides him has ever had his fingers in me… But my point is, I ran from Drew that night because of my feelings for Ashton. So, before I try to see what there might be between Brayden and me, I need to make one hundred percent sure Ashton doesn't see a future with us. Chances are he'll tell me the kiss was nothing, but before I move forward, I need to know one way or another.

**Me: Give me a minute.**

**Brayden: What?**

**Me: BRB!**

I drop my phone on my bed and run out of my apartment and over to Ashton's before I lose my false bravado. Since I forgot my key, I bang on the door. A minute later, a tall, shirtless, sexy as hell man answers.

"Is there a fire?" Drew asks, raising a single brow in question.

My jaw drops as I take in his tanned, muscular chest that's on display. I've seen him before, that night we were together... but I was too focused on what we were doing to take the time to appreciate the view. As my gaze descends, I notice he has a tattoo on his ribcage: a quote of some sort. I would have to get closer to read what it says.

As my eyes rake farther down his body, counting each of his abs, he clears his throat, forcing my gaze to go back to his face.

"How long are you going to stand here and eye-fuck me?" he asks. "It's kind of chilly. Think you could finish in here with the door closed?"

He smirks cockily and I groan, embarrassed. How did I go from having no sex life to being attracted to three guys? Well, actually, technically I still have no sex life, since Drew is the coach and off-limits, and even if he wasn't, I still bailed on him because of my feelings for Ashton, who is gay...

"Mia." Drew laughs, making me snap out of it. "Get in here."

"Oh, sorry." I step inside. "I'm here to see Ashton."

"I'm in here," Ashton calls from his bedroom. "Please tell me you brought breakfast."

"No, I didn't," I yell back, stepping past Drew and heading straight to Ashton's room.

"MiMi, I'm starving," Ashton whines, when I get into his room and close the door behind me so we have some privacy.

He glances up from his video game and then pauses it. "Are you okay? You're looking a little flushed."

"Yeah, it's, umm…" I clear my throat. "It's cold outside." When he un-pauses his game, I step in front of the screen. "We need to talk."

Ashton pauses the game again and releases an annoyed sigh. "Can we talk after you feed me? You know it's hard for me to think or communicate before I eat."

"The kiss between us the other night. What did it mean to you?"

Ashton's eyes bulge out and then fly back down to his controller. "My stomach is going to eat my insides if I don't get some food in me soon."

"Don't do that," I plead. "Don't change the subject. I need to know if the kiss between us was just that, a drunken kiss, or if it was more."

When Ashton remains quiet, I add, "Brayden asked me out."

"Rapey Dude Bro Bray, really?"

"He's not rapey," I argue. "He's actually really sweet and funny, and he wants to take me on a date, but I need to know if there's something between us first. I mean, I know you're gay but—"

"That's right," Ashton says, cutting me off. "I'm gay."

My heart sinks into my stomach. I knew this was a possibility, but a piece of me had hoped…

"So, the kiss?" I ask, needing him to verbally confirm it.

"Was just that… A drunken kiss," he says, looking anywhere but at me. I'm not sure if he's doing it because he's full of shit, or because he feels bad.

I kneel in front of him, making him look at me. "So, you're okay with me going out with another guy?"

"Well,      I think you could do better than that asshole jock, but yeah." He shrugs a single shoulder.

"Fine, then I'll tell him yes."

"Just make sure you don't leave your drink unattended."

"Ashton…"

"I'm kidding," he says. "Now, can you please feed me? If I get any skinnier, I'm going to wither away."

"I can't," I tell him, standing. "Brayden and I are going on a date."

His head shoots up. "Now?"

"Yeah, now. Looks like you'll have to get your own food today."

I stalk out of his room and through the apartment. I knew what his answer would be before I came over, but it still hurts. It's my fault, though, for falling for a guy I knew wasn't available. And now it's time to move forward. Ashton and I are best friends, and that's all we'll ever be.

When I get back to my place, I snatch my phone up and text out a reply to Brayden.

**Me: I'll be ready in an hour.**

Then I jump into the shower to get ready for my date.

An hour later, as I'm double-checking my appearance in the mirror, there's a knock on my door. I kept it casual, in a cream-colored V-neck sweater and a pair of black skinny jeans that have rips going down both legs. I'm wearing my cute UGGS and my hair is in a loose ponytail. My face is natural, with only a hint of mascara and lip gloss. I'm also wearing my contacts today instead of my glasses.

The doorbell goes off, and I scoop up my phone, pushing it into my back pocket, and head out to answer the door.

When I open it, Brayden is standing on the other side holding a beautiful bouquet of flowers in his hand with a sports looking bag flung over his shoulder. He's wearing a white long-sleeved Ice Hawk's shirt and a matching hat, a pair of dark-wash jeans that are slightly snug along his muscular thighs, and white tennis shoes.

"Well, don't you clean up nice."

Brayden laughs. "These are for you." He holds out the bouquet for me to take, as I open the door, so he can come inside.

"Thank you, they're so pretty." I bring the flowers up to my nose to smell them.

"You're welcome." He leans in and kisses my cheek. "You look beautiful."

Butterflies swarm in my belly, and I take that as a good sign. I might have feelings for Ashton, *and have a little crush on Drew*, but I'm also very much attracted to Brayden. And unlike the other two, he's available and wants me back.

I set the flowers on the table and grab my keys. "Ready?"

"Absolutely."

I assumed when Brayden asked me out, he meant going somewhere off campus, so I'm confused when, instead of heading out to the parking lot, he takes my hand in his and steers us toward campus.

"Tell me something about yourself," he says as we walk down the sidewalk.

"Like what my favorite food is, or about how I moved here to escape my shitty family?" I ask, unsure how deep he wants to go.

Brayden laughs, and the melodic sound hits me in the chest and slides down, landing between my thighs. I've noticed the few times I've been around him, he doesn't laugh often, but when he does, it's beautiful. His entire face softens, making him look younger, more carefree.

"My motto is usually go big or go home," he says, "but I'm determined to make this date perfect, so, let's go with your favorite food. If you get upset and cry, you might ask to end the date early… And I haven't had enough time to charm you into that kiss yet."

Now it's my turn to laugh. He really is a damn charmer.

"So, food?" he prompts.

"Pineapple pizza. Yours?"

"My mom's lasagna. Favorite band?"

"Hmm… that's a hard one. I'm going to go with Eminem circa two thousand. You?"

Brayden laughs. "I would have to say the same."

"It's a shame we weren't alive back then. I bet he was amazing live."

"Speak for yourself," Brayden scoffs. "I was alive."

"Whatever, you were like two."

"True. Umm… favorite video game."

"That's easy. Super Mario World. Duh. My turn: favorite… sport."

Brayden snorts. "Really? Hockey, of course. Is there any other sport?"

"Well, you could play it but like others…"

"I love it," he admits. "Hockey is my life. My mom swears I could skate before I could walk."

"I believe it. You kicked ass out there last night. I was impressed."

"Thanks," he says. "Umm… favorite color."

"Pink," I tell him before I can think too hard. *Well, it was before Mom ruined that color for me.*

"Really?" He eyes me. "I can't really imagine you wearing pink."

I glance down at my clothes. Today, my outfit is probably considered dressed up compared to how I usually dress in my gamer shirts and baggy pants and overalls.

But I didn't always dress like this… When I was little my mom would dress me up in frilly pink dresses and pink ribbons like I was a beautiful doll. I felt girly and pretty, and she would tell me so. At one point, I wouldn't even leave the house unless I was wearing one, knowing she would coo over me in them. But then one day, when I was wearing my pretty pink dress, she told me I looked fat and insisted I change. And from that day forward, I never wore another pink dress. But it didn't really matter what color I wore, because for the next several years, nothing was good enough. I was too fat, my hips too wide, my breasts too big. And with every put-down, my style changed to hide my imperfect body.

Brayden and I come to a halt, and I notice we're standing in front of the arena where he plays.

"I've changed my mind," he says. "I want the deep."

"What?"

"Just now, when I mentioned I couldn't imagine you wearing pink, you went somewhere else. I want to know where."

"Trust me, you don't want to go there."

"Yes, I do," he insists. "I want the light and the dark, the shallow and the deep. I know we just met, but I want all of you."

I swallow thickly at his request. Not even Ashton knows about my past. When I came here it was to escape and leave all that shit behind. In order to give Brayden a piece of that, I would have to open that box, and I'm scared once it's open, it'll be hard to close.

"My mom and I have a… difficult relationship. Pink symbolizes my past, the happy times before everything changed for the worse." I glance at Brayden and a look of longing comes over his features, like he understands what I mean.

Not wanting to ruin the mood, I ask, "What about you? What's your favorite color?"

"Red." He unlocks the door to the arena and we walk in.

"Are we here for our date, or did you need to stop by to grab something?" I ask while he locks the door behind us.

"Our date," he says, giving me nothing more.

We head down the same hallway, where I ran into him last night, and through a set of doors that take us into the locker room.

"Are we allowed to be here?"

He reaches into what I assume is his locker and grabs his skates. "Nobody comes in on Sundays." He sets down the bag he was carrying and unzips it. "And other than a few people who work here, like the janitors and coach, nobody has a key." He pulls out a pair of white ice skates and hands them to me.

"I glanced at your shoe size the other day when you were asleep," he admits sheepishly. "They should fit."

"You bought me these?" I don't know how much ice skates cost, but it seems like a little much for a date.

"Yeah." He grabs my foot and removes my boot. "You can't live in Michigan and not know how to skate. Don't worry"—he winks—"I won't let you fall and kill yourself."

After he laces up my skates, he helps me stand.

"Here." He pulls a white Ice Hawks hoodie out of the bag. "It's cold on the ice. You'll need this."

I smile at his thoughtfulness and pull the hoodie on. It smells like him—masculine and clean. I try not to inhale too hard. When he leans in, I think he might kiss me, but instead, he brushes his fingers over my ass, making me blush furiously. He pulls my phone out of my back pocket and waves it at me, a grin tugging at his lips.

"You won't want to keep this in there." He slides it into the front hoodie pocket. "Might break if you fall."

"You just wanted an excuse to touch my ass." My body warms when his dark eyes flash devilishly.

He shrugs, neither confirming nor denying my words. "Come on. I've got you."

I wobble the entire way to the ice, but Brayden holds me up so I don't fall. The moment my skates hit the ice, I cringe, knowing this isn't going to end well for me.

"Stop worrying," he says, skating behind me. His hands land on my hips, and he slowly pushes me forward.

"Whoa!" I shriek, my feet slipping and sliding.

"Steady," he murmurs into my ear. "I got you. Just focus on keeping your feet steady. I promise I won't let you fall." I take a deep breath and relax, and the second I do, my feet stop slipping.

"Good girl." He squeezes the sides of my hips in encouragement. "Now I'm going to move. Just let yourself glide with me. Don't resist."

"Okay," I breathe, doing as he says.

We take off slowly, and Brayden skates us around the outside of the rink. We're both silent, as I focus on the ice and making sure I don't bust my ass.

The longer we skate, the more comfortable I feel, and the next thing I know, Brayden's letting go of my waist and taking hold of my hand. "You're doing great," he says. "Keep doing what you're doing."

I chance a glance at him and his eyes lock with mine. He grins a boyish grin and butterflies attack my chest. I'm so absorbed in him, I lose focus. My feet slip and slide and I grab hold of Brayden, hoping he'll save me. But I must catch him off guard, because instead of him steadying us both, I take him down with me. Our asses hit the cold as hell ice, and Brayden and I both crack up laughing.

When I try to stand, my skates slide forward and my back hits the ice.

"Are you okay?" Brayden asks through a laugh.

"Sure," I groan. "Who needs a working tailbone anyway."

He crawls over and hovers above me, until our faces are close together. "I'm sorry," he says, pushing a wayward hair from my face. His eyes drop down to my mouth and I know what's coming next.

"Mia," he murmurs. "I want to kiss you." My heart picks up speed, fluttering against my ribcage like a bird flapping its wings. "Tell me I can kiss you."

Stupidly, I nod.

"I need the words, Mia. Can't have Ashton calling me rapey." His words are meant as a joke, but the mention of Ashton has my stomach churning. I close my eyes briefly to get the thought of him out of my head. I can't let him be here on this date. He made his decision, and now I have to move on.

"Yes, you can kiss me," I tell him, opening my eyes.

He grants me the most gorgeous smile and then his mouth is on mine. Softly, his lips curl around my own. My hands find his beanie, and I remove it, so I can thread my fingers through his hair. He deepens the kiss, his tongue gently seeking entrance.

Unlike the passionate kiss I shared with Ashton, this one with Brayden is tender and sweet. Not better or worse, just different.

And then my phone dings with a text message, ending the moment.

"Next date, we're playing video games," I tell him once we separate. "Where we'll be safe and I won't fall and die."

Brayden's lips curve into a cocky smile. "Next date, huh?" he taunts. "We haven't even finished this one."

"Whatever." I roll my eyes. "You know what I mean."

"Oh, I do," he says, pulling me onto my feet. "You mean, you're enjoying this date so much, you're already planning our next one."

"Keep telling yourself that." I pull out my phone to see who texted, and when I see it was Ashton, my heart drops.

**Ashy C: We need to talk.**

"Everything okay?" Brayden asks, his tone turning serious.

"Yeah, just Ashton." I push my phone back into my pocket without responding.

Brayden eyes me curiously. "Did he say something that upset you?"

"Nope, just that we need to talk."

Brayden helps me off the ice and I plop onto the bench, where it's safe, to rest.

"You and him seem really close," he says, sitting next to me. He lifts my skate and places it into his lap, then starts undoing the laces.

"Yeah, he's my best friend."

"You're a freshman, right?" he asks. "So, you just met him a few months ago."

"Yeah, in the beginning of the summer. Some guy was hitting on me and I used Ashton to scare him away." I laugh, remembering that night. "We hit it off and have been inseparable ever since." He drops my foot and grabs the other skate. "Speaking of which… What's up with you and Drew?"

My eyes are on his hands, so I see when they momentarily still. "We were friends, then we weren't," he says tightly.

"Oh, c'mon," I push. "I gave you a deep. Your turn. What happened?"

He drops my now unlaced skate and looks at me. His brown eyes, which moments ago were bright and full of life, are now dark and stormy. "Life," he says. "Life happened." The raw emotion that emanates from his tone sends chills up my spine, and I decide not to push him on the subject.

"So, does this date include food?" I ask, changing the subject and hoping to lighten the mood.

"Of course," he says, his expression softening. "Let's go grab our shoes and then we can go. Do you like Mexican?"

"Umm, who doesn't?"

# FIFTEEN

*Ashton*

'm gay.

Gay.

Fucking gay.

So why does sending Mia away feel like the dumbest goddamn thing I've ever done in my life? She was so brave. Waltzing right into my room, determined to be an adult about it all.

And me?

I panicked.

Froze up.

Was not prepared to be confronted about my feelings.

Truth is, I don't know what my feelings are. They're a mess. I love Mia. As a friend. But that kiss? The annoying niggling I feel when I see her talk to Brayden? It pokes at other parts of my heart. I'm jealous as fuck over Brayden. When I'd found out she bailed on Drew to come to me, possessive pride washed over me.

I'm not a dick. Definitely not to her.

Yet the way I've been feeling is right there in Brayden dickhead territory. He probably knows all about feeling like a douchebag over a girl. If I didn't despise the prick, I'd ask him for advice.

Problem is, he's the problem.

The guy actively pursuing my girl.

She can't be my girl, though.

I'm. Fucking. Gay.

Am I bi?

Cringing, I can that idea right away. It's not girls. It's Mia. Imagining her naked and beneath me does things to me. Excites unknown areas of me. Opens up dark cavities in my heart that I didn't know existed.

Am I willing to destroy our friendship to use her to test out new avenues regarding my sexuality?

Absolutely not.

Why?

Because I love her.

Back to square fucking one.

*Knock. Knock. Knock.*

"Come in," I grumble.

"I brought food. Overheard that you were hungry and that Mia was bailing on you," Drew says as he opens my door. "Hope you like peanut butter and jelly."

Under any other circumstances, a hot half-naked coach bringing me food in bed would have me giddy and blow-job ready in three seconds.

This isn't under normal circumstances, though.

I'm in the fucking Twilight Zone.

"You okay?" he asks, approaching the bed, a frown on his handsome face.

"Not really."

To my surprise, he hands me the plate and sits down on my bed beside me. With our backs against the headboard and legs stretched out in front of us, I eat my sandwich in silence, pouting. When I finish, he lets out a sigh.

"Spill. Your thoughts are loud and you clearly need someone to talk to. I'm here. Ready and waiting."

I can't help but glance over his broad, sculpted chest. Heat prickles across my flesh, only further reminding me that I like guys, not girls, and this whole Mia thing is a mess.

"Mia left in such a hurry that night with you because she…" I trail off, unable to figure out how to explain this. "She's my best friend. But…"

"She's hot?" he offers.

A laugh barks out of me. "Yeah, if you're into girls."

"But you're not?"

"Nope." I set my plate down on my end table and start fidgeting with the drawstrings of my sweats. "But she's not like other girls."

"That, I can agree on."

"Sorry," I grumble. "This is weird for you."

"Weird, sure, but nothing I can't handle. My whole life's been weird and fucked-up. At this point, I roll with the punches."

I study his sad, forced grin. It makes my chest tighten. If I wasn't feeling selfish and sorry for myself, I'd pry into the mystery that is Drew. One day, whether he likes it or not, I will.

"She came onto me. Kissed me. It got hot. You walked in on the tail end of it."

"Not awkward at all," he deadpans, making us both laugh.

"I've never felt that way about a girl. She consumed me in that moment…"

"But?"

"But then reality hit. I reminded myself I was gay."

"So you're a labels guy then, huh?"

I frown at him. "What?"

"The kind of guy who sticks everyone into a category. Mia: best friend and a girl. Brayden: asshole jock. Me: dad's live-in spy." He smirks at me. "You: openly gay, sarcastic little shit."

My lips curl into a wicked grin. "You forgot to add hot for me."

"And hot," he indulges, making the hairs on my arms stand on end. "Sound about right?"

"It's why I love psychology. Everyone has a warning label."

"Warning labels, huh?"

"Yep."

"What exactly are you protecting yourself from, Dr. Carter?"

I bristle at his words. "I just like knowing what people are so I can deal with them."

"What if people are more than one thing? What if they're not bad?"

"You're starting to sound a lot like my therapist."

"You deflect with jokes and sarcasm. You're cynical and standoffish. People want in, Ashton, but you won't let them because you're a pussy."

"Fuck off. Is this the shitty pep talks you give your players? If so, you should rethink your methods."

"If you like Mia, then go after the fucking girl, man. Ignore the labels you've placed on each of you and just let your feelings guide you."

His words burrow their way deep inside me.

"Too late," I tell him bitterly. "Already let her go off on a date with your bestie Brayden."

He tenses at the mention of Brayden, which only makes me want to pick at that scab more.

"What's your story with him anyway? No offense, but I like you. How were you two ever anything that would require you to be protective over him even when he's a total dick to you?" I ask, frowning at him. "I'm not blind. You want to be in his life in some capacity and he blocks you out."

Drew drags his palm down his face before turning his icy blue eyes my way. "He was my best friend. We were competitive as shit, but when it came down to it, we had each other's backs."

"Until?"

He searches my eyes for a long moment before putting it in a way I completely understand. "I was a labels guy too." He shakes his head in frustration. "I'm trying like hell to get my friend back. It's probably too little too late, but I'm going to damn well try."

"Need me to run interference?"

He frowns.

"Whatever. I don't know jock sports jargon. I'm asking, do you want me to help? Not that I can talk to him, but I could probably terrorize him enough to send him your way needing a friend." I chuckle darkly. "It's the least I could do for him stealing my girl."

Drew's eyebrows fly up. "Your girl?"

I flinch at how that sounds. "You know what I mean."

"I can handle Bray," he states. "But now that he's set his sights on Mia, I'm not sure you can. He's a relentless, competitive brat when he wants to be." He smiles like he's proud of this.

"I'm going to talk to her," I say with growing confidence. "When she gets back, I'll go over there and tell her how I feel."

"You should shower first."

"There's enough room for two in there," I offer. "You look as though you could use one yourself."

His blue eyes flash in a deviant way that makes my dick twitch. "Nah, I can wash my dick all by myself like a big boy."

With those words, he leaves me to myself.

And I absolutely rub one out in the shower to the image of him doing just that.

The second I start hearing sounds through the wall of Mia's apartment, signaling she's home, I bolt. I took Drew's advice and pulled myself together. My hair is fixed, I have on cologne, and I'm wearing something Dad would approve of. I texted her earlier that we needed to talk, but she never responded. Now, I'm going to get my girl.

She screams out in surprise when I fling open her front door.

For a moment, I simply stare at her. Mia really is beautiful. Today, her brown eyes seem soft and her pink lips look puffier than usual. The thought of kissing them has me prowling toward her, a man on a mission. She gasps in shock when my hand grips her jaw. I dart my gaze all over her soft, pretty features before inhaling her scent.

Him.

She smells like Brayden.

And that has an annoyingly possessive need to claim her rising up inside of me.

"You said we were going to talk," she says, her words breathless.

"We'll talk later."

I crush my lips to hers, desperate to see if the kiss we shared before was a drunk mistake. But the moment my lips fuse to hers, I'm starved for her. My free hand slides into her mussed up hair and I clutch onto her, needing her to stay here with me. A small, surprised moan escapes her. Greedily, my tongue slides across hers, wanting to taste the sound straight from the source.

Sweet.

I've never kissed someone so sweet.

Mia is Twizzlers and Fireball and Skittles and happiness.

I could develop cavities from this kiss, and it'd be worth it.

As our kiss deepens, and her breath comes out in pants, I start thinking ahead. Mia naked. Mia's tits. Mia's pussy.

Does a pussy feel good?

What if it doesn't?

Images of us in bed, me unable to perform, threaten my sanity. That would be fucked up. She would hate me. I would hate me.

The kiss turns sour.

Breaking away from her lips, I shake my head.

"I'm sorry, MiMi."

*Sorry for being an asshole.*

*Sorry for not understanding who I am.*

*Sorry for the label I want to slap right over your mouth so you won't fucking frown at me.*

"Ashton," she hisses.

"I'm sorry," I blurt out again, bailing as quickly as I arrived.

Sounds grow distorted and the room spins as I bolt. I'm disgusted. Not with Mia, with myself. I'm a dick. A total, fucking brainless dick.

She calls after me, but I'm already pushing back into my apartment. Drew seems to be headed out based on the fact he's now dressed, but when I stumble, colliding with him, his strong hands grip my shoulders to steady me.

"What happened?" he demands. "You're pale as a fucking ghost, man."

I want to cry. I want to puke. I want to fucking die right now.

"I, uh," I croak out, slamming my eyes shut. "I fucked up."

"How? How did you—"

"No," Mia yells from my doorway. "You do *not* get to do this."

Drew gently smacks at my cheek, forcing me to look into his probing blue eyes. "Ashton. What's going on?"

"What's going on is he's stringing me along," Mia accuses, her words sounding choked with emotion. "He's trying successfully to break my heart." A sob.

I wince. "I'm not," I mutter to Drew, begging with my eyes for him to believe me.

Drew eases me around to face Mia, never letting go of my shoulder. Her cheeks are tearstained, which guts me. My shoulders hunch. I'm unable to look her in her accusing eyes any longer.

"Mia," Drew says softly. "He's your best friend."

Another choked sob.

"You two have a friendship most people would die to have. Are you really going to do this to each other?" he asks. "Blow up on him?" And then to me he says, "Or shut her out?"

She sniffles, breaking my heart.

I chance a look at her. "I don't want to hurt you, MiMi. Fuck, that's the last thing I want."

"Then stop using me to explore your feelings," she rasps out. "I can't take it. I'd rather have my best friend back. All this other stuff is too hard."

"Get over here," I rumble, finally stepping out of Drew's comforting grip.

She rushes over to me, throwing her arms around my neck. I hug her to me, my heart beating out of control and stuck in my throat.

"I'm sorry I fucked up, MiMi. Please forgive me."

She snorts out a humorless laugh. "As if I had a choice. I love you, Ashton Carter, even when you're a confusing asshole."

The jingle of keys can be heard as Drew silently lets himself out of the apartment. Later, I'll have to corner him and thank him for not letting me retreat. For forcing me to deal with this shit with Mia. Having him there, standing behind me, felt more comforting than I'd like to admit.

He was wrong.

I don't see him as Dad's live-in spy.

I see him as my gorgeous, intelligent roommate and now friend.

Maybe people can have a few labels.

Or… fuck labels.

Mia and I, though, our label of best friends, will always be my favorite.

"I get jealous of Brayden. I think you're beautiful. Lately, the urge to kiss you is out of control," I whisper against her hair. "But I'm not enough for you. My mind is too messy. I'm afraid if I ventured out to try something with you, I'll fail. I can't ruin us, Mia. I need you."

"I need you too." She sighs heavily. "I had a wonderful date with Brayden. We kissed. Thought you should know that."

Guilt eats me alive.

I ruined her date because of me.

"MiMi…"

"I'm going to see him again. And I'm going to need my best friend to be just that. My best friend."

"You got it," I promise, hating how my heart doesn't completely like that idea. "Want to eat ice cream and build pig pens on Minecraft?"

"Now you're just sucking up," she says with a laugh.

"Is it working?"

"Kinda."

"Are we good, Mia? I can't bear to think we're not."

She tilts her head to look up at me. "We're good. Now go make me an ice cream sundae while I change out of these clothes."

I can't help but grin down at her. "You're a bossy brat."

And beautiful and brave and my best friend.

"And you're a bitchy boy," she sasses. "That makes us even."

I tickle her ribs, sending her screaming out of my apartment.

We fixed it.

I'll be damned if I break it again.

# SIXTEEN

## Drew

"Hey, Dad. I know it's been a while since I've visited. But in my defense, it's been one helluva a year." I swallow thickly. "I can't believe it's been five damn years since you've been gone." I drop my ass onto the cold grass. Sometimes it seems like I talk to him more now that he's gone than I did when he was alive.

"So, as you can see I'm back in Hawk's Landing. Coaching at Atlantic Pointe. Not exactly what you dreamed for me… Hell, it wasn't what I dreamed for myself. But that's just the way shit shook out."

I pull the hockey puck I brought with me out of my hoodie pocket and roll it around in my hands, mentally preparing for what I'm about to say next. Even if I know my dad can't talk back, saying the next words are still hard because I have to hear them. "Brayden plays for the Ice Hawks… and he still hates me. I don't blame him. Not really. What I did was so stupid and if I could take it back I would."

I take a deep breath and drop my face into my hands. Over the years, after my dad passed away, I used to come here to talk to him. Get shit off my chest since I had no one else to talk to. But right now, as I attempt to spill my guts to him, I feel like maybe I'm talking to the wrong person. Maybe the person I need to be talking to is the guy I'm talking about… "I miss him so fucking much, but I have no clue how to fix shit. If it's not too late, that is."

"Who do you miss?" a masculine voice says, making me jump. I twist my head around and find Brayden standing behind me, dressed in an Ice Hawk's hoodie identical to mine and jeans. His hands are stuffed into his front pockets and his brown eyes are locked on me.

Breaking our stare, I lean forward and place the hockey puck on top of the others I've left over the years and then stand and face him.

For a long minute, I consider how to answer his question. I could lie, but the advice I gave Ashton earlier is still on my mind: *let your feelings guide you.* I think it's time I take my own advice.

"You," I tell him honestly. "I miss you."

And then I wait with bated breath to see how he's going to respond.

Brayden's eyes flicker with a hint of raw emotion before he quickly schools his features, feigning indifference. "Looks like we had the same idea." He juts his chin out toward my dad's gravestone, changing the subject. My heart drops into my stomach at the way he ignored my attempt at telling him how I feel, but I can't fault him. I fucked up first and now I have to deal with those consequences. I hurt Brayden, and I don't blame him for the wall he's erected to protect himself.

"You here to visit Ben?" I ask dumbly. Because really, who else would he be here to visit?

Brayden flinches as his brother's name leaves my lips, and my heart breaks for him.

"Damn it, Bray." I step closer to him. "How long are you going to blame yourself for his death?"

Brayden's eyes cut into thin slits, and his back goes ramrod straight. I probably shouldn't have brought up his brother's death, but Jesus, he's been blaming himself for years, when it wasn't even his fault.

"You can't keep carrying that guilt on your back," I tell him. "Eventually that shit's going to break you."

"Maybe, but I'll still be in better shape than Ben since he's dead," Brayden chokes out.

"But not because of you." I move forward until we're face to face. "What happened was a goddamn tragedy, but it wasn't—"

"Don't fucking say it," he barks. "It *was* my fault, and we both know it. You were there. Mom left *me* in charge of looking after him. She told me to keep him inside, and instead of doing so, I let him convince me to go have a fucking snowball fight in the dead middle of winter." He jabs his fingers into the center of his chest. "I did that. He made me promise not to tell her, and I agreed. He's dead and it's my fault."

"You couldn't have known he was sick," I say, wishing like hell he would stop blaming himself. After all these years, I'm surprised the stress from the guilt hasn't eaten him alive. "He had no symptoms. And you don't even know if taking him outside is what caused the pneumonia. And you'll never know. Maybe if you talk to your parents…"

"I don't want to discuss this." His eyes are rimmed with unshed tears. "I just came by to drop off the puck from the game."

The promise he made to Ben during their last conversation at the hospital. I shouldn't have been listening in, but I was thirteen and worried for my best friend and his brother.

*"Am I gonna die?" Ben asks as Brayden sits next to him on the bed.*

*"No," Brayden tells him, even though only minutes before the doctor told his parents Ben's pneumonia is critical and they should consider saying their goodbyes just in case.*

*"If I do, do you think I can see you play hockey from heaven?"*

*"I don't know, Ben, but I'll raise my stick high after every goal just in case," Brayden promises.*

*I peek in, and Ben is frowning. "Who will you give your winning puck to?"*

*"You're not dying, Ben," Brayden chokes out. "You'll get it like always."*

*"But if I do…"*

*"I'll make sure you still get them."*

Ben died a couple hours later, taking a large piece of Brayden with him.

"I gotta get going," Brayden says, snapping me back to the now. He stalks off down the sidewalk and I chase after him, not wanting our conversation to end like this.

"Wait," I yell after him. He doesn't stop, but he does slow down enough that I'm able to quickly catch up to him. "I know you hate me, but—"

Brayden stops short, and I damn near run into him. "I don't hate you," he says. "In order to hate you I would have to give a shit about you, and I stopped doing that the *second* time you ran away."

"You know that's not true," I say, determined not let him push me away. "I know I fucked up." I step closer to him. "But we're both here at the same school, playing for the same team…"

"I'm playing… You quit, remember?" He crosses his arms over his chest. "Care to explain why?"

I open my mouth to tell him what I haven't been able to tell anyone but my dad, but I can't make the words come out. Because once they do, it'll make it all too fucking real. As long as nobody knows, I can pretend a little longer that my hockey career isn't over. That I'll never play another sixty-minute game in front of thousands of fans. That everything I worked for my entire life hasn't been destroyed.

When I don't speak up quick enough, Brayden laughs humorlessly. "Didn't think so."

He takes off toward the parking lot, and again, I follow after him. "Wait, please."

"What?" he barks, stopping and facing me again.

"Can we please just start over?"

"And what, go back to before my brother died? Before you left me? Sorry, I can't do that," he says. "My brother isn't coming back, and I can't pretend like you didn't run away… twice."

"Then how about a truce?" I ask, trying a different angle. "The fact is you play for the team I coach, and yeah, we have a past, but if we don't do something, call some sort of truce, it's going to be one long ass season. And it's not fair to the other guys on the team who are left having to pick sides."

Brayden releases a harsh breath, his gaze searing into mine, as he contemplates what I'm asking. "Fine," he finally says. "A truce… for the season."

"Thank you."

"I'm taking one for the team."

We walk to our vehicles in silence, and just as I'm about to get inside my truck, Brayden calls out my name. "I'm going by the rink to run through some drills, if you want to join." Without waiting for me to answer, he jumps into his SUV and takes off.

I'm not turning down any invitation he throws my way. Not ever again.

When we get to the arena, neither of us says a word. We stay silent as we get changed and lace up.

The second my skates touch the ice, my heart thumps against my ribcage.

Brayden throws me a stick and drops the puck, and even though it's freezing inside, my body breaks out into a cold sweat, as if remembering the last time I played hockey. It's been over a year since then. But this isn't like then. I'm not actually playing, I'm just messing around.

Brayden skates toward me and passes the puck my way. "Let's go," he says, already skating backward toward the net. "One on one." It's a drill players do to work on their defensive skills.

I take off with the puck and skate toward him, trying to figure out which way he's going to try to defend me. Predictably, he tries to take me to the outside, but because I'm already expecting it, I'm able to fake, which opens up the lane for me to shoot. I drive the puck straight into the net, as Brayden curses under his breath.

"Gonna have to try harder than that," I tell him, grabbing the puck and passing it back to him. I forgot how good it feels to play, and my entire body is thrumming with pent-up adrenaline.

Brayden heads down the center and I stay on him. If he were doing this during a real game, I'd be yelling at him—everyone knows you don't go center—but since we're only fucking around, I let it go. When he realizes he won't be able to pass me, he pivots, skating behind the net. I crash him into the boards and steal the puck. My heart is pumping in my chest, and my breaths are labored, reminding me how out of shape I am, but fuck if it doesn't feel good to be able to get physical again.

"Oh, so that's how you want to play," he yells from behind me, his competitive side making its appearance. "Okay, game on."

For the next twenty minutes, we take turns defending each other. With every possession, it gets more intense. More physical. More heated. Our focus turning to knocking each other down instead of trying to score. As if we're taking the last eight years out on each other. And instead of saying the shit we need to say, we're slamming each other into the boards.

*I hate you.*

*I miss you.*

*You shouldn't have left.*

*I regret it.*

When he checks me extra fucking hard, sending me flying across the ice, I get up and do it back to him, only instead of him getting back up and starting again, he must reach his breaking point, because he chucks his stick and skates toward me, pulling his helmet off his head and dropping it onto the ice.

"What the fuck, man!" He shoves me against the wall as I take in huge gulps of air, trying to catch my breath. My lungs and heart screaming at me for going from zero to sixty.

I remove my own helmet and shove him away from me. "How was what I did any different than the last ten times you checked me?"

"You're playing like an asshole," he hisses. "If you got something to say, just say it."

"I already did at the cemetery." I step closer. Our eyes lock on each other, and it's as if something in the air shifts, the tension suddenly growing thick. "I miss you."

"No," Brayden snaps. "You don't get to miss me. You chose to leave." He turns his back on me, and I grab his shoulder, flinging him around and pushing him against the boards. I don't know what's come over me, maybe it's the conversation from earlier with Ashton… But I suddenly have the need to tell Brayden just how I feel.

"I miss you every fucking day." We're so close, our faces are only inches from each other, our chests touching as they both rise and fall in sync.

"I know I fucked up," I tell him, "but I was young and scared…"

"We both were," he barks. "But you ran." He sighs. "I needed you and you ran. And then even after all that, when you needed me, when your fucking dad died, I still showed up. I had your back."

His eyes close momentarily, as if he's trying to get control of his emotions. His tongue darts out, running along the seam of his lips. And before I can think about what I'm doing, my mouth is crashing against his. His lips are firm yet also soft in their own way. Just like they were the last time I felt them against my own.

Time slows to a stop.

Like the last few seconds of a championship game, it's over in an instant.

And then he shoves me away, ending the kiss before it even began.

"What the hell," he hisses, his eyes filled with a myriad of emotions: hurt, shock, and if I'm not mistaken, lust. "This"—he waggles his finger between us—"is not part of our truce."

He skates off the rink and I stay where I am, trying to figure out what the hell I was thinking.

# SEVENTEEN

*Brayden*

Truce?

Yeah, fucking right.

Our truce lasted all of three seconds until he pressed his lips to mine, starting a war.

I'm so pissed at him, I can't even see straight. Yesterday, after he pulled that shit on me at the rink, I went back to my dorm room and paced all evening until I ran my roommate off. I'd wanted so badly to march over to Drew's apartment and tell him off.

Again.

What's there to say, though?

Instead, I attempted to study until I was bleary-eyed and the anger that flowed through my veins finally cooled. Today, I just feel tired.

Tired of Drew.

Tired of the way he makes me so furious.

Tired of the past always dictating my life.

This morning's practice reflected just that. He was relentless, too. Riding my ass the whole time, bitching at me to skate harder, move faster, and pay attention. I'd wanted to kill him, but for the team, I managed to bite my tongue.

"You okay?" Finn asks, dragging me from my thoughts. "You kind of played like shit earlier."

I flip him off. "Tell me how you really feel."

"You know I love you," he states, laughing. "Whatever it is, you gotta get over it, man. Do some fucking yoga or get laid."

Thoughts of Mia come to mind, which has me smiling. "I'll try."

"The yoga or the sex?"

"Can't it be both?" I playfully shoulder check Finn on my way out of the locker room. "See ya later."

I'm rushing down the hallway to avoid a run-in with Drew when I do exactly that.

Run into him.

We both grunt in surprise, and I jolt back, hating the fire that's once again burning angrily through me.

"Bray," he starts, but I shake my head as I pass by him. "We need to talk eventually."

"Talking with you always ends badly."

His hand clasps over my shoulder, stopping me. "Please…"

"I'm late. Maybe later."

He releases me without a word and I haul ass out of there. Rather than head out to the parking lot where I know other guys will already be hanging out, I take a different turn, winding my way through the athletic buildings. I'm about to turn around and head back the way I came when a guy enters through a side door.

A familiar guy.

Mia's best friend.

There's something about Ashton that rubs me. His maddening smirks. The arrogance that practically drips from him. All his snide-ass remarks.

And Mia? She just laughs.

When we'd all gone out last weekend after the game, I watched their interaction with jealous interest. There was a time Drew and I ribbed each other the way they did. Laughed at each other's jokes. Had whole conversations with just our eyes.

The way he stared at her…

I know he's gay, but that night I caught him staring at her like he fucking forgot that fact.

He's wearing a thin zip-up hoodie and stops just inside the door to dust snow out of his hair. His bag starts to slide off his shoulder. With a grunt, he pulls it back up and then strolls over to another doorway.

I don't know what compels me to follow him, but I do.

Every time I've seen him, he acts like he doesn't give two shits about anything or anyone but Mia. I haven't really seen him without her company.

I'm surprised to see him enter an Olympic-sized indoor pool area. He drops his bag onto the bleachers near one end of the pool. I walk along the perimeter of the pool that's already splashing with swimmers, and make my way closer. He kicks off his Doc Martens and then unzips his hoodie. In a way, I feel like a creep watching him, but I'm curious about what makes him so special. Mia clearly adores him.

Someone calls out to him from the water and he gives them one of his douche-y head nods like he's the coolest motherfucker at this school, and then peels off his jacket. After he tosses it, he reaches behind his head to grab the fabric of his T-shirt.

I stand there just watching.

Knowing he's undressing to swim.

Waiting to…

Compare myself to him?

I'm not sure.

He bends slightly as he peels off his T-shirt, revealing hard back muscles. His pants are hanging off his waist just low enough I get a glimpse of a hint of his ass crack. With a swift flick of his wrist, he undoes his belt and sends his jeans to the ground.

Tight ass blue fuckin' spandex shorts.

I'm about to bust my ass up laughing, but then he turns to the side as he pulls off his socks, revealing a form that's not all that funny. Instead, I'm impressed. His legs are long and lean, but his upper body is cut with muscle, especially his upper back and shoulders. How did I not realize this guy was an athlete? He looks like your typical stoner metal-head weirdo who apparently moonlights as an underwear model.

Once he's shoved all his clothes into his bag, he rolls his head on his shoulders. I set my own bag down on a bench and sit so I can watch him. It's probably best I leave, but I'm too invested now. I want to see him swim.

He grabs a white swim cap from the zipper of his bag and then folds the edges back. His biceps flex as he pulls it over his forehead and then begins peeling it down over his hair. He makes quick work of stuffing any stray hairs beneath the latex. After grabbing a pair of goggles, he tugs those into place and then starts to stretch.

It's fascinating watching him.

I've never given two shits about swimming.

But as he bends and swivels and stretches his long limbs, I grow more curious about his abilities. I wonder what sort of stroke he normally swims. I wonder a whole lot about this guy who gets on my nerves.

My eyes do skim over his dick, because it's almost like he's putting his junk out there on display wearing that shit. He's packing, much to my surprise.

"Carter, you going to be at the meet?" some dude calls out from the water.

Ashton's shoulders tense and then he gives that dude a cocky grin. "Yeah, man. Why wouldn't I?"

"Right on," the dude says.

Ashton spends the next few minutes bouncing on his feet and shaking out his arms. Then, he shakes out his shoulders. I'm given no warning for what happens next. He hops onto a small black platform, bends over, then dives in.

And just like that, the place goes quiet as they watch him.

I can see why, too.

He's a fucking dolphin or some shit.

When he resurfaces a quarter of the way down, he comes out of the water with impressive power. All of his shoulder muscles bulge with each movement. With powerful kicks of his legs that seem fused together, he slices through the water with inhuman speed.

I'm amazed at this asshole's incredible ability.

He makes it to the end within seconds, flips under the water, and kicks off the edge, then goes at it again. By the time he makes it to the other side, no more than forty or fifty seconds have passed. I'm exhausted for him, but he surprises me when he climbs back out, glares at the water, and then steps back onto the platform.

"Wait for me," the dude calls out to him.

"Brady, that's all I do when we race." Ashton laughs at him.

The dude—Brady—just grins back. They both perch onto their spots and then someone blows a whistle.

Again, Ashton flies through the water. Brady is so far behind him, it's almost laughable. When I hear a laugh—one that sounds bitter and nasty—I reluctantly drag my gaze over to the sound of it.

Some dickhead is standing near Ashton's stuff. He manages to stop glaring at the pool long enough to edge closer. There's intent written all over his twerp face. When he bends over Ashton's bag, I abandon my own to stalk over to him.

"Yo, not your shit."

His head whips up and he winces. "What?"

"You know what," I say lowly. "You're lingering like you're going to do something to his bag. Beat it, asshole."

His lip curls up in disgust. "You don't belong here, hockey prick."

I narrow my eyes at him. Something clicks. I know this guy. He was fucking with Mia at the game she came to. Stepping up to him, I poke his chest.

"You don't belong here, standing over Ashton's fucking bag, fuckface."

He tries to stand up to me, but I'm taller, stronger, and meaner. I'm not about to kick someone's ass and get booted from the hockey team, but I'm also not about to let him creep around Mia's best friend's shit.

"What's up, dick licker?"

Ashton's smartass words arrive moments before he does. Then, he's standing beside me, dripping and rippling with a storm of adrenaline and barely suppressed rage. I figure it's aimed toward me, but he's staring right at fuckface.

"I can't figure you out, Ashton," the guy says. "First you're with guys. Then you're fucking around with girls. Now you're blowing jocks like this asshole. I thought you were gay. Maybe you're bi. One thing's for sure, you're a fucking whore."

I snort out a laugh. "No, wiseass. Your mom's a whore."

It's so juvenile, but it has Ashton laughing.

The guy's face turns purple, but I have to give him credit, he isn't backing down from this standoff.

"All this time off, Travis," Ashton says lowly, his voice a menacing growl, "has given me time to practice. I'm pretty sure I shaved two seconds off my best time on the one hundred-meter butterfly. What was your best time again?" Ashton shoves past him, scooping up his bag before sneering at Travis. "Oh, that's right. Always several seconds behind me."

Ashton storms off toward the locker room without looking back. I smirk at Travis before heading back over to my bag. My phone buzzes in my hoodie pocket. I pull it out to read the text.

**Mia: Did you study, mister? You have a test Thursday.**

Grinning, I reply.

**Me: Too busy thinking about you.**

I really have been studying for it, but it's more fun to tease her.

**Mia: Gag. Ew. Don't say corny pickup lines like that. I'm allergic.**

**Me: Fine. I studied, ice princess.**

**Mia: I think you meant ass princess since that's where I ended up on our date.**

**Me: We could always go on another date soon… somewhere softer for that cute ass. Like my lap.**

**Mia: Gag. Again. You're killing me.**

**Me: Friday, after the game, I'll take you out for dinner and I'll throw all my pickup lines at you. I won't be able to get rid of you after that. You'll be a goner for my maddening charm.**

**Mia: Definitely maddening. As enticing as that is, I can't. For real this time.**

**Me: Ashton?**

The dots move and stop a few times before she replies.

**Mia: No. Why?**

**Me: He's your best friend.**

**Mia: Oh, lol. No, I'm going to California to visit my mom and dad.**

**Me: The mom you don't get along with? Need a wingman?**

**Mia: I wish. I'll manage a way to get through.**

**Me: When you get back, I'll reward you with pineapple pizza, even if it is the grossest shit I've ever seen.**

**Mia: Sounds like a date!**

Dates with Mia distract me from things like unwanted kisses from Drew.

Asshole.

"Why are you here?" Ashton grunts, no longer half naked and wet. He's changed back into his clothes and has his bag slung over his shoulder. His hair is wet on the roots around his ears and along his neck where the cap rode up.

"Watching you."

"Got that, stalker. Why?"

"You didn't tell me you were half merman."

He lifts a brow. "Of all the fucking shit you could come up with? Merman?" He shakes his head and walks back toward the doors.

I snag my bag and trot after him. "Would you prefer whale?"

He shoots me the bird over his head.

"Fine, fucker, you swim like a dolphin. Happy?"

His head turns so he can sear me with his probing hazel eyes. "A little."

Laughing, I follow him out into the hall and then out the side door. As soon as we step outside, snowflakes flutter around. We've been having small flurries, but nothing's sticking yet. It's going to be one helluva winter if we're already getting hit with snow.

"It's fucking cold out here," he whines, squinting against the wind. "Why are you following me?"

I reach into the side of my bag and yank out a beanie. "Put this on, whiny."

Rather than glaring at my Ice Hawks beanie like it's a snake, he yanks it out of my hand and pulls it on over his head. I'm surprisingly grateful he took it without argument.

"You're a good swimmer," I tell him when we reach the parking lot where his car sits beneath a thin layer of snow.

He hits the fob, unlocking it, before turning to flash me an arrogant grin. "I'm the best."

After seeing him destroy that Brady kid, I have no doubt.

My phone buzzes in my pocket.

**Mia: I can fit you in Thursday.**

**Me: For our date?**

**Mia: No, dork. For a tutoring session.**

**Me: Your place?**

**Mia: The tutoring center. I'm on to your tricks.**

**Me: I can still steal a kiss there, babe. No one's going to kick me out.**

**Mia: If you're good and stay focused, maybe you won't have to steal it.**

Challenge accepted.
Hopefully Mia's kiss will help me erase the one Drew gave me.
I'm tired of Drew taking up space in my mind.
So fucking tired.

# EIGHTEEN

*Mia*

"**A**nd what's one of the main themes from 'The Yellow Wallpaper'?"

"Gender," Brayden says, "because she was a woman and during that time that meant she was confined to the home. When she speaks, it's for all women and not just her."

"Good." I glance over the questions we've been going over before his quiz on the short story. "And what about—"

"Nope." Brayden plucks the paper from my hands and tosses it to the side. "Every correct answer equals a kiss." He frames my cheeks and presses his mouth to mine, his tongue wasting no time delving past my parted lips. My fingers go to his nape, and I'm about to deepen the kiss, when there's a throat clearing that has me remembering where we are: at the tutoring center.

Breathlessly, I push Brayden away and adjust my glasses. He smirks, no doubt loving that he got me all hot and bothered.

"The last I checked, Brayden was failing English and History, not Sex Ed," Drew says, glancing from Brayden to me.

"Nope, definitely not failing Sex Ed." Brayden winks at me, making me roll my eyes. "I'm passing that class with flying colors, especially when the teacher is Mia."

"Funny," I say. "I wasn't aware you were even enrolled in that class."

Brayden grins. "Oh, I'm enrolled. We're just covering the basics right now. We'll get deeper into the course soon, though."

When Drew snort-laughs, I remember he's here and just heard everything Brayden said.

"And on that note," I say, my face and neck heating up in mortification. "You better get to class before you're late."

Brayden checks the time on his phone and stands. "I'll call you when I get out." Then to Drew he says, "You don't need to check up on me. I told you I would handle it and I am."

I don't miss the way Drew flinches at his words, and I wonder, not for the first time, what their story is. "If I don't answer, I'm on the plane," I remind Brayden. I'm flying out tonight to California for three days.

Brayden turns his attention back to me. "All right. Text me before you fly out." He dips his head and kisses me softly before he takes off. I don't know when kissing each other goodbye became such a normal occurrence between us, but I must admit, I kind of like it.

"See ya later at practice," Drew calls after him. Brayden doesn't turn around, but he throws a hand up to indicate he heard him.

"How's he doing?" Drew asks once Brayden is gone.

"Who's asking? His friend or his coach?"

Drew flinches again. "We're not friends, so his coach."

"He's doing well. He just needed someone to help organize his thoughts." I pack my books and laptop into my backpack and zip it up.

"You heading home?" Drew asks. The question has my heart bottoming out into my stomach. Texting and talking with Brayden these last few days has been the perfect distraction from my life. Between having to psych myself up to go home and deal with my mom for seventy-two hours, and the way Ashton's been acting toward me since we agreed to just be friends, it feels like I've developed five ulcers.

But when I'm talking to Brayden, he keeps my mind occupied with his flirting, and for a little while, I feel like I'm able to breathe again. Until he leaves and I'm left worrying about everything that's going on.

"Yeah," I tell him, slinging my backpack over my shoulder.

"I'm heading home too. Wanna walk together?"

"Sure."

We step outside and the ground is free from all the snow from the last few days. It's warmer today and the sun is out. We walk in silence. I should probably try to make conversation, but I can't stop thinking about everything that's going on. I'm leaving in a few hours and Ashton is acting weird. I need my best friend right now more than ever and he's been MIA all week, and even when he is around, it's like he's somewhere else.

When we step into our apartment building, I realize neither of us said a single word to each other. "Sorry, I wasn't the best walking partner," I joke.

"It's okay." Drew steps in front of his and Ashton's apartment. "I have a lot going on too." He unlocks the door and opens it. "Are you coming in to see Ashton?"

"Yeah, I'll see if he's around before I go home to pack."

I check Ashton's room and he's not here. I should probably just go home, but I'm afraid if I don't stay here and wait for him, I won't see him before I go, and I hate the thought of leaving while we're in this weird place.

"Would you mind if I waited?"

"No." Drew opens the fridge and tosses me a bottle of water. "So, based on the way you let Brayden kiss you without kicking his ass, I'm assuming things are going well," he says, sitting next to me on the couch.

I glance over at him, unsure if he's the right person to be talking about whatever's happening between Brayden and me.

"What?" he asks.

"Nothing… It's just…" I nervously laugh. "Isn't it weird talking about Brayden and me?"

Drew falters and his eyes dart over to mine. "Why would you say that?" His tone is slightly defensive.

"Well, you know… A few weeks ago we almost…"

Drew releases what sounds like a relieved sigh and laughs. The tension in his shoulders melts away as he flashes me a devilish smirk. "We almost what?"

"You know what." I slap his arm. "When we were in that room at The Lodge."

"Know what?" His brows furrow together in false confusion.

Fine! He wants me to spell it out for him, two can play this game. "When you stuck your fingers in me… and I had my hand on your dick."

Drew chokes on his water, clearly shocked I would come out and say it, then coughs to cover it up. "Well, now it's weird." He laughs. "Since I now have the image of you spread out on that bed, with my…"

The door swings open and Ashton storms in like a tornado. His face is down, looking at his phone, so he doesn't notice me at first.

"Hey," I say, making my presence known.

His head snaps up, and a look of shock and… disgust flashes over his features. My stomach roils. Something is wrong. Way wrong.

"What are you doing here?" he asks with irritation in his tone that has me regretting waiting for him.

"Didn't you get my text?" My eyes dart to his phone in his hand. He obviously did and ignored it. "I'm leaving soon."

"I didn't know your text required a reply," he says, walking past me. "I reek of chlorine. I need to shower." He disappears into his room, leaving me sitting here, almost in tears.

"Hey." Drew covers his hand with mine. "You okay? I know some stuff has happened between you and Ashton…"

My gaze darts over to him. He knows? Has Ashton confided in him? It would make sense since they're roommates.

"Has he been acting okay this week?"

"He's been a little more distracted than usual," Drew notes. "Not as many witty comments."

"I'm worried," I admit softly. "Maybe I should cancel my trip."

"Don't do that. I'll keep an eye on him for you."

"Thank you." I sigh in relief, feeling a little better about leaving. "Give me your number." I pull my phone out and open it to my contacts.

"Aren't you already juggling enough guys?" Drew jokes.

"Ha-ha." I hand him my phone. "So you can keep me updated."

He types in his info, then hands it back to me. When I glance at what he typed, I'm confused. "Guy Number One?"

"Well, I was the first guy in the picture, before Brayden and Ashton fell for you." He laughs, mischief twinkling in his eyes.

I'm laughing at his remark, when Ashton's door creaks open and he steps out into the hall in nothing but a towel slung low around his hips. Water dripping down his firm chest and washboard abs. My girly parts clench at the sight of his nipple piercing—something he religiously wears when he's not swimming. A simple tiny metal bar shouldn't have such an effect on me, but it does. I wonder what it would feel like to run my tongue along the metal and—

Drew clears his throat, shaking me from my thoughts. My eyes slowly rise to meet Ashton's, knowing I've been caught checking him out. I'm expecting him to make some cocky comment about it, and with the way things are going, I'm actually hoping he does. I don't even care at this point that he caught me drooling over him.

But he doesn't.

"What are you still doing here?" he asks, making me gasp in shock and hurt.

"I was waiting for you." I stand. "I thought we could hang out before I go."

He stares at me for a long moment and then sighs. "All right. Let me get dressed and I'll meet you over at your place."

Once he disappears back into his room, Drew says, "I'll watch out for him. I promise." He takes my hand and squeezes it. "Go on your trip and if you need to know anything, I'll text you." He smiles softly and his sexy dimple pops out.

"Thank you." I lean over and kiss his cheek. "It means a lot to me."

I'm in the middle of packing my luggage when Ashton saunters into my room, dressed in a gray long-sleeved Jane's Addiction shirt and holey jeans, complete with his black Doc Martens. The guy puts like zero effort into what he wears and somehow it makes him look even sexier.

"What's up?" he says, dropping onto the edge of my bed, his eyes never leaving his phone.

"Packing. You gonna miss me?" I joke, hoping to lighten the mood.

When he doesn't respond, my mind races with worry. He told me we were fixed, that things would go back to the way they were, but he lied. Everything is broken and nothing is the way it was.

I grab two tiny dresses and hold them up to get his attention. "Which one should I wear to the dinner party?"

I expect him to make a comment about them being too short, but he only looks up and says, "Both look fine."

His comment is my breaking point. I drop the dresses and round the bed, stopping in front of him. "Hey." I snatch his phone from him. I want to ask him if everything's okay between us, but I'm scared of what his answer will be. So instead I say, "You know you can talk to me, right?"

"Yeah, I know." His eyes dart all over the room, looking everywhere but at me. I don't know what to say, how to fix this, and it's breaking my heart. I hate that I'm leaving while we're like this, but I don't have a choice.

"Okay." I sigh in defeat. "I better get going." I stand and zip up my luggage, then drop it onto the ground. I roll it to my front door and Ashton follows. When we get outside, I lock my door then turn to my best friend. "I'll see you when I get back."

"Yeah." He plasters the fakest smile on his face, and I have to force back the tears. I can literally feel myself losing my best friend. I want to jump into his arms and beg him to talk to me, to not shut me out, but I have a plane to catch, and I'm not sure I want to know how he would respond.

"I'll miss you," I tell him.

"Me too," he says back, already walking down the hall. When he gets to his front door, he turns quickly and says, "Safe travels, MiMi," then disappears into his apartment, leaving me standing there speechless. A single tear escapes down my cheek, and I swipe it away, refusing to cry right now. I need to be strong for my trip or my mom will eat me alive.

"Mia Lynn," Mom says for the millionth time tonight, making me roll my eyes. "Have you tried applying serum to under your eyes? Those dark circles add several years to your age and not in a good way."

"I'll definitely check it out," I say stiffly, reminding myself that in less than three days I'll be on a plane heading back to Michigan. I just need to get through this first.

This isn't the first comment she's made since I arrived a few hours earlier, and it won't be the last. It's what she does, her way of making it clear I'm not enough. Flawed. Imperfect.

*"Have you put on weight? Because your hips look wider. I've heard about the freshman fifteen but never experienced it."*

*"Are you taking care of your hair? It looks dry."*

*"Maybe you should wear close-toed shoes to dinner. Your pedicure doesn't look fresh."*

*"When's the last time you got a decent manicure? I guess it's to be expected in a town like that one."*

*"Oh, is that the dress you're wearing to the dinner party?"*

My phone vibrates in my hand, and I glance at it. It's Brayden. Funny how just his name on my screen has my heart fluttering in my chest.

"It's rude to walk around with a phone while we have guests over," Mom says, glaring at me.

"I'm sorry. I've been waiting to hear from a guy I've been tutoring. He took his quiz and is waiting for the professor to post the grades."

"Maybe you should focus on your own studies," she says. "I saw your grades the other day. A B in creative writing. How do you expect to ever be taken seriously in the writing world with grades like that?"

I open my mouth to argue that it's a senior level class and there's only one grade so far, but stop myself. I made straight As all through school and she never once complimented me. Of course the one time she comments is when I have one B, which is only two points away from an A.

"I'll bring it up," I tell her as my phone vibrates again. "I better answer this." Before she can argue, I slip away, quickly running up the stairs to my room. I close the door behind me, taking a deep breath. Now that I'm far enough away from her I feel like I can breathe a little easier.

I click on Brayden's name to return his call, as I kick off my heels and start stripping out of my dress. I've been mingling for hours down there and have fulfilled my obligation for the evening. I have no intention of returning.

"Hey," he says, his masculine voice husky and sexy. "Guess who got a B on his quiz?"

"What? Really?"

"Yep! And I'm thinking I deserve something extra special for it."

"Oh, really?" I laugh, already feeling lighter. "And what do you think it is you deserve?"

"Well, if getting a right answer equals a kiss, I imagine getting a B on my quiz is worth way more... At least some tongue action."

His words make me think of Ashton's and my kiss, both times, and how it ruined everything, changed everything. And now I'm not sure anything between us will ever be the same.

"Mia," Brayden says.

"Huh?"

"I asked you a question." Shit, I was lost in thought and zoned out. Brayden deserves better than that.

"I'm sorry. I got distracted." I put the phone on speaker so I can get dressed into my pajamas.

"Everything okay?"

"No," I blurt out, taking the phone with me to the en suite bathroom so I can remove my contacts and clean off my face. "My mom is a monster, and my dad is too busy kissing her ass to see how horrible she is. I'm stuck here, like Cinderella pre-fairy godmother, while my best friend is acting weird, and I think our friendship might be over because we kissed...

twice… and now everything is all messed up and I miss him and I don't know what to do. And honestly, I'm not even sure there's anything I could do even if I were there. I don't think he wants to be friends anymore, and it makes me so damn sad." My voice cracks on the last word, as tears well up and fall down my face.

We're both quiet for a long moment, and I cringe, realizing I just word vomited all over Brayden and he's probably ready to bolt. And I wouldn't blame him.

"I'm sorry." I sigh. "You were probably looking for an easy lay, and instead you jumped on the crazy train. I won't blame you if you jump off," I tell him, as I laugh through my tears. God, can I get any crazier?

"One, I'm not looking for an easy lay. If I were, you would be the last person I would go to. I told you on our date I want all of you, and I meant it." Butterflies swarm my belly. "I'm completely okay taking a ride on the crazy train," he jokes.

"And two?" I prompt.

"I thought Ashton was gay."

Oh, yeah, I admitted to kissing him… twice.

"He is. He regretted it the second it happened… both times. And now things are all weird between us. He's barely spoken ten words to me all week."

"Maybe it's not you," Brayden says. "I ran into him at the pool on Monday and that guy who was giving you shit at my game was there. Seemed to piss Ashton off."

"Travis?" I set my phone down and remove my contacts, placing them back in their holder.

"Yeah, he was looking shady as fuck, and when I confronted him, he got pissed. Words were said. Maybe Ashton is dealing with that."

"Maybe," I say, upset that Ashton never once mentioned Travis giving him shit. "Wait, you got in the middle of it?" I wet a washcloth and start cleaning my face.

"He's your best friend," Brayden says as if him being my best friend is all the reason he needs to have Ashton's back. My heart does a weird flip-flop and I find myself smiling.

"Thank you. That means a lot to me." I take the phone off speaker as I walk back into my room and then climb into bed.

"No problem. Wish I could do something to make you feel better."

"That's sweet." I cuddle up into my blanket. "I wish you were here." I sigh into my pillow, more than ready for this day, hell, this weekend, to be over.

"Me too," he says, his voice low.

A yawn escapes my lips and my eyes grow heavy. "Can you maybe talk to me until I fall asleep?"

Brayden chuckles. "Sure, what do you want to talk about?"

"Anything. Tell me a story."

"Hmm, okay. Once upon a time there lived a princess…"

I try to keep my eyes open, but before he even finishes the first sentence, I'm already falling asleep to the sound of his soothing voice.

# NINETEEN

*Ashton*

A real laugh bubbles out of me.

Loud and obnoxious.

Mom's green eyes glitter with delight. At least she's a fun drunk. When we've both been sucking down the wine, I turn into her dancing monkey that makes her laugh, and Dad glares at us both with that look of disappointment he's long since perfected.

Mom dabs away the tears of laughter with her linen napkin. We're at Roadman's Steaks, an upscale restaurant in Hawk's Landing, tucked away in a corner. Family dinners for us always turn weird.

"How's swim practice?" Dad grinds out, trying desperately to keep us on normal topics.

"If you're asking if I've been smuggling in weed in between swimming circles around Brady, then the answer is no. Been too busy," I deadpan.

Dad sets his steak knife down with a clank on his plate and frowns at me. "Enough with the pity party. We know it wasn't you. Your drug test was negative."

"Just like I told you," I remind him.

"But you *did* have the drugs on you." He sighs and pinches the bridge of his nose. "I'm the dean, Ashton. I couldn't let that go."

"Of course not, Dad. Of course not." My tone drips with sarcasm. "So, Mom, got any new nose jobs lately?"

This sends her into another fit of giggles. I love my mom, I really do, but sometimes she's a fucking embarrassment. Everyone in this town kisses her ass, though, because she's loaded. Long before Dad ever swept her off her feet, she was wealthy beyond means. From the moment he took her out on their first date, he's been proving to her family that he's a worthy husband who isn't reliant on their money.

So that makes us doubly rich.

But when you have a flighty mother and a career-hungry father, you're left with an emotionally neglected kid with fucked-up genes added to it.

"Kathy, my esthetician, says she has a little brother your age. Offered to set you up," Mom reveals. "But he's a bartender." She cackles. "I told her you were dating someone."

"Wendy," Dad mutters. "It's inappropriate to set your son up on a date."

"I didn't set him up," Mom huffs. "If I did, it'd be with that gorgeous new resort owner. What's his name, Curtis? I can't remember."

"Peter Lombardi. And he's not…"

My brow lifts, waiting for him to finish that statement.

"He's not like Ashton," he finally grits out.

"No one is," I tell Dad with a wolfish grin.

"I just don't understand why you get weird about the whole thing," Mom says after she drains her fourth glass of wine. "It's just two boys. Nothing wrong with that. You always wanted two sons. Maybe one day you'll get your wish. All that hard work is paying off."

Dad's nostrils flare. "You've had enough to drink."

"I'm gay. I sleep with men. If we don't talk about it, it becomes a dirty little secret." I laugh when Dad cringes at my words. "Kind of like that time

Mom was getting plowed by her yoga instructor. Remember that, Mom? What was his name? Raul?"

Dad slams his fist down on the table, making all the dishes clatter and the glasses slosh. "Enough."

"Raul was just a phase." Mom waves her hand in the air like it's nothing. "You got your apology."

A black 1965 Porsche 356 SC Cabriolet.

Apparently, your Latino lover mishap can be forgiven to the tune of three hundred thirty-four thousand dollars. Mom promised to go to marriage counseling. I got dragged into therapy for shits and giggles. Dad got a fucking car.

Fun times in the Carter family.

"Am I excused?"

Dad growls. "You're shitfaced, Ashton. No, you're not excused. You're going to get some coffee in you before you go anywhere."

That would mean too many hours to sober up while under Dad's disapproving stare.

Hard pass.

"I'll call an Uber."

Mom's overly filled upper lip curls up. "Lord no, baby. Those things are filled with needles and coke dust and ejaculation."

I snort out a laugh, earning another glare from Dad. "Where the fuck did you learn that?"

"Esther from the club. She saw a news program about it."

Mom's second favorite thing, only slightly behind getting wasted just to piss her husband off, is gossiping with the other Stepford wives at the country club they're members of.

"Steven can drive you home," Dad grumbles. "I'll drop your car off tomorrow."

I don't want to hitch a ride from their driver—yes, they have a goddamn driver—because Steven has hated me ever since high school when he had to drive me around to every place my parents dictated I go, all the while I was making out with whatever guy I could con to come along with me.

I'm pretty sure Steven's been an unwilling witness to a couple of back seat blowjobs too.

He never seemed so happy as to see me go off to college.

But riding with Steven is still the better of the two options. If I have to sit here for another minute with Dad, I'll slit my wrists with a fucking steak knife.

"It's been real, and it's been fun," I say, standing and subsequently swaying, "but it hasn't been real fun." I toss my key fob at Dad.

Mom starts giggling again. "Come here, rascal, and give me a kiss goodbye."

I round the table and bend to kiss her cheek. "Until the next torture dinner, Mommy Dearest."

She starts laughing again, much to Dad's annoyance.

"See you around, Daddy-o."

"Try it again sometime when you're sober," Dad snaps.

I give him an exaggerated thumbs-up and cheesy smile before strolling out of the restaurant. I'm wearing a stupid dinner jacket—this place won't even let you in unless you're wearing one—and I'm eager to strip out of it. The host at the stand, a guy close to my age and a little on the small side, blatantly checks me out. Usually, I'd take the bait, flirt in front of my dad to get a rise out of him, and then have this dude choking on my dick before poor Steven even pulled out of the parking lot.

Not tonight.

Tonight, I just want to get the fuck home and go to bed.

My thoughts keep drifting to Mia. Always Mia. Everything with us is a fucked-up mess. I don't even know how to fix it either.

She's all the way in California and probably pissed at me.

I'd be pissed at me too.

"Hey, Stevie Boy," I chirp when I drop into the back seat of my parents' car.

Steven, always the professional, ignores my taunting. "Where to, young sir?"

"My place. Unless you want to hang out."

He puts the car in drive, not bothering to answer. I lean my face against the cool glass, watching the scenery fly by quickly.

*Watch your back.*

Travis's words are like acid on my brain. Before I left to have dinner with my parents, I saw him heading into my building. He'd hissed out those words, successfully pissing me off. Sure, he got one over on me once, but I'll be damned if I let it happen again.

Still, his words got to me.

I hadn't been watching my back when he planted that shit in my bag. If it hadn't been for Brayden on Monday, he would've done it again. Travis is such a pussy.

Why did Brayden intervene? Why the fuck was he even there?

All too soon, I'm at my place. I don't bother saying bye to Steven and head inside. Drew's voice can be heard on the other side of the door as I fumble to unlock it. It makes me realize it's late and the hockey game is clearly over. I'd wanted to go—to watch Brayden again—but when Dad demands a family dinner, I usually bite the bullet and just go to get him off my back for a while.

"I said I don't mind," Drew says to his phone on FaceTime. "It's not a big deal."

His hair is wet from a recent shower and he's shirtless. I shut the door behind me, flipping the lock, and lean my back against it to steal a moment to stare at him. He's stretched out on the sofa, his jeans low on his hips, revealing too many grooves that make me want to run my tongue across them. My dick twitches in agreement.

"Kace owes me. Seriously. You don't have to use your credit card. I've got it." Drew's dimple pops out as he grins.

"Thanks, man." Brayden. "I hope she doesn't freak."

"Nah, Mia's cool. She'll be happy."

All the heat that was simmering in my veins freezes.

"Right. I better pack a bag and catch some Zs. That's an early flight in the morning," Brayden says. "Thanks again. I guess this truce shit is working."

Drew chuckles. "I guess it is."

After Drew hangs up the phone, he tosses it onto the table. His eyes lazily skim my way, but when he sees me, they widen in shock. It's then I remember I'm wearing this stupid outfit to please my dad. I start to roughly yank at the knot on my tie.

"Brayden?" I ask, my voice shaking with anger.

He rises to his feet, frowning. "Yep."

"Why is he going to see Mia?"

"You know why. He likes her."

*I like her!*

Storming away from him, I make my way into my room. I strip out of the stupid preppy shit and throw on some swim team sweats. Once I'm not feeling like such a freak, I stalk back into the kitchen to find something to drink. Drew follows me and leans his hip against the granite countertop and crosses his arms over his massive chest.

"You okay?"

I yank a bottle of tequila from a cabinet and unscrew the cap. "Does it look like I'm okay?"

"No, it looks like you're seconds from losing your shit," he says slowly. "Having mixed feelings again?"

Tilting back the bottle, I suck down the fiery liquid. When I can't drink anymore without a break, I slam it down, glaring at him. "Again? They never left. It's been real fucking confusing for a while now."

"You could've talked to her," he reminds me. "You didn't have to treat her like shit before she left."

His words wound me. "I treated her like shit?"

"Dude, you were a total dick. Barely even spoke to her. If you like her, you sure as hell could have fooled me."

"It doesn't matter anyway. Her date rapey dude bro knight in shining fucking armor is on his way to bed her like a fucking princess!"

Drew takes several quick steps, crowding me. "You're drunk and pissy, I get it. But you can lay off Brayden. This is between you and Mia."

"Sure thing, boss," I spit out, grabbing my tequila. "If you need me,

I'll be drinking myself into oblivion, wondering how the fuck I turn my-self not gay."

"You and your goddamn labels," Drew growls out. "Get over your-self already."

I flip him off, stumble over his shoes on the floor, and then kick them before making my way back to my room. Flopping down on my bed, I try not to spill my tequila. My head is spinning with all sorts of confusing thoughts, half of which involve Mia in this bed with me.

The other half are a little more on par with normal Ashton fantasy ma-terial, including a coach and a cocky hockey player. By the time I've drunk myself into a stupor, my dick is hard and my heart aches.

I want Mia.

So bad.

But I don't think I'm enough. I don't think she's enough. That's the part that hurts so fucking badly. What happens when I finally convince myself I can pursue something with Mia? Everything's all fun and games while we kiss and flirt. But what happens when we fall into bed together? My dick goes soft mid-fuck. No big deal. We'll laugh and get over it. Wrong. I'll fucking die if it comes to that.

Because as much as I want Mia, I can't turn off how I feel toward guys. Take Drew, for instance. If I wasn't so fucked-up over this stuff with her, I'd absolutely flirt with him until I had those jeans down and my lips on his dick. You can't live in the same apartment with someone like Drew and not want to fuck around naked with him.

And Brayden? My nemesis? Looked pretty goddamn hot standing off with Travis. I don't know why he was there, but I liked it. I liked him seeing me be really fucking good at something. I liked him doing his damnedest to protect me. It was invigorating and something I might allow my curiosity to poke at and explore if he weren't the one trying to actively fuck my girl.

Jesus.

I can't even sort out my mind.

My eyes droop. I slam the bottle down loudly onto the end table before rolling onto my stomach. I squeeze my eyes shut, trying to find answers. I need direction and help. I'm about to pass out, exhausted and stressed to the max, when Drew clears his throat.

"I'm sorry."

I grunt against the mattress.

"I know it's messy for you and I shouldn't have been an asshole earlier." The bed sinks down with his weight. "I promised Mia I'd look after you. So here I am. Watching your crybaby ass."

A laugh rumbles out of me, making the bed shake. "You took it literally?" I clench my ass. "What's my ass doing now? Looking hot, big guy?"

"Even when you're depressed as hell, you find a way to give people shit, huh?"

"It's my superpower."

"You want to talk about it?"

I roll onto my side. "I don't know what to say. I like Mia. I want Mia. I love Mia."

"But?" He mimics my position, stretching out on my bed like it belongs to him.

"But this…" I reach a hand forward and run my fingertips down his chest toward his abs. "So much this."

His breath hitches when my fingers dip into his belly button. A strong hand grips my wrist, stopping it from exploring further.

"So being a bitch to Mia somehow makes all the confusing feelings go away?" Drew asks, his thumb brushing along my wrist in a comforting manner.

"No," I admit. "It makes it worse." My eyes skate up to his. His blues seem electric with intensity. I know he was with Mia before he moved in here, but it feels like a lifetime ago. He hasn't shoved my hand away. It makes me wonder why not.

"Are you bi, Drew?"

His eyes drop to my lips for a brief second. "I don't do labels."

"Well I do," I murmur. "I think you're bi."

He scoffs but doesn't argue. His hand releases my wrist and he rolls onto his back, scrubbing a palm over his face. I don't miss the way he's sporting a semi in his jeans.

"Have you fucked a man?" I probe.

He ignores me. I inch closer, taunting him, my foot brushing against his.

"Has a man ever fucked you?"

"Ashton," he grinds out in response. "Stop your bullshit."

"You sound guilty. Which was it?" I tease my finger up and down his abdomen. He doesn't push me away. "Who fucked who?"

"I fuck whoever I want, whenever I want, because I don't have any labels stuck on my box telling me what I can and cannot do." He scowls at me.

His abs flex when I drag my finger all the way to the button on his jeans.

"Teach me your ways, Coach," I murmur, loving the war that flickers in his blue eyes. "Since you're so fucking smart."

"You're such an asshole."

I pluck at the button on his jeans. "It's one of my endearing qualities."

"Ashton." His voice trembles. "You should stop."

"Should, but I'm really bad at doing what I should."

Leaning forward, I bring my lips nearly to his. He sucks in a breath at my nearness, and then another one when I pull down his zipper.

"Ash—" he starts, but I shut him down with a kiss.

His hand goes to my chest, as though he might push me away, but then his thumb brushes over my nipple ring, making my dick strain against my sweats. I groan when his tongue swipes eagerly against mine.

Holy fuck.

Fiery lust surges through me, making me desperate to strip him down and drag my tongue all the way to his dick.

I want to suck him until he's empty and crying out my name.

*I guess you really don't like Mia.*

The thought hits me right in the gut, souring my mood. I do fucking like Mia. I love her. And that's why it's been so damn hard.

Because this.

Men.

Fuck.

Drew sucks on my bottom lip, nips at it, and then pulls away. "You're drunk. You need sleep."

I boldly rub my palm over his dick in his jeans. "You could sleep with me."

"Nah," Drew rasps out, gently pushing my hand away. "You're going to regret this shit tomorrow."

Maybe.

Maybe not.

I roll onto my back and watch as he slides out of my bed. A chill settles in my bones. Lonely and aching. Maybe Drew letting me suck him off isn't the answer, but letting him go after that hot kiss doesn't sit right with me either.

"Drew," I grunt out.

He stops with his hand on the doorknob. "Yeah?"

"You're a good kisser."

His head turns and he flashes me one of his one-dimpled grins. "You too, man."

"We should do it again sometime."

He grunts out a laugh. "Go to sleep, Ashton."

"Think of me when you take care of that boner," I tease. "I'll be thinking of you."

I'm not rewarded with an answer. He leaves without another word. I shove my hand down into my sweats and grab my neglected dick.

I think of Drew, just like I promised.

Problem is, I think of Mia too.

And fuck, if that doesn't make everything more confusing.

# TWENTY

## *Drew*

I can't believe we kissed.

What the hell is wrong with me?

All week, I'd agonized over what happened with Brayden. It tore me up, but I resigned myself to the fact he was going to want to act like nothing ever happened. He did just that. Once he cooled off, we went back into truce territory.

What I never expected was to end up in Ashton's bed with my tongue down his throat. I don't like guys. It'd only ever been Brayden. I've fucked around with girls and girls only. Brayden and I are on a totally different level that is based on friendship and history. But guys? Never. Until Ashton.

Fucking hell.

It was nice, too. He kisses like he talks. Taunting. Teasing. Just fucking with you because he can. I was sucked into this energy that Ashton puts out. My horny-ass body, once again, forgot all the fucking rules and was ready to get naked with a guy—this guy.

Thank God I managed to pull back and put space between us.

Kissing him was a mistake.

Ashton is in love with Mia. It's sad to watch the anguish in his hazel eyes. To see him fight everything he's ever known to try and get to the place he wants to be with Mia. Last night he was drunk and vulnerable. I'm an asshole for kissing him back.

I try not to think of the way he'd touched my dick over my jeans. It's been so fucking long since I've been with someone. A few more reckless seconds and there's no telling what could have happened between us.

Ashton and I can't be anything.

As much as I give him shit about the labels, there's a reason for some of them. Like my being a coach here and his dad being the one who got me the job. I can't lose this job. Not over a kiss.

My thoughts drift back to Bray.

I close my eyes, remembering the unfiltered emotions rippling from him. With Bray, he's always just bursting with everything he's feeling. It manifests itself into anger, but he can't mask his pain no matter how hard he tries. Each time I'm around him, I want to gather him in my arms and try to alleviate some of it so he doesn't have to feel so much. After kissing Ashton, it makes me realize that Bray and I have more than just history pulling us together. There's a sexual energy and attraction infused with it too.

Ashton thought he was a mess.

I'm the goddamn mess here.

My phone buzzes.

**Unknown: Hey, it's Mia. How are things?**

I glance at the time. It's almost ten.

**Me: Okay.**

My phone starts to ring. With a sigh, I answer it, my voice gravelly from having just woken up. "Hello?"

"Hey," Mia greets, her voice sounding sultry and sexier than usual over the phone. "That didn't sound like a good text. Ashton okay?"

Her concern for him has guilt clawing up my throat.

"He's… upset." But then I made out with him to make it all better. "About me?"

I can't exactly tell her all the details, so I leave it vague for now. "He came home all dressed up, but he was wasted."

"Ugh," she groans. "Dinner with his parents. It never ends well."

A pang of sadness hits me in the chest. My dad was a good parent and so are Bray's mom and dad. I couldn't imagine having parents who drive you to drinking.

"Why? Curtis seems cool."

"I like Curtis too," she agrees. "He's always nice and seems worried about Ashton. You can't tell him that, though."

I sigh, knowing full well what she means. It's like when I try to tell Bray anything. He refuses to hear it.

"Are you okay?"

"Yeah," she murmurs.

"Could have fooled me."

She laughs. "I hate being here. My mom is my issue. She's just so…"

"Bitchy?"

Another laugh. "That too. Pretentious. Overbearing. At times, borderline cruel." Her voice cracks. "I love her. She's my mom."

"But you wish you could throttle her ass?"

"Yes," she says with a giggle. "I'm sorry I left you to babysit Ashton. I just… I can't bear to see him in pain."

"You're a good friend."

"A friend. Seems as though that's all I'll ever be." Her tone isn't bitter, just resigned.

"Sometimes, we want to do so much for our best friend, but they won't let us. It's maddening."

"You speak from experience," she says. "Does this have something to do with you and Brayden?"

"Yeah. I want to be there for him…" And more. "But I hurt him, Mia. I hurt him and I hate myself for it. All I want is to repair that hurt. I just don't know how."

"Maybe give him time. Start small. Be there for him even when it's hard."

"Are you following your own sage advice with Ashton?"

"I guess I need to." She's quiet for a minute. "I'm sorry for what happened between us."

"It's okay. I get it, short stuff. I really do."

"It wasn't fair to you." She swallows audibly. "For what it's worth, I enjoyed that night. Where it was leading. Who it was with. My mind's just a mess. And now you're…"

"Same," I grunt out. "It was a good night…" I let my words drift off so she can repaint the picture in her head.

"Very good," she whispers. "Thank you. I needed that."

The line goes silent and her breathing soothes me.

"How do you normally cheer that asshole up in there?" I ask. "Last night was hell."

"Feed him. Ashton loves food."

"For someone who has such a sweet tooth and eats everything in sight, he's extremely fit. It makes me hate him a little."

We both laugh.

"I agree—hold on. Someone's at the door. Probably my mom."

I smile as I think about what comes next.

"Brayden! Oh my God! What are you doing here?"

Her squeal of delight and then giggles warm my heart.

"Drew, I have to go. Call me later."

"Bye, short stuff."

The phone clicks off and I rub at the ache in my chest. It's bittersweet knowing Brayden is happy. He likes Mia. Mia deserves someone like Bray. Just sucks when you're on the outside. I'm attracted to Mia and obviously we had a connection, but Bray is just…

He's everything I'll never have.

After a quick shower, I start on breakfast. Ashton hasn't surfaced from his room until I begin cooking the bacon. Then, like the human garbage disposal he is, he stumbles out of his room following the scent of food. His hair is wet and he's dressed, but he still looks like shit thanks to his obvious hangover.

"Hey," I greet. "Hungry?"

"Like a hippo."

I smirk because sometimes he seems so much younger than me. Truth is, we're the same age.

"Grab us some juice while I finish up," I tell him.

Ashton starts some coffee and then roots around in the fridge for the orange juice. We move in amicable silence until it's all done and ready.

"How do you like your coffee?" he asks.

"Two sugars and a teaspoon of creamer is fine."

He makes a face but obeys. "Just like Mia."

I watch in absolute horror as he dumps way too much sugar into his own glass. Then, he pours in the creamer until his coffee can no longer be considered that. It's damn near white. Fucking sick. It reminds me of how Brayden likes his. The total opposite. Straight with nothing. Black like his hair. I'd find this humorous in some way or even ironic since I kissed them both this week, but it only makes me miss Bray.

"What?" he asks.

"You. I bet your dentist hates you."

He flashes me his pearly whites. "Dr. Redkin loves me."

"Because he makes a shit-ton of money off you."

"Yeah," he agrees. "Used to send me home with suckers after each visit. It's probably his fault I'm this way."

We both chuckle and set our plates down at the coffee table. He flips on the television, landing on a music station while I bring in our coffee and juice. As guitar riffs fill the silence, we eat. Even hungover, Ashton is a sight to behold. His black T-shirt fits him well and his holey jeans look good on him. He's what I'd call effortlessly cool. Guys probably want to be him, but can't pull it off because they don't have his devil-may-care attitude.

"Want to hit the gym with me later?" I ask. "After eating this, I'll need it."

He inhales his pancakes, shrugging, and talks over his mouthful of food. "Maybe."

We make it through breakfast, and Ashton surprises me by cleaning up. His apartment stays fairly clean now that I think about it. It's just him that's messy.

He makes us more coffee and then turns on his Xbox.

"Here." He tosses me a controller. "Time for you to eat your words."

NHL 20 comes on and I grin. "Man, this is my game. Sorry about your loss."

"We haven't even started yet," he says, laughing.

"I'm about to whip your ass. Apologizing in advance."

We start the game, and I learn very quickly that video games and real hockey aren't the same. You can be Ashton, having never played a day of hockey in your life or even understand the rules, and annihilate.

"That's another one, loser," he says after every goddamn goal he gets.

He starts pissing me off and I shoulder check him. Not in the game, but on the couch. His smile is vicious and taunting.

"That's another one, los—"

He doesn't finish his statement because I steal his controller. We wrestle over it until I have him pinned on the couch.

"You're such a sore los—" he starts, but I don't let him say the word again.

My lips crash against his, noting how he tastes sweet like syrup. He groans in surprise, but then his fingers are sliding beneath the hem of my shirt and skating up my bare ribs. I'm hard as fuck and greedily grind my hips against him, noting he's just as excited as I am. Our dicks rub together through our clothes, making us both moan.

Bad idea.

Such a bad idea.

But, goddamn does it feel good.

His tongue dominates mine and it only makes me want to take control more. Ashton is used to winning at everything he does. I kiss him like he's mine and he has to obey me. His fight for the upper hand is a ruthless war done with his lips, tongue, and the taunting way his hands now grab my ass.

Fuck, this guy makes me crazy.

Last night, he grabbed my dick, clearly satisfied as fuck with himself over making me squirm. This morning, I don't let him get there first. I nip at his lip and then jaw and then ear. He freezes when my hand tugs at the button on his jeans.

"I don't like to lose," I murmur against his ear.

His hips buck up. "Me neither."

I manage to get his zipper down and then my hand is diving into his boxers. We both breathe heavily as I grip his thick cock.

"Fuck, Drew." His voice is gravelly and sounds like a complaint. Everything out of Ashton's mouth sounds like he's bitching, but I'm starting to learn more about him. It's just the way he is. His eager fingers ripping at my shirt and panting tells otherwise.

"Looks like you lost," I taunt, running my thumb over the bead of pre-cum on the tip of his dick.

"I can tell you with one hundred percent certainty, I'm the winner right now." He groans, thrusting his hips up. "Fuck."

Our mouths meet again and I kiss him brutally while stroking him. Based on his breathing, I can tell he's close to coming. The moment he loses it, I smile against his lips. He makes a choked sound and then hot cum is soaking my hand. I stroke him until he's good and messy and wrung dry.

"That was fun," I tease against his lips.

"Game's not over," he growls.

I don't try to stop him when he undoes my own jeans. No, my compliant ass lifts up to give him the access he needs. We both stare between us as he pulls my dick out of my pants. He wraps his hand around my cock and strokes it with that taunting ability he has.

I'm worthless right now.

Reduced to fucking his fist and begging to come.

He knows it too based on the triumphant gleam in his hazel eyes.

"Who's the loser?" he teases, his hand jerking me off oh-so-fucking-good.

"You," I volley back.

He laughs. "I got to come first. That makes me the winner."

"You're an asshole."

"For some reason, you're into assholes," he challenges back. "Say it and I'll let you come."

Our eyes meet and I shake my head.

"So help me if you stop moving that hand," I warn, "I'll find some other place to stick my dick in."

He laughs, wild and wicked, and continues stroking me. "I guess it's a tie then."

I close my eyes as he brings me to the brink of ecstasy. Then, I'm diving over the edge with a groan. My hot cum jets out, shooting all over him. I'm exhausted and overrun by lust-filled emotions. I fall against him, my heart racing in my chest.

My brain decides to catch up, reminding me this was a bad idea.

Too late now.

Ashton's fingers run through my hair in a surprisingly tender move. Stupid me melts at the touch. I close my eyes, inhaling his clean, soapy scent. A smile tugs at my lips, knowing he'll have to take another shower because he's a fucking mess with both our cum all over him.

"What are we going to do now?" His loaded question is shockingly worried and unsure. I don't think he regrets what just happened, but I also think he's having reservations like me.

"Go to the gym," I grunt out, giving him the simple answer.

*What are we going to do now*... about us? About this? I don't have a simple answer for that.

"Can we nap instead?" he jokes, injecting his usual humor in his tone.

"No," I tell him, lifting up so I can see his stupidly sexy face. "We're going to the gym because apparently I'm a loser." I smirk. "But when we get there, the only loser will be you. That's a motherfucking fact."

"Oh no," he says in a dry, sardonic tone, "I'll be forced to watch you lift weights and see all your muscles bulge. You really showed me."

And because I can't help myself, I press a kiss to his sarcastic mouth.

"Get dressed, loser. I'm ready to whip your ass now."

His deviant hazel eyes flash, making my dick twitch, but I move away from him before he makes good on whatever wicked thoughts he's thinking.

"Now, Carter," I bark out as I step back. "Stop looking at me like that."

He drags his eyes over my wrecked state. I can't help but do the same to him. His shirt is soaked with our cum and his dick is hard again, bouncing against his lower abs.

"I'll be ready in ten," I grunt, turning away from him. "Be ready to work your ass off."

"Yeah, yeah. I'll be ready."

# TWENTY-ONE

*Brayden*

"**B**rayden! Oh my God! What are you doing here?"

As Mia stands in the doorway, wearing nothing but a tiny tank top and even tinier pajama shorts, with a huge grin splayed across her face, I know I did the right thing coming here.

"Drew, I have to go. Call me later," she says, quickly ending the call. She shucks the phone onto her bed and pulls me inside, closing the door behind her. I drop my overnight bag on the ground as she drags me over to her bed.

"I can't believe you're here." She plops onto the edge of the bed and spreads her thighs, tugging on my shirt so I'm standing between her legs. She glances up at me with her caramel-colored eyes shining with happiness.

I try to focus on her, but I'm stuck on who she was on the phone with. Drew. Since when does she talk to Drew? Did he call her? And if there's something going on between them, why would he offer to help me charter a plane to see her?

"Brayden," Mia says, framing my face with her delicate hands. "What's wrong?"

"Why were you on the phone with Drew?" I ask, unable to help myself. My question comes out harsher than intended, but I'm confused as hell and kind of pissed. One minute he's kissing me and the next he's talking to the woman he knows I'm interested in.

Her brows dip in confusion, but before she can answer, I continue. "If you and Drew have something going on, you need to let me know." I can handle her and Ashton kissing. I get it, shit happens. The two of them are best friends and close, and wires get crossed, but I will not be pinned against Drew.

Her face morphs from confusion to anger, and I take a slight step back.

"You asked me a question. Can I answer?" she quips.

"Yeah."

"Thanks. I called him to check on Ashton. He told me he would keep an eye on him for me. I'm worried about him and Drew lives with him."

I look into her eyes, trying to find any hint of a lie, but all I can see is concern for her best friend.

I release a sigh of relief, and Mia eyes me curiously.

"What exactly happened between you and Drew?"

"It's not about what happened between us," I deflect. "I know something happened between you two and—" Fuck, if I finish what I'm saying I'm going to sound like a jealous asshole. Oh well, fuck it. "I can't be sloppy seconds to Drew."

Mia's eyes widen in fury. "Sloppy seconds? What are we, in high school?" She scoffs. "What happened with Drew and me was a one-time thing… Actually, it wasn't *even* a one-time thing."

"What do you mean?"

"It doesn't matter." She pushes the center of her glasses up her nose and then crosses her arms over her chest. "It was before I met you. How about you tell me about *you* and Drew?" She raises a single brow.

"There isn't much—"

"Nope." She cuts me off with a shake of her head. "You said you wanted all of me, including the deep. I told you the other night about Ashton and me kissing, now it's your turn. Give me your deep."

I turn her desk chair around behind me and drop into it. My elbows dig into my thighs and I stare at Mia for a long second. She doesn't understand what she's asking of me. This isn't just deep, this is dark and gritty and so fucking raw. I've never spoken about what happened between Drew and me to anyone. And once I tell her, there's no taking it back. And there's a good chance she'll never see me the same again.

Mia stares at me, chewing on her bottom lip nervously, as she waits patiently for me to speak. I've only known her for a short time, but I already know she's a game changer. I can feel it when I'm around her, when I hear her voice. When I see the way she smiles at me, the way she laughs. The way she lets me in. And if we have a chance at going anywhere, I'm going to have to let her in as well.

"When I was thirteen and my brother was nine, I killed him."

Mia gasps, and I clarify, "Not literally, but it was my fault." I swallow thickly, trying to explain without letting the images swarm my head and take over. "I took him out in the cold and a few days later he was in the hospital with a horrible cold and pneumonia."

"Oh, Brayden," Mia murmurs.

"We were hanging out. It was winter break and our parents were out Christmas shopping. Drew was over and it started to snow. Ben begged me to go out and play in the snow. My mom had made it clear we weren't allowed to leave the house, but he kept begging and I gave in."

"Things happen," she says, her eyes filled with sympathy. "You didn't kill him. You were a teenager who loved his brother and wanted to make him happy."

"Drew said the same thing too many times to count, but it doesn't matter. I made a choice and it led to his death." And I'll have to live with that choice for the rest of my life.

"People get pneumonia all the time without ever going outside. He could've gotten it regardless. What did your parents say?"

"They don't know."

Mia's eyes go wide in shock and confusion.

"Ben made us promise not to tell our mom that we snuck out. He didn't want us to get in trouble. They don't know. Only Ben, who's dead, Drew and me, and now you, know." No matter how much I wanted to tell them, so they would have someone to blame, I couldn't break my promise to Ben.

Mia stands and comes over to me, sits in my lap and wraps her arms around me. She smells like vanilla and comfort, a heady combination I've quickly become addicted to. And I hate that what I have to admit next might mean I'll never get to smell her scent again.

"I can't tell you what to do," she says, pulling back slightly and looking into my eyes. "But I really think you should tell your parents." She shifts, trying to get comfortable, and I hold on to her tighter. "You've been carrying this guilt with you all these years and you don't even know if it was your fault."

Not wanting to break our connection, but needing to get us more comfortable, I lift her and walk us over to her bed. I lie down, leaning against the headboard, and she stays straddling me. My dick feels her warmth and begs to come out, but I ignore it. Now is not the time…

"So, is that why you and Drew don't talk?" she asks, her curious brown eyes boring into mine, begging for answers.

"No. We stopped talking because when Ben died I was in a really bad place, and Drew was comforting me, and…" I close my eyes, not wanting to see her expression when I admit what I've never said out loud. "I kissed him."

The room goes quiet, and after several seconds of Mia not saying a word, I open my eyes. "That's it?" she says, sounding sad as fuck. "You kissed him?"

"Uh, yeah, I kissed him. I was crying in bed the day of my brother's funeral and he was trying to comfort me. We were lying close to each other, and something felt like it shifted… and I kissed him. He told me he needed some time, so I gave it to him. Every day I waited, hoping he would come around. But he never did. I tried to talk to him, but he shut me down.

Ended our eight-year friendship. We went to high school and continued to play hockey for the same team, but we never spoke. Not until…"

Fuck, this is so embarrassing. She's going to think the worst, and I'm not even sure she'd be wrong. "His dad died. And like a dumbass, I tried to be there for him. He was crying and I was just trying to comfort him the way he had comforted me, but then it happened again. I fucking kissed him, and that time he didn't just stop talking to me, he ran… all the way to the NHL."

Mia tugs on her top lip, her brows furrowed, but doesn't say anything. I don't know whether I've shocked her into silence or if she's afraid to say whatever is on her mind.

"There's more…"

"Okay," she says, her voice holding no judgment.

"Last week I ran into Drew after our date. I was at the cemetery visiting my brother and he was visiting his dad. We talked and he asked to call a truce of sorts. Said it was for the team, so I wouldn't give him shit in front of the guys. In return, I threw out an olive branch and invited him to the rink. We were playing some one on one. It got kind of heated since we're both competitive as fuck." I smile at the memory of the way we were beating on each other. I missed the hell out of those days.

"Anyway," I continue. "I don't know how it happened, but one second we're slamming each other against the boards and the next Drew is kissing me."

Mia's eyes go wide, like something you would see in a cartoon, and I find myself chuckling. She's so fucking adorable.

"So, what happened?" she asks, now nibbling on her bottom lip in suspense.

"I ran." I shrug. "He shouldn't have done that shit," I hiss. "We were finally getting back to a good place. Sure, shit wasn't perfect. But I could feel us getting there. Now it's like we're back at square one." Well, except for the fact he did me this solid by calling in a favor to charter me a plane to come see Mia.

"So, the whole reason why your friendship ended was because you kissed him?"

"Yeah."

"Great." Her lips pull down into a frown. "So, pretty much what you're saying is Ashton and I are screwed. We kissed… twice… and now he's pushing me away like Drew did to you."

Is she serious right now? I just told her I sucked face with a guy three times and her only concern is her friendship with her best friend?

She tries to climb off my lap, but I hold on to her hips, refusing to let her go. "You're not going to ask me if I'm gay?" I ask incredulously.

"Umm… no, I wasn't," she says, looking at me like I've got three heads.

"I kissed a guy. Three times."

"I know." She laughs. "But you've also kissed me, and a lot of other girls, if the rumors are true." She shrugs. "But since you clearly want me to ask, I can… Are you gay?"

I chuckle at how well she's taking all this. "I don't know."

She giggles and the sound shoots straight to my dick. "Well, if you are, you better let your dick know that. Because he's been poking me…"

I shake my head and breathe in a sigh of relief. I was so worried about telling her and she handled it fucking perfect. "I don't think I am."

"Well, have you ever liked any other guys? Found anyone besides Drew attractive?"

My thoughts go back to the other day at the pool, Ashton in his speedo… His taut chest and muscular back…

"Uh-oh," she taunts with a laugh. "Your face is all red and… Oh my God. Your dick just got super hard. Who were you just thinking of?"

Nope, no fucking way. It was one thing to admit what happened between me and Drew. There's no way I'm telling the girl I'm seeing I checked out her gay best friend.

"Brayden, tell me," she pushes. "I won't tell anyone, I promise."

Needing to distract her, I grip her by the curves of her hips and roll us over. "I don't want to talk about this anymore," I say honestly. "I came here for you, to cheer you up, and instead it somehow became all about me." I press my lips to hers and my dick stirs. I may not know what the fuck I am, but I know for a fact Mia turns me on.

She could easily push me to answer, but instead she wraps her arms around my neck and murmurs against my mouth, "Thank you for coming. I didn't realize how much I needed you here until I saw you standing in my doorway."

Her fingers thread through the strands of my hair and she pulls me close, deepening the kiss. My heart hammers against my chest. She may've needed me, but in a lot of ways, I think I needed her just as much. We kiss like this for several minutes, getting lost in each other, until there's a knock on her door.

"Mia, it's time to get up," a whiny, female voices says from the other side.

"Oh shit!" she whisper-yells, pushing me off her. "I'll be down in a few minutes," she calls out. Then to me, she says, "Who let you in?"

"Some old guy… Umm… Regi…" I can't remember the guy's name. I was too nervous to get up here to see Mia, worried she'd freak out that I showed up as a surprise. We've only been seeing each other for a minute. I wasn't sure if flying across the country and showing up at one's childhood home would be considered too much too soon.

"Reginald," she says. "He's the butler."

What the hell… her family has a butler? I knew they were more than well-off when I arrived and the neighborhood was locked down like Fort Knox. Then, I pulled up to the house, which is more like a mansion, and found another gate. Like, who needs two gates? And a butler? You would never know when you hang out with Mia that she's loaded, or at least her parents are. She's sweet and laidback and dresses like a book nerd-slash-gamer… and fuck, I'm totally judging her. Drew comes from a wealthy family and never acted like he was better than me. So, why would I expect Mia to?

She sighs. "My mom is going to totally flip when she finds out you're here." Instead of sounding upset, she almost sounds… excited. "Guess we better go down and have breakfast with them." There's an evil glint in her eye, and I would be upset that it's clear she's about to use me to fuck with her parents, but that's why I came here. To make her feel better. To be her support.

"Ready when you are," I tell her, placing a soft kiss against her neck. "Bring on the 'rents."

"Ha-ha." She laughs. "Famous last words…"

After she finishes getting ready, looking more like those Kardashian chicks on that reality show than the Mia I've come to know, we head downstairs. I'm confused as to why she's so dressed up—wearing fancy clothes and tall heels and a face full of makeup—until we walk into the dining room, where a man and a woman are seated at the table… together. Except they aren't really together since the table seats twelve people and they're both located on opposite ends.

At our arrival, they both look up from their phones. Their eyes landing on Mia and me. I glance at, who I assume, is her father first. He's older, his full head of gray hair making him look to be in his fifties, maybe even sixties. His eyes are the same color as Mia's, soft and warm and welcoming, and he's dressed in what looks to be an expensive suit.

My eyes skate over to the other end of the table, where I know without a doubt Mia's mom is sitting. Same color hair, same nose, same lips. They almost look more like sisters than mother-daughter. Either she was really young when she had Mia, ages extremely well, or she pays a lot of money to keep her youth. She's sporting diamonds in her ears and around her neck. I can't see her pants, but her top is see-through black silk. I glance down at myself, in my jeans and T-shirt and Reeboks, and feel out of place. Now, Mia dressed the way she is makes sense.

"Mom, Dad," Mia says, "this is my friend, Brayden." She gestures to her parents. "Brayden, this is my mom, Claire Voss-Lexington." The name sounds familiar, and then it hits me. She's a famous actress. And not just any actress, one who has won a helluva lot of awards if I'm not wrong. My mom forced me to watch a bunch of her movies, and she's also been in several action flicks. No wonder they live in this huge damn house. She's practically Hollywood royalty.

"Nice to meet you," I choke out, trying not to sound like a crazy fan or something. Mom would die if she knew I was here with *the* Claire Voss-Lexington.

Claire simply nods, scrutinizing me with narrowed eyes.

"This is my dad, Harold Lexington."

Unlike Mia's mom, Harold smiles. "Nice to meet you. Are you from Michigan?"

"Yes, sir. I decided to surprise Mia and flew over to check out where she's from."

Mia gestures for us to sit next to each other, and I try to ignore how odd it is to have everyone so spread out. At my house, we all sit together so we can be close and talk.

A woman dressed in a black and white outfit sets a plate in front of me and offers me coffee. I nod and then thank her.

"Help yourself," Mia says, grabbing a plain bagel from a basket that contains an assortment of breads.

"Mia," her mom says, her tone chiding. "Maybe you should focus more on the fruit. The bagel will cause bloating and I can't have someone alter your dress *again* before tonight."

Mia nods once and sets the bagel down, grabbing the bowl of fruit.

My gaze darts between Mia and her mom in shock. Who the hell does this woman think she is, telling her own daughter to watch her weight?

"What is your major?" Claire asks, addressing me.

"Business, ma'am," I say to be polite. "But I play hockey. My goal is to get drafted into the NHL."

Claire skims her gaze down my bicep in an appreciative way. "Oh, so I bet you work out a lot. Keep fit."

I try not to shudder at her cougar-like gawking.

"I work out every day. Kind of a prerequisite for hockey."

Claire continues to stare, making everyone feel uncomfortable as fuck.

Mia sighs under her breath. "Mom, please."

"What?" Claire asks. Then, to me, she says, "Maybe you could show my daughter how to eat properly. She's struggled with her weight her entire life. She lacks all the discipline. I had to have her dress altered last night because she's let herself go once again."

The mean bite to her voice has my hackles rising.

"Have you thought about what we discussed last night?" Claire continues, her attention back on Mia, a sneer plastered on her plastic face.

"Mom," Mia warns, almost begging her not to continue.

"There's nothing wrong with getting a little help," Claire states. "The surgery would curb your appetite."

What in the actual fuck?

"Claire," Harold warns, his tone failing to sound firm like I'm sure he intends.

It's one thing to hear Mia tell me her relationship with her mom is strained, but it's another to hear a mother talk shit to her daughter about her weight like she's obese.

"I think Mia's weight is perfect. She's beautiful just the way she is," I tell Claire, my voice rumbling with the authority to put this woman in her place that Harold so clearly lacks. I grab two bagels and drop them onto our plates. I slather them each with cream cheese and hand Mia one. Then, I lean in close and whisper just loud enough I know her mom can hear me, "I happen to think you're hot as hell."

Mia cracks a smile and takes the bagel from me. I notice her eyes are glossy with unshed tears, and I make a mental note to not only never watch another one of Claire's stupid movies again and make sure my mom never does either, but to buy Mia something with carbs every damn day just to stick it to her asshole mom.

Claire, though, isn't done circling us like a panther ready to strike. Her sculpted brows are furrowed, reminding me of a fucking villain.

"I'm assuming your *friend* will be staying at a hotel," Claire snips, her gaze flitting to Mia coldly.

Mia's back goes ramrod straight. "I was thinking he could stay here." She looks at her dad for help. "We have the room."

Claire scoffs, at the same time Harold says, this time sounding like the goddamn man of the house, "We have plenty of room. He can stay here."

It's as if the temperature in the room goes down seventy degrees, with the icy glare Claire shoots at her husband. Mia's gaze darts between her parents, and I'm about to say I can stay somewhere else, even though it will mean putting it on my credit card, when Harold speaks again.

"We have twelve empty rooms. He can stay here," he repeats, making Mia smile slightly.

Claire throws her napkin on the table and stands. "If you're bringing him to the charity function tonight, he better be dressed appropriately," she says before storming out. I could be wrong, but when she leaves, the temperature rises back to a nice seventy-five degrees.

# TWENTY-TWO



Brayden is here. With me. He flew all the way from Michigan to California just to be here for me. Nobody has ever done anything like that for me before. When he first arrived, he opened up to me about him and Drew. I think he assumed when he told me about them I was going to call him gay and push him away, but how can I judge him when Ashton and I are in a similar situation? If I've learned anything from this whole ordeal it's that we can't choose who we love or who we're attracted to. Ashton might label himself as gay, but I know deep down he's attracted to me, yet for whatever reason he doesn't want to be.

And I can accept that. I really can. If he doesn't want to be with me, if he doesn't want to accept that there's something between us, I can respect it. But what scares me is him pushing me away, the same way Drew pushed Brayden away. I love Ashton, and as much as I would've loved to see where things could go with us, his friendship is more important to me. Now I'm scared to death he's going to pull a Drew and I'm going to lose him for good. All I want is to hop on a plane and run home to beg him not to do this to us, but I can't do that. Because I'm stuck here until tomorrow night.

But at least if I have to be stuck here, it's nice to have Brayden with me. This morning at breakfast Mom did what she always does. She put me down. I'm used to just taking it, because God forbid Dad ever stick up for me. So I was shocked when Brayden jumped in like a white knight.

And then the unthinkable happened. Dad actually stood up to Mom. When she suggested Brayden stay at a hotel out of spite, I thought for sure Dad would agree. But he insisted Brayden stay here, and my heart swelled with hope that maybe Dad is capable of standing up to Mom.

Of course she had to have the final word by reminding me that Brayden would need a tux for tonight. I could've argued, but she's right. Brayden will stick out at the event like a sore thumb if he's not wearing a tux. Which is why our first stop after we ate breakfast—and I changed into something more comfortable since I wouldn't be around my mom—was the tuxedo shop my father frequents to have Brayden fitted for a tux. I told the salesman not to let him see the price and offered to pay extra to have it altered on rush.

Once that was out of the way, we spent the rest of the day playing tourists—well, Brayden wasn't playing… he really is one. I showed him all the popular sights, and we ate lunch at my favorite bistro. Being here with him made me realize I don't hate this city, just my mom. I love everything else about it. Its fast pace, the over-the-top, extravagant people. The way it's full of life and character and contains so much diversity. I can see myself making a life here. The problem is, in order to do that, I would be near my mom. And I like my sanity too much to be close to her ever again. Maybe one day I'll be able to come back, but for now, I'm glad I have Michigan to go back to.

I also realized how much I really like Brayden. Away from the stress of school and our personal issues, we were able to focus on each other. We spent the day laughing and flirting and having a good time. I stopped checking to see if Ashton had texted and enjoyed my time with a guy who wants me. A guy who enjoys my company and isn't afraid to show it, and it felt really good. So good, I was sad when the guy from the tuxedo shop called to let me know we could pick up Brayden's tux. It meant our fun, carefree day had to come to an end.

"What do you think?" Brayden spreads his arms out wide. He's dressed in a three-piece black Tom Ford suit with Armani loafers, and I can't take my eyes off him. His shirt is white and his tie is black and white checkered. Brayden is sexy on a normal day, when he's dressed in his jeans and T-shirts, but right now, dressed to the nines, he looks exceptionally delectable.

"I think you look damn good," I tell him honestly, not caring that I'm blatantly eye-fucking him in front of the salesman. All day our flirting has gotten more heated. It started with sweet kisses, then moved to hand holding. At lunch, Brayden's hand landed on my thigh, and while we were walking to the tuxedo shop, he pushed me into a small alleyway and devoured me against the wall. At this point, I have no doubt I'm soaking wet and needing to find some kind of relief—hopefully by the hands of Brayden.

"Perfect," the salesman says. "Are you planning to wear it out?"

"Yes," I tell him, checking the time. "We actually need to get going. I still need to stop by the house to get ready."

"Oh, uh… How much do I owe you?" Brayden asks. I can see it in his eyes he's nervous. He didn't consider how much it would cost. But I'm not about to let something like money ruin today.

"It's no charge," I tell him. "My dad has an account with them."

He looks like he wants to argue, so I stand on my tiptoes and kiss him, hoping it'll distract him. I know it works when he groans into my mouth, his fingers fisting my mane, as he deepens the kiss.

The salesman clears his throat and Brayden smirks.

"Let's go," I say, taking his hand and pulling him out of the store. "My parents are already on their way to the event, which means we have the house to ourselves." I glance back and see Brayden's eyes turn molten with lust.

We jump into my parents' town car, and the second the door closes, Brayden's mouth is back on mine. While we drive through the streets of Hollywood Hills, we kiss, our tongues frantically moving against each other.

When the car pulls up to the front, we both jump out. And the moment we're in my room, I'm back on Brayden, ripping off each layer of his tux. It's like opening a beautifully wrapped present on Christmas morning. The wrapping paper is nice, but what you really want is what's underneath.

When he's bare from the waist up, I admire his fit, muscular body. My eyes land on a tattoo on his left pec of a hockey puck and a stick with his brother's name and a set of dates scrawled over it. Knowing the meaning behind it, breaks my heart. I place an open-mouthed kiss over it, wishing I could heal his heart with my kiss.

When I step back, he lifts my shirt over my head and then yanks the cups of my bra down, my breasts spilling out of their confines. His lips wrap around one of the hardened peaks, and he sucks on my nipple. My back arches at the delicious feeling of his mouth on my body.

As he massages my breasts, giving them his full attention, I unzip his pants and tug them down, along with his briefs. My fingers wrap around his shaft. It's thick and smooth, similar to... *Oh no, don't go there, Mia.* I close my eyes and shake the thoughts of the way Drew's dick felt out of my head.

"On the bed," Brayden growls, lifting and tossing me onto the center of my bed. He kicks off his pants and loafers, while I push my skirt and panties down my legs.

As he crawls up the bed, I take in how beautiful he is. From his corded muscles, to his six-pack abs. It's obvious he takes good care of himself. For a second, I wonder what he thinks when he sees me. My stomach and thighs are soft in contrast to his hard, toned body. My thoughts flit to my mom's comments about my weight, but I push them away, refusing to let her ruin this moment.

He crawls up my body, and I shiver slightly at the way our naked bodies rub against each other. The night I was with Drew, I was nervous... He was a stranger. But with Brayden, it feels different. It feels right.

Brayden's hands land on either side of me, as he rains kisses all over my face: each of my cheeks, my forehead, the corner of my mouth. My top lip. Bottom lip. Then he works his way down, trailing kisses across my collarbone. He licks each of my nipples, and my body goes into a frenzy.

"You're so fucking perfect," he murmurs, kissing his way down the center of my torso and landing at the apex of my legs. My heart beats erratically as I watch Brayden spread my legs and kiss the inside of my thigh. I sigh in contentment, which has him glancing up and grinning at me.

This is how it should be.

A guy who wants me.

Appreciates me.

Needs me.

And isn't ashamed to admit it.

Brayden buries his face between my legs and licks up my center. He strokes my clit, working me over with his fingers and tongue, until I'm crying out my release as my body trembles in pleasure. Somewhere in my room, I can hear a phone vibrating, but I ignore it. It's probably my mom wondering where we are.

Or Ashton… I push the thought from my head. He has no business being in this room with us—with me.

When I've come down from my orgasm, Brayden climbs back up and our eyes meet. His strong arms cage me in, and his hard-as-steel dick presses against my center. His body feels warm against mine.

"Do you have a condom?" he murmurs. It takes a second for the words to sink in, but once they do, the fog of lust disappears and the reality of what we're about to do, appears.

"I'm a virgin," I blurt out. Brayden's eyebrows shoot up to his forehead and he sits up, taking his warmth with him. Leaving me lying here, naked and vulnerable. Instinctually, my arms cross over my breasts in an attempt to somewhat cover myself. "I'm sorry. I didn't mean to kill the mood."

"No, I'm glad you said something." He falls onto his side, then pushes my hair off my face, tucking it behind my ear.

"I don't know if I'm ready… for that," I admit, hating how young I sound, when Brayden is no doubt experienced. "I'm sorry," I repeat.

"Hey, don't ever apologize for wanting to wait." He presses a soft kiss to my lips that has me sighing into his mouth.

"It's not that. I just… I've never been with someone I wanted in the way I want you… until now." My eyes meet his, and he smiles the most beautiful boyish grin. "I don't have a condom, but I'm on the pill and…"

A phone vibrates again somewhere and Brayden groans. "We need to get to that charity function," he says. "I want to be with you so fucking badly." Our lips once again meet for a moment before he pulls back. "But not like this, not for your first time. Your first time should be slow and romantic. You should be worshipped." He kisses the sensitive spot behind my ear and butterflies attack my belly. "We should get ready to go."

He sits up and his dick juts out. It's so thick and hard and the head is purple like it's angry. "What about you?" I ask.

"I'll take a quick shower and rub one out," he says with a wink.

"Just because we aren't having sex right now, doesn't mean I can't make you feel good the way you made me feel good." I sit up and push him onto his back. Before he can argue, I grip his erection and stroke it up and down.

"Mia," he breathes. "Are you—"

His words are cut off when I wrap my lips around the head of his dick and suck him into my mouth, inch by delicious inch. I've never tasted a dick before, but I'm pleasantly surprised. He tastes clean mixed with a slight masculine musk. I have no clue what the hell I'm doing, so I just do whatever comes to me.

Using my hands and mouth and tongue, I suck and pump and lick. Brayden moans and curses under his breath, so I assume I'm doing something right. Then his dick swells beneath my touch, and a salty taste hits my tongue, just before Brayden fists my mane and lifts me off him. I watch with fascination as ropes of cum shoot from the slit of his head, landing all over my breasts and his thighs.

"Was it good?" I ask, curious if my first blowjob went okay.

Brayden laughs. "It was mind-blowing."

A phone vibrates again, snapping us out of the moment. "We better get cleaned up and ready to go." I lean over his cum-covered dick and kiss him. "And in case I haven't said it enough, thank you for being here."

"You ready to go?" Brayden asks, stepping into my room. He's dressed in a pair of jeans and an Ice Hawks hoodie with his bag slung over his shoulder.

"I am," I tell him, zipping up my luggage and rolling it behind me.

Since I didn't want to risk my mom throwing a fit, after we got home from the charity function last night, we went to our separate rooms. I had left my phone at home, not wanting to deal with whoever was calling, but after I got changed into my pajamas and laid in bed, I let my curiosity get the better of me and checked.

Three calls from my mom.

One from my dad.

One from Sasha—along with a text asking where I've been.

None from Ashton.

I laid in bed and debated whether to call or text him, but couldn't bring myself to do it. Then I called Drew, but it went to his voicemail.

Maybe it's for the best. What Ashton's doing to me hurts, and I don't want to hurt anymore. If he's going to act like this, then as much as it kills me, maybe it's time we go our separate ways. But even as I thought those thoughts, a lump formed in my throat and my stomach roiled.

And then Brayden FaceTimed me, and we spent the rest of the night from our separate rooms talking and laughing, until we both fell asleep with our phones next to us.

Now it's morning and after having brunch with my parents, we're going to head home. Since Drew chartered him a plane here, instead of us flying separately, we're going to fly together on my family's jet.

We get downstairs and both leave our luggage by the staircase. We enter the dining room and it's empty.

"Nancy," I call out to the maid who takes care of the house full-time.

"Yes, Miss Lexington?"

"Are my parents here?"

"No, your mother got a call this morning that the producer needed to do some reshoots and your father was called into emergency surgery."

"Oh." And of course neither of them thought to tell me… "Okay, thanks."

"You okay?" Brayden asks, his voice etched with concern.

"Yep."

"You can tell me the truth." What he means is, he's witnessed my parents' behavior firsthand and knows how fucked-up my family is.

"It's just so typical of her. She demands I come here and once I've fulfilled my obligation, she drops out of sight. And my dad…" I shrug. "I shouldn't even care. I didn't even want to come here. You saw the way my mom treats me…" I had hoped Brayden sticking up for me at breakfast would've put her on her best behavior, but nope. The entire time at the event, she picked at me. She made sure to steer clear of the food conversation, but she had no problem finding other things wrong with me. At one point Brayden was so sick of her digs, he abruptly cut her off and told her he needed to show me something.

"They're still your parents," he says. "And you love them."

"They are… and I do." But I also love myself and don't ever want to sink as low as I did before.

"Wanna get something to eat on the way?" Brayden offers. "I was thinking something with bread." He shoots a wink my way and I laugh.

"Sure."

We stop at a small deli and grab sandwiches and coffee, then head to the airport. The flight is long, and I find myself falling asleep in Brayden's arms, not waking up until we're landing.

When we arrive back to campus, Brayden insists the Uber stop at my apartment complex and he'll walk back to his dorm from there.

After the driver takes off, Brayden closes the space between us and cups my jaw. His mouth descends on mine and his tongue delves past my parted lips. The kiss doesn't last long, but when he pulls back, I'm already breathless.

"Do you, uh, want to come up?" I ask, even though I could really use some time to myself to decompress.

"I do, but I'm not going to. I need to get home and get some reading done before my tutoring session tomorrow." He shoots me a flirty wink and throws his bag over his shoulder. "My tutor is a real ballbuster."

I laugh as I watch him saunter through the parking lot and disappear down the sidewalk. It's crazy how quickly life changes. Who would've thought Brayden Murphy would end up being my white knight?

Definitely not me.

# TWENTY-THREE

*Ashton*

'm an idiot.

Every time my fingers hover over my phone, hell-bent on texting Mia, I stop myself. She deserves better. Especially after the douchebag way I've treated her. I need to get over myself and talk to her. Explain myself. Beg for forgiveness.

Truth is, I can't stop thinking about her.

It's not a phase or something that'll go away.

I need her.

*But what about Drew?*

Guilt niggles at me, but I can't let that cloud my judgment. What we did was just something fun to pass the time. Two guys fucking around to get off. It happens all the time with me. Sure, I like dick, but I like Mia too. Right now, that has to be enough.

Because, without her, I feel pretty fucking empty.

Biting the bullet, I type out a message to Mia.

**Me: Text me when you get home.**

**MiMi: I'm home.**

**Me: I'm coming over.**

**MiMi: I'm tired.**

Ignoring her message, I throw on a hoodie and slip my socked feet into my Adidas slides. Drew's door is closed. After our intense gym session, we came back and retreated to our own corners. A part of me craves to dwell on how good it felt to be with him, but my heart, for once, has taken lead on this one, making my dick sit the fuck down.

I slip out of my apartment and head over to hers. She's locked it, but I anticipated this and use my key to enter. The apartment is quiet, so I meander my way through, looking for her. I find her in her closet, hanging clothes up. Gripping the top of the doorframe of the closet and leaning in, I clear my throat.

"Jesus! Fuck, Ashton! You can't sneak up on me like that." She shoves the hanger on the rod before putting her hands on her hips, glaring at me. "Why are you here?"

Her fiery words poke holes in my resolve, but I don't let it sink me.

"I came here to talk."

"Now?" she seethes, her nostrils flaring. "After you let me feel like shit all week? Especially right before I left? Screw you, Ashton."

If only...

"MiMi," I grit out, releasing the doorframe and stepping toward her. "I'm sorry."

"Sorry isn't good enough." Hurt cracks along her angry façade, blinding me with its intensity. "Sorry is just a word that you've been throwing around all too many times lately."

I scrub my palm over my face and sigh. "I've always liked guys, MiMi. Ever since I could remember. It's just a part of me." I frown, stepping even closer to her. "But then you kissed me."

Her brown eyes dart away. "It was a mistake."

"A mistake typically means it was an accident or something that never should have happened. But, the kiss was good," I remind her. "So good, you completely fucked my mind with it." A heavy breath of frustration escapes me. "Years of knowing my own brain suddenly felt like a lie. Everything was confusing. When I kissed you that second time, I absolutely wanted it."

She chews on her bottom lip, her eyes darting all over my face, trying to understand.

"It's taken all week, especially this weekend, to realize I love you, Mia," I admit, "and not in just some friendly way. I love you with parts of me I didn't know existed. I can't turn it off. You're here." I tap my chest over my heart. "I thought maybe I wanted to get rid of that part. But the truth is, I can't without killing me in the process."

A gasp tumbles past her lips when I grip her jaw, tilting her head up. I press my lips to hers, desperately craving another taste of her sweetness. My tongue teases hers, as I apologize soundlessly for the way I've behaved. Kissing her feels good. It feels right.

Her palms press to my chest and she pushes, breaking the kiss. My hand slides down to the side of her neck and I caress her jaw with my thumb.

"You can't do this." She presses her lips together.

"I've figured it out, though," I explain, leaning in to kiss her again.

"So?" she snaps, pushing me back. "I didn't realize I was supposed to wait until you figured your shit out."

I clench my jaw. "Mia…"

"No," she hisses. "I went away this weekend stressed about seeing my mother. I needed you and you weren't there." She swallows. "Know who was?"

Fucking Brayden.

"Yeah," I grind out. "I know."

She lifts her chin, leveling me with a hard stare. "We messed around."

I don't flinch. She didn't say it to hurt me. Just stating facts.

"I don't care," I tell her gently.

"Well, you should," she says, "because I like him. I like being with him."

Now, I really do cringe at her words.

"What about us?" I mutter. "MiMi, I can't lose you."

"There is no us... not like that."

I reach forward, running my knuckles along her cheek. Her eyes glisten with unshed tears. Mia forgets I can read her better than I can read myself. She's upset and angry with me—justifiably so—but that doesn't mean she hates me or can turn off the way she feels about me. I drag my thumb across her wet lip, searing her with a determined stare.

"I'm not going anywhere," I vow, my words low and husky. "This thing between us won't just disappear. Believe me, I already fucking tried to make it go away."

She swallows hard and a tear races down her cheek. Leaning in, I kiss the wet streak and then pull her to me for a hug. I'm happy as fuck when she hugs me back.

"You're making this hard on me," she whines, making me smile.

I stroke my fingers through her hair and kiss the top of her head. "It's one of the things you love about me. I'm a hot mess. One you signed up for when you looped your arm with mine and told everyone I was your boyfriend."

"Totally regretting that now," she mutters.

I chuckle. "Nah, you love me. Want to know why?"

"Oh God. Don't tell me you made a list."

"I couldn't find enough paper. I guess I'll just have to tell you."

"Why do I love you, Ashton?"

Pulling away, I smile down at her, admiring her pretty features. "I honestly don't know why, MiMi, but I'm glad you do."

Yesterday, Mia and I made progress. Not in a romantic sense, but in the way we got back to our normal friendly ways. Last night, we laughed together at stupid shit, ate junk food, and played video games until late. This evening, I plan for more of the same.

I manage to avoid Drew again today, which makes me feel like shit, but I can't have him distracting me. It'd be smart to confess to Mia about what happened between Drew and me, but I can't bear what that would do to our fragile relationship. Knowing her, she'll see it as more uncertainty on my end.

That's anything but the truth.

I'm completely certain where she's concerned.

I want to kiss her and hold her and one day go to bed with her. It's the natural progression of us. I won't rest until we've tried. If we fail, so be it, but I need to try first.

After grabbing a big bag of Skittles, I head over to Mia's once I know she'll be home from class. I'm just letting myself in when I hear her giggles. I'd smile if it weren't for the fact I'm not giving her the giggles. Someone else is.

My irritation is further ratcheted up the moment I see Brayden. He has her pinned against the back of the couch, planting teasing kisses on her. Jealousy coils around my heart, making the world turn green around me. I want to rip her out of his massive arms and pull her to me. But I know Mia. That'll just piss her off when I really can't afford to do that right now.

"Hey," I grunt out, trying to keep my voice level.

Mia flashes me a guilty look before forcing a smile my way. "Hey. I invited Brayden too. Thought we could all hang out."

His smug, stupidly hot smile gets on my last nerve. He lifts his head at me in greeting but doesn't say a word. The satisfaction gleaming in his chocolate brown eyes has my hand tightening around the bag of Skittles as anger threatens to drown me.

"Cool," I grumble. "We watching a movie or what?"

"Yeah, Brayden thought we could watch that new Chris Hemsworth movie. We went ahead and ordered food."

I walk past them into the kitchen and start opening cabinets on a hunt for booze. Mia shows up, hugging me from behind. All my fury bleeds away, forcing me to relax.

"I missed you today," she tells me, her hand patting my abs over my T-shirt.

"Missed you too, MiMi. What are we drinking?"

"Water?" she offers, making me snort. "Fine. There's vodka in the freezer."

She pulls away to go back into the living room. I play bartender, dumping Skittles into three tumblers and then filling them partway with vodka and then the rest of the way with Sprite.

"Come and get it, kids," I call out.

Mia, ever the adventurous one, grins when she sees her drink. "What do you call this one?"

"Rainbow Barf."

Brayden snorts. "It looks sick."

"The longer it sits there, the sicker it'll look. Better drink it while you can still see the colors," I warn. "Don't worry. I didn't roofie you, bro."

The corner of his lips kicks up in a maddening smirk. "Good to know."

Mia darts her gaze back and forth, seemingly tense about our exchange. I refuse to piss her off because I'm jealous as fuck over Brayden. I'm smarter than that. If I really want to win Mia over, then I need to do it the right way.

Be the Ashton she knows and loves.

I'm about to open my mouth to say something dreadfully charming, but then Brayden wraps an arm around her waist. I'd think he was taunting me, just to piss me off, but he seems desperate to touch her. I can't fault him, because I get it.

Mia is special.

I fucked up.

Frowning, I suck down my Rainbow Barf and then chomp angrily on the Skittles. The vodka concoction burns down my esophagus and starts an inferno in my stomach. I make myself another drink before walking into the living room, needing space. Just to be a prick, I park my ass down in the middle of the sofa. When they walk up to the sofa, I pat the cushion beside me for Mia to sit. Brayden's dark eyes flash with challenge and then he takes their drinks, sets them on the table, and then sits beside me with her in his lap.

"I have an away game this weekend, but maybe Thursday night I could take you out," he says, patting her thigh.

"That sounds nice," she agrees. "I'll miss you while you're gone."

Gag.

Fucking gag.

I level Brayden with a glare that says, *"I kissed your girl last night."*

He smirks back with a look that says, *"I know."*

Leave it to Mia to be upfront and open about everything. Makes me feel like an even worse douchebag for what happened with Drew, because I can't tell her about it. I just can't.

Brayden pulls her back against his chest, nuzzling against her neck, kissing her there. She giggles because she's ticklish there—a fact I knew long before him. His eyes meet mine as he sucks on the flesh there.

Fuck him.

"Stop," she warns him, though her voice is breathless and needy. It does shit to me. Makes my dick hard in my jeans.

He does it again, his eyes flashing with triumph. That he got the fucking girl. With my eyes burning holes into him, I take her hand and thread our fingers together. It's something I would have done long before she kissed me that day. We're affectionate like that. I bring her hand up and kiss one of her knuckles.

The room goes quiet aside from the way Brayden suckles on her neck. She squeezes my hand. I don't know if it's an apology or a reminder that she's still here with me. Either way, I take it, squeezing her back.

Brayden's hand cradles her cheek, turning her face to him. His challenging stare locks on mine, even after his lips fuse to hers.

I don't back down or look away.

He nips at her bottom lip, making her whimper. My dick strains against my jeans. His eyes close and the tension bleeds away. I watch them, hating how much I enjoy the sight of them together. He's fucking hot and Mia is gorgeous. I shouldn't like it as much as I do.

*Ding-dong!*

Mia shrieks in surprise. Brayden grabs her hips and moves her aside to snatch his wallet up from the table beside his phone and keys. As soon as he walks off to greet the delivery person, Mia glances my way, her cheeks flushed.

"I'm sorry," she murmurs. "That was probably awkward for you."

"Let me tell you a secret," I say lowly, crooking a finger at her to urge her closer.

She leans in so close I can smell his masculine scent lingering on her. "What?"

"It wasn't awkward because I can still do this." I kiss her soft lips and then pull away with a smile. "I haven't lost you yet."

Her lashes flutter against her cheeks and she presses her fingers to her lips, surprise shining in her eyes.

"What'd I miss?" Brayden practically growls as he drops the bag of food on the coffee table.

I wink at him. "Mia'll tell you later. She doesn't keep secrets."

The look on his face is murderous because he knows what that means. I kissed his girl—*my girl*—and I'll do it every damn chance I get.

He might be a big, hot jock with eyes for my girl.

But I'm a spoiled boy who's spent twenty-one years getting everything he wants.

If Brayden wants Mia, he's going to have to fight a little harder for her because I'm not going fucking anywhere, and when it comes to getting what I want, I'll fight dirty.

# TWENTY-FOUR

## *Drew*

"**C**an I get a Guinness?" I call over to the bartender, who's locked eyes with me from across the bar. With his brown, messy hair and hazel eyes, he reminds me a little of Ashton. Fucking Ashton. I mentally shake my head at how awkward shit's been this week since our *weekend* together. Ever since Mia and Brayden returned, he's barely been home, and when he is, he's practically hiding out in his room. I'm going to need to get on Curtis about finding me another apartment for next semester. There's no way I'm going to continue to live like that. Especially since instead of regretting it, I can't get the night out of my head. And instead of wishing it never happened, I keep thinking about when it could happen again.

The bartender sets my beer in front of me. "I'm Kaleb. You new around here?"

"Just passing through," I tell him, taking a sip of my beer. "Only here for the night."

His lips curl into a grin. "And you're spending it at the bar of the hotel?"

"Do you suggest I spend it somewhere else?" I ask, finding it too easy to flirt with this guy. For years, I focused my attention on women, but now that I've spent some time with Ashton, as well as kissed Brayden, I find myself giving the same sex equal amount of attention. Does this make me bi? Maybe… But I'm going to take the advice I gave Ashton not too long ago and not smack a label on it.

"Right here is fine with me," Kaleb says, his eyes sparkling with lust and mischief. My gaze slides down past his strong nose and chiseled jaw, landing on the tattoo peeking out from under the collar of his shirt. I wonder what—

"Picking up bartenders in bars now?" a masculine voice I would recognize from anywhere says, cutting off my thoughts. I glance over and find Brayden sitting on the barstool next to me.

"I'll take a Heineken," he says to Kaleb.

"Good fucking game," I tell him, patting him on the shoulder and ignoring his dig about the bartender.

"Damn right it was," Brayden cockily replies. "We got this season on lock."

"Don't get too comfortable," I warn, taking a sip of my beer. "You've won three games. You still have thirty more to go."

"Thirty more we'll fucking win." Brayden scoffs as Kaleb sets his drink down, his attention coming back to me.

"Let me know if you need anything else," Kaleb says with a wink. "I'll be around all night." He saunters away and I can't help but check out his ass as he goes.

Brayden tilts his beer back and takes a long gulp. My eyes land on his Adam's apple and the way it bounces as he drinks. An Adam's apple shouldn't be sexy, but it is. These are all things I'm noticing now that I never paid attention to before.

Brayden sets his beer down and his gaze lands on me, as if he's caught me checking him out.

"Why aren't you out with your teammates?" I ask, knowing full well the guys made plans to hit up the local bar so they could try to get laid before curfew. We just finished our game with New Hampshire and since it's one of the colleges that are too far to drive there and back in one day, we're in a hotel for the night and will drive back in the morning. I've given the guys a 2:00 a.m. curfew since the game ended late. I'll have to check their rooms good to make sure they don't have any women hiding in their closets and tubs.

"Not in the mood." Brayden shrugs.

I finish off my beer and catch Kaleb's eye, tipping my bottle so he knows I want another one. He flashes me a smile, and I wait for my insides to burn the way they did when Brayden kissed me all those years ago. The way they did when I kissed Brayden when we were alone. The way they did with Ashton last week. But it doesn't happen.

"Here you go," Kaleb says. "Need anything else?"

I'm about to tell him I'm good when Brayden speaks up first.

"Yeah, asshole. For you to quit flirting with the customers and do your damn job," Brayden hisses, shocking the shit out of me.

Kaleb blanches. "I'm sorry, man. I didn't know you two—"

"We're not," I correct him, my eyes going from Kaleb to Brayden.

When I give him a *what the fuck* look, he glares my way before he returns his attention back to the bartender. "It's none of your business what we are."

Once the bartender walks away, Brayden says, "So, what? You're gay now?"

I swing my head his way. "The fuck?"

"You're clearly checking out the bartender, and he, you. Is that what you want?" His brown eyes are blazing with unreadable emotion and his jaw clenches. "To fuck him?"

His label and accusation rubs me the wrong way.

"I kissed you," I taunt. "And the last time I checked, you pushed me away. Now you're trying to cockblock me?"

Brayden blinks rapidly. "So you are… gay?"

"I hooked up with a guy last weekend." I shrug, playing nonchalant while trying to rile up Brayden.

It fucking works too because he glowers at me.

"Who?" he barks.

"I don't kiss and tell." I throw a fifty-dollar bill on the counter and stand. "Have a good night."

I enter the empty elevator and press the number of my floor. The doors are shutting when they suddenly pop back open, and in walks Brayden.

"This conversation isn't over," he growls.

I smirk on the outside, but on the inside, my heart is smacking against my ribcage, making it hard to breathe. What does he mean, it isn't over? Does he want to talk now? Later?

We stand in the elevator in silence, but the tension in the small area is damn near suffocating. I consider asking him what he means several times, but I can't find it in me to get the words out. Instead I stare at the screen as the numbers go higher. Neither of us says a word, but it's the loudest damn silence I've ever heard.

My questions are answered when we step out of the elevator and, instead of Brayden going into his room, he follows me into mine. Fuck, this is a bad idea. Me and him alone in my room… This last week we've finally settled into a comfortable coach and player relationship. I might even say we're making progress toward getting our friendship back. If we cross over that invisible, thin line, I'm not sure we'll ever be able to come back from it. But I can't find it in me to tell Brayden to leave. To insist we finish this conversation somewhere in public, where I can't fuck anything up.

"What is it you—" Before I can finish my sentence, Brayden is on me, his mouth crashing against mine. Tasting me. Coaxing my tongue to duel with his. Unlike our previous kisses, when only one of us has been on board, this time, we're both giving as good as we're taking. My tongue strokes his as I devour him.

All too quickly, though, he breaks the kiss.

"That's how our first kiss should've been," he murmurs with a shake of his head. Our bodies are so close, I can feel his hard dick against my own, telling me he's turned the fuck on. Just like I am. My eyes land on his mouth, glistening from our kiss. I want to lick his lips to get another taste of him.

"I was young and didn't know what was happening." I was scared shitless about what us kissing would mean for us. "I fucked up."

Brayden takes a step backward, and all I want to do is pull him back to me.

"You ended our friendship instead of talking to me," he says, his features saturated in hurt as he stares at me. "I fucking needed you, loved you, and you left me like I didn't mean shit to you." His voice cracks on the last word, breaking my heart in the process.

"I know, and I wish I could go back and change the choices I made, but I can't. But I can tell you that I've thought about you over the years, missed you every second of every damn day." I beg him with my eyes and words to hear me, believe me, forgive me. "And when we kissed… well, when I kissed you, I felt that shit to my core. I wanted you like I've never wanted anyone else in my life."

"And you show me that by letting me know you dicked someone else last weekend."

He takes another step back, his face contorted in pain, but this time I refuse to let him distance himself any farther.

I grab the hem of his shirt and pull him back to me, until our faces are close… too close. I can smell the beer lingering on his breath. The same beer I was just tasting on his tongue a few moments ago. "And I thought about you the entire time."

His eyes go wide in shock and then his mouth is back on mine, pushing me against the wall. His lips curl around mine, stroking, teasing, caressing. He lifts my shirt and slides his palms over my abs. His skin is hot and I crave his warmth. I should stop this, but he tastes too good, feels too good, and I've fantasized too often about being with him.

So, instead, I spur him on, my hand skating down his front, until I get to the bulge beneath his pants. I squeeze it gently, waiting to see how he'll react. When he groans into my mouth, deepening the kiss, I dip my hand into his pants and wrap my fingers around his hard shaft.

His strong lips caress mine, and I stroke his dick, using the beads of precum to create fiction. I push his pants down slightly, and then I do something bold.

I break our kiss and drop to my knees, my eyes rising to meet Brayden's smoldering gaze. "I'm going to taste you," I warn him, just in case he wants this to stop now. When his eyes roll back and his fingers thread through the back of my hair, I take that as my cue to continue.

With my fingers wrapped around his dick, I lick the swollen head, tasting the saltiness of his precum as it seeps out of his slit, and then lick my way down his entire length until I get to his ballsac.

"Jesus, Drew," Brayden groans. "You're a fucking tease."

His words make me feel powerful. Like I'm in charge of his pleasure.

Starting back at his head, I take him, inch by inch, into my mouth, not stopping until it taps the back of my throat. I gag slightly and glance up to find Brayden's eyes locked on me.

"Fuck," he breathes. "That feels so fucking good."

With his fingers intertwined in my hair, he pulls my head back slightly, then pushes me back onto his dick, showing me how he likes it. He does this several times before I take over, fucking him with my mouth. In and out. In and out.

All too soon, Brayden's dick swells inside of my mouth. He tries to pull me off of him, but I'm not a damn quitter. I grab ahold of the back of his legs and take him in as far as I can go. Jets of cum shoot down my throat. It's thick and salty and I damn near choke, but I don't stop. I suck and swallow, taking every last drop, until his dick goes flaccid in my mouth. And then I release him and stand, my eyes meeting his. Refusing to regret what we just did.

"Holy fucking shit," he mutters, out of breath, backing up and stuffing his dick back into his pants. I expect him to run, but instead he drops onto my couch and scrubs his face with his hands. "Fuck," he murmurs. "I can't believe that shit just happened."

"Why?" I ask, flinching at his choice of words, scared I fucked up. I might've been letting my heart guide me, but what if he was guided by his dick, and now that it's been drained, he's thinking clearly. I'm not sure how I'll handle it if he pushes me away. I've gone too long without him, and now that I have him back, I can't lose him again. I *won't* lose him again.

He lifts his face, which is filled with anguish. "Because I'm with Mia."

Fuck. Shit. Fuck. Mia. I was so lost in Brayden, I wasn't even thinking about anyone but the two of us. Wait…

"You two are together?"

"We haven't had the talk or anything, but we've been hanging out a lot. Why?"

I think back to the few times I've run into Ashton this week. The way he and Mia were cuddled on the couch. They've always been close, but this last week it seemed like more, like they were…

"I thought they were finally together." I don't have to say who *they* is for Brayden to know who I'm talking about.

Brayden raises a single brow. "Ashton and Mia are only…" And then, as if it's suddenly clicked, his eyes bulge and he changes directions. "Is that who you fucked around with? Ashton?"

When I don't say anything, he laughs humorlessly. "Fucking A. That little fucker. He's not only going after Mia but you too."

"It was just a one-time thing."

He stands. "Yeah, and so was this."

He stalks out of the door and slams it behind him. I consider going after him, but I pussy out, worried he'll push me away. Instead, I jump into the shower to rinse the night off me. As I let the hot water rain down on me, the events of tonight come back to me. Brayden kissing me. The sweet and bitter taste of his tongue mixed with mine.

I grip my shaft and tightly wind my fingers around it, stroking and pumping it, remembering the way Brayden's dick felt in my mouth, full and thick, slightly veiny. What would it feel like to have him return the favor? To have his mouth on my dick? Or better yet, what would it feel like to fuck him? To push my dick through his tight ass and claim him?

I get he's with Mia, but he wanted me first, and now that I'm no longer running scared, I'm not sure I can sit back and watch them be together.

The thought has my dick thickening. The vision of Brayden and Mia, Mia and Brayden. Her in the middle of my bed at The Lodge, her legs spread while I fingerfuck her. Brayden kissing her while he strokes my dick. My hand slaps the wall and I drop my head, closing my eyes, as I shoot my load to the fantasy.

One thing I know with absolute certainty…

I want Brayden. I need Brayden.

I will absolutely fight for Brayden.

# TWENTY-FIVE



'm tired as fuck, but I can't wait. I have to see Mia. I need space from Drew.

Jesus.

Every time I let my mind drift back to Saturday night in his hotel room, my dick grows rock-hard.

He blew me. Drew—the guy who freaked the fuck out when I kissed him years ago—got on his knees, pulled out my cock, and sucked me off.

Sad part is, I really, really liked it. To the point I jacked off the moment I got back to my hotel room because I was so amped over what that did to me—what *he* did to me—and was already hard again.

But it was wrong.

Right?

It's wrong because I've been seeing Mia. Fooled around with Mia. Really like Mia. I can't, though, turn off a lifetime of feelings I've had for

Drew. Even when I was pissed as hell at him, I loved him. Everything's a fucking mess.

I have to be upfront with her, though. I also need to find out what the fuck Ashton thinks he's doing to her. And to Drew. It makes me want to knee him right in the nuts.

*Hypocrite.*

Ignoring my internal bitch boy, I head over to Mia's once we roll back into town. I knock and wait for her to answer. The door flings open. She's wearing a wide smile that tightens when she sees me.

"Not expecting me?" I ask, arching a brow.

She laughs and shakes her head. "I thought it was Ashton."

"Hmph."

"Hmph?"

"Can we talk?" I step closer, tucking a dark tendril of hair behind her ear.

Her brows furrow. "Yeah. Is everything okay?" The way her voice shakes slightly, it seems as though she's anticipating this conversation. But how could she know Drew gave me a blowjob?

"Not really," I grunt. "Everything's a mess."

"Do you want to come inside?"

"Not really. I'm tired. I just… I needed to talk to you before I went back to my dorm to crash."

"Well, talk, Brayden. You're beating around the bush."

I scrub my palm over my face. "I, uh, I had a good night with Drew."

Her eyes widen and her plump lips part. I crave to kiss them in this moment, but that won't get me any closer to sorting out this confusing mess.

"We sort of kissed. A lot." I close my eyes, remembering the way it felt.

"You're smiling," she whispers.

I swallow down the emotion clogging my throat. "I missed him."

When I reopen my eyes, her bottom lip is trembling. It makes me feel like shit to hurt her. Stepping close to her, I cup her cheek and lean my forehead to hers.

"I'm so fucking confused, Mia," I admit. "I like you so much. So fucking much, but…"

"You have history with Drew."

I nod. "I'm afraid if I push too hard away from him, I may never get him back. It's all I've ever wanted for so long. He's here. He's fucking here. And it's up to me to do something about it." I press a quick kiss to her lips. "I'm so sorry I've done this to you."

"Hey," she coos, wrapping her arms around me. "It's not just you." She sighs. "Things are… different with Ashton. Better. This week, we've been close in ways we've never been before. He's my best friend, but I think he wants to be more."

"Be careful with him," I warn, unable to curb my irritation.

She tenses, pulling away to frown. "It's Ashton. I don't have to be careful with him."

"I'm just saying after what happened with him and Drew—"

"What?" Her word slices through the air like a blade, cutting me off.

"Nothing," I grind out. "I shouldn't have said anything. It's not my place."

"What happened?" she demands.

"You'll have to ask him, Mia."

"Why wouldn't he tell me if something happened with them?" she asks, hurt shining in her dark eyes. "I've been upfront with Ashton about everything. With you, too. It's not like he'd be afraid of my reaction. It's probably nothing."

If you call sword fighting nothing…

I sat far away from Drew on the way back to Hawk's Landing, but I texted him the whole way, demanding to know what all he and Ashton did. I'd expected to be pissed about it, not so fucking jealous. What I really didn't expect was how I imagined every little detail Drew gave me. How they made out and jacked each other off…

"I'll text you later and check up on things," I say to her, leaning in to kiss her forehead. "Just because I need some time to figure this shit out with Drew, it doesn't mean I want to stop being around you. I don't have tons of friends, Mia, but you've been one of the best to me. I can't lose Drew after everything, but I can't lose you either."

"I'll be right here." She forces a smile. "Now go study."

I give her an exaggerated salute as I back away from her door. "Yes, ma'am."

This time her smile is real. She closes the door, but rather than feel like a weight has been lifted, I feel the crushing sense of disappointment.

As I walk down the hall toward the elevators, I can't help but think this is all Ashton's fault. All of it. He's the wrench in all of this. Fucking with Mia and Drew. At least with me and Mia, I really like spending time with her. I wasn't using her to experiment with my sexuality. I wanted her. Hell, I still want her. But I can't ignore this thing with Drew. I need to face our past and try to work through it with him, even if it lands us back to being best friends again. He's such a huge fucking part of my heart that's been detached from me for so long. I feel like now my heart is starting to beat again.

I can't let Ashton fuck Mia over, though. He didn't tell her about him and Drew, which means he probably won't ever. She doesn't deserve to be involved with some lying asshole. If he's lying about that, who the hell knows what else he's lying to her about.

*Sorry, Mia, but as your once-almost-boyfriend, it's my duty to threaten this dickhead.*

I take the long hike across campus to the building with the pool. Once inside, I make a beeline toward the chlorine smell. I slam right into someone exiting.

Travis.

His stumbles back, his water bottle hitting the floor, but he rights himself just in time before he falls with it. Quickly, he bends to pick it up. When he stands back up, I crowd him, sniffing.

"You stink, douchebag."

He stumbles back, away from me with eyes wide from fear, and then bolts out the side door. Fucking freak. Ignoring his weird ass, I stalk into the pool area. I march my angry ass over to where Ashton left his bag last time and plant my ass beside it. It reeks of chlorine, I think. I don't know how he puts up with the god-awful smell all the time. My eyes drag along the pool like a net until I find him.

I hate that the asshole has to demand attention.

I further hate that I unwillingly give it to him.

Ashton glides through the water, faster and more furious than before. I've never seen anything like it. I'll admit, since the last time I watched him, I looked up swimmer videos. The only swimmer I'd ever heard of was Michael Phelps. Ashton makes that guy seem like a novice. He owns the pool like he's Poseidon. All the other swimmers watch in awe as he does his thing.

Back and forth.

Back and forth.

He swims with speed and grace and it's fucking mesmerizing.

Finally, he climbs out and stands near the pool edge. His muscular body drips with pool water as he looks my way, cocking his head in confusion. I pin him with a hard, challenging glare.

He begins sauntering my way as he peels off his blue cap and goggles. His dark hair flops over one of his hazel eyes that gleam with wickedness. I hate that I once again have to scope out how he compares to me. My gaze roams down his chiseled abs, taking in the way his obliques flex with each step he takes. Today he's wearing skintight red spandex shorts that leave very little to the imagination.

Swim team is basically eye porn for everyone else.

I jerk my gaze back up to his, finding his lips curled into a knowing smirk. It pisses me off. He tosses his cap and goggles into my lap.

"To cover up your hard-on," he taunts.

"Fuck off," I growl.

He smirks as he snatches up his towel and dries off. "Why are you here?"

"We need to talk."

"No shit, Sherlock. Talk." He drops the towel and grabs his water bottle. After he unscrews the cap and pulls it off, he lifts a brow. "Dude, stop staring at my junk and say what you need to say."

My nostrils flare as I jump to my feet. He lifts his bottle to his lips. I smack it hard out of his hand, sending it flying to the ground.

"What the fuck?" he snarls, getting in my face. "Is this about Mia—"

"Not now." I push past him to pick up the bottle. Bringing it to my nose, I inhale. "What the fuck?" Whirling around, I shove it in Ashton's face. "Is that—"

"That fucking bastard," Ashton hisses. "Bleach? Is he trying to kill me?"

My blood runs cold. Travis. I thought he smelled funny. Looked guilty as fuck, too.

"I'm going to beat that motherfucker's ass," I rumble, my hand curling into a fist.

Ashton shakes his head at me. "You can't."

He just tried to make him drink bleach! The hell I can't.

Ashton snags his shit up and storms off to the locker room. I stalk after him, not ready to end this conversation about Travis. That guy needs to lay the fuck off. As soon as we're in the locker room, Ashton starts stripping out of his red shorts, flashing me his toned ass. I cross my arms over my chest, refusing to leave.

He dresses in record speed, before turning to glower at me. "Enjoy your peep show, dude bro?"

"Nah, man," I grind out. "I'd rather check out Drew's ass."

His eyes narrow and his jaw clenches.

"Now you're thinking about it," I taunt. "How you jacked each other off last weekend… How my fucking best friend's tongue was down your throat." I stride right up to him and poke his hard chest. "Drew told me every sordid detail. Best friends and all. Makes me wonder. Did you tell *your* best friend?"

"Back the fuck off me, Brayden, or so help me I will knock your ass on the ground." His hazel eyes flash in warning.

"What's wrong? Can't have Mia find out you prefer dick over pussy?"

"I said back the fuck off." His words are low and threatening. "Now."

"You want to beat my ass for telling you the truth, but I'm not allowed to throat punch that pussy Travis for trying to poison you?"

What the hell is wrong with this guy?

"I'll tell her," he mutters.

"She knows."

He lets out a murderous roar and shoves me with surprising force. I trip over his bag, landing hard on my ass. He pounces on me, his hands on my throat. I land a punch in his ribs, but he's snarling like a fucking mountain lion. We grapple, each of us trying to get the upper hand until it happens.

We both freeze.

He's hard. He's fucking hard. But so am I.

"Told you," I bite out, triumphant. "You can't just turn off the fact you like dick."

His hips flex as a hateful expression crosses over his features. "And what are you going to do when Mia finds out that your dick is a fan of dicks too?"

I let out a dark chuckle. "She already knows. Now get the fuck off me."

"Or what? You'll beat me up?" he taunts. "You gonna poke my eye out with your hard-on?"

Fucking asshole.

"You have to the count of three," I warn. "One."

His mouth curls into a sinister grin. "The jock can count. All that tutoring paid off after all."

"Two," I spit out.

"Like the number of dicks Drew had in his hands when we spent the weekend together and we came all over my stomach together."

I don't even get to number three because his words set me off.

Red.

I see fucking red.

# TWENTY-SIX

*Mia*

The second Brayden disappears from the hallway, I'm stalking next door. My heart is pumping, my blood boiling. This last week Ashton's been all over me, trying to convince me that I'm who he wants. I think I knew deep down, contrary to what he preached, I would never be enough for him. But to find out from Brayden that Ashton hooked up with Drew is like a slap to my face. He's the same guy I left for Ashton the night at The Lodge. The same Drew I pushed from my thoughts, telling myself he was off-limits because he is. He's the man Brayden loves and cares about. Can't live without.

As I bang on the door, I'm not sure what I'm even mad about at this point. Everything is so confusing and complicated. Am I pissed that Ashton might've fucked Drew? And if so, shouldn't I be upset that Brayden also kissed the same guy? My heart hammers in my chest. I am upset, I am mad. At Brayden, at Ashton…

The door opens and Drew makes his appearance and suddenly I realize I'm also really freaking mad at Drew.

"How could you!" I shout, tears of anger pricking my eyes.

His eyes go wide. "Mia, I…"

"Ashton is my best friend." I swipe the falling tears. "And Brayden." I take a deep breath that does nothing to calm my nerves. "I really care about him."

"Mia…"

"Why? Why, Drew? You can't have them both! It's not fair. Why did you do this? Was it because I left you hanging that night at The Lodge?" But even as I say the words, I know they aren't true. I know Drew isn't like that. He cares about Ashton and Brayden, just like I do.

I stare at Drew for a second. His eyes are glossed over with guilt and he looks crestfallen. I want to yell at him some more, take out my hurt and anger and frustration on him, but it's obvious he's going through this as well.

"Where's Ashton?" I look past him, hoping to see my best friend so he can explain why he kept this from me.

"He's at the pool," Drew explains, his features etched with pain and sorrow.

"Fine, let's go." I grab his hand and pull him along, giving him barely enough time to close the door behind him. "I'm sick of these secrets and lies." I stomp down the hall.

Since neither of us has our keys, Drew and I walk across campus to the sports complex. Neither of us saying a word. I don't want to hear it from Drew. I want to hear it from Ashton. I want him to tell me what happened and why he didn't tell me. I want him to tell me if Drew is who he wants…

Then I remember about Brayden. Where does he fit into all of this? He loves Drew. But what if Drew wants Ashton? He'll be crushed.

We get to the pool and I search for Ashton. There are swimmers in the pool, on the small platforms diving in, but no Ashton anywhere. It's hot and sticky in here, and I struggle to breathe easily.

"He's probably in the locker room," I mutter, dragging Drew behind me.

The anger surging through me is quickly getting doused by sadness. I knew with everything in me it was a bad idea to kiss Ashton. It set events into motion that I'm no longer able to stop. Like a wrecking ball, this thing I started because of a stupid, drunken kiss is now destroying every aspect of my life. I'm nearly in tears by the time I push into the men's locker room.

I freeze in the doorway, Drew's heat burning into me from behind. Drew sucks in a sharp, shocked breath. I, on the other hand, can't breathe.

I don't understand.

Ashton is…

And Brayden is…

Why are they kissing?

Drew's hands come down on my shoulders just as the first tear leaks from my eye and races down my cheek. I shake my head in disbelief, a small whine escaping my throat. Both Ashton and Brayden pause from their kissing, where they're sprawled out on the floor in an intimate way with Ashton on top of Brayden. Ashton's back tenses and then he jerks his head my way.

"Fuck," Brayden mutters, covering his face with his palm.

Ashton, however, is horror-stricken. He scrambles back, falling on his ass, as crimson creeps up his neck and blazes across his cheeks. "Mia, I can explain—"

"No," I choke out, sending more tears dropping from my eyes like raindrops of regret.

I try to step back, but Drew is behind me, no doubt just as upset as I am. Brayden won't get up off the floor or look at us. Ashton is approaching with anguish in his hazel eyes.

"Mia, please," he begs, his voice cracking.

"No," I hiss.

He reaches for me and I shriek. "Don't touch me!"

My words are like a gunshot wound to him, because he clutches his chest, stumbling back slightly. "Mia," he whispers. "Mia, please."

"I have to go," I utter, turning in Drew's arms.

Drew is as tense as I feel, but he drapes an arm over my shoulder to guide me away from the horrible scene, sheltering me in this moment. I know he's hurting every bit as much as I am. Now's not the time to compare war stories, though.

"Mia!" Ashton calls out, his voice pained. "Mia! Please, wait!"

I don't wait.

I can't.

My heart is broken in too many ways I don't understand.

"Mia!"

It keeps breaking, each time he says my name like he's dying.

"MIA!"

# BOUND TOGETHER

YOUR CAPACITY TO LOVE IS LIMITLESS. THE ONLY THING
STOPPING YOU IS THE WAY YOU THINK.–UNKNOWN

# ONE

*Ashton*

**W**hat have I done?

Fuck.

My lips feel bruised from the kiss Brayden and I just shared, but it's my heart that's taken a beating. I fucked up. Badly. One minute I was pissed at him, taunting him, and the next we were kissing.

It was me.

I leaned down and planted my lips on his.

I just didn't expect him to kiss me back.

"Mia," I rasp, staring at the now closed locker room door.

Movement to my left steals my attention. Brayden rises to his feet, the erection straining in his jeans still on full display. My heart is broken and my world is fucked, and yet I still can't help but think he's hot as hell.

This is so bad.

"You told her," I bite out, shoving my hormones down to harness my anger. "*You* did this."

Brayden's features morph from shock at what happened to fury. "Fuck you, Ashton. You did this to yourself when you messed around with Drew and then dry fucked me on the tile floor when you were supposed to be pursuing Mia!"

The fucking gall of this guy!

Stalking over to him, I shove my middle finger in his face. "Get lost, asshole."

He smacks my hand out of the way and grabs the front of my shirt, yanking me until our noses nearly touch. "You can't pin this shit on me," he growls. "You fucked up. Own it."

It's true.

I did this.

It's easier to blame him, though. To make him feel one iota of the hurt I'm aching from.

"Are *you* owning it?" I sneer, noticing his slight flinch at my words. "Drew didn't look too fucking happy either."

Low blow but fuck him for acting holier than thou.

He shoves me back, hard against a row of lockers. "What happens between Drew and me is none of your goddamn business."

I struggle in his grip, but the fucker is strong. His hips pin me. I hate that fire lights a path down my spine and zings to my dick. Now, of all times, my dick needs to calm the fuck down. This is so fucked up.

"Fuck," I complain, as sadness creeps in. "I hurt her. I fucking hurt her."

Brayden's brown eyes darken. He smells good—too good—and I would push him away if I had the strength. "You're not the only one," Brayden rumbles. His eyes dart over my face, an unreadable expression on his features, before he pulls away, taking his heat with him.

"I need…" I spear my fingers through my hair and tug at the strands. "I need to talk to her."

The intensity that was burning between us only seconds before is snuffed out as reality seeps in. Everything is a mess. We both know it.

"Maybe you should give her a chance to cool off, man," Brayden suggests as I snatch up my bag.

Ignoring him, I storm out of the locker room and past the pool. I don't need to let her cool off. I need to find her, hold her, kiss her. I need to apologize for being a rotten asshole. I need to do something… anything.

"See you at the meet," Aaron, another swimmer, calls out as I pass.

I tip my head in acknowledgment and keep walking. Brayden is following me, which pisses me off. What the fuck is he even doing here? All he did was blow shit up with Mia and me. I'm not even sure he planned to do it either. He clearly had every intention of showing up to put me in my place. But then…

I try not to think about the few seconds leading up to the kiss.

He was so fucking pissed, but sexy as hell too. I'd thought nothing in that moment except for the fact I wanted to taste him. I didn't make a split decision, rather just gave in to instinct. My lips brushed along his for a teasing taste, but then he groaned. Needy and curious. I craved to swipe my tongue over his. To nip at his lip and grind my dick against his.

Curiosity ruined everything.

It ruined her.

Now I'm hauling ass across campus, hoping to save my relationship with Mia. She hates me. I hate me. I'd begged her to let me explain before she bolted, but the truth is, I don't know that I can explain it to her. I sure as fuck can't explain it to myself.

"Ash," Brayden clips out. "Stop, man."

"Can't," I grit out when we make it to my apartment building. I fling open the door and choose the stairwell rather than the elevator, taking the steps two at a time to the third floor. By the time I reach the landing on the third floor, I'm losing energy fast. After my swim session, where I put in everything I had, to the kiss with Brayden, and then to this, I'm running on fumes.

I trot down the hall until I make it to her door. It's locked, so I start beating on it.

"Mia! Let me in! I want to talk to you!" I bellow. "Mia!"

No answer.

I'll just go grab my key from next door and let myself in. I turn on my heel, rushing to my apartment. After letting myself in, I hunt for the key in the kitchen drawer, but feel a presence behind me, making me pause.

"Why are you still here?" I snap, refusing to look at Brayden.

"What are you doing?"

"Getting a fucking key. You can go now."

He walks up to me and pushes me away from the drawer. His hip knocks it closed before he leans against it. "You can't barge in over there."

"The fuck I can't!"

"She locked her door for a reason," Brayden says in a calm voice that gets on my last nerve. "Give her some space."

"Move."

"I can't let you do this."

"This is not your fucking problem to worry about!" I yell, shoving at his immovable form. "Go the fuck away!"

His jaw clenches, but he makes no move to leave. "Are you done throwing a tantrum?"

"Seriously, asshole, get the fuck out of my apartment."

He shakes his head. "Sorry, man. Not until you cool off."

He's serious.

Douchebag Brayden is going to play the goddamn hero.

With. My. Fucking. Girl.

"You think I'd hurt her?" My fury threatens to explode into a thousand pieces. "Because if you're insinuating that—"

"I'm not insinuating shit," he snarls, his dark eyes narrowing, "but I know Mia. This isn't the way to deal with it. Making demands and being a total prick. Just calm the fuck down before you ruin it beyond repair."

His words cut deep. I've fucked up. I don't want to make it worse.

"How are you so calm right now?" I demand. "Things with you and Drew are fucked too."

He flinches and it makes me feel like a dick.

"Whatever," I grumble, digging around a cabinet until I find a bottle of tequila. I unscrew the lid and take a long, burning pull of the liquid.

*I'm so sorry, Mia.*

I wish I could say the words to make her understand. That I love her and need her, but… there's this craving that pulls me away from her all the same. It's unfair that I'm wired the wrong way. I just want to hold her and keep her.

I take a few more swigs, feeling all kinds of sorry for myself, until I realize Brayden has approached. It pisses me off that my hairs stand on end and my dick fucking reacts. My heart is screaming at me to go plead my case to Mia, but my body isn't completely on board with my sudden epiphany with my sexuality. It knows a fine-looking man and is reacting accordingly.

"I can't lose her," I admit, my voice cracking with emotion.

His brows are furled together, but his eyes have softened. It's in this moment—right in this second—that I see why Mia was so enamored with him. There are sides of him he guards. Right now, he's not guarding shit. The antagonistic side of me wants to poke at this softness. See how deep I can go. Explore it. My therapist calls that destructive behavior. I call it curiosity.

"You won't," he assures me in a gritty voice that does unspeakable things to me, taking the bottle from my hands to drink some. "It's Mia. She's sweet and caring. But she's going to need some time."

Fuck, I know he's right.

I know Mia.

We both do.

I steal the bottle back and make my way into the living room. Brayden follows me and makes himself at fucking home on the couch next to me.

"What are you doing with her anyway?" he asks, angling himself to face me.

Question of the fucking year.

What am I doing with her?

Trying like hell—and fucking failing—to keep her.

"None of your business."

"It is because it involves me," he reminds me. "Just out with it."

I scrub my palm down over my face and frown. "I want to be with her. I do."

"But…"

"Maybe there isn't a but," I snap.

He thumps me on the arm hard, making my skin sting. "Don't be a dick."

"Says the dick who just thumped me." Scowling, I rub at the spot that'll now be bruised.

"Tell me the but, Ashton."

I let out a heavy sigh of frustration. "But I still kissed your dumb ass. That's the problem."

"Mia deserves more than someone whose heart isn't fully in," he mutters. "Trust me. I already came to that decision tonight."

"But my heart is in," I argue. "I love her."

His eyes dart back and forth between mine like he's trying to pry inside my brain. I know how I feel about Mia. I'm just confused about the other shit.

"You know this is messed up, right?" I pass him the bottle. "I hate you and yet here you are fucking consoling me over this. It's your fault for that kiss."

A dark eyebrow arches up. I hate the way my gaze automatically falls to his lips as he drinks from the bottle—lips that were on mine twenty minutes ago. Full, soft, pink lips.

"Hate?" he asks. "Why do you hate me?"

"I wish I could hate you," I amend. "But…"

"But I'm so hot it's kind of hard."

I flip him off, stealing the bottle back. Instead of letting go, he tightens his grip. His fingers are hot beneath mine. Fuck if I don't imagine them wrapped around other things besides bottles.

Not. Fucking. Helping. Ashton.

"Ash." Brayden releases the bottle but pins me with an intense stare. "You love Mia? Well then, fight for her. At the very least, you talk to her about your chaotic feelings." His brows furrow and his head dips down, despair leaking into his features. "Losing your best friend because you can't communicate over your emotions fucking sucks." His brown eyes lift to meet mine, and the sadness in them reflects my own.

"How is it that you of all people understand what I'm going through?" I complain.

He chuckles. "I think God is punishing you for being an asshole."

"I'm commiserating with you. Is God punishing you, too?"

Brayden recoils slightly, his entire body turning stiff. "Yep."

Now it's my turn to be concerned. We were joking, yet it's clear to me he believes he's being punished for something. For whatever's happened between him and Drew? It's on the tip of my tongue to ask, but he clears his throat and stands.

"I probably better go." His voice is gravelly and pained. "You going to be okay now? I'm not going to get a call to come bail you out of jail for breaking and entering or stalking or some shit?"

A snort escapes me. "If I go to jail, I'd much rather call Dad. It gives me great joy to see how many shades of crimson his face can turn when he's equal parts pissed and embarrassed. But you could totally come along to film it."

"You're such a dick." His tone is no longer despondent, and I'm surprised that I'm thankful about that. "Seriously. Will you be okay?"

I don't know why he cares.

*Because we kissed and he liked it.*

My blood heats, but I blame the tequila.

"I'm not going to drink myself to death if that's what you're wondering," I tell him.

He stares at me for a long beat before turning his back on me. I can't help but run my gaze over his muscular, masculine form. I fucking kissed him. I kissed this guy I supposedly hate because he's hot and maddening and it felt good.

Mia deserves better than me.

Not some asshole who bounces—literally—from one dick to the next.

"Brayden," I call out when he opens the door.

He glances over his shoulder at me, the sharp angles of his jaw clenching. "Yeah?"

"Thanks for…"

The pep talk. The unexpected quasi-friendship. Stopping me from further fucking things up with Mia.

And the kiss. The kiss. The fucking kiss.

"For what?" he asks, his husky voice setting fire to my alcohol infused blood.

"For tonight." My eyes drop briefly to his lips, a painful memory lingering in my chest.

"See you around, Ash."

The door clicks closed behind him. Misery clouds around me, reminding me I'm once again all alone. When Brayden was here, comforting me in unexpected ways, it was easy not to let this thing with Mia consume me.

He's gone, which means my dick has gone back into hibernation.

My heart, though, is back to bleeding for the girl I love.

# TWO

## Drew

"**M**ia! Let me in! I want to talk to you!" Ashton yells from the other side of Mia's front door. "Mia!"

I encircle my arms around Mia and bring her closer to me on the couch. "I can tell him to go away."

"No." She shakes her head, sniveling loudly. "Don't open the door. If you do, he'll slip right through the cracks." She rests her head against my chest and her entire body shakes as she cries. "I can't let him in. I can't handle him hurting me anymore."

My phone vibrates in my pocket with a text, but I don't answer it, telling myself it's because I want to give Mia my full attention. But the truth is, I'm scared to check it. Right now, I'm focusing on Mia. Her hurt. Her anger. Her pain. And in doing so, I'm ignoring the myriad of feelings that are stirring in me and threatening to break free. If I check my text and it's either of them, I have no doubt those feelings will erupt, and then I'll have to deal with them.

My thoughts go back to earlier.

*Ashton kissing Brayden…*

*Brayden kissing Ashton back…*

If I hadn't seen it with my own eyes, I wouldn't even believe it. Ashton kissing Brayden, sure. He's an equal opportunist. But Brayden… *my* Brayden was kissing him back.

Just as the knocking and yelling stops, my phone vibrates again.

"It's one of them," Mia says, glancing up at me. Her glasses are removed and her eyes are red-rimmed. Her cheeks blotchy. She must've been wearing a little bit of mascara because it's slightly smeared under her eyes. Her hair is up in a messy bun. She looks so damn sad.

"Probably."

"How could he do this?" she asks, sitting up and crossing her legs, bringing them up to her chest like she's trying to protect herself from the big bad world.

"Which one?" I raise a brow, and she releases a shaky breath.

"I was referring to Ashton, but I guess both of them." She closes her eyes and swallows thickly. "How did this happen? How did we get here?"

Here meaning her being in love with her best friend and caring deeply about mine.

Here meaning me being in love with my best friend and caring deeply about hers.

Here meaning our best friends kissing, who, the last time I checked, hated each other.

"I don't know," I murmur, wishing I had the answers, but at the same time not wanting them.

My phone vibrates again, and Mia's glassy eyes meet mine. "Maybe you should check it."

"I don't know if I can."

"I get it," she agrees. "My heart… it hurts so much." Fresh tears well up in her eyes and fall over, racing down her cheeks. "I love him, but I'll never be enough." Her body racks with fresh sobs as she covers her face with her hands. I pull her back toward me, wrapping my arms around her, hoping to comfort her.

"He loves you too," I assure her. "He's just so damn confused."

I shouldn't be defending Ashton, not after what I witnessed. But I can't help the way I feel about him. I care about him, even when he does stupid shit like kiss my best friend. It's who Ashton is. He acts without thinking. Makes irrational decisions. But it's half of what I like about him. I wish I could be a little more like him. Act impulsively, consequences be damned.

"I know," she says. "But it doesn't change the fact he hurt me. He told me he loved me and wanted to be with me, and I believed him."

"What about Brayden?"

Mia chews on her bottom lip for several seconds. "Brayden knows."

"And he was okay with that?" Doesn't sound like the Brayden I know.

"I think…" She sighs. "I think he understood because he feels the same way… about you."

Her sad as fuck eyes lock with mine and my first emotion breaks free. Guilt.

"I'm so fucking sorry for my part in all of this." I beg her with my eyes to forgive me. "I don't know how this all got so twisted. It's like one minute, I was trolling for a woman to hook up with at The Lodge and the next, I'm fucking around with two different guys."

Mia does some weird snort-laugh-cry thing and then grants me the smallest smile. "I get it. They're both… oddly irresistible in their own ways."

Her smile falls and she takes a deep breath. "Where do we go from here?"

"I guess the question is, where do *you* want to go from here?"

She chews on her bottom lip in thought before she says, "Right now, I think I need a little breather."

I get exactly how she feels. "If you want me to go…"

"No." She shakes her head. "Unless you want to go…"

"Right now, I think I need a little breather as well."

"Wanna watch a movie?" she suggests. "Try to take our mind off the shitstorm that's waiting outside for us."

"Sure."

She clicks the television on and presses play on the first movie that pops up. The opening credits have barely even begun, when I hear her sniffling.

"Hey, what's wrong?" I take the remote out of her hand and press pause.

"It's 'No Strings Attached.'" She hiccups through a sob. "It's about two best friends who fall in love." Her lids fill with tears and her chest falls up and down heavily. "Drew," she cries. "I love him. I need him. I don't want to lose him." She's crying so hard, it's difficult to make out what she's saying. "And I really, really care about Brayden," she adds. "I'm so sorry. I know you love him…"

"Shhh… It's okay." I guide her closer so I can comfort her. She lays her head across my lap, and I run my fingers through her hair, trying to calm her down. When she shifts her body, getting comfortable, her face brushes against my crotch, and my dick stirs, thinking he's about to get some attention. I close my eyes. Breathe in, then exhale harshly, praying she doesn't notice.

But she does…

"Umm… Drew," she says softly. "Are you…?"

I clear my throat. "Hard? You're rubbing your face against my dick, Mia."

"Oh," she breathes, sitting up. "I'm sorry." She eyes me sheepishly. "We're a hot mess, aren't we?" She laughs, and I chuckle at how up and down her emotions are. One second she's in tears and the next she's laughing. It would be amusing if not for the circumstance.

My phone vibrates and she eyes my pocket. "Can I ask you a question?"

"Of course."

"If you could be with one person, who would you be with?"

"Damn," I say through a laugh. "Hitting me with the hard questions."

"The fact that you think it's a hard question says a lot."

I let her words soak in. She's right. I should've immediately said Brayden. He should've been the obvious answer, but that would mean never being with Ashton again, and for some crazy reason, the thought of not being with Ashton again doesn't sit well with me. Then there's the fact I was just sporting a chubby over Mia touching me. Jesus fuck, she's right. We're a hot damn mess.

"What about you?" I ask without answering.

She raises a knowing brow. "If I had to pick one person…" She considers her answer for several seconds. "I want to say Ashton…"

"But…"

"But I think it's clear I'm missing an important piece he obviously needs, and I want him to be happy. I don't think I could ever truly make Ashton happy." Her eyes roll to the ceiling as she tries to stop herself from crying, but she fails, and the tears skate down her face. I reach over and wipe them with my thumbs, hating how badly she's hurting. Hating how fucked up this situation is.

"Nothing has to be answered tonight." I pull her into my chest. "Why don't we pick a different movie and just tune it all out for tonight? Tomorrow, all this bullshit will still be here."

She nods in agreement against my chest. "Okay."

I find an action flick and press play. Not even twenty minutes into the movie and Mia is snoring softly. Carefully, so I don't wake her up, I lift and carry her to her room and lay her down in her bed.

I'm pulling the blanket up when her eyes flutter open. "Stay the night," she says groggily.

"You sure?"

"Yeah," she insists. "It's safe here." In other words, if I go home I'll be forced to face Ashton.

"Thanks."

I climb into bed with her and she rolls over, her head landing on my chest and her soft body snuggling against mine. I try to ignore the way my entire body relaxes at her touch. She curls up closer, and her arm falls across my torso. I close my eyes, trying and failing not to notice how perfectly she fits against me.

It makes me wonder how Brayden—or Ashton—would feel in this position. Could I give up women altogether in order to be with Brayden?

Could he? As my eyes close in exhaustion, my thoughts go back to Mia's question: if I had to pick one person to be with, who would I pick? If only that question had a correct answer, then we all wouldn't be in this damn situation.

I wake up to the sound of my alarm going off. Fuck, it's 4:00 a.m. Practice. I glance over at Mia, who at some point rolled over and is facing the other way, and carefully climb out of the bed so I don't wake her up.

I consider going straight to practice without changing and then remember my keys are at the apartment. The only other person with a set of keys who would be there as early as me would be Brayden, but I'm not sure if he'll be showing up to practice.

After leaving Mia a note that I had to go to practice but will be by after to check on her, I lock myself out of her apartment and walk next door to my own.

Shit, no keys means I don't have keys to my apartment either. I try the doorknob and sigh when it opens the door. At least at this hour, he'll be asleep.

But the moment the door clicks shut behind me, I know I'm wrong.

Ashton is not asleep.

He's fucking wrecked and waiting.

"Where were you?" His words are cold and filled with accusation. He pushes his hair back from his face, his bloodshot eyes meeting mine.

"You know where," I mutter, not wanting to look at him, yet unable to look away either.

Not when he's like this.

Burning with a mixture of anger and something else.

His hair is messy and sticking up. Dark circles ring his eyes. He's shirtless and wearing his swim sweats. Despair practically drips from him. A perfectly tormented man, and somehow too beautiful to look away from.

"Did you sleep with her?" Hate ripples from him, but the pained expression on his face indicates it's directed at himself. As though he's hoping for the lash of my words.

Rather than hurt him, I walk over to him, gently clutching his shoulder. "No."

He doesn't say anything. Simply bows his head. I squeeze the powerful muscle that only years of swimming can create.

"I'm sorry I fucked everything up," he whispers, barely audible. "I'm a fuck-up."

"Everyone's fucked-up," I say with a sigh. "Including me."

With those words, I leave him hopefully feeling not so alone, because it's the truth. All four of us have a play in this situation—each aiming for the goal and always missing—but no one's winning shit.

# THREE



**H**e won't look at me.

Not that I'm surprised.

I royally fucked up.

All through practice, I felt Drew's intense glare on me, but by the time I would glance at him, his stare was elsewhere. His jaw clenched, the only tell of his pain.

Not anger. Pain.

I fucking hurt him.

"You going to Marcus's party tonight?" Finn asks as he shoulders his bag.

"Nah," I grunt, toweling my wet hair. "I need to study."

Finn smirks. "Is this about that girl? Naked studying?" He waggles his brows. "Need a study partner?"

"Go away," I say with a laugh, shoving at him.

"I'll text you the address in case you change your mind. See ya, Murphy."

"Later."

The moment he's gone, I steel my nerves. I need to talk to Drew. He may have been able to avoid me at practice, but he won't be able to avoid me when I march right into his office. I'm just grabbing a clean shirt from my bag when I hear keys jangle. I dart my eyes over at Drew's office to find him locking up.

He's trying to escape.

Fisting my shirt, I charge over to him, my heart clenching and blood buzzing through my veins.

"We need to talk," I grit out, hating how he still won't meet my eyes.

"I have a meeting."

"Liar."

His blue eyes finally—fucking finally—lock onto mine, blazing with anger. Good. I can deal with anger. I can't deal with breaking his heart.

"I have a meeting," he says, his voice turning icy.

"So cancel it." I take a step closer, needing to be near him. "I want to talk to you."

A muscle ticks in his jaw and his nostrils flare. "There are things I want too, but clearly that's not going to fucking happen."

His words are a punch to the gut.

"Drew," I choke. "What happened with Ashton—"

"Stop," he snaps. "Just stop."

I step until we're nose to nose. "We were fighting and then…" I close my eyes, frowning. "Then we were kissing. I'm sorry."

"It's fine." His words are cold. "Can I leave now?"

I open my eyes to look at him. "I fucked up."

"It was just a kiss," he mutters. "Not a big deal."

"It was, though." I fist the front of his shirt, aching to kiss him until he forgives me. "After what you and I did this weekend, I shouldn't have done that. I'm sorry."

"Brayden…" He sighs. "I'm more worried about Mia right now than my feelings."

His words make me flinch—a stab from a double-edged sword. They're a reminder that another person was hurt by that kiss. Mia. And that he holds her feelings above his own.

I'm storming with confusing emotions.

"I'll talk to her," I assure him. "I'll make this right."

Drew snorts in disbelief. "It's too fucked up to ever be right."

"Please don't shut me out," I beg, hating the vulnerability in my tone. "Please."

His blue eyes soften as he studies me, seemingly searching for answers as to what is going on in my head. I'll tell him. Whatever he needs to hear to make it right again.

"I'm not shutting you out." His hand grips my wrist, but he doesn't pull my hand away from where I hold on to his shirt. "I just need space to think."

"About us?" My voice cracks. "I've been thinking a lot about us."

I know I fucked up and kissed Ashton back. I'd gotten so caught up in the way he was taunting me that it just sort of happened. I'd be a liar if I said I wasn't attracted to Ashton. Seeing him swim is what changed things for me. From hating him to admiring him. When he had me pinned and was fucking with me to piss me off, I got turned on. That kiss was… un-fortunately, really fucking nice.

It was just with the wrong person.

"I need to leave," Drew reminds me. "We can talk later."

I crave to kiss him and hug him. To show him that we really can be okay. All we have to do is try. I'm not confused right now. I want Drew. I want to make it right.

"Tell me we'll be okay."

He lets out a heavy sigh. "We'll be okay."

Even though he doesn't sound convincing at all, I'm fucking elated. I release his shirt to hug him, burying my face against his neck. My heart tightens inside my chest when he hugs me back. Everything is fucked-up and messy, but being like this with Drew is one of the right and good things in my world.

Someone clears their throat.

Drew and I fly apart. My skin prickles with worry when I whirl around to find Dean Carter staring at us, wearing a frown that looks so much like Ashton's it's frightening.

"Dean Carter," Drew rasps out. "I was—"

"My brother," I choke out. "Comforting me about my brother. He knew him too."

I feel like shit throwing Ben out there, but I sure as hell don't want Drew to get his ass reamed for hugging me. We were friends long before he was my coach. But, to an outsider, I know it looks bad, especially since I'm half-naked from my shower.

"I'm sorry," Dean Carter says to me before turning his attention to Drew. "I just came by to congratulate you on the win. Again. This is going to be a great season."

I throw on my shirt and then scoop up my bag. "Later, guys."

I'm buzzing with worry as I head for the tutoring center where I have an appointment with Mia. Now that I've put some distance between Drew and me, I can't help but mull over his words. She's probably feeling all kinds of betrayed. Not only did she catch the boy she's stupidly in love with kissing someone, but it had to be me. The same guy who flew all the way out to California to surprise her. The same guy who took her on a date and was intimate with her. The same guy who broke things off with her in order to pursue something with Drew.

I'm a fucking mess.

Mia doesn't deserve this.

If Drew and I will be okay, maybe Mia and I can be too. She's sweet and trusting and caring. Not the type to hold grudges forever. Maybe one day we can go back to being friends. I owe her an apology and I won't feel right until I've made it.

I bump into a girl and steady her so she doesn't fall. It's a familiar girl I've seen around a few times.

"Sorry," I grunt out. "Didn't see you there."

"Brayden Murphy?"

I grin because it's what my fans expect. "That's me."

"Sasha. Remember me?"

I'm nodding even though I had no fucking idea what her name was. "That's right. How's it going?"

"Just busy. My daddy's been planning the athletic program's annual fundraising event, so I've been hunting down items for the auction." Ah, I don't know her, but I do know her dad. From what I've heard, he graduated twenty years ago and still holds half the football records. Could've gone pro, but he blew out his knee. Now he's just an old man living vicariously through the younger generation. Can't complain, though… It's because of the fundraising events he organizes that the hockey team got all new equipment and uniforms this year.

"I'm planning a dating auction." She smiles, batting her fake lashes at me.

"I'm sure you'll earn lots of money with that." I scan the tutoring center behind her, looking for Mia. "Let me know how it goes."

Her fingers wrap around my bicep, stopping me. "I thought maybe you'd like to offer a date for an auction item. A portion of the proceeds do go toward hockey after all."

"Me?" I frown at her. Drew's already told the team we have to go, but I was just planning to make an appearance and then dip the fuck out.

"You're the most loved hockey player this school has," she explains, her pink lips quirking up on one side. "I've already wrangled the quarterback of the football team and the starting center of the basketball team. I tell you, it's fate we bumped into each other. Literally."

"Uhh," I groan, running my fingers through my wet hair. "I guess, yeah." Anything to get the hell out of here.

"Wonderful," she says, flashing me her mouth full of perfect veneers. "It's a good thing this is for a good cause. I won't mind one bit outbidding everyone for a date with you."

The thought of going on a date—albeit a paid-for one—with this chick is nauseating.

"Right," I grunt out. "So I gotta go."

"I'll have my assistant, Bianca, email you with the details." She gives my bicep another squeeze before releasing me. "See you soon."

Glad to be away from her, I stalk over to the guy running the tutoring center reception desk. Some nerd with glasses and a face full of pimples. As soon as he sees me, he blushes.

"What?" I demand, confused at his sudden embarrassment.

"N-Nothing," he croaks out. "Can I help you?"

I study this dude for a second. He's nervous and his face keeps turning redder by the second. Is he afraid of me?

"I'm here to see Mia Livingston."

He averts his gaze to the computer. "She's not in today. Looks like her appointment with Brayden Murphy—"

"That's me," I confirm.

"Canceled. It looks like it's been canceled." He blushes again. "Depending on the subject, I could tutor you."

All the puzzle pieces snap together. He's attracted to me. Something, before all this recent shit with Drew and then Ashton, I would've chalked up to him being a dweeb. Now, I recognize it for what it is. This guy is apparently also into guys, namely me. I'm slightly annoyed at the fact I'm starting to notice the opposite sex—even when not attracted back. I feel like I should blame Ashton for this. Definitely Ashton.

"Nah, man. I'm good." I give him a head nod and then stalk out of the tutoring center.

She canceled because of what I did.

I hurt her.

Just like I hurt Drew.

I'll need to see her soon and repair things. Apologize. Grovel. Sure, Mia and I were technically "off" whatever it is we were attempting, but it doesn't mean I still didn't hurt her.

Since I'm fucking starving after practice, I make my way over to the cafeteria and grab a sandwich. I see a few guys I recognize and tip my head to them, but never stop to talk. I pause for a second, letting that sink in.

I never stop to talk.

Never party with Finn or the others.

Rarely meet up with the other teammates outside of practice or games.

I'm a damn loner.

It wasn't always this way. Before Ben's death, I was popular and liked at my school. I had ride or die friends, including Drew. I went to sleepovers and terrorized the mall with my buddies. I went on trips out of town with my friends and their families. I allowed myself the pleasures of friendship.

When Ben died, I began to retreat.

I didn't feel deserving to have fun when he'd never be able to again.

It all felt so unfair.

And now I'm a goddamn man who has no friends because the ones he does have, he tries to stick his dumbass tongue down their throats.

Fuck.

"Hey, Nick," I grunt out, walking up to the table of guys who were just waving to me. "Your brother still play for that Canadian hockey team? How's that going for him?"

Everyone blinks at me, seemingly surprised that I approached and engaged in conversation.

Okay, so I'm really shitty at this.

"Yeah, man," Nick says, his brows furling. "Want me to put in a good word?"

"No," I rush out quickly. "I was just making conversation."

"Oh."

The uncomfortable silence wanes on.

"Right, so if you ever want to hang, hit me up," I state, giving him a forced smile.

Nick nods, but confusion glimmers in his eyes. "Sure thing."

I grunt out a goodbye and then walk away, hating how fucking awkward that was. Why do I have to be this way? All I care about is hockey, my parents, and Drew. It's all it's been for as long as I can remember.

What about Mia and Ashton?

Mia's a no-brainer. I do care about that girl.

Ashton…

I don't want to think about Ashton. He's problematic.

On the way over to Mia's, I wolf down my sandwich, my mind spinning with all the confusing shit I'm dealing with. I don't know how to make sense of the way my heart speeds up at the thought of seeing her. Or how it seems to stop altogether when I think of the kiss with Ashton. My heart just fucking explodes when my thoughts return to Drew—always Drew.

I finally reach Mia's door and knock, hoping like hell she'll answer. Heavy footsteps thud toward the door. The lock flips and then the door opens enough to reveal Drew.

My Drew.

Why the hell is he here?

"This was your meeting?" I bite out, flames of anger licking at my insides. I know it's irrational, but I feel duped somehow. "What's going on here?"

He still looks hot as hell wearing his Ice Hawks long-sleeved white shirt and dark wash jeans. I want to yank him to me and kiss him, but after the shit storm that was last night, I don't dare. We're on thin ice and one wrong move could lead to dire consequences.

I can't lose him again.

Not when we're so close to… something.

The something feels right and I need it.

"My meeting was canceled," he states in a gruff tone. "It was an academic probation meeting with advisors, but since all my players got their grades up, it was unnecessary. Anything else you'd like to interrogate me about, Officer?"

I tear my gaze from his lips that have twisted up in an angry sneer to peek past him into Mia's apartment. "I need to talk to Mia. She canceled her tutoring session with me."

He crosses his arms, blocking the doorway with his big body. "You should reschedule with someone else."

"I don't want anyone else," I throw back, heated at his words. "I want Mia!"

We both flinch at my words.

It's not like that, but it kind of feels like that.

"She doesn't want to talk to you or Ashton right now. Give her some space."

I have the urge to yell for her to come to the door but then that'd be going against the advice I just gave Ashton about Mia last night. I know this girl. It'll only piss her off more.

"Can you tell her I stopped by?" I ask, deflating like a balloon. "Please."

"I will."

"Tell her I'm sorry."

His blue eyes flash with pain that stabs me right in the gut. "You've been saying that a lot today."

I want to pull him to me and say it a thousand more times because now that my head's out of my ass, I know what I want.

Drew.

For most of my life, it's been Drew.

A beautiful, sweet girl and a hot, sarcastic asshole aren't going to change that.

"Drew," I mutter, wanting nothing more than to close this divide between us.

He uncrosses his arms and starts to turn to go back inside. On impulse, I grab his hand. It's warm and strong in my own. He doesn't pull away, which feels like progress.

"Tell me we're okay. Say it again," I plead.

His jaw clenches, but his thumb is gentle as it strokes my hand. "We're okay."

Uncertainty flickers in his blue eyes, unsettling me.

"Bye, Bray."

I reluctantly release his hand, hating how cold I feel when our connection is severed. "Bye, Drew."

I'm still staring his way when the door closes in my face. Resolve begins to build up inside me, fiery and hot. Sure, over the years Drew and I have danced around this thing that has always seemed inevitable between us. At certain times, our grief only stirred up the messy emotions, never letting them settle. Anger took the wheel more often than not.

But now?

Now we're back on the path to an us.

I can feel it with utmost certainty.

It's going to be rocky as fuck, but our path so far has been that way.

Who wants a smooth road when they could take the bumpy, frustrating road with Drew Thompson?

I've fought tooth and nail to get to where I am with hockey.

I'll do the same for him because I'm tired of pretending like he doesn't mean the entire fucking world to me. I'm tired of this push and pull. I'm going to fight for him rather than against him. It's about damn time, too.

*We're going to be okay, Drew.*

*Just wait and see.*

# FOUR

*Mia*

"He said he's sorry," Drew says, closing the door. He glances at me with the saddest eyes and I hate that I'm being a coward and forcing him to run interference. I might've been hurt by what Ashton and Brayden did, but so was Drew.

I bring my knees up to my chest and encircle my arms around them. "I heard… Thank you for that." I nod toward the door. "I know eventually I'm going to have to talk to them."

"You don't have to thank me," Drew says, sitting back down and wrapping his comforting arms around me. "And you don't have to rush to see or speak to anyone. They'll both be here when you're ready."

"Have you, um, spoken to either of them?" I look up at him and he nods solemnly.

"A little. I saw Ashton this morning when I went home to get ready for practice."

"How is he?" I shouldn't care how he's doing, but I can't help it. I know how my best friend is, and he doesn't handle shit well.

"Not good," Drew says truthfully. "Beating himself up in typical Ashton fashion. Blamed himself and called himself a fuck-up." The thought of not being able to hug my best friend makes me sad. One of the reasons Ashton and I clicked was because we're the same: both natural loners. Right now, I have Drew, but who does Ashton have? Who will be there to talk him down, to hold him the way Drew is holding me? He's not a fuck-up. He's just confused, the way we all are. The only difference is, where I think through every decision I make—from years of my mom berating me over every bad choice—Ashton flies by the seat of his pants. It's one of the things I love about him… and it's also what led to him hurting me.

"Saw Brayden at practice," Drew adds, snapping me from my thoughts. He's quiet for several seconds before he continues. "When we were younger, the reason we stopped talking was because Brayden kissed me." My mind goes back to the night Brayden and I talked while he was visiting me in California. He told me about this, and I couldn't help thinking how similar our situations were. Best friends torn apart all because of a kiss— an act of love. Something that should bring two people together, instead tore them apart.

"I ran because I was scared of what that kiss would mean," he says, looking down at me. "We were best friends and with one kiss, everything changed. I just kept thinking, if I reciprocate, will that make me gay? Or bi? Back then athletes weren't gay… well, at least not publicly, and I was scared of what my dad and the kids at school would say."

Drew releases me slightly so we can face each other. His features are etched with pain, and I can tell he's been holding this all in for years.

"You were young," I tell him. "And being different is scary."

"Maybe, but Brayden put his heart on the line twice for me. Once when we were thirteen and again when my dad died. He kissed me twice, not giving a shit about the consequences or what people might think. We both felt it, this pull between us, but he wasn't scared to act on it. And I ran like a fucking coward."

He scrubs his palms over his scruff that's grown in the last few days since he hasn't shaven. "I want to be so mad at Brayden for what he did with Ashton, but…"

"But you love him, and he's your best friend," I choke out, missing the hell out of mine.

"Yeah, but more than that, I want to be with him." Drew's glassy eyes meet mine. "I spent eight years without him, and I don't think I can do that again. I came here to coach, but the truth is, I also came here to get my best friend back."

My heart both swells and clenches at the same time because the man he wants is the same man I was falling for. God, this is so messed up.

I close my eyes and take a deep breath, and when I open them, I say the words I think he's needing to hear. "Then you should go after him."

Drew's eyes lock with mine.

"He loves you, Drew, and after spending this time with you, I can see why. Go to him, work it out. At least one of us can have that elusive happily ever after."

Drew nods. "I'm not ready yet. I need to forgive him first, so when I do go to him, I'm not still angry and hurt by what he did."

"You of all people know that what happened wasn't Brayden's fault." I huff out a laugh. "I love Ashton to death, but we both know he was the instigator there. It wasn't too long ago you were with Ashton as well. I'm not saying Brayden didn't do anything, because we both saw him kissing Ashton back, but…"

Drew groans. "But Ashton is hard as fuck to resist."

I laugh harder. "I miss him so much." Fresh sobs rack my body, and Drew pulls me into his arms so I'm straddling his thighs. I wrap my arms around his neck and he holds me tight while I cry into his neck. "Why can't I be enough?"

"Fuck, Mia, you are," Drew murmurs. "You are enough."

"Not for Brayden… and not for Ashton…" And not even for Drew. I've fallen for three men. Three sweet, funny, thoughtful, sexy men, and I'm not enough for any of them.

Memories from when I was younger hit me hard.

*"You aren't skinny enough."*

*"You aren't motivated enough."*

*"You aren't pretty enough."*

*"You aren't coordinated enough."*

*"You aren't popular enough."*

My entire life, I've never been enough. My mom made sure I knew it, and as much as I hate to admit it, she wasn't wrong.

I pull away from Drew and climb off his lap. "If it's okay with you, I think I really just want to be alone." I swipe the tears that won't stop falling.

"Are you sure?" he asks, worry in his tone.

"Yeah," I choke out. "I'm sorry. I just… I need some time to think."

"Okay, yeah." He stands. "But if you need anything…"

"I know, thank you."

"You sure?" he asks again as he opens the front door.

"Yeah."

Once he's out the door, I lock it and then slide down the door until I'm sitting on the floor, and then I let go and cry.

I want to be enough for someone.

My parents. Ashton. Drew and Brayden.

Seems like I'm almost good enough, but not quite.

I guess Mom was always right.

There's a knock on the door, and I drag myself out of bed. The first couple days of me being at home and wallowing, Ashton and Brayden would stop by and try to get me to open the door, but after Drew told them I needed time, they stopped. Not ready to leave and deal with the real world, I emailed my professors and feigned sick. They were nice about it, letting me know the work I need to do to stay caught up, and it bought me a few days.

Now, it's Friday and Drew and Brayden are leaving for an away game, so I could probably get away with leaving my apartment, but there's still Ashton. I haven't seen or spoken to him since I caught him and Brayden lip-locked, and I don't think I'm ready yet. I haven't even turned my phone on. It's been quiet and peaceful… and lonely.

The knock sounds again, and my heart picks up speed at the thought of Ashton being on the other side of my door. I bring my eye to the peephole, mentally preparing myself for seeing the man who's stolen my heart and shattered it, but instead, I see Drew.

"Hey," I say, opening the door so he can come in. "I thought you had a game."

"We do." He closes the door behind him. "But when I stopped by before, I noticed you didn't have any food in your fridge." He raises his arms, holding a coffee in one hand and a bag in the other.

"Thanks," I mutter, taking the items from him and setting them on the counter. "But you don't have to take care of me."

"I know, but I'm worried about you. You've been holed up in this apartment all week, and you haven't eaten anything…"

"I'm fine," I snap. "Anyway, what about you? Yeah, you've gone out, but have you talked to Brayden or Ashton?"

His look of guilt tells me my answer: he hasn't.

"I'm planning to. I just need some time."

"And so do I."

He nods. "Okay, I have to head out. The bus is leaving soon, but if you need anything—"

"I have your number. Now go." I playfully push his shoulders. "Focus on the game and don't worry about me."

I pull the door open and Drew and I come face to face with Sasha. "There you are," she says, raking her eyes down the length of my body. "Where the heck have you been?" Her nose bunches up in disgust. "And why do you look like… that?"

Then, as if just realizing there's someone else here, her eyes land on Drew. "Who are you?" Her brows furrow in thought.

"I'm just leaving," Drew says stiffly. I'm confused by his abrupt answer, until I remember… He's the coach, and I'm a student. And…

"Are you the guy from the club?" Sasha asks, quickly putting the pieces together.

"I'll talk to you later," I say to Drew, practically pushing him out the door, while pulling Sasha inside, so she can't berate him with questions.

The second the door closes, she says, "You and the hockey coach?"

Shit, I was hoping she wouldn't recognize him as anything other than the guy from the club. "Nothing happened between us," I tell her point-blank. The last thing we need is for Sasha to start gossiping.

"Sure didn't look that way on the dance floor…" She hits me with an accusatory stare.

"Sasha," I groan. "Don't make something out of nothing, please. He's the coach and I'm a student and once we knew that, we both walked away."

"So, then what's he doing here?"

"He's roommates with Ashton." I don't want to give her anything more, but if I want to get her off the Drew train, I'm going to have to distract her with something else. "Ashton and I kissed and then… he kissed someone else." There, that ought to do it.

"What a slime ball. I've told you before he's a bad egg." She lifts her chin so her nose is pointed up, all too ready to step on her high horse. "Did you know he was caught with drugs on campus?"

"It was weed," I say in his defense. "And it was planted."

Sasha harrumphs. "He's bad news. My mother says his father can't control him. Plus…" She leans in, like we're not alone, and she has a secret to tell me. "I heard he's gay."

"Nooooo." I mock gasp, mentally rolling my eyes. Everyone knows Ashton is gay. He's never made it out to be a secret. *And only your dumb ass would think he would suddenly switch teams for you…*

"Yep." She pops the P. "Looks like you dodged a bullet with that one." My chest constricts. It feels more like I was hit by said bullet, right in the center of my heart.

"We're going out tonight," she transitions. "It looks like you can use some fresh air. Take a shower, get dressed…" Her eyes land on my hair, and her face contorts into a pained expression, like it's personally offending her.

"And please, do something with your hair." She saunters over to the door. "I'll text you the name of the lounge and the address. We're meeting there at nine o'clock." And then she disappears out the door.

For the next couple hours, while I watch reruns of crappy television that I'm not even paying attention to, I consider whether I should go out tonight. Sasha's annoying, but she's right, I need some fresh air. I haven't left this apartment in days. Ashton, Drew, and Brayden are all continuing with their lives while I'm here, wallowing alone. It wouldn't hurt to take a shower, get dressed, and get drunk. If nothing else, maybe it will help me forget. Because clearly sitting in this apartment, crying and sulking, isn't working.

After I'm showered and dressed in a sexy little black number—I might not have my shit together, but at least I can look like I do—I turn my phone on so I can call for an Uber. The second my phone lights up, it's overcome with texts and missed alerts. I spot Ashton's and Brayden's names but quickly swipe them away. Not going there... I pull my Uber app up and request a car, and then, after putting my phone on silent, I shove it into the front of my dress.

As I step out of my apartment and walk past Ashton's, I slow down slightly, hoping maybe, like he always does, he'll hear me and come out. But he doesn't.

Fifteen minutes later, I arrive downtown at an upscale lounge called The Brasserie, one I've always thought was too uppity for me to ever step inside. There's a line of people waiting to get inside, and since we're experiencing a rare early winter, it's chilly outside. I consider just telling the driver to take me back home, since I didn't bring a jacket, and I'm not in the mood for freezing to death, but I don't want to waste actually showering and getting dressed.

After thanking the driver, I pull my phone out and shoot a text to Sasha, who immediately replies that my name is at the door. Thank God!

Once I'm in, I make a beeline straight for the bar.

"What can I get you?" the good-looking bartender asks, blatantly checking me out.

"Umm… A martini, please. Any flavor is fine." I should probably find Sasha and her posse, but I'm not in the mood yet. I'll need a little bit of alcohol in my system to deal with her tonight.

The bartender nods and goes about making my drink. While I'm waiting, my phone vibrates against my breast. It's probably Sasha… I pull it out to let her know I'm grabbing a drink and I'll find her soon, but when I swipe up to check the message, I freeze. It's not Sasha… It's Ashton. And before I can demand my brain to abort, I'm reading his text.

**Ashy C: This is my daily message to remind you that I love you and I'm here when you're ready to talk.**

The bartender sets my drink down and I swallow the entire thing in one fell swoop.

"Want another one?" he asks, his brows knitted together in confusion.

"Actually, I'll take a double shot of whatever you have that's the strongest," I shout over the blaring music.

*I love you.*

The bartender raises a brow but doesn't argue, grabbing the shot glass and setting it in front of me. He pours the liquor, and I down it before he's even had time to put the bottle back. The liquor stings its way down my esophagus and when it reaches my belly, it feels like it's on fire. My throat and stomach burn, but I welcome the pain. Craving it.

*I'm here when you're ready to talk.*

"Another one?" he asks, holding up the bottle.

"Yep, keep 'em coming."

"Bad day?"

"Bad week," I tell him, downing the shot. "You know what, can I just keep the bottle?"

He laughs. "This is a two-thousand-dollar bottle of liquor."

I pull my credit card out and drop it onto the bar. "I'm good for it."

He nods with a smirk. "It's all yours."

After I pour another shot and swallow it back, I glance at my phone.

*This is my daily message…*

I already knew there were more, but I haven't read them. I close my eyes, refusing to go there. If I read them, I'm going to want to respond. And then I'll have to deal with everything.

I open my eyes, and the phone is still there, lying on the bar top, beckoning me.

Pick me up. Read me.

*Oh, great, Mia, in your drunken state, your phone is talking to you.* I roll my eyes, and just as I'm about to pour myself another shot, my phone lights up with another message.

**Ashy C: I miss you more than Skittles and gummy bears.**

His words are my breaking point, and before I can stop myself, my fingers are firing off a text.

**Me: You don't love me! If you did, you wouldn't have hurt me. Now stop messaging me. I'm at The Brasserie having a good time without you. I hope your Skittles and gummy bears keep you warm at night.**

There, take that!

He certainly doesn't need me to keep him warm.

And I don't need him either.

I have a two-thousand-dollar bottle of gin and bartender eye-candy to do that for me.

I'm okay.

I may not be enough for anyone else, but I'm enough for me.

"Fuck fuck-boys!" I call out to the bartender, raising my bottle.

He laughs and tips his head in agreement.

I'm doing fine and dandy all by myself, thank you very much.

# FIVE

*Ashton*

The Brasserie.

One of Mom's favorite hoity-toity hangouts. I know exactly where this place is and I'll be damned if I let this opportunity pass me up. I take the world's fastest shower and dress in something that'll grant me access into that rich bitch martini lounge. Black slacks, a black button-up, and a slate-colored tie. I hate dressing up, but if I want to go get the girl, I need to actually be able to get in to get her. I break the rules with my black Doc Marten lace-up combat boots because if I have to crawl into society's box, at least I can leave the lid off.

I shove my wallet in my pocket, grab my leather jacket from the closet, and snag my keys in record time. It's cold as fuck outside, so I'm glad I wore a jacket. I'm thrumming with pent-up energy, though, too wired to be cold.

I'm going to see her.

Mia.

My Mia.

I'll make this right. I know I can. I just need her in my arms so I can hold her. Our severed connection has left me hemorrhaging without her. Mia needs to know that I can't exist without her in my life. I'll take her any way I can get her.

This week, I've thought about it a lot. I'm a player. Worse than I gave Brayden shit for when I first met him. I use people for my own entertainment. It's sick and fucked up. Hell, I even called my damn therapist this week to ask why I'm that way. It led to a surprisingly eye-opening session that helped me realize I'm a self-destructive shithead. That explosive behavior of mine draws people close enough that when I detonate, they're all destroyed along with me.

Mia.

Dad.

So many others.

I hurt people because I like to hurt myself. They become casualties of my destruction. I need to learn to stop wrecking my own heart, and as a result, saving those around me.

Baby steps.

It only solidifies my desire to pursue my degree in psychology. If people like me could figure out how to handle ourselves, imagine how many others like us we could also help. For the first time since I started therapy all those years ago, I had respect for the person trying to help me.

I'm not delusional enough to think I'm going to magically be a better person, but this is the first time I *wanted* to be better. I had someone I needed desperately to be better for.

Mia.

She deserves to have a best friend who will keep trying to do right by her, even when he fucks up. And if it leads to something more, then so be it. If it doesn't, I'll be perfectly content seeing her smile directed at me and to have my gamer buddy back.

Mia is like the sun.

Bright and hot and penetrating.

She gets inside you and lights up all the shadowed corners of the darkest parts of you.

For some strange-ass reason, she decided to walk into my life and shine her sparkly light on me. When you're used to being a cold-hearted dick, it's a little alarming to grow so warm just by being exposed to another person.

Mia is my world.

A huge piece that completes the puzzle that is me, pulling all the fragmented, jagged parts together and making them somehow fit and make sense.

I'm not whole without her.

In no time, I'm pulling my Audi up to the curb in front of a long-ass line. I fling open the door, cringing against the biting cold, and then pull out my wallet to meet the approaching valet guy.

"Keep it running or drive it around the block a couple of times. I'll be out in a few," I tell him as I flip open my wallet. "Here. Keep it warm."

He smiles at the handful of hundreds I thrust at him. "Sure, man. It can stay for a few."

I hand him my keys and then trot to the front of the line. A man dressed in a suit arches a brow at me, daring me to try and enter.

"Wendy Worthington-Carter. She's my mom," I bark at him. "I'm just going in to fetch my girl and I'll be out of here."

The guy's face curls into a devious smirk. "Tell your mom Bo says hi." He winks in a way that makes my skin crawl.

Fucking gross.

"Yeah, dude. I'll tell her."

He waves me inside. I scan my gaze across the room, looking for the hottest brunette in this place. Eventually, I settle my stare on the saddest girl to ever drink expensive-ass gin straight from a bottle.

My girl.

I stalk through the crowd, a man on a mission. I'm almost to her when a snobby bitch steps right in front of me.

"What are you doing here?" Sasha sneers, curling her lip up at me.

I hate this bitch.

"I'm taking my girl home." I grit my teeth. "Move, princess."

"You're gay," Sasha spits at me as though I'm supposed to fucking recoil or some shit.

"And you're a bitch, but here we are. Move or I'll do it for you." I crack my neck, leveling her with a hard glare. I didn't come all this way to be sidelined by a stuck-up sorority brat.

"How did you even get in here?" Sasha demands. "You're… you."

Gripping her dainty shoulders, I move her aside, ignoring her snarling. I prowl the rest of the way up to Mia, crowding her from behind. She stiffens her body when I wrap my arms around her.

"Missed you, MiMi," I murmur, nuzzling my nose in her hair near her ear, inhaling her sweet scent I've craved so badly.

"Ashton." Her choked out word slices my already butchered heart.

"I'm here," I say, hugging her tight.

"You shouldn't be."

She's drunk. There's a slur in her words and her dumb friend isn't exactly the nurturing type. It's a good thing I arrived because based on the way she falls against me, her head lolling to the side, it was only a matter of time before some douchebag took advantage of her.

"I know," I croon, "but I'm here anyway. Let's get you home."

The bartender shoots me a worried look. "Want me to call her an Uber?"

"I'm her best friend," I snap at him. "She's going home with me where I can keep her safe. Next time, look at the fucking ID before you sell a college freshman the whole damn bottle."

His face pales. Fuck him.

I slide Mia's arm over my shoulders and wrap an arm around her waist, holding her up. Sasha steps in front of me again, her face bright red with anger.

"Move," I growl.

"Come on," Sasha says to Mia, holding her hand out. "I'll take you home."

"I don't feel good," Mia groans.

Sasha's nose scrunches. "I'll call an Uber."

"I'm taking her home," I snarl. "Get the fuck over it."

She gasps in shock at my words. Unlike Sasha, I don't give a goddamn about pretenses. My girl is wasted and sick and heartbroken. I'm the only one who will take care of her like she needs to be cared for.

I walk Mia almost to the doors when the cold draft rushes in as more patrons do, making her shiver. Pulling away from her and leaning her against the wall beside the door, I peel off my jacket and then set to putting it on her. Her brown eyes are shimmering with sadness and her bottom lip pokes out, wobbling.

Fuck.

I broke her damn heart.

Threading my fingers into her soft hair, I tilt her head up so I can see her pretty, distraught face up close. Her eyes flutter closed when I lean in. I press a soft kiss to her lips.

"I've got you, MiMi."

When I pull away, a tear is streaking down her cheek. I quickly wipe it away with my thumb and tuck her under my protective embrace once more. We step outside, both of us flinching against the cold. I make my way back over to my Audi and retrieve my keys from the valet. Once I have the passenger side door open, I assist Mia into the seat before closing her inside.

Finally.

I won't lose her again.

Once I'm inside the still-warm car, I reach over and take her hand. I expect resistance, but my girl threads her fingers with mine. Like old times.

She leans her forehead against the glass side window, groaning as I take off. My heart is pounding out of my chest, overcome with elation that I managed to not only talk to her, but to finally touch her again.

The drive home is quiet, but my mind is loud. I want to tell her I love her. Apologize. Beg for forgiveness. Instead, I opt for silence, afraid to disrupt the moment.

"I don't feel so good," she mumbles again. "Ashton, I think I'm going to be sick."

I pull into a parking spot in front of our building and shut off the car just as she flings open the door. Something splatters on the pavement. I don't do puke. At all. But this is Mia. I'll swim through a pool of it if that means I get to have her on the other side.

"Yuck, MiMi," I grumble as I reach her. Vomit drips from her chin and her eyes are teary. "How much did you pay for that bottle of regret?"

"Two thousand dollars."

I chuckle as I help her step over the mess. "Let's go wash that fifty bucks off your chin."

We barely make it to the building before she wretches another two Benjamins out of her system. Once inside the building, I scoop up her tiny body and carry her through the halls. She presses her face against my neck, groaning like she might puke some more. The stench makes me want to gag, but I'll endure it for her.

Eventually, we make it inside my apartment. She doesn't protest, so I consider it a win. I carry her right to my room and into the bathroom. Once I set her on the counter and peel my jacket off her that'll need dry cleaning, I start the shower. Her eyes are closed, and she's a mess with puke in her hair and down the front of her dress.

"Can you shower?" I ask, frowning at her. "You need to. I'm not letting you in my bed like this."

A crazed laugh bubbles out of her and then she starts to cry. "You want *me* in your bed?"

"I want you everywhere, Mia."

I yank off my tie and toss it to the floor as steam begins to fill the bathroom. "Do you need my help?"

Her teary eyes roam up my chest to my face and she nods.

"Okay," I say, sucking in a breath. "Try not to get dazzled by my dick. It's so pretty, it hurts to look at. It's best if you avert your eyes."

She laughs but then starts to gag again. I scoop her up and carry her over to the toilet, gripping her messy, sticky hair as she heaves into the toilet. Her chokes turn into sobs.

"Shh, baby, shh. I'm going to take care of you," I assure her. "Get it all out so we can clean you up."

She grips the bowl, no longer puking, just shaking. I release her hair so I can strip out of my fancy shit. Then, I crouch to unzip her dress. I help her stand up and something clatters to the floor. Her phone, ID, and credit card.

"Were you hiding those in your vag?" I ask. "I may not know much about pussies, but your phone seems a little big to be shoving up your snatch."

"That's what boobs are for," she slurs. "To hold stuff. Like an extra pocket."

"Another one of life's mysteries explained. Thanks, MiMi."

I turn her to face me, allowing my eyes to roam down her body. My heart does a flop inside my chest as I admire her curvy body. Tits normally don't do shit for me. Mia's intrigue me. I have the insane urge to taste each nipple. My dick thickens and I thank every god in existence for the fact it's working.

Now's not the time to consider if I can actually ever fuck Mia. Right now, I need to care for my girl. I snag my toothbrush and toothpaste from the holder on the way to the shower. Once inside, I lead her under the spray. She sighs, tilting her head up as the water drenches her face and hair. With her eyes closed and the water sluicing down her tits, I decide I really, really like her tits. Her nipples are hard, just begging to be bitten.

*Love knows no labels.*

Maybe Drew was right.

Before my mind can drift to Drew and his naked body, I focus on my girl. I squirt some toothpaste on my brush and then grip her now clean chin.

"Open up, MiMi. I need to wash that expensive mistake out of your mouth."

She opens her big brown eyes and parts her lips. Jesus. I love this girl. I want her and need her. I can't believe I ever doubted it.

I brush her teeth for her, enjoying immensely how cute she is foaming at the mouth. Once I've scrubbed her clean, I lead her back under the spray. As she rinses, I drop the toothbrush on a shelf and grab the bar of soap.

My hands are eager to clean her, but she's drunk and I don't want her to be pissed later. Instead of touching her like I want, I hand her the bar of soap.

Sloppily she cleans her body while I shampoo her hair. My dick is hard, much to my delight, as I wash the puke out of her hair. She turns to face me, the soap slipping from her grip and hitting the floor with a thud.

"Ashton," she whimpers. "Why am I not enough?"

I rinse the shampoo out and then grip her hair, tilting her face up to look at me. My lips press to her forehead, then her nose, and finally her lips.

"Mia," I rumble. "You're more than enough. You're too much. I don't deserve one sliver of you, but I need you all the same."

Her lips part and I kiss her. Softly. Gentle at first. And then my tongue is greedily lashing against hers. She slides her soapy palms up my chest to my shoulders, her body pressing against my front. Her tits are firm and an odd sensation pushed against me, but one I like. My dick is stone against her stomach.

The urge to grip her ass and lift her is strong.

I could fuck her right now.

I'm hard. I could do it. I know I could.

But the first time I attempt this with Mia, it needs to be once we've cleared the air between us. She's drunk and I would die if she regretted this in the morning.

*Don't be destructive, Ashton.*

*Think of your girl, not your dick for once.*

"Let's get you dried off and into bed, baby. You need sleep," I murmur against her lips. "In the morning we can talk."

She nods. "Thank you for rescuing me."

"I'll always rescue you, Mia."

Her groan wakes me up. The room is still dark, but dawn is creeping into my bedroom. I roll over onto my side, staring at her pretty face that's barely visible in the dim light. A dark, still-damp tendril of hair is draped across her face. I gently brush it away.

"Morning," she murmurs, her eyes opening just a bit. "Is this a dream?"

"Hmm," I tease. "I'd call it more of a fantasy. Some hot swimmer rescues you from a pedophile bartender and wicked sorority sister and bathes you after you showered yourself in two-thousand-dollar gin. Are you into it?"

She scrunches her face. "Yuck. That's more like a nightmare."

"Which part?" I murmur, dragging my thumb along her jaw.

"Maybe not the naked shower part with the hot swimmer." Her smile undoes me. "Definitely the barf part, though. Yuck. You hate puke."

"But I love you," I tell her, no longer joking. My voice drips with conviction. "You know that, right?"

Her head nods as tears well in her eyes.

"Mia," I murmur. "I'm so fucking sorry. For everything. I've acted like a total asshole and it's unforgivable. I swear, I can be better than this. For you. You have to let me try, because if you don't, what the fuck am I even living this life for?"

She blinks hard, sending tears skating down her temples. "Don't talk like that."

"It's true," I say with a sigh. "My life is a fucking mess. My parents hate me and I have no friends because I'm a difficult piece of shit. Somehow, I got you. Like the universe forgot it was supposed to punish me, but tossed me a reward instead. And, as you know, I'm spoiled and wanted what it gave me. I wanted you."

Her sob guts me. Tears a hole inside my chest, stealing not just a part of my soul, but all of it. I want to make it better. I want to heal her. I want to make her smile and laugh and be fucking happy.

I want her.

My lips press to hers for a chaste kiss and she whimpers.

"Ashton…"

"Mia, listen," I whisper against her lips. "I wanted you as my friend, so I thought. I wanted your light brightening my dark world. I just wanted you. But then you kissed me and I realized I wanted you in more ways I didn't realize I could have you. I'm greedy as fuck, baby. It's been a mental adjustment, but I'm getting there. I've made some terrible mistakes concerning you, but I will always try to undo them or get better when it comes to you. You have to believe me. I'd never hurt you on purpose."

This time, when I kiss her, her fingers thread into my hair, deepening our kiss. I want to throw out a morning breath joke, but now's not the time to be playful. If I'm willing to swim through puke for her, I'll kiss her when we both need to brush our teeth, because when it's the one you love, you'll do whatever it fucking takes to have time with them.

"I like you in my clothes," I murmur, my hand skating up under her shirt to feel the tit I wanted to touch last night. "I think I like you out of them better, though."

Her laugh is pure gold—honest and sweet. "Do you use that pickup line a lot? Because even though it's corny as hell, it's oddly magical."

"Funny," I tease as I pinch her nipple, "no one's ever called my dick oddly magical before."

"I was talking about you, not your dick."

I nip at her bottom lip, loving the gasp that escapes her when I pull at her nipple. "Know what else is oddly magical about me?"

"What?"

"My mouth."

Her eyebrow arches up. "Ashton, what are we doing?"

I pull away from her, sitting up on my knees. My dick is hard and straining against my boxers. Her eyes slide over my bare chest, lingering on my nipple ring.

"We're doing what feels right, Mia. No labels, just us."

Her eyes widen when I pull my sweats down her sexy thighs, baring her to me. My heart rate speeds up as she shakily tugs off my borrowed T-shirt.

Naked.

Mia is naked and in my bed.

"I thought…" I choke out, frowning. "I thought I'd fail and you'd be disgusted with me."

Her brows furl. "You have to put yourself out there. You have to try."

"With you, I realized I don't have to try. It just comes naturally," I admit. "I didn't know if I could do this or want to be with you this way, but now I can tell you with absolute certainty, I want and need to be with you. I love you, Mia, and if you let me, I want to show you with my body just how much."

"I'm a virgin," she croaks out. "I don't exactly have experience. I want to be good for you. The best. What if I'm not enough?"

I prowl over her, pressing kisses up her soft stomach to her breasts. They jiggle as she breathes heavily. I nip one of her breasts, delighting in the firmness of it, before tonguing her nipple. Sucking hard on the peak, I revel in the surprised yelp that escapes her.

"Ashton," she whimpers.

"You're everything to me."

Her back arches up when I start licking and nipping at her breast. I may have never fucked a woman before, but I know how to pleasure a body. Her nipples are sensitive, and she clearly likes the attention. When I've made them red and swollen from my teeth and tongue, I kiss my way back down to her pussy. Her dark hair is trimmed neatly and her scent is alluring. I'm not a complete dunce. I know how the female anatomy works, but I've just never been exposed to it. I run my tongue along her slit, thankful that I enjoy the taste of her. It makes me eager to continue. I part her pink pussy lips to expose her clit. It's cute and begs, like her pert nipples, for a kiss.

Her body jolts up off the bed when I tease the nub with my tongue. She moans—a low, seductive purr that strokes my fucking soul—and then I'm lost to her. I'm desperate to bring her pleasure. To show her how fucking amazing we can be together. The more I suck on her clit, the wetter her pussy gets. I want to go slow with her, but my dick is seeping with the need to be inside her. All it takes is a little more tongue play on her needy clit and then she's coming hard, crying out my name like I'm the god she prays to.

As she shudders and writhes, I reach into the drawer and pull out a condom. I rip it open and roll it over my dick. I'm not sure if chicks need lube like guys do, so I yank out the bottle from my drawer and slather my condom-covered cock just in case.

"Ashton," she murmurs. "Kiss me."

I crawl up her body, locking my eyes with hers. "You're my first…" I tell her, needing her to understand that if I fuck this up, I'll try harder the next time to make it better.

"Woman," she finishes, wincing slightly as she lets her insecurities—ones I no doubt put on her—creep into her mind.

"*Only* woman," I correct. "There's only one you, Mia."

Her breath hitches when I grip my dick and slide it against her slick hole. I press into her just a bit and then stare down at my pretty girl.

"I love you," I remind her.

"I love you too—ahh!"

I thrust my hips hard, growling as her tight body stretches to accommodate my thickness. My world tilts around me as I'm overcome with pleasure.

She feels better than good.

She feels fucking amazing.

Our lips connect and our tongues greet each other happily. Like we've finally figured out the steps to a dance we've been trying to learn. I thrust into her, desperate to connect her to me in such a physical, deep way. We kiss and moan, each of us tearing at the other like we might be able to climb inside one another. All too soon, I lose control, coming with a relieved groan. Rather than disconnect from my girl, I fall against her, sliding my arms around her and crushing her to me.

I know I should dispose of the condom.

Ask her if I should make her come again.

Clean her up.

Let her breathe.

For now, I just want to keep her like this.

In my arms.

Mine.

# SIX

*Mia*

On. Cloud. Nine. That's the only way to describe how I feel right now as I wait for Ashton to come back to bed. After we made love and Ashton held me for several minutes, I excused myself to the bathroom to take a quick shower so I could clean up. When I got out, I got dressed in Ashton's hoodie and sweats and then went in search of the man himself.

At first I was nervous maybe he would regret what we did. I think it would be naïve of me not to have little doubts in the back of my mind. We kissed twice and both times he freaked out. And this was bigger. This was sex. Something neither of us had ever done before.

But the moment I stepped foot into the kitchen and Ashton's eyes locked with mine, I felt like I could finally breathe. He smiled that sexy, boyish grin, and butterflies attacked my belly. He cut across the kitchen and kissed my lips, then he told me to get my ass back in bed, so he could bring me breakfast in bed.

While I wait for him, my thoughts go back to earlier, to the way he let me completely in.

*"I thought I'd fail and you'd be disgusted with me."*

I felt anything but. The way he took care of me… I can't imagine doing what we did with anyone but Ashton.

*"We're doing what feels right, Mia. No labels, just us."*

This is all I wanted for so long and now I finally have it.

*"You're everything to me."*

I have to hope that what he said is true, and that I'm enough for him. Because with every kiss, every thrust, I fell even more in love with Ashton and I don't know what I would do, if it turned out I wasn't enough for him.

"Hey," a masculine voice says from the doorway.

I shake myself out of my thoughts and turn toward the direction of the voice. Standing in the doorway is Drew with a confused expression on his face.

"Hey," I say back, trying and failing to contain my smile. "Did you guys win?"

"Did we win?" He laughs incredulously. "I just walked through the door and found Ashton cooking breakfast… while whistling. I thought for a second I was in the wrong damn apartment. Then, after double checking and seeing that I was in fact in the right apartment, and wondering why the hell he's in such a good mood, I find you lying in his bed… In Ashton Carter's fucking bed. The man you've been avoiding all week." Drew's eyes go comically wide. "And your first question is 'Did we win?' What the hell is going on, Mia?"

"What's going on is I made my girl breakfast in bed," Ashton says, pushing past Drew and setting a tray of food down on the bed next to me. "And now I'm going to feed it to her." He drops on the bed on the other side of the food and winks at me. "I have a swim meet this morning, so we're going to need to make this quick. You're coming, right?" he asks me.

"Of course. I can't wait to finally see you compete." I run my fingers through his floppy hair and push it out of his eyes. Ashton playfully reaches up and snags the tip of my finger, biting gently on it.

"Good, because I want you to be there when I kick Travis's ass."

"So, what, I'm gone like fifteen hours and you two are together now?" Drew asks, his tone a mixture of hurt and disbelief.

I glance over at him and my heart drops. I was flying so high on my Ashton cloud I didn't think about how this would affect Drew. He's been there for me every day, whether it was bringing me over food or coffee, or just stopping by to make sure I was hanging in there.

I move to stand, but Ashton must sense it, because he wraps his fingers around my forearm, stopping me. "I need to talk to Drew for a minute," I tell him, silently begging him to understand. His eyes dart back and forth between us, but he lets go of my arm and nods.

When I gesture for Drew to follow me out, he shakes his head. "We can talk here." His gaze swings back over to Ashton. "You forgave him?" His tone isn't judgmental, but it isn't happy either. He's worried, and if I'm not mistaken I think sad—and I wonder if it's because he and Brayden aren't talking yet or if he's upset that Ashton and I are together.

"I did," I tell him. "We talked and he apologized."

"And you're together now?"

"Yeah," I say softly. "We are."

Drew nods. "That's good. I'm happy for you." He clears his throat, then looks around me at Ashton. "I know you regret what you did. I saw it in your eyes all week. The way you sulked halfway to depression over what happened. But what you didn't see… what she didn't let you see was how badly you hurt her."

"Drew," I start.

"No. He needs to hear this." Drew turns his attention back to Ashton. "You didn't see her refusing to eat all week. You didn't see her crying to the point I thought she was going to pass out from exhaustion. I know you love her, and I don't doubt right now you think you have it all figured out, but I'm warning you right now, if you fucking hurt her again, I will kick your ass."

"Drew," I repeat harshly. "Stop."

"No, MiMi," Ashton says. "He's right. I hurt you. I saw it last night when I brought you home wasted. I felt it when I held you. You've lost weight…

because of me. And if I hurt her again," he says to Drew, "you have my permission to kick my ass."

"I don't need your permission," Drew volleys. "Let's just hope it doesn't come to that."

"It won't. He won't hurt me again," I say, even though deep down I'm scared of exactly that. Ashton may have the best of intentions, he may love me, and I may be everything to him, but what if I'm still not enough?

"You know I'm here, right?" Drew says to me.

"I know, but I don't want it to be like this…" I don't want to lose Drew in order to be with Ashton. We've become close and I care about him. "Come to the swim meet with us," I blurt out. "Please."

Drew opens his mouth, most likely to say no, but Ashton speaks first. "Don't even think about saying no. I told you this before. What MiMi wants, MiMi gets. It's a home meet, too, so you don't have to travel far."

Drew groans. "Fine, but I need to shower first."

"Yay!" I jump into Drew's arms. "Thank you for everything," I murmur softly. "I couldn't have gotten through this week without you."

Ashton clears his throat and I pull back. "The food's getting cold."

"I'll meet you guys at the pool," Drew says before retreating.

"You and Drew have gotten close," Ashton observes once he's gone. He averts his eyes, grabbing a piece of pancake and dragging it through the bowl of syrup.

"Hey." I tip his chin up. "He was there when I needed a friend… But that's all he is, a friend."

Ashton nods then brings the drenched pancake piece to my mouth. I take a bite and flinch at how sweet it is. Typical Ashton, a little pancake and a lot of syrup. I'm actually surprised he didn't throw some candy in there while he was at it.

"Good?" he asks, his eyes homing in on my lips, which are now sticky from the syrup.

"Why don't you come over here and find out?" I taunt, licking my lips.

Ashton growls and reaches across the tray of food—the plate clatters and the cups spill—but neither of us pays it any mind as his mouth crashes against mine. His tongue darts out, licking across the seam of my lips before he pushes through, tangling his tongue with my own. "Mmm…" he murmurs against my mouth. "Delicious."

"So, how are you really doing?" Drew asks. We're sitting in the bottom row of the bleachers, watching the different events. Up until now, we've been watching in silence, neither of us sure what to say to each other. Ashton is on the other side of the pool with his team, looking the most focused I've ever seen him.

"I'm good. It's cool to see Ashton in his element."

On our way over, Ashton explained to me that a swim meet has several events, but each swimmer can only participate in four max, and today he'll be swimming in four different events. He mentioned the names, but all I can remember is free and butterfly—not sure how much that will help me. He also said last year he held the record in three different events. It was interesting to see how animated he got while talking about swimming. Since I only met him this summer, and that asshole Travis got him removed from the first swim meet, I've yet to actually see him compete. So far, he's swum in two events, winning both of them.

"I mean with everything that's—"

"What are you guys doing here?" a voice says, cutting off Drew. I glance up and find Brayden, dressed in a pair of jeans and an Ice Hawks hoodie, with a beanie on his head, standing in front of us. My heart pitter-patters in my chest at the sight of him, and I have to close my eyes to shut those thoughts down. I'm with Ashton… I love Ashton… but seeing Brayden for the first time since he hurt me makes me realize you can't just will your feelings to go away. Brayden and I connected on a deeper level and those feelings are still there.

"We're here to watch Ashton," Drew says, speaking up, since my voice wouldn't work quick enough. "You?"

Brayden flinches but quickly schools his features. "Same. I had to submit an essay online, so I'm a little late."

My first thought is, why is he here? Since when does Brayden support Ashton? The last I checked they hated each other—until I caught them kissing. Then it hits me that he had to submit an essay, and I feel bad that I haven't been around to tutor him all week. I committed to help him and I've let him down. But at the same time, he let me down too.

"I didn't know you and Ashton were close." Drew voices my own thoughts.

"We, uh…" He averts his eyes. "We've been hanging out this week."

A sharp pain lances through my heart. Ashton and Brayden kissed. Now they're hanging out. The two men I care about and hurt me found comfort in each other. I shake the thought away. Ashton is with me now. He wants me. He said I'm enough.

When Drew doesn't say anything in response, Brayden's face falls slightly, and my stomach knots. Instinctually I want to go to him, hug him and tell him it's going to be okay, but I refrain. That's not my place—not anymore. But just because it didn't work out between us, doesn't mean I can't still care about him, and if I can forgive Ashton, I can forgive Brayden.

"Why don't you sit with us?" I offer, moving away from Drew so Brayden can sit between us. "Ashton still has two more events."

Brayden's eyes widen slightly and dart over to Drew. It takes a couple awkward seconds, but Drew nods once and edges slightly over as well.

"I'm a little shocked to see you here," Brayden says carefully, once he's seated. "When I saw Ashton before I left yesterday he was still acting like a growly, pouting little shit."

I laugh softly, able to imagine Ashton just as Brayden described. "We made up…" I can't say what I need to say next while looking at him, so I turn my attention to the pool as Ashton and several other swimmers prepare for their race. "We're, um…" I clear my throat. "We're together now."

The horn blows and the swimmers start their race. The crowd erupts in cheers, and I'm thankful for the break in silence. Ashton warned me the races are quick, and he was right. Not even twenty seconds later and the race is over, and Ashton's the winner. The other two events at least lasted a good forty seconds…

Ashton climbs out of the pool and grabs a couple towels, throwing one over his shoulders and wrapping the other one around his trim torso. His teammates pat him on the shoulder, no doubt congratulating him on his time. I don't know what's considered good, but the fact he was the fastest at only eighteen-point-thirty-three seconds is just crazy to me.

My eyes descend along his taut chest and lean abs, my lady parts tingling in memory of the way his hard body felt against mine this morning as he made love to me. The way he took such sweet care of me.

As he saunters over, his gaze meets mine. At first the expression on his face is cocky, like he knows exactly what I'm thinking, but then I can see when he notices Brayden next to me, because his face contorts into… is that guilt? No, I have to be seeing things that aren't there. My insecurities are messing with me. I expected jealousy, anger maybe. The way he acted when I hugged Drew earlier. But I wasn't expecting the pained look on his face he's sporting as he walks over to us.

"You did so well," I tell him, popping up from the bench and wrapping my arms around him. He smells like chlorine mixed with Ashton. My favorite smell.

"Thanks." He pulls back slightly. "I still have one more race, but I have a small break." His eyes land on my lips, and his tongue darts out, licking his own, like he's warring with himself as to whether or not he should kiss me.

Instead of waiting for him to make a decision, I do it for him. The kiss isn't long, but it's enough to make me wish we were back at his place, where I could remove those towels and take my time exploring every inch of his body. When the kiss ends, I back away slightly.

Brayden stands and walks over. "Sorry I'm late, Ash. School is kicking my ass. Good job on the win, though."

"Thanks, man."

He and Ashton share a hug, which in itself is strange, but when they pull apart, the heated gaze in Brayden's eyes is enough to make me feel sick. He's attracted to Ashton. I glance over at Drew, wondering if he's seeing what I'm seeing, and based on the way his jaw is tight, I would say he is. I move slightly so I can see Ashton's face, but before I can catch his expression, he shakes his head and turns his attention to me.

"I'm in the last event, so once I'm done, after I meet with my team to go over the points, we can go."

"No rush," I squeak out. "We'll be here."

Ashton's eyes bounce over the three of us, and then with a tight nod, he heads back over to where his team is.

"How are your classes going?" I ask Brayden after a few minutes of awkward as hell silence as we watch some relay type of race. When I asked Ashton why he doesn't do those, he told me he doesn't play well with others.

"Okay," he says, "definitely miss my tutor." He smirks playfully, but when he realizes what he just did, he tones it down.

"Don't do that," I tell him. "Don't not be yourself. I know things are weird, but before we… dated, we were friends. And I hope we can go back to being friends again."

"Yeah?" he asks.

"Yeah." I smile. "Monday, I expect to see you at the tutoring center on time with my Starbucks coffee."

Brayden chuckles. "Yes, ma'am."

A little while later, Ashton's race begins. Once again, like the damn fish he is, he blows everyone's time out of the water, winning his fourth and final event. When he gets out of the pool, pumping his fist in excitement, I don't miss the way Travis, who only won one race from what I can recall, glares at Ashton.

The team disappears into the locker room and Brayden excuses himself, saying he still has more schoolwork to do, leaving only Drew and me.

"I think I'm going to get going as well," Drew says. He steps toward me, until our bodies are close… too close. He reaches out and tucks a wayward hair behind my ear and smiles softly. "I know you said you're good, but if you need me, day or night, I'm here. Okay?"

Before I can answer him, a squeaky feminine voice calls my name.

"Mia!" Ashton's mom, Wendy, says, waving her manicured hand in the air. "I knew that was you!" I laugh to myself as she saunters over, dressed like she's at a dinner party instead of at her son's swim meet, while Curtis follows behind.

"How are you, my dear?" She pulls me into a hug, her strong perfume nearly knocking me off my feet. "Did you see my Ashton in action?" she gushes. "Like a dolphin!"

I laugh, wondering not for the first time why Ashton thinks his parents hate him. The few times I've been around them, they've done nothing but be supportive of him.

"I did. He's amazing."

"Andrew," Curtis says. "I'm surprised to see you here. The last I checked you were in Flint kicking some Raptor butt."

Drew laughs tightly. "We did, sir. Got back earlier. Just thought I would come out to support my roommate and school."

Curtis eyes him speculatively, then a wide grin splits across his face. "Good man."

We chat while we wait for Ashton. He shows up, dressed in sweats and a hoodie, his hair messy and sticking up in several different directions. It's apparent he showered in the locker room when he normally waits until he gets home.

"What's everyone talking about?" Ashton says as he steps between Drew and me, each of his hands on one of our shoulders. "My ass in my speedo?"

Curtis groans while Wendy laughs.

"Tell 'em, MiMi. It was the highlight of the event." He kisses the top of my head.

"He's not wrong," I say, giggling.

Curtis, used to our antics, shakes his head at Ashton. "We're all proud of the way you won all your matches. Impressive."

Ashton shrugs off his dad's words. "Did you expect anything less?"

"I didn't," Wendy says, grinning. "Let's go to Edmond's and celebrate. Bring your friends, love. We have to discuss the Atlantic Pointe athletic program's fundraising event."

"Sounds boring." Ashton wraps an arm around my waist. "Nah, we'll pass. Ready to go, babe?"

"Babe?" Curtis's brows furl together as his eyes bounce back and forth between Ashton and me.

Ashton flashes me a wicked grin that says he's about to take great pleasure in fucking with his dad *again*. "Yeah, about that. I'm into chicks now. Well, one really. You can stop being ashamed, Dad." He smacks my ass playfully. "Now you can have grandkids. You're welcome."

Oh my God.

# SEVEN

Ashton

**M**om laughs, always the first to enjoy my inappropriate jokes. Dad's face turns beet red. I guess this fucking embarrasses him too. Whatever. No matter what I do or say, it's never the right thing.

"Ignore him," Mia says to Dad, trying to smooth out my words. "We're not having kids right now."

"Check back in six weeks, though," I throw out. "My girlfriend and I fuck—ow!"

I let go of Mia to rub my arm where Drew elbowed me. He shoots me a warning glare to knock it off. Who made him Daddy Junior?

"We're going on a date," I grumble. "We'll have to take you up on that super boring fancy dinner where we watch Mom get plastered another time. Right, babe?"

Mia just shakes her head. "You're such a brat."

"I'm holding you to it." Mom's eyes glitter with amusement. "Bring your friend, too. The more the merrier."

Fuck that.

Drew can stay his ass home. I'm not about to let my mom flirt with my fucking roommate. That's sick. Thankfully, Dad shuts her down.

"I'll text you and we can set up a dinner," Dad says. "Come, dear, let's head to Edmond's and give these kids their privacy."

Mom hugs me and then Mia before waltzing away with Dad stalking after her.

"Mommy Dearest is a fucking cougar," I tell Drew. "Stay away or I'll cut your dick off."

"Dude," Drew chokes out. "Don't sweat it. I'm not going to hook up with your mom."

"Good." I hold out my fist, waiting for him to bump it with his. He reluctantly bumps my fist. "See you later, man. Mia and I are going on a date."

Drew's lips thin out. I know he's annoyed at the fact Mia and I made up while he was gone, but he'll just have to get over it. We fixed our shit. The end. Drew can be pissy, but he knows how much I want this thing with Mia to work. He and I played around, and while it was hot and fun, I don't love him like I do Mia.

"Thanks for coming," Mia says, pulling away from me to give Drew a hug. "See you later."

Drew frowns, but eventually nods. "Later."

As soon as he's gone, I tuck Mia back under my arm and lead her out of the building. We pass by Travis and I grin at him. Fucking loser. He glares at us and it makes me giddy as fuck. I hate that guy.

"Watch your back," Travis mutters.

"No, dude, that's what you do since you can't ever catch the fuck up to me. Go home and cry in your Cheerios or call your mommy. No one here cares."

I flip him the bird as we leave.

As we drive down Main Street downtown, my chest squeezes with anxiety. I don't date. I fuck around. So the fact I have to take Mia out on the perfect date now, I'm kind of panicking. Where the hell do chicks like to be taken to on dates?

I see a few restaurants that are fancy as fuck, but quite frankly, we're not dressed nice enough. I didn't think this through when I decided to take her out right after the meet.

"You okay?" Mia asks, squeezing my hand. "You're tense."

"I'm just trying to think up the perfect place to take you to dinner."

I see a swanky steakhouse and whip into an open spot right out front as a car leaves. Shutting off the car, I glance up at the place hoping like hell they'll let us in dressed like college slackers.

"Ashton…"

"You love steak," I tell her. "Let's go."

I pop out of the car, thrumming with nervous energy. I'm overwhelmed by the feeling that I'm not doing this right. Quickly, I round the vehicle and open her door. She frowns at me. Fuck. I'm definitely screwing this up. I reach down and take her hand, pulling her out of the car and into my arms. I start to walk toward the door of the steakhouse, but Mia's feet are planted firmly to the ground.

"Ashton."

I clench my jaw, hating how my stomach is flipping like it's in a barrel tumbling down a hill. "What, my beautiful girlfriend?"

She rolls her pretty brown eyes. "That."

"What?"

"All this"—she waves at me and the steakhouse—"isn't you."

I scowl. "Neither is dating a woman, but we're here, Mia, and I'm just blindly navigating this unknown territory."

Her palms slide up my chest, calming the storm of emotions brewing inside of me. She stands on her toes and kisses my lips. "Can we go to the pizza place with the arcade? It's right across the street. Please?"

I love that place.

Slowly, I nod, because I'll give her whatever the hell she wants. "Yeah, MiMi. Whatever you want."

Her fingers thread into my hair and she pulls me down to her lips. "I want you to be yourself. Just be you, Ashton. Fancy steakhouses aren't you. Can you do that?"

This fucking girl.

"Yeah, brat, I can do that. Let's go."

We walk hand in hand across the street, the anxious weight lifting with each step we take. Once inside of the pizza parlor, the scent of garlic and melted cheese chases away any lingering doubt.

It's just Mia and me.

This is natural for us.

I guide her over to a booth near the arcades and slide in next to her. It feels good to put my arm around her as we share a menu. I thought maybe it'd be weird dating a girl in public, but I find it easy because it's Mia.

The server comes by and we order a pizza half with that nasty pineapple shit on her side and something more fucking human on the other side. While we wait, we head over to the games. I put a twenty into the machine and get us a bunch of quarters.

"What do you want to play?" I ask, nodding at the ancient machines that have been around since the '80s.

"Pac-Man." She bounces over to it and sits in one of the chairs. "See if you can beat me, boyfriend."

I laugh as I sit opposite of her. "Gotta warn you, MiMi. I'm going to whip your ass at this game just like always. Your girlfriend card has been revoked for the duration of this game."

"What if I show you my boobs?" she taunts, her brown eyes wickedly gleaming.

"We could negotiate then," I say with a smirk.

I put in some quarters and we begin a heated match. She yells at me and I laugh, but ultimately, I destroy her in Pac-Man. Every time she gets mad, she throws a quarter at me. A kid, maybe seven or eight, lingers nearby, snagging up all the abandoned coins.

"You're such a cheater," she whines. "You probably came out of the womb playing this game."

"Nah, I was like five when I begged my mom for the arcade game in my room."

She shakes her head. "You're so damn spoiled, Ashton Carter."

"You say that like it's a bad thing."

Her eyes roll and she stands up. "Since you're a big winner, win me something from the claw machine."

I let her pull me up from the machine and guide me over to the one filled with stuffed animals. I shove a few quarters in.

"Which one do you want?" I ask, analyzing which toys are easiest to snag.

She stands on her toes and points at a dolphin. "That one."

Easy.

I maneuver the claw over to the dolphin and mash the button to send it down to grab it. Luckily, it scoops up the dolphin and deposits it into the bin.

She squeals and pulls it out. "Look. A dolphin. Like you." She hugs it. "I love it."

I throw in some more quarters, my eyes set on the Mario in the corner. It'll be tricky since it's buried under some others. I'll just win those too. I fish out the two in my way, focused on my prize. She gleefully collects each one. Finally, I nab the Mario and drop him into the bin. I pull it out and waggle it in front of her.

"Look, it's you." I smirk at her. "Mario girl."

"I don't have a mustache," she deadpans, "but I'll take it. And these can be Brayden and Drew." She holds up the two matching hawks holding hockey sticks.

"The dolphin's the cutest," I tease, dropping a kiss on her lips. "Am I right?"

She playfully sighs. "Yeah, he is."

I kiss her deeply and then pull away, taking a moment to appreciate the fact I got the fucking girl. Mine. She's mine. Finally.

"Why do you hate your parents?" Mia asks after I pay the bill and we're walking out to the car.

I cringe at her question. "I don't hate them. They hate me. Well, Dad does. Mom just thinks I'm her dancing monkey."

She's quiet as we approach my Audi. It's not until we're inside and driving off that she speaks up again. "I don't see it. Curtis wants to be in your life so bad and Wendy is funny. They love you. Today, at your meet, they were proud."

Her words echo that of my therapist. I don't know why I don't believe them. Maybe it's because I remember the time Mom cheated on Dad and hurt him so bad, I thought they were going to divorce. They yelled so fucking much. I would try and lighten the mood with jokes, albeit inappropriate ones. Mom would laugh to piss off Dad, who would ultimately storm away. They fixed their marriage, but I'd already settled into the role of jokester. If Dad was mad at me, he wasn't mad at her. If he wasn't mad at her, they stayed married.

Hollowness settles in my gut.

I guess in some deep-down way, maybe I feel like I somehow keep them together in my weird-ass, black sheep way.

Can't wait to drop that epiphany bomb on my therapist.

"What about your parents?" I probe. "You hate yours."

"Because they're actually the worst. Just ask Brayden."

The car grows quiet again. *Just ask Brayden.* Because he fucking flew out there like a goddamn knight in shining armor to comfort her when I was being an asshole. Fuck. I stew over that the entire way back to the apartment. When we park, I shut off the car and sigh, but make no moves to get out.

"It kills me that he knows things I don't know about you," I murmur, slicing my eyes her way.

"You never ask."

I feel the sting of her words, a painful slash through my heart. "Why do you hate them, Mia? Tell me more than the surface bullshit you've told me in the past."

"Dad is Mom's puppet," she says sadly. "Mom is a vicious wicked witch who never fails to tell me how I'm not smart enough, not pretty enough, not skinny enough, not proper enough. Never enough."

"Fuck your mom," I growl. "Get over here."

She unbuckles and climbs across the console, settling in my lap. It's squished in my little car, but she fits snugly between me and the steering wheel. I stroke her hair and kiss her neck.

"I think you're perfect. My sweet, perfect Mia."

"He always chooses her over me," she whispers. "Like I'm just an accessory that comes with the title of husband." She turns and meets my stare, her lips inches from mine. "When I met you this past summer, I felt like I finally belonged to someone. Sure, we were just friends, but I felt like you'd chosen me of all the people to be yours."

"You *are* mine," I remind her.

"For a bit I wasn't," she says, her bottom lip wobbling. "You chose…" Her eyes water. "You didn't choose me."

"I'm sorry."

"I know." She kisses my lips. "I'm glad you eventually did."

I slide my palm up her throat and grip her jaw, caressing her with my thumb. "I'll always choose you. Don't let your pussy dad or your mean-ass mom ever make you doubt that again."

She smiles, warming me with her light. "I don't. Not anymore. Thank you for the date. I had fun."

Dates are supposed to be romantic, not fun, but she seems happy and that's all that matters.

"Plenty more pizza dates in our future." I pull her down for a dizzying kiss. I dominate her mouth with my tongue until we're both breathless and my dick is painfully hard. "Ready to have a naked video game date now?"

Her giggle is cute as fuck. "No way. Drew might walk in and see."

"Like we're not the two hottest people he's ever laid eyes on?" I tease. "Oh, what a hardship on Drew's poor virgin eyes."

She laughs, swatting my arm. "You're insane." Then she covers my mouth with my palm. "Don't say it."

*Insane for you.*

My eyes must say it for me because she laughs again.

I mumble out words and nip at her hand until she releases me. "I wasn't going to say that," I lie.

Her dark eyebrow quirks in challenge. "That so? What were you going to say?"

I stare at her for a long time and then shrug. "I forgot. You distracted me with your pretty dick sucking lips."

"Ashton!"

"MiMi," I throw back, pretending to be just as scandalized as she is.

Her phone buzzes from her hoodie pocket. She retrieves it to read the text. The beautiful smile fades away, giving me a glimpse of the girl her mother has spent her entire life belittling to the point she has a fucking complex.

"What did she say?" I growl.

Her lips part, her brows furrowing. "How did you know it was my mom?"

"Because I've never seen that look before, and after you explained what a bitch she is, I connected the dots all on my own. You're not the only smart one around here."

Her smile is back. "Cocky dork."

"Don't call my cock a dork."

"Oh my God," she groans. "You're an idiot."

"And you're dating a cocky dork." I smirk at her. "What did the wicked witch of the west say?"

"I'm being summoned to another bullshit ball."

"Good." I level her with a hard stare. "This time, you won't have your knight in shining armor. This time, you'll have a fucked-up prince who would love nothing more than to slay the fucking she-devil dragon for his princess who has the prettiest dick sucking lips he's ever seen."

"I think that was romantic," she says slowly, narrowing her eyes at me, "in some bizarre, so Ashton kind of way."

I guess I *can* be romantic then.

Who knew?

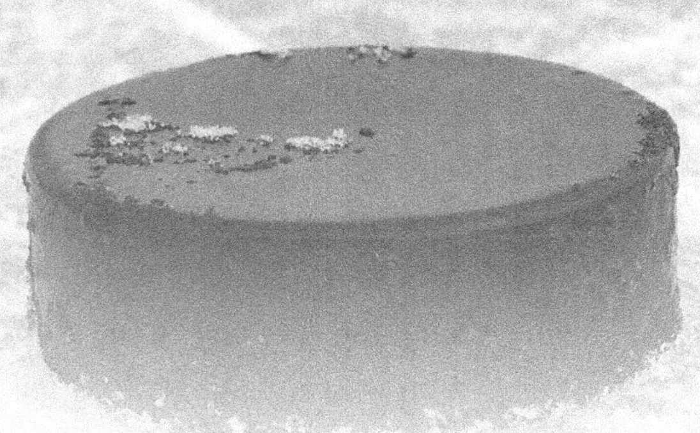

# EIGHT

## *Drew*

I walk through the kitchen and go straight to the cabinet where I know Ashton keeps his liquor.

Fucking Ashton.

Fucking Mia.

I scrub my hands over my face. I want to be happy for them. I do. All I want is for her to be happy. Every day this week as I held her and comforted her while she cried in my arms, all I wanted was to take the pain away and for her to smile again. But when I walked in and saw that very smile, while she was lying in Ashton's bed—the room smelling like sex—something in me broke.

Because I wanted to be the one to make her smile.

Ashton hurt her.

Brayden hurt her.

I wanted to heal her.

But Ashton, like the goddamn tornado he is, swooped in and scooped her up.

I'm happy that they're happy, I am. But I have to wonder how long this happiness will last. How long until Ashton fucks it all up and Mia is sad and crying again.

After the meet, I tried to keep busy at my office going over plays, but I was too pissed to focus and eventually came home. Maybe I can drown the noise in my head with rum instead.

There's a knock on the door, so I set the bottle down and go answer it. I swing it open and standing on the other side is Brayden. I was shocked as shit to see him at Ashton's meet. This entire week I've been avoiding the apartment. When I'm not at practice, I've been bouncing between the office and Mia's place, so I had no clue how close Brayden and Ashton have gotten.

Fucking Ashton.

Fucking Brayden.

How is it that Ashton fucks everything up and still gets the girl *and* the guy?

"Ashton's not here."

Brayden glares. "I'm not here for Ashton."

"Oh, sorry, I just assumed since you've apparently been hanging out with him all week that you were."

"What the fuck is your problem?" Brayden hisses. "I know you're not really pissed that, while you've been avoiding me all week, I've been hanging out with Ashton."

"The guy you kissed," I correct.

"The guy who's now with Mia," he volleys.

I scoff. "It'll never work out."

Brayden's brows hit his forehead. "Is that what this is about? Mia? What happened this week between you two?"

"I comforted her… You know because the guy she was supposed to be dating kissed her best friend."

"And now they're together." He shrugs nonchalantly.

"Until he hurts her again. Kisses another guy… fucks another guy."

Brayden eyes me for several seconds, like he's trying to figure me out. Good luck with that, buddy. Not even I know what the hell is going on with me. "You're not worried about Mia getting hurt again…" he finally says, shaking his head. "You fell for her."

"What?" I splutter, thrown off guard by his statement.

"You. Fell. For. Mia. The same way I did. The same way Ashton did. And now you're pissed they're together and you're alone."

"I guess you failing your classes makes sense," I spit, trying to deflect. "Since you apparently don't pay attention."

"What the fuck is that supposed to mean?" Brayden asks, stepping over the threshold and into my face.

"It means, I don't want Mia—"

"Bullshit."

"I want you!"

My words echo around in my heart for the longest second known to man and then Brayden pounces. His mouth crashes against mine, forcing me to stumble back. He slams the door shut and pushes me up against it. "You want me?" he taunts. "Then show me."

His mouth is back on mine, his tongue slipping past my lips. He kisses me hard and deep, and I kiss him right back, giving myself completely over to him. It's been too damn long since the last time I touched him, tasted him, and I'm jonesing for a hit.

As he reaches for my pants, I remember where we are. "Wait," I murmur against his lips, grabbing his wrist. "I don't want to rush this." The last time we were together, in the hotel room, it was rushed. We were both angry and desperate. This time, I want to take our time. He demanded I show him that I want him, and I plan to do just that.

Brayden pulls back, misunderstanding me, confusion and hurt swimming in his eyes. "Let's go to my room," I clarify. His eyes light up at my words, and I vow to make sure Brayden is always happy, so he never looks sad again.

The second we're in my room, Brayden is on me. Placing kisses along my jaw. His lips are firm yet soft, and every kiss is filled with intent and passion.

"Wanna know why I was here every day?" he asks, nipping at my bottom lip.

Our eyes meet and I wait for him to tell me.

"I was hoping to run into you," he says. "Yeah, I wanted to be there for Ashton and somewhere along the way we actually became friends, but we could've hung out anywhere."

He pulls my shirt over my head and places a kiss to my left pec, swirling his tongue around my nipple. The sensation shoots straight to my dick, forcing me to let out a groan.

"Every day I kept waiting for you to show up," he says, kissing my right pec. "But you never did."

He licks my nipple, then bites down on it, and I groan louder, silently wishing for him to never stop touching me.

"I was at the office and Mia's place," I choke out, trying to focus on what he's saying but distracted by the way he's licking my nipples.

"Do you want her, Drew?" he asks. "Do you want her to be the one kissing you?" He kisses my lips. "Do you want her to be the one sucking on you?" He runs his tongue down the side of my throat and sucks on my neck. "Do you want her to be the one licking you?" His tongue laves at my left nipple.

I swallow thickly, unsure how the fuck to answer those fucking questions.

"You do, don't you?" he asks, grabbing the button of my jeans and undoing them.

"I want *you*," I choke out. "I came here for *you*."

He pushes my pants and boxer briefs down my thighs and then he drops to his knees. "You might've come here for me," he says. "But you want Mia too now. What about Ashton?" he asks, taking my hard as steel dick in his hand. "Do you wish Ashton were the one stroking your dick right now?"

I shake my head, but I can't speak. I can't answer him. I can't lie to him. It's all fucking confusing.

"I want *you*," I tell him again. "I came here for *you*."

Brayden nods. "But you fell for them too, didn't you?"

He releases my dick and stands, taking my face in his strong palms. "I did too," he admits. "I fell for them both too."

"It doesn't change how I feel about you," I tell him. "I came here for you."

"I know," he says, "and it doesn't change how I feel about you."

"And how is that?" I ask, needing to hear the words. "How do you feel about me?"

"I love you. I always have," Brayden says, and then his mouth is back on me. He steers us over to the bed, where we both scramble to take our clothes off between kisses.

Once we're both naked, we drop onto my bed. Brayden pushes me onto my back and then kisses along my neck and down my chest and torso. He settles himself between my legs and takes my dick in his hands. "I've imagined what it would be like to do this for years," he says, licking the swollen head. "But I never thought it would happen."

My heart clenches in my chest, an overwhelming pain spearing straight into it. He didn't think it would happen because I ran. I wasted eight years running from him instead of to him. We could've had this years ago.

Brayden slowly licks his way up my dick, from root to tip, and I momentarily close my eyes, enjoying the feel of his mouth on me. "Open your eyes," he demands, stopping his ministrations.

My eyes snap open.

"I can't take the chance of you imagining someone else with his… or *her* mouth wrapped around your dick."

His words are like icy water poured straight over my dick. I scramble up, pushing Brayden off me. "Is that what this is about?" I ask, hurt evident in my tone. "You want me because you think I want Ashton and Mia?"

I push him backward and cup his face with my hand. "You think, with your mouth wrapped around my dick, I could ever, hell, *would ever* imagine someone else?"

Brayden swallows loudly, his Adam's apple moving, and I can see the insecurity written all over his features.

"I. Came. Here. For. You." I run my tongue along the seam of his lips. "Yeah, you're right. I developed feelings for Ashton and Mia, but so did fucking you."

He releases a harsh breath, but doesn't argue.

"But I would choose you," I continue." Always you. You are who I want, who I imagine when I'm fisting my dick in the shower. You're the one who fucking hurt me. Not Ashton, not Mia. You."

"I'm sorry," Brayden croaks out.

"I know you are. And I get it… But if we're going to do this, there can't be anyone else in this room but us. Ashton and Mia are together. The way it's supposed to be."

Brayden nods. "Just us."

"Just us," I repeat.

And then my mouth crushes against Brayden's, trying to show him that it's him. Always him. I will always choose him. I already lost him once and I'll never let that happen again.

Rolling to my side, I take Brayden with me, until we're lying side by side, our bodies grinding against each other. As we both grip each other's dicks, neither of us is leading or following, because neither of us really knows where the hell we're going. What we're doing. All we know is that we want to be with each other. Our emotions are guiding us.

"Fuck," Brayden murmurs against my lips. "I've missed you so much."

He squeezes the hell out of my dick, stroking it up and down slowly.

"I've missed you too." I stroke him the same way he does me. Beads of cum seep from his tip and I use it to create a bit of friction.

"I need to taste you," he says, kissing me.

"Then taste me."

I assume he's talking about my mouth, so when he moves out of my grip, I'm confused. He edges down the bed, until he's between my legs, and then it clicks. He wants to taste my dick. But I want to taste him as well…

And then an idea strikes. "Wait," I tell him, crawling over to where he is.

"What's wrong?" he asks with a sexy pout.

"I want to taste you too." I lie across the bed, taking his dick in my hand. "Go on," I urge. "Taste me."

Brayden obeys, lying in the opposite position. I spread my legs and he does the same, then both our mouths are on each other. I suck and tease his dick while he does the same to mine. One day I'm going to take my time, explore every inch of him, but right now, I'm too turned on, too worked up. It seems to always be that way when we come together.

I take him all the way down my throat, and his dick swells. His fingers caress my sac, and my dick throbs. "Bray," I choke out, warning him.

That single word spurs him on, making him suck me harder, until I'm coming inside his warm, wet mouth. A few seconds later, he's doing the same. I swallow everything he gives me, then I lick him clean.

"Fuck," he breathes, releasing my dick.

I do the same, dropping onto my back. I close my eyes, reveling in what just happened. When we were younger, it was Bray pursuing me. At the rink and in the hotel room, it was me pursuing him. But tonight, for the first time, it was the two of us, together.

"Hey," he says. His voice is so close, I startle. Opening my eyes, I find him lying next to me again.

"Hey," I say back.

We both stare at each other for several seconds, unsure of where to go from here. And then I speak up because, even though I know what it's like to be with a man, this was Brayden's first time. Sure, we've kissed, and I've blown him, but neither is the same as having someone's dick down your throat.

"What did you think?"

He laughs. "About what? You sucking my dick? In case you forgot, you've done that before."

I shake my head. "No, about… sucking mine."

His face goes serious, and my stomach knots. What if he hated it? What if after all these years, I'm not what he wants? Where would we go from here? "I tried to be with a guy once," he admits. "It was during our senior trip."

"I didn't go on the trip." My grandma wasn't feeling well and I wasn't comfortable leaving her alone.

"I know," he says. "I got drunk and broke away from everyone… met this guy… I figured it would be the perfect way to figure out if I was gay."

"What happened?" I considered doing the same thing over the years, but every time I couldn't go through with it—until Ashton. I quickly push him from my thoughts. I meant what I said to Brayden—it can only be the two of us in this room.

"We kissed… But the second he touched my dick, I ran." He chuckles lightly, running his hand along my shoulder and landing on my ass. "But with you… it feels right."

He tugs me toward him, and I release a breath. "It does," I agree. "It feels damn right."

"I want this. I want you… I want us."

"Then you can have me. It's why I came back… for you."

Brayden nods, but the expression on his face looks like he has something on his mind.

"What?" I prompt.

"You keep saying you came back for me, but you also came back because of hockey…"

My heart picks up speed, knowing exactly where he's going. What he's about to ask. I hold my breath, praying he doesn't ask it…

"What happened, Drew? Why did you leave the NHL?"

# NINE

*Brayden*

His blue eyes that had been shining with a mixture of love and lust dim. He completely shuts down, avoiding eye contact. What the hell happened?

I know it's not because he lost his ability to play or some shit like that. Drew is fucking amazing on the ice.

The very best.

It's something else. Something he's ashamed of. He did something, I think. But that makes no sense because he's so by the book about everything.

Except us.

He breaks the rules of his coaching position by being with me.

Definitely not by the book there.

I shove that thought down and run my fingers through his messy hair. "Drew," I rumble. "You can talk to me."

Pain flashes in his eyes before he slams them shut. As though he can block out my questions and the world around him. Whatever happened kills him.

I could push and probe, because that's what we do, but not now. Not when he's so fucking vulnerable and sad. I'll tug this information out of him eventually. Leaning forward, I press a kiss to his mouth that felt so good around my dick, and his eyes pop back open.

"Tell me when you're ready. Might not be today or tomorrow or next week, but you'll tell me because not only are we this now"—I wave at our naked bodies tangled together—"but you're my best friend in the whole goddamn world."

He nods. "I'm sorry."

Rather than let him feel like shit, I palm the back of his neck and draw him to me for another kiss. We're just getting hot and heavy again, our dicks hard and pressed together, when we hear voices.

Fuck.

By the time it registers, Drew barely has a chance to pull the covers over our bodies when someone fills the doorway.

"*Holy* shit," Ashton says, gripping the top of the doorframe as he leans into Drew's room. "I leave you two unattended for two hours and look at the trouble you get yourselves into."

Beautiful fucking Mia peeks her head around him, her brown eyes widening in shock at the scene before her.

"Oh. Oh my God. Ashton, leave them alone," she chokes out, her arms going around his waist to pull him away.

Ashton is wearing one of his devious smirks, but his hazel eyes are gleaming with an emotion I can't quite put my finger on. Not jealousy. Because he has Mia. Right? Not anger because we're cool now. It certainly isn't fucking happiness, that much I do know.

"If you guys are done fucking, put some clothes on and come hang out with MiMi and me." His gaze lingers for a moment longer before he releases the top of the doorframe to grab Mia and toss her over his shoulder, making her squeal with laughter.

"I guess there's no hiding what we just did," I say with a nervous chuckle.

Drew gives me a quick peck to my lips. "I don't want to hide what we just did. Felt pretty damn good to me. Long overdue too."

We crawl out of bed and I throw on some St. Louis Blues sweats I find folded neatly on the dresser. Drew smirks at me but doesn't tell me no. He grabs another pair from the drawer and throws them on. I'm too hot for a shirt, so I head into the living room to see what Mia and Ashton are up to while Drew makes a beeline for the bathroom.

"Where's Mia?" I ask, scanning the space.

"Ran next door to change," Ashton says, not looking up from whatever he's doing in the kitchen. "You two kids have fun?"

I walk into the kitchen to find him cutting oranges. "Yeah. How was your date?"

His eyes cut over to mine, a smile playing at his lips. "We didn't have a happy ending like yours, but I did feed my girl."

"Hopefully lots of carbs," I tease, stepping closer to steal an orange wedge.

He stiffens and his hazel eyes take on the despondent look they had all week. "I fucked up with her, man. It should have been me who went to see her."

I try not to take offense at his words. What Mia and I shared that weekend was amazing. I don't regret one second of it. "But it wasn't. I made sure she was okay."

Rather than get jealous, his shoulders hunch. "Thanks for that. Was her mom really a witch?"

A disgusted snort escapes me. "She's more than a witch. She's a rotten, evil cunt. I fucking hate her mom."

Fiery eyes meet mine. "I'm glad you were there to protect her from that horrible woman."

"Me too." I bring the orange wedge up to my lips and bite down.

Ashton's gaze peruses from my mouth to my pectorals to my naval and then he shakes his head, continuing on his task.

"What are you making?"

"Bahama Mamas. Apparently some douchebag was after my rum." He points his knife at the bottle on the counter. "MiMi wanted something fruity, so I figured I'd please everyone." His eyes are once again taking in the way I eat the orange.

A flash of heat zapping through me has me quickly stepping away to toss the peel in the trash. Drew saunters into the kitchen smelling like fucking paradise and I can't help but grin at him. He throws a wink at me before leaning a hip against the counter to watch Ashton.

Ashton darts his gaze between us and then laughs. "You two are way gayer than me. Look at you in your matching pants. So fucking cute."

We all laugh as Mia returns, dropping her bag on the floor just inside the door.

And then nothing's funny at all.

She's changed out of her clothes she wore to the meet. Her dark hair has been braided into pigtails and her cute glasses are perched on her nose. I'm not sure she's even wearing pants because the white Nintendo hoodie hangs halfway down her thighs. Her bare, naked thighs. Thighs I've kissed and been between. She has on knee-high red and white striped socks and stupid unicorn slippers.

That whole ensemble should not be sexy.

I should not be reliving every second of our time together where I tasted her and touched her.

I'm with Drew. She's with Ashton.

"What?" she asks, her eyes bouncing between the three of us who've gone silent. "Do I look stupid or something?"

Ashton snorts. "Fuck no, MiMi. You're so damn cute, you gave everyone a boner just by being you. Now come over here and help me make these drinks."

Tearing my gaze from her, I discover that Drew's eyes are snared on the way Ashton now has Mia pinned against the counter. Ashton playfully nips at her neck while she places the orange slices into each of the glasses. I walk over to Drew and grab his hand. As though breaking from his trance, he threads his fingers with mine.

"Let's play NHL 20," I say to Drew, tugging him out of the kitchen.

Ashton cackles. "Drew sucks at that game, dude bro Bray."

"I do not," Drew grumbles as he sits on the floor in front of the television.

I smirk at Drew as I set up the game. He's such a bad liar. Once the game is on, I plop down next to him and begin whipping his ass, loving how pissed off he gets each time I knock the puck into his net. Ashton shows up with drinks. We absently drink while we play and before long, I'm getting a refill.

"Fuck you," Drew barks out, tossing his controller to the floor. "I'm not playing this dumbass game."

"Aww, Drew's a sore loser," Mia taunts. "Need a hug?"

"I need a shot," he mumbles back.

Ashton drops down next to me, grabbing the abandoned controller. He's a lot harder to beat. We spend the next hour in a heated match, neck in neck. If Mia stopped refilling our glasses, maybe I could focus on the screen a little better.

"Pause it," Ashton says. "I gotta take a piss."

He stands and slightly staggers before heading out of the living room. Finally tearing myself from the game, I glance around, looking for Drew. Mia—no longer wearing her hoodie, but a tight red camisole—is curled up next to him and his arm is around her. They're talking lowly, both of them wearing serene expressions. Her tiny shorts have crept up her thighs, showing a lot of silky skin.

My gut twists in a weird way and I'd like to think it's jealousy at the way he holds Mia when he could be holding me, but I don't think that's it. It reminds me of how it felt to hold her too. She's so soft and sweet and—

"Mine," Ashton says, a playful lilt in his voice as he returns and scoops Mia out of Drew's arms. He sits down at one end of the couch with her in his lap. "Game's over, man. Put on a movie."

"I'm not your bitch," I grumble back.

Ashton laughs. "You're just mad I was gonna beat you again and you won't have a chance to try and win. Later, loser. Later I'll whip your ass so hard you won't be able to sit for a week." His eyes drag down my shirtless front for a second and then he pulls his stare away, jaw clenching.

I flip off the game and turn it to some Brad Pitt movie where he ages in reverse. Drew looks like a king sprawled out on the other end of the couch, his blue eyes blazing with heat. Bypassing the recliner, I sit down next to Drew, angling my body where I can watch Ashton and Mia right along with the movie. Drew absently strokes his fingertips over my hardened nipple, making my dick all kinds of hard in my sweats. Luckily, Ashton is too wrapped up in Mia to notice what Drew does to me from one simple touch.

"Love you, MiMi," Ashton murmurs, his thumb hooking one of the straps and pulling it down her shoulder.

The movie is forgotten as I watch the way he caresses her skin so reverently. It makes me wonder if he'll take her shirt off with us here. My dick twitches at that thought. Then, my dick twitches for a whole other reason when I feel warm lips at my neck. Drew's tongue is hot as he licks my skin. His teeth nip at my flesh and then he sucks, making me groan.

The loud, desperate sound that escapes me has both Ashton and Mia pulling from their kiss to look over at us. Drew's palm rubs over my abs, his fingertips teasing the waistband of my sweats. I can't help but buck my hips up, wishing he'd push his hand down beneath the fabric and grip my aching dick. Ashton's gaze is fiery lust as he rakes it over me and then his attention is back on Mia. He pulls her thighs until she's straddling him, kissing her like he might be able to steal her soul—the little devil. Her moans have me reminiscing back to that weekend. When I made her moan like that. He grips her hips, dragging her over his dick, dry fucking her right in front of us.

It's hot and it makes me feel guilty for thinking it.

I hate that I'd totally watch them go at it if they were up for it.

Needing distance from the scene before me, I turn to meet Drew's lips for a kiss. He kisses me with such hunger, I feel like he might devour me whole. The couch moves and then Ashton is stumbling away with Mia locked in his arms. They barely get the door closed to his room before her moans really kick up.

"Ready for bed?" Drew rasps out.

"I'm spending the night?" I tease with a grin.

"Damn fucking right you are. I'm going to keep you in my bed as long as you'll let me."

Forever.

He can keep me forever.

I wake with a splitting headache and a naked body wrapped around me. I'm not used to a dick rutting against my crack, but I can't say I hate it. Based on the way Drew is still softly snoring, I'd say he's having a good sex dream. I fight a smile as I lie in the dark, contemplating last night. After a shower where we took turns blowing each other, we fell into bed exhausted but happy.

I thought it was the sun shining in that woke me, but when I hear murmured voices, I realize it's Mia and Ashton. His door is closed but Drew's remains open. Mia's sounds of pleasure filter through the wall, making my dick hard as stone. Every so often Ashton lets out a feral snarl or the headboard will thump hard against the wall. The sounds are erotic. I feel like a voyeur listening to them fuck. A strong hand wraps around my dick, making my heart shudder.

"Someone's turned on this morning," Drew rumbles against my neck. "Want me to take care of you?"

I push my ass against his dick, loving the hiss he makes. He punishes me back by stroking me hard, his hand gripping me to the point of pain. Fuck, it feels good. Our breathing becomes ragged as he rubs his dick along the crack of my ass, never attempting to enter, and jacks me off.

God, he feels good.

This feels good.

Like I've been waiting my whole life for this moment.

"Drew," I groan. "Fuck."

"I know," he agrees. "So fucking good."

He carries us over the edge together. As soon as my nuts seize up to come, his hot cum rushes up my lower back, soaking me. His dick slides through the mess he made, rubbing against my crack. I come hard, nearly growing dizzy from the pleasure. I've barely come down from my high when my phone buzzes from my abandoned pants on the floor.

"Better answer that while I get the shower started," Drew says, kissing my neck.

He climbs out of bed and tosses me my pants. I fish out my phone to see I've missed a call from Mom. With a sigh, I ring her back, putting her on speaker.

"Hey, sweetie," she chirps. "I thought you were avoiding me again."

Guilt swims up inside me.

"Never, Mom. What's up?"

"Your dad and I thought you'd like to come over for steak tonight. He's about to head up to the butcher to grab some meat. We were wondering if we'd need to get one more." She pauses. "I know you and Drew don't always get along, but I was hoping—"

"Yeah," I say, cutting her off. "We'll be there. Drew loves steak."

"Fuck yeah he does," Ashton says, smirking from the doorway.

I shoot him a glare. "Go away, man."

"Who's that?" Mom asks, her voice growing higher with excitement. "A friend?"

"Yeah, Mom, an annoying friend," I grumble.

Ashton laughs as he walks into Drew's room. He crosses his arms over his bare chest that's red from Mia's fingernails scratching over the flesh. I have to look away.

"Bring him, sweetie. The more the merrier."

"I'm sure Ashton has shit to do," I grumble.

Ashton's hazel eyes gleam with devious wickedness. "Nope. Me and my girlfriend have no plans. We'll be there, Mrs. Murphy."

Fucking suck-up.

I shoot him the bird.

"Wonderful! Your father is going to be so pleased. We'll pick up six steaks then. See you around six, honey." Then to Ashton she says, "Can't wait to meet you, sweetheart."

He struts around the room like a fucking rooster. "Me neither. Can I call you Mom? My mom is a drunk—"

"See you then," I bark out, cutting him off. "Love you. Bye."

"This is going to be so much fun." Ashton grins like the fucking devil. "Maybe Mom will show me pictures of you from when you were little. Lots of embarrassing shit that I can fuck with you over from now until eternity."

"Fuck off and don't call her Mom."

"No can do, dude bro. Already did. It's a thing now." He nods to the bathroom where the shower is going. "Go fuck your boyfriend and then help me make breakfast. Mia is going to need her energy after last night."

I fling the blanket off my body and stride over to the bathroom, secretly delighted over the fact that I just shut Ashton up—the guy with a never-ending commentary—with my naked ass.

A small part of me is apprehensive over the idea of Ashton and Mia being in my childhood home, but a bigger part is kind of excited.

I have friends now.

I'm happy.

Mom and Dad are going to be so fucking shocked.

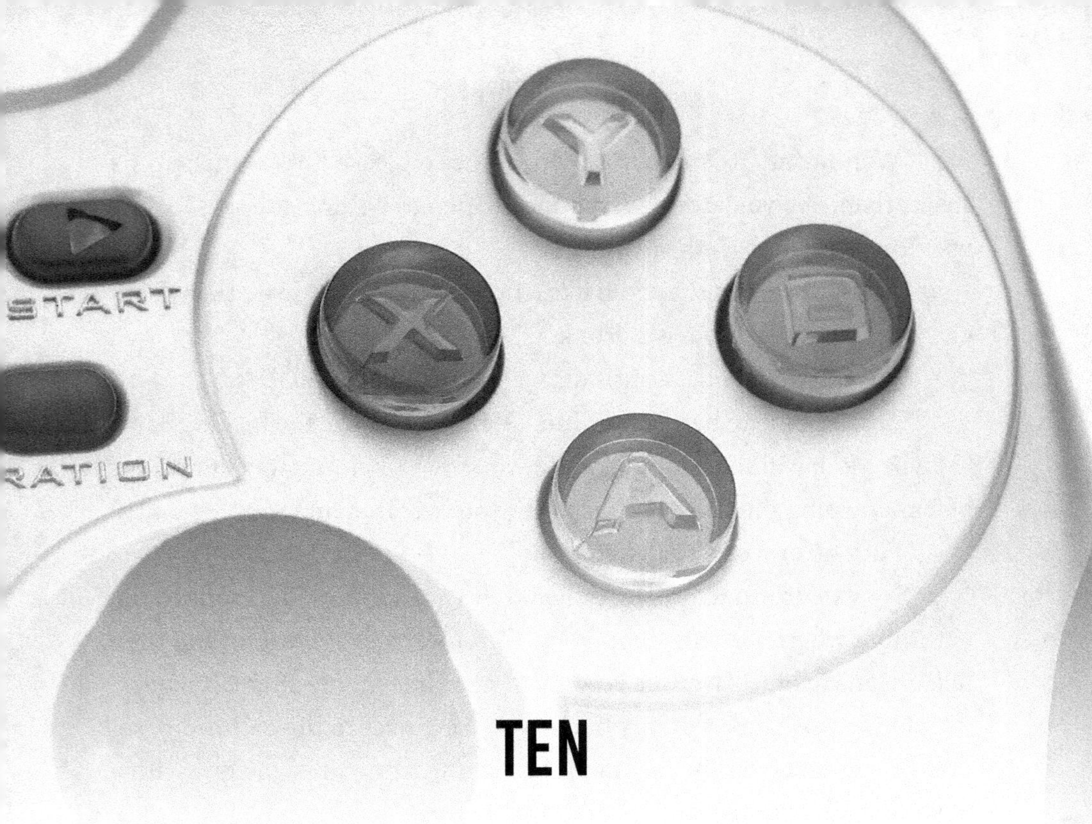

# TEN

*Mia*

This is weird, right?

I'm going with my boyfriend to have dinner with my ex-almost boyfriend and his boyfriend at my ex-almost boyfriend's family's house. God.

It's so weird.

Ashton laughs, already reading my mind. Bastard.

"What?" I grumble as we park behind Drew's truck in a driveway to a normal, ranch-style home—a home that would probably fit inside my parents' palatial living room back in California.

"Relax, MiMi. Brayden's parents can't possibly be any worse than ours. And if they are, we can all go back to my place after and toast to horrible parents everywhere." He grabs my hand and tugs me close so he can kiss my lips. "If it gets weird, we'll bail. Promise."

The tension bleeds out of me as I climb out of Ashton's Audi. Drew and Brayden are already walking inside. Ashton takes my hand and guides me up the steps, squeezing to let me know he's there.

The scent of brownies fills my nostrils as we enter the small home. My stomach grumbles and I bite back a grin, knowing Ashton will be thrilled to eat brownies.

"My babies," a woman with dark hair says. "I missed you two."

She pulls Drew and Brayden in for a hug. It's cute seeing them together, though I wonder how Brayden's parents will deal with learning they're an item now. It makes me wonder if they'll tell them at all.

"And who are these two cuties?" she asks, grinning at me with a smile that matches Bray's.

"I'm the hot friend Ashton," Ashton says, "and this is my even hotter girlfriend, Mia."

"Lovely to meet you," she chirps, pulling us in for a motherly hug too. "I'm Molly."

I don't expect to get choked up over a hug from a woman I don't know, but I do. I have to bite on my lip to keep from crying. Why can't my mom be like this?

"Tim's outside, checking the grill. I'm working on a salad," Molly says. "It's so nice having a full house. I'm happy you all could come tonight."

"I like my steak still mooing," Ashton says. "Does your husband know how to cook steak or does he char everything like your son's boyfriend? Drew's bacon is shit."

Drew shoots Ashton a sharp look and Brayden just rolls his eyes. Molly laughs, clearly entertained by Ashton.

"Come on, rude ass," Drew says, grabbing Ashton's arm. "Let's go say hi to Tim and he can smack you around with his spatula a bit."

Brayden shakes his head as they go out the back door.

"You kids want to help me in the kitchen?" Molly asks.

I nod, completely out of my element. I can't remember the last time I helped my mom in the kitchen. I once tried to help the chef, curious about how to cook, and my mom flipped out on me and said never to embarrass her like that again.

Molly hands me several different vegetables and a cutting board and knife. I take the tomato and slice it down the middle, and then again. Then I realize, aside from cutting up the occasional piece of fruit or making a sandwich, I've never actually made a meal. I get all my food from the cafeteria or order in. I try to imagine how I like my tomatoes in my salad. Usually a bit smaller, but since I have no clue how to cut them any smaller, I nervously move on to the next vegetable, hoping I'm not messing up her salad too much. Mom is super picky about the presentation of the meals that are served in her home. Everything is about appearance with her. Hopefully Molly isn't the same way. Because there's no way the hack job I'm doing on these vegetables is going to look pretty.

"So, how did you all meet?" Molly asks.

"Mia's my tutor," Brayden says, locking eyes with me. "She's the reason I'm currently passing all of my classes." He shoots me a playful wink and I shake my head.

"Oh, that's so nice of you." She beams at me as she washes and chops up the lettuce.

I sigh in relief that he didn't tell her I'm his ex-almost girlfriend, then go back to eyeing the vegetables, picking up a carrot next. Molly hands me some weird contraption and I eye it, having no clue what to do with it. Not wanting to look stupid, I consider Googling it or taking a picture of it and sending it to Clancy, my parents' chef, but instead I set it down and move on to the green pepper. I turn it around in my hands, unsure how to slice it. I glance over at the other color peppers and realize I need to pick one because I'm running out of vegetables to skip.

As I'm about to admit defeat, muscular arms cage me in against the counter. I know based off the woodsy scent it's Brayden, and when I glance up, it's confirmed.

"Here," he says softly, his warm breath against my ear. "Let me show you." I should be concerned about how close we are, especially in front of his mom, but as he wraps his hand over the top of mine and shows me how to slice a pepper, all I can do is sigh in relief.

Molly grins over at me, not even fazed that her son is this close to me.

"I know Brayden really wanted to go straight into the NHL," she says, pride in her tone. "But it was so important to us that he get an education first. God forbid something happen to him, he needs a backup plan."

I nod in agreement, as I watch Brayden show me how to cut each of the vegetables. Molly must notice by now that he's showing me, but she doesn't say a word, and for that I'm thankful.

Brayden takes the contraption she gave me and says, "It's a peeler." He slides it along the outside of the cucumber, then lets go of it, so I can take over.

"Thank you," I whisper, turning my head to look at him. He grins and then pecks a sweet kiss on the side of my neck before stepping away.

"You're doing a great job," Molly says, scooping up the vegetables we've already sliced and placing them all into a big salad bowl. Her gaze meets mine and a smile spreads across her face. I can't help but beam back with pride.

"Damn, MiMi," Ashton says as he enters the kitchen. "Look at you going all Rachel Ray up in here." Brayden moves to the side and Ashton takes his place, planting a kiss to my cheek. "Keep this up and I'm going to have you barefoot and pregnant in the kitchen in no time."

"Ashton," I whine, jutting out my arm to elbow him. He dodges my elbow and snags a slice of cucumber, popping it into his mouth.

Molly laughs. "You two are so cute."

"Don't encourage him," Brayden groans, also grabbing a slice of cucumber. I pretend to stab his hand and he laughs, pulling his hand away.

"Dinner's ready," Tim calls out.

Molly hands me the finished bowl of salad and then we all join Drew and Tim in the dining room. It's a small, cozy room with a circular wood table and chairs. It looks like it should seat four people tops, but enough chairs are squeezed together so we can all sit.

Ashton plops into a seat then pulls the one next to him out for me. Brayden and Drew sit next to each other with Brayden on the other side of me, and Molly and Tim do the same, across from me.

As Ashton is about to reach for the plate of steaks, Molly speaks up. "Who would like to say grace?"

Ashton pulls his hand back. "I will, Mom."

"Have you ever even said grace?" I accuse, knowing damn well he hasn't since his family isn't religious.

Ashton shrugs. "No, but I've seen it on TV."

We all groan and Molly giggles. "Thank you, sweet boy, that would be great."

I catch Drew rolling his eyes and laugh under my breath, before I follow Molly and Tim's lead and lower my head, waiting to hear Ashton's speech.

"Grace," Ashton says. I wait several seconds for him to continue, before I realize that's it. He literally said 'grace.' My head pops back up in shock, ready to stab him with my steak knife, when he chuckles. "Kidding."

He shoots me a devilish wink and I groan on the inside, afraid of whatever is about to come out of his mouth next. "Lord, thank you for the delicious food I'm about to devour, for the people I'm about to devour it with, and for MiMi, who I'll most *definitely* be devouring later. Amen."

I groan.

Tim laughs.

Brayden and Drew both snort.

And Molly giggles, winks my way, and then says, "Dig in, everyone."

We're all grabbing our food, when my cell phone vibrates in my back pocket. Not sure who it is, I quickly pull it out to check, immediately wishing I didn't.

**Mom: I'm having your dress designed for the event. Can you try not to gain another ten pounds between now and then? With the holidays, they won't be able to alter it.**

Without even bothering to reply, I shove my phone back in my pocket. When I glance up, Ashton is watching me curiously. "My mom," I murmur with an eye roll to play it off. The last thing I want to do is ruin everyone's dinner with talk of my family.

I watch everyone grab their food, as they make small talk about Brayden's team's winning streak, but I'm suddenly not all that hungry. I grab a piece of steak and a salad, since they're the healthiest items, but bypass the macaroni and cheese, mashed potatoes, and buttery rolls.

"MiMi, don't you love mac n cheese?" Ashton asks, eyeing my half empty plate. Before I can answer, he plops some down on my plate. "Try it, it's good," he says, taking a bite.

"So, tell me what's new," Molly says.

"Well—" Ashton begins with a glint in his eyes that tells me he's about to out Drew and Brayden. Earlier, he joked about it, but no one actually took him seriously. I kick him under the table and shake my head. It's one thing to mess around, but it's another to mess with someone's family.

"Drew and I are together now... like a couple," Brayden says, shocking the hell out of me with the way he just comes out and announces it. I hold my breath, praying his parents don't ridicule or disown him. But at least if they do, we're here and have his back.

Molly glances from Drew to Brayden several times before a huge smile breaks across her face and tears fill her eyes. She stands and walks over to Drew, pulling him into a hug. "Finally," she says through a watery smile. "Congratulations." She hugs Brayden next, telling him how happy she is for him before she sits back down.

Ashton stares at her in shock, for the first time in his life speechless. My eyes dart to Tim, wondering if he'll be this happy, or if he'll be the one to give them a hard time.

"How is that going to work with you being the coach?" Tim asks Drew.

Drew stiffens. "I don't know, sir. It only just happened, so we're still figuring it all out."

Tim nods, as if that answer is good enough for him. "I imagine this road will be a bumpy one. I'm glad you boys made it back to each other. If you need anything, we're here."

"Thank you," Brayden and Drew both say.

And that's it... Just like that both of Brayden's parents accepted them being together. My heart thumps behind my ribcage, wishing these people could be my family. Wondering why my own can never be that accepting.

As if he can tell what I'm thinking, Ashton reaches over and squeezes my leg. I grant him a forced smile and go about eating my salad.

"Here, MiMi," Ashton says, "try this." He extends his fork of mashed potatoes toward me. I try to shake my head, but he keeps going and I'm forced to take a bite. "Good, right?"

"Yeah," I say after I swallow my bite.

"Did you try my mom's rolls?" Brayden asks from the other side of me. He tosses a roll onto my plate, and I groan on the inside. What the hell is up with these boys trying to feed me?

I glance over at Brayden and catch the weird look passing between him and Ashton, and it hits me. He told Ashton about my mom. Freaking great.

Not wanting to be rude, I have no choice but to eat everything they place on my plate. After the meal is over and everyone has helped clean up, Molly brings a massive plate of brownies over.

"Would you like one or two?" she asks me sweetly.

"Oh, none for me, but thank you," I tell her.

Her brows dip together. "Is there something wrong with my brownies, honey?"

"Maybe it's the pregnancy hormones," Ashton quips, grabbing three for himself.

Molly's eyes go wide, and my head swings over to him, my face heating up in embarrassment.

"Ignore him. He's an idiot," Drew says, grabbing his own brownie. "You can only believe a quarter of what comes out of Ashton's mouth. She's not pregnant."

"Yet," Ashton adds with a wink. I make a mental note to go get on birth control as soon as possible. Too many pregnancy jokes are coming out of his mouth.

"Just have one, please," Molly insists.

Because I don't want to offend her, and because they look and smell delicious, I nod.

"Good girl," she says with a wink.

As I take a bite of my brownie, I notice Ashton and Brayden both smiling at each other. And I know Brayden definitely told Ashton about my mom.

After dessert is over, Molly insists we all go out back and have an after-dinner drink by her chiminea. It's cold outside, but the warmth from it makes it nice. Ashton and I cuddle up into one of her lounge chairs together, while everyone pairs off in the other two.

"This is nice," Molly muses. "We should make this a weekly tradition. Remember when you used to come over every Sunday for dinner?" she asks Drew, who nods in agreement.

"Yeah, I've missed this," he says, wrapping his arm around Brayden. "Being on the road got old quick."

My phone buzzes in my pocket again, and I plan to ignore it, but Ashton pulls it out. "Sasha has formally invited you to the DELTA DELTA DELTA Halloween party," he says with a snort. "Hell no. No one wants to see her dressed as Slutty Sorority Barbie. Oh wait. She's Slutty Sorority Barbie *every* day."

"Be nice," I say, smacking his thigh. "It could be fun. Maybe Drew and Brayden could come."

Before Ashton opens his mouth and says something super inappropriate about that, Brayden chimes in. "I got a text earlier from Finn. The whole team is going. I think I'll go. I've been trying to be more present with them. Being team captain means you actually have to talk to the team." He laughs. "You can be my date, Mia." He winks.

"If he's going," Ashton grumbles, "then Drew and I have to go to make sure you don't get roofied by Brayden's dude bro friends."

Molly laughs. "You're such a silly boy."

Ashton beams like it's a compliment.

"I can't," Drew says, though he has a wistful expression on his face. "I wish I could."

"It's a Halloween party," Ashton says to Drew. "Wear a damn mask. No one will ever know."

"I think it will be wonderful for you four to dress up and have fun," Molly encourages.

"As long as you're careful," Tim adds, his attention on Drew.

"Halloween used to be your favorite holiday," Molly says to Brayden. "Remember when you and Ben went through your phase of dressing up together?" She smiles. "Brayden wanted to be Papa Smurf and convinced Ben to be Smurfette. Poor thing had to walk around the neighborhood in a dress and blond wig, but he didn't seem to mind."

Everyone laughs, but when I look over at Brayden, he isn't. He's not even smiling.

"Oh!" Molly continues, completely oblivious to the change in Brayden's demeanor. "And what about the time you three boys all dressed up as your favorite hockey players? I think I have a picture somewhere."

At that, Brayden jumps out of the chair and mutters, "I'll be right back."

Molly stops talking, a frown marring her features. "I shouldn't have—"

"No, dear," Tim says. "It's okay to talk about Ben. All we have left are the memories."

My thoughts go back to the time Brayden and I spent together in my childhood room at my parents' place when he surprised me by showing up for the weekend. The devastated look in his eyes when he told me about his brother's death. The guilt dripping with each word as he confessed to me that he was to blame. Had he not agreed to take his brother outside in the cold that day while his parents were out, he believes his brother never would've caught pneumonia and died. I can't even imagine living with a weight like that on my shoulders.

"I'm going to go talk to him," I say, my eyes meeting Drew's to make sure I'm not overstepping. He nods once and I take off into the house to find Brayden.

I search the kitchen and living room and then head down the small hallway that's filled with family photos. The second door on the right is slightly ajar, so I poke my head in. "Hey, can I come in?"

Brayden nods.

I sit next to him on the twin-sized bed and glance around. There are hockey trophies and pictures filled with happy faces. Hockey posters are hanging on the walls and there's a corkboard with a collage of more photos.

I admire how homey the room is. You can tell a teenager lived here. I think back to my room at home and how it looks more like it's staged than lived-in.

Brayden is clutching a small picture frame to his chest. "Can I see?"

He hands it over and I admire the photo. There are three boys in the picture. Two older and one younger. I can tell right away that the two older ones are Drew and Brayden. Drew's signature dimple is on display as he smiles over at Brayden, who looks to be laughing at something someone said. The youngest of the three is glancing over at the other two boys with a look of awe.

"This is your brother," I guess.

"Yeah. It's the last photo I have with him."

I notice then they're all wearing hockey uniforms. It must've been Halloween.

"Bray, you have to tell your parents… You can't keep living with this guilt."

Brayden shakes his head. "I can't. I promised Ben."

"Though I didn't get to know Ben, I think he would be okay with you telling them. The little boy in this picture loved you. He wouldn't want you to suffer in silence."

"What if they hate me?" he whispers, staring down at the picture. "What if I tell them and they blame me?"

"The way you're already blaming yourself?" I set the picture down and turn to face him. "You announced over dinner you're not only gay but dating your best friend and they barely batted an eyelash. I don't see them blaming you or hating you. I think you need to trust them. I've only just met them, but I can see it in their eyes, they love you so much."

I choke up as I say the words, wishing my parents loved me the way Brayden's love him.

"I'm not ready yet," Brayden chokes out. "I know that makes me a wuss, but…"

"No, it doesn't," I argue. "It makes you human." I pull him into a hug. "But one day, when you're ready, I believe that when you tell them, they'll be there for you and a huge weight will be lifted off your shoulders."

By the time we make it back outside, Ashton and Drew are standing, getting ready to leave.

"Well, we gotta bail," Ashton says, snagging my hand. "Have to get started on making some grandbabies, Mom."

Tim shakes his head, chuckling. "I don't think he's kidding."

"He's not," Bray, Drew, and I all say at once, making Ashton grin evilly.

"Please come see us again soon," Molly says, hugging each of us. "This was a wonderful evening."

Once we've bid our goodbyes, we all walk out and I can't help but think this is the best family dinner I've ever been to.

# ELEVEN

*Ashton*

"I can't believe I got talked into this," Drew complains, fussing with his mask. "It's just asking for trouble."

Mia hooks her arm with his once we get out of Brayden's SUV at the party. "No one will know it's you," Mia assures Drew. "Plus, you have enough blood on your shirt and mask, I don't think anyone is going to mess with you. You look scary."

Scary hot.

I try to unthink that thought, but it already happened. When we went to the Halloween shop yesterday, we were left with the most generic shit to choose from. Drew got a Jason Voorhees hockey mask and opted for regular clothes splattered with fake blood. I'd tried to encourage him to be Chippendale Jason and wear a bowtie with no shirt—even offered to oil him up—but he just rolled his eyes and ignored me.

"I look scary," I throw in. "Right, Kurt?"

Brayden looks my way and busts out laughing. Again. My costume is wicked cool. Fuck him. Drew starts to laugh and then Mia cackles too.

"Fuck the three of you," I grumble.

"It's just… I can't…" Brayden wheezes, trying to speak through his chuckles. "I can't fucking take you serious with those eyebrows."

I waggle them at him, making him howl even more. "I'm the devil. These are my evil eyebrows." I'd taken a lot of time to white out my face with makeup and then draw on these cartoony evil brows with black eyeliner. They're overexaggerated and pretty awesome if I do say so myself.

"I can't look at you, man," Brayden says, tears rolling down his cheeks.

"At least my costume is fucking cool," I snap. "Unlike whatever that is." I wave at that. Him. All his '90s grunge glory. He's such a poser, though. Who wears a Nirvana T-shirt to dress like Kurt Cobain? Kurt Cobain never wore his own band T-shirts. His blond wig was supposed to be for a female flapper, but it had been opened and was a little fucked up, so he thought it made him look like Kurt. No, it makes him look stupid.

"Don't pout," Brayden says, grinning. "If you don't look at your face, you're all right."

My face is cool, but he's right. The rest of me is even better. I found a devil horns headband and a tail that I attached to my black, metal studded belt, but the rest is just cool shit I had. A red tank, tight, holey black jeans, and my high-top red, Doc Marten combat boots with black laces. MiMi painted my nails black. I look hot. Like the devil's supposed to be.

"Mia looks the best," Drew says, glancing over his shoulder as Brayden and I follow. "An angel is fitting."

*Barely fits* is more like it.

And I'm so fucking into it, too.

I admire her cute ass as it bounces with each step she takes. Her tight white dress barely covers the ass I love to bite. She has on white and silver striped thigh-high socks and white platform shoes. The dress is sleeveless and dips low in the front. It's super slutty and I can't wait to fuck her in it. Her dark hair is in cute pigtails that make for great handlebars when she gives me head. Instead of her glasses, she put in contacts and white false eyelashes. She found a headband with a sparkly halo and her lips are painted silver with glitter all over them.

"I cannot wait to get my cock messy with that glitter shit," I say, reaching forward to pinch her ass.

My angel glances at me, a devilish grin on her face. "You're so bad."

"It's literally my only job in life, MiMi. To be bad. Devil and all."

We make it inside the packed party house, immediately swarmed by people. Drew lingers by me while Mia gets attacked by Sasha, who wears a skanky nerd costume complete with black-rimmed glasses. I find it funny that her attempt to be a nerd is a failed one. Mia rocks her nerd outfit every day and looks hot as shit too without having to show one quarter of the skin Sasha does. Brayden gets hauled away by a group of big, beefy dudes.

"Stop being so tense, man," I say, nudging Drew. "You really do put off serial killer vibes right now."

He snorts out a laugh. "Sorry."

"Don't be sorry. Let's make fun of people instead. Like Sasha. What the fuck does Mia see in this girl? I would rather my girlfriend not enroll in the Stepford Wives program."

"A lot of the girls here are like that. Mia's just special and different. She's not going to ever try to be like Sasha," Drew says. "Mia's smarter than that."

"Oh fucking great," I grumble, turning to face Drew so I don't have to see that dickhead Travis. "Douchebag in a cowboy costume twelve o'clock."

Drew steps closer, peering over my shoulder past me, looking creepy and intense in his Jason mask. Okay, so maybe it suits him, but I still prefer the Chippendale version better.

"He's coming this way," Drew warns.

"Because he'd recognize this ass from a mile away," I grumble.

"It's a remarkable ass," Drew says, chuckling.

Our eyes meet for a second and Drew's intense blues burn into me. I'm forced to remember things between us that I've kept a pretty good damn lid on since I've been with Mia. Flashes of us kissing. In my bed. On the couch. Touching, grunting, rutting. Cum. Hot cum.

"Fuck," I curse, annoyed that I'd even go there mentally when I have

Mia. "I'm going to grab my girl and dance. You coming?" I break my gaze from his penetrating one and seek out my girlfriend. My super-hot girlfriend. My girlfriend I'm loyal to and love more than anyone in the world.

I find Mia locked in an uncomfortable conversation with Sasha and her bitch squad. Sneaking up behind my girl, I wrap my arms around her and playfully grab her tits.

"Want to dance, angel?"

Sasha's mean girl glare is in place, but she cracks a grin at seeing my face, then turns purple trying to hide it. "We were discussing the sorority chapter, responsibilities, and obligations for the sisters and—"

"Sorry, all I heard was blah, blah, blah, boring shit, blah, blah, blah and then I fell asleep. Come on, MiMi, let's dance so I can wake up." I ignore Sasha's heated glare as I haul Mia over to where people are dancing. Some Lizzo is playing, which feels like an appropriate song to grind to.

I pull my angel against me, my palms settling on her ass, and dance with her, my eyes locked on hers. She grins, her dark eyes glittering in the blinking party lights.

"The devil's going to fuck the innocence right out of you, angel," I tease, dropping a kiss to her sparkly lips.

"He already did."

We dance through each song, the rest of the world slowly fading away around us. Mia's body feels good grinding against mine. I'm practically dry fucking her by the time Brayden and Drew find us. They stand around like a couple of big-ass bodyguards, which is comical.

"Tell me the popular guys know how to dance," I taunt. "We're nerds and we can fucking do it."

"I can dance," Brayden grumbles. "See."

I smirk as he grabs Mia's hips and shows me just how good he can dance. With my girl. Drew's blue eyes are alight behind his mask, watching with a mixture of curiosity and heat. He's probably into that kinky shit—watching his boyfriend flirt with his roomie's girlfriend. Hell, I'm kind of into it.

My mind reflects to last week when we'd all hung out together, right after I made things official with Mia. Bray and Drew were suddenly a thing, too. I'll never forget the thrill that raced down my spine to see them watching as Mia dry fucked me on the couch while we kissed. I'd seen how aroused Brayden was by the boner he was sporting in his sweats, but even had I not seen that, I still wouldn't have missed the matching expressions on their faces.

Curious.

Turned on.

Eager.

I wanted to strip Mia down and make her ride my dick in front of them. To see what they'd do. I'd kind of hoped they would've stripped down and rubbed their dicks against each other for Mia and me to watch. It was so fucked up to feel that way—especially since I'd just gotten the girl—that I was in a hurry to get the fuck out of that living room with her. When I fucked her that night, my fantasies inside my head tangled with the beautiful reality in my bed. I still feel guilty about that shit.

Thank fuck nothing like that has happened since. Sure, we hang out and chill, but since we've left alcohol out of the equation, everyone has behaved.

I just can't ever drink again.

Mia's head falls back against Brayden's chest as she sings her cute little heart out. He's laughing, moving his hips with her, earning the stares of every jealous motherfucker in this party.

Hell, I guess I do need alcohol.

"Who wants a drink?" I ask.

All three of them nod.

"Great, Drew, make sure no fuckers like one of Brayden's roofie buddies come over to dance with my girl." I grab his arm, forcing him to break out of his serial killer stance to come stand on the other side of Mia. "Dance with the angel."

He's hesitant at first, his eyes darting to Bray, who nods, and then he starts working his hips in tandem with them.

Fucking hell.

I want to stare at the way the three of them move together so effortlessly. Mia is having the time of her life, all smiles. It's hot as fuck seeing her sandwiched between two muscly hockey players. That's a fantasy I am definitely beating off to the next time I'm alone.

Just a fantasy.

I love Mia, but I can't exactly become un-gay. As long as I don't act on my fantasies or obsess over them, it's fine. I'm loyal to Mia until the end. Still, a guy can appreciate the hottest goddamn vision he's ever seen.

Finally, I break away to head over to the kitchen that's bustling with people grabbing drinks. I walk over to a stack of plastic cups, ready to mix up some Ashton specials, when someone crowds me from behind.

"When you dress like this, you think everyone believes you're suddenly straight now?" a masculine voice growls. "We all know you still love dick."

To punctuate his point, he rubs his dick against my ass.

"Travis, you have exactly two seconds to get the fuck away from me…"

"Or what?"

"Or I'll beat your fucking face in with a vodka bottle."

"You know I like it rough," he rumbles. "We were good in the sack because I'd let you do wild shit to me. I bet the angel is too delicate and breakable. I bet she doesn't satisfy you like I did."

Spinning around, I grab his neck and shove him against the cabinets. "Don't fucking talk about her."

"Aww," he taunts. "Poor Ashton Carter. Defending his girlfriend's honor from his ex-fuck. Is her ass as tight as mine?"

"Fuck off," I snap, releasing him.

"Better hope that shit doesn't bruise," Travis sneers. "I wouldn't want to have to tell the dean that his son is an abusive prick. Not only would you be kicked off the swim team, he might be forced to make you leave the school altogether."

"What the hell do you want from me?"

"Well, I wanted you," he snarls. "But then you were too good for me. Now, I'll settle for you to quit the team. Your parents are loaded. You don't need swimming like I do. You make me look bad."

I laugh cruelly. "You do that all by yourself."

Turning away from this dickhead, I set to making our drinks. He creeps up behind me, his hand going to my throat, this time catching me off guard. I struggle to shake him off.

"Just. Quit. The. Team," he barks out.

I'm about to kick off the cabinets and slam him to the floor when he's jerked away. Kurt fucking Cobain has him smashed against the wall, his fingers digging into the prick's jaw.

"Stay the fuck away from my friend," Brayden warns.

"Or you'll kick my ass?" Travis taunts. "Fuck you, Murphy."

Brayden's massive hand tightens, making Travis cry out in pain. "I'll take joy in breaking your jaw. They'll have to wire it shut and you'll never suck cock again."

I walk up to Brayden, skimming my knuckle down his spine to calm him. "The asshole's not worth it. It's what he wants. Probably been waiting for this moment so he can tattle. Just ignore him." I hook my finger through the belt loop of Brayden's jeans and pull him back.

"Keep it up," Brayden warns Travis. "Just keep it up."

Travis rubs at his red face before pulling his cowboy bandana back up over his mouth. He storms away. Good fucking riddance.

"Come on," I tell Brayden. "Let's go dance before our lovers decide to make babies without us."

Brayden laughs. "Those fucking eyebrows, man."

We both chuckle as we make our way back over to Mia and Drew. She has her arms in the air as she dances in front of him, grinning up at him. I grab onto her hips, rubbing my dick against her round ass. Brayden surprises me when his hand fists the back of my shirt as he starts dancing behind me.

"It's fucking hot," Drew complains, pushing his mask up to rest on top of his head so he can swipe at the sweat. His blue eyes burn with lust. "Mia never runs out of energy."

"She's got stamina from all those dumbass Wii games she plays," I tattle.

She pushes her butt against me, which in turn makes me push my ass against Brayden. His hand grabs onto my hip. The laughter fades as we continue to dance, this time all synced up to the music. I try to ignore the fact that a big-ass hard dick is pressed against me. That's what happens with dicks. You rub them on something, they get hard. It's just dancing. I grab Mia's tits to remind myself that I'm hers. My hand slides down to her hip where Drew's already is. Rather than pushing his away, I leave it there, sorta liking the feel of him as he touches my girl.

This is so fucked up.

And hot.

I can't even blame it on the alcohol.

Brayden's fingers brush against a sliver of my skin beneath the hem of my tank. My dick is hard as stone as I grind into Mia. It's hot as hell watching Drew dart his glance from Brayden to me to Mia, as though he can't decide where he wants to look. I understand the feeling. Because Mia feels good to touch and kiss, but I can't help but admire Drew's lips and the way his tight, bloody shirt fits his muscled shoulders that my girl has her hands on.

"If Travis fucks with you again, let me know," Brayden says, his breath hot against my ear. "I'll kill him."

His words are vines, wrapping around me and choking me. I like the tangled feel. The strangulation of them. It does shit to me knowing he's got my back. Right now, literally.

"I can handle Travis," I tell him, turning my head slightly so I can see him.

With our faces inches apart, my entire body heats by a thousand degrees. Fuck him for being so goddamn hot, even dressed as a horrible poser Kurt. His brown eyes are locked on my mouth and he licks his lips. Fuck if that doesn't send a current of want straight to my dick.

I don't want him.

I want Mia.

It's not my fault he makes me stare at him. Actually, we can blame Molly and Tim for making a hot kid. Definitely gonna throw that in his mom's face next time I see her. Then, because he's secretly a sadist, he presses a soft kiss on the side of my neck before pulling away. I try to remember that Mia and I have always been affectionate friends. It's not unheard of to touch and kiss your friends. Mia and I are a testament to that.

But then we started fucking…

His eyes finally lift to my eyebrows and then he starts to laugh. "Those eyebrows, man. They're fucking ridiculous."

I waggle them, sending him into another fit of laughter. "Tell your dick that."

He shakes his head, uncaring that his boner is about to rip out of his jeans. "My dick is not into devil eyebrows." He walks over to Drew, pulling him away from Mia. His lips brush against Drew's before he pulls Drew's mask back in place. "You kids ready to bail? We made an appearance. I could go for some Pancake House right now."

"I'm so in," I state, grabbing Mia and hugging her to me. "What do you say, MiMi? Want to leave this hell and let me lick syrup off your pretty titties?"

She laughs, smacking my arm. "We can leave, but you're not licking syrup off my boobs at Pancake House."

I pull her to me for a dizzying kiss. "Fine. We'll sneak some of those little bottles. I'll lick it off you when we get home."

"I like that idea much better."

# TWELVE

## *Drew*

"**A**ll right, guys, bring it in!" I yell to the team as we finish up our afternoon practice. They all skate over, stopping in front of me. "That was a damn good practice. I have no doubt tomorrow night we're going to destroy Ohio." The team cheers, pumped for the game. We're still undefeated so far this season and everyone is hoping to keep it that way as long as possible. "Next week, we'll be meeting to go over how the game went, but Monday will be the last practice before Thanksgiving break."

Everyone hoots and hollers, ready for the upcoming five-day break. Classes and sports shut down on Wednesday and won't reopen until Monday. Most students go home, but the campus is still open for those who stay. Brayden's parents invited us over for Thanksgiving, but aside from that, I'm looking forward to spending some downtime with Brayden. It's definitely not easy dating a guy in secret. But until I can figure out how to coach his team and date a player on it, we don't have much of a choice.

"What time is that fundraising crap?" Finn asks, snapping me from my thoughts.

"It's not crap," I say, hitting him with a hard stare. "The event supports the athletic program, which means it's helping to support this team. It starts promptly at six and I expect you all to be there on time and dressed nice." They groan in unison, some of them cursing under their breath.

I shoot them all a warning glare, so they know I'm not playing. "And nice, meaning dress pants, dress shirt, and tie. And iron that shit too. Got it?" Curtis made it clear this event is a big deal. It's how the athletic program earns nearly thirty percent of their funding.

The guys all mutter their understanding. "All right, get out of here and I'll see you tomorrow morning for practice… six a.m."

The guys scramble to the locker room, ready to get on with the rest of their afternoon. I head into my office, while they shower and bullshit with each other about who's throwing what party. I never knew college was like one long-ass party. I guess because I went from high school straight to the NHL, I skipped the whole college experience. Sure, the guys partied, but it was different. More sophisticated. I was surrounded by luxury and class. Here, I'm surrounded by immature college students who are chasing ass.

Some days it's hard to remember that I'm the same age as these guys. Like my few years in the NHL forced me to grow up. As I type up an email to the transportation company we'll be using next month for our away game, I think back to the Halloween party a couple weeks ago. I wasn't keen on going at first, scared someone would recognize me, but in the end I was glad I got to go. For a single night I got to be my age… Dancing with Brayden and Ashton and Mia, drinking shitty liquor—just having a good time. It was the only time Brayden and I have been able to be out in public together, and to a certain extent, act like a couple.

"What's going through that sexy head of yours?" a gravelly voice says. I glance up and quickly dart my eyes around to make sure nobody heard him.

"Everyone's gone." He steps into my office and closes the door behind him. With the blinds shut, the only way someone can see inside is through the window of the door.

I look at the time and realize I've been lost in my own head for close to thirty minutes. Brayden comes to my side of the desk and props his ass up against the edge. He's dressed in his usual Ice Hawks sweats and hoodie. He's sporting a matching blue beanie and wet strands of hair are sticking out from having just taken a shower. My eyes ascend until they meet his and he smirks, knowing I was just checking him out.

I don't give a shit, though. He's used to it. I spent years without him and sometimes I just need to look at him to remind myself that I have him back in my life. That he's mine. And I'm his.

"So…" he prompts. "What's going on in your head? You looked like you were lost in thought."

I roll my chair back slightly and fist the front of his hoodie, pulling him over so he's in front of me, standing between my legs. His fingers thread through my messy hair, that's long overdue for a haircut, and I tug on the front of his hoodie, pulling him down to kiss him. The second our mouths connect, it feels like we've entered our own world. Just Brayden and me. No college, no hockey, no hiding. Just us.

"What's wrong?" he asks when he ends the kiss. His brows are furrowed in concern, and I find myself rubbing the crease away on his forehead.

"I was just—" My words are cut off, when there's a quick knock on the door and then it swings open. Brayden jumps back as Curtis walks through the door. My heart pumps extra hard as my entire body drains in nervousness.

Curtis's gaze ping-pongs from me to Brayden and then back to me. "Everything okay in here?" he asks, obviously feeling the tension in the room, not knowing he's the cause of it.

"Yeah," I choke out, then clear my throat. "Bray… den and I were just going over some plays for tomorrow night's game against Ohio."

Curtis nods slowly. "How're you feeling about it?"

"Good," Brayden answers for me. "The chemistry of the team is solid this year. I think we have a chance of making it to the championship and taking the trophy home."

"Good, good," Curtis replies, a small smile finally forming on his lips. "And you're ready to schmooze the donors on Saturday?"

"Yes, sir." Brayden smirks. "I've even agreed to be auctioned off."

Curtis chuckles, as my head swings his way. What the hell is he talking about?

"That's right," Curtis says. "I saw your name on the roster. Can't wait to see which lucky lady wins a date with you." He pats Brayden on the shoulder. "All right, I better get going. Dinner with the wife… Just wanted to touch base, Drew. I'll see you guys Saturday."

With one final look between the two of us, he exits, leaving the door wide-open. I wait a few seconds, until I hear the heavy locker room door slam shut and then I'm up and on Brayden. "You didn't tell me you were being auctioned off."

Brayden groans. "It honestly slipped my mind until the dean walked in."

"Why the hell would you agree to that?" I accuse, hurt as hell that my boyfriend would be willing to auction himself off to the highest bidder. "It's bad enough we can't even go on a fucking date, but now you're going to go on a date with someone else."

"It's not like that," Brayden argues. "It's for a good cause."

"So, I'll donate to the fucking fundraiser." I know I sound like a jealous asshole. "Back out."

Brayden scoffs. "I'm not backing out. I already agreed to it. Blow your money on something else."

"So, what? You're just going to go on this date with whichever woman wins you? Take her to dinner? You don't think whoever spends thousands on you isn't going to be expecting to get her money's worth?"

Brayden snorts out a laugh. "It's for a fundraiser. I'm not being pimped out."

"Might as well be," I argue, grabbing my jacket and throwing it over my shoulders. I had a meeting earlier with the athletic department, so I'm dressed in a fucking monkey suit, complete with a tie and dress shoes.

"It's not like that," Brayden says, following me out of the office. I flip the light switch then lock the door.

"Whatever, Bray," I hiss. "Enjoy your fucking date."

"Stop," he commands, grabbing my bicep and turning me around. He pushes me up against a wall and his body presses against mine. "You don't think I want to show up to that function with you, arm in arm? You don't think I hate that every night we have to hide out in your room, that I can't post a single picture of us on social media? That the only people who can know about us are my parents and Ashton and Mia?"

His brown eyes sear into mine. "I love you, Drew, and I want to shout that shit to the fucking world. Let everyone know that you're mine." He sighs. "But we can't. I have seven months of school left and then we have the rest of our lives to be together in public."

Brayden eyes me for a few seconds, then says, "You don't think I would cheat on you, do you?"

I close my eyes, hating myself for being insecure. I know Brayden is committed to me, but I also know up until a few weeks ago, he was straight, and if the rumors are correct, fucking lots of different women.

"Drew…" he prompts.

I open my eyes and he's staring at me with hurt etched across his features. I hate myself for even considering the notion that he would cheat on me. Brayden loves me. He tells me every chance he gets and shows me every time we're alone.

"No." I shake my head to emphasize my answer.

"I wouldn't." He cages my face between his rough hands.

"I know. I just hate this shit. I'm sorry."

"I do, too." He presses his lips to mine. "But it's not forever."

I nod in agreement. "Yeah… You coming over tonight?" I don't know why I'm even asking. Brayden has spent every night in my bed with me since the day we got together. Most of his clothes are in my drawers and hanging in my closet.

"Actually, I was thinking we should go out."

"You know we can't do that." I take his hand in mine, threading our fingers together while we walk through the locker room.

"How about you go home and change into something more comfortable, and I'll be over in an hour to pick you up."

"Bray… You don't have to do this." I groan. "I was acting stupid."

"No, you weren't." We stop in front of the entrance door and he palms my cheek and kisses me. "Now go home and get ready because I'm taking you out on our first official date."

When I get home, the apartment is empty. I quickly change out of my suit and jump in the shower. As I'm deciding what to wear, Brayden sends me a text, telling me to dress casual. I get dressed in pair of nice jeans and a Henley. I throw on a pair of Chucks and put on my Tag Heuer watch— it was my first purchase when I received my signing bonus. I step into the bathroom, brush my teeth, and then spray some cologne on me. I have no idea what Brayden has planned, or how he plans to pull this off, but I'm excited nonetheless. I can't remember the last time I went on a date.

When there's a knock on my door, I chuckle to myself. Brayden never knocks. He and Mia might not officially live here, but they both come and go like they do.

I swing the door open and find Brayden standing on the other side, looking sexy as hell. He's changed out of his sweats and hoodie and is dressed in a pair of jeans, a long-sleeved Reebok shirt, and matching Reebok tennis shoes.

When I get done eye-fucking him, I notice he's holding a small bottle of whiskey in his hand. "I didn't want to get too girly and shit," he says with a shrug, "so I went with a bottle of liquor instead of flowers." He hands it to me and my heart warms at the sentiment.

"Never understood why women always want flowers," I joke.

"Right?" he deadpans. "Flowers just wilt away and die, and I swear every girl who sniffs them always says they smell beautiful. Have you ever smelled flowers? They're so fragrant they make your eyes water." His nose scrunches up in disgust, and I laugh.

"You ready to go?" he asks, stepping inside and giving me a quick kiss.

"Yeah, let me just put my bottle in the freezer. For later." I wink, and he laughs. It's the best fucking sound in the world.

As Brayden drives through town, we make small talk about the game tomorrow night, the upcoming holiday break, and how he's doing in his classes. I don't know where we're going, and I guess I could ask, but I'd rather wait to see what he has planned.

When we get out of town, my heart drops. I should've known wherever we're going would require us leaving Hawk's Landing. I know Brayden is only doing what he has to do so we can be together in public, but it's still a reminder that in order to do so, we have to drive past the town limits.

An hour later I'm starting to wonder where we're going when he gets off the interstate and I see the sign. "Bray…"

"Yeah?"

"Tell me we're not going where I think we're going." There's no way he would bring us here of all places.

"Where do you think we're going?" he asks, pulling into the parking lot of the Michigan Wolves stadium.

"To watch a Wolves game."

"Yep," he says as he swings into a parking spot.

"This is awesome, but we can't go in there." I might've only played in the NHL for a short time, but I was one of the top paid players. Any smart hockey fan will recognize me.

"Trust me?" he asks, turning the vehicle off.

"Of course I do."

"Then, c'mon." He drops a Wolves ball cap into my hands. "And put that on." He shakes a matching one out and pulls it over his head.

As we walk through the parking lot, memories of when we were younger flash through my mind. Coming to this stadium to watch the Wolves play—my dad play. My dad would offer to get us seats up close, but Brayden's dad insisted we sit in the higher level cheap seats. He said you have to work your way down to appreciate the view up close. So, we would come to the games and, with our binoculars stuck to our faces, commentate the entire game. Some of my best memories with Brayden were up in those shitty seats.

When we get to the ticket window, Brayden tells the woman he purchased tickets online and gives her his confirmation number. She hands him the tickets and we head inside.

"Let's get our food," he says, stopping at the concession stand. "Two boxes of popcorn, an order of nachos, two blue raspberry slushies, and two hot dogs, please," he orders. "Did I get that right?"

My heart damn near explodes in my chest that he remembers exactly what we used to order. Since Tim insisted on buying the seats, my dad insisted on paying for the snacks. Looking back, it's kind of ironic that we probably paid more for the food than the seats.

"Yeah," I choke out. "It's right."

With our food piled high in our arms, we head into the stadium. The game has already started, but it doesn't fucking matter. This is already the best damn date I've ever been on.

"What are our seat numbers?" I ask, glancing at the signs.

"Q 42 and 43," he says with a smirk.

I laugh, fucking elated that he got us the nosebleed seats.

On our way to our seats, he stops a man selling binoculars and buys two pairs. I laugh, remembering how we used to bring our own to every game. Once we find our seats, we drop into them and set our food down in the empty seats next to us. Then, we both bring our binoculars up to our faces so we can see what's going on.

We spend the next couple hours watching Michigan kick New York's ass. We commentate the game, eat the shitty food, and laugh as we reminisce about the past.

"What'd you think?" Brayden asks on our way home. "Good first date?"

I take his hand in mine and bring it up to my lips, placing a kiss to his knuckles. "You set the bar pretty high. Next date I'm going to expect you to top that."

Brayden laughs. "Nah, next date is all yours. That's the great thing about dating a guy. I don't have to be the one to plan it all."

# THIRTEEN

*Brayden*

*A Few Days Later*

"**...T**hink it's wonderful you've donated a date to raise money for the athletic program. I know I'll certainly be bidding."

I stifle a groan as I smile at Mrs. Vanworth. "All for the cause."

"Mother," Sasha says tightly. "Don't embarrass Daddy. I already told you, he's spoken for. I'll be bidding on Brayden and going on the date with him. You just write that check into my account."

Both women titter and plaster on fake smiles.

Jesus Christ.

Where are my friends?

I scan the room, flooded with people dressed in their fancy attire. The tie around my neck feels like a noose, tightening with each second I have to spend rubbing elbows with Sasha and her mother. When I spot Drew, I finally have an excuse to bail.

"Just saw Coach," I say, gently gripping Sasha's shoulder. "If you'll excuse me."

"Make sure you're by the podium around nine," she reminds me. "We'll figure the date out later. I'm thinking a weekend trip to New York City. My treat. The least I can do to help with the fundraiser."

Drew will shit his pants if she tries to take me to New York for the weekend. Not sure how I'll get out of this, but I'll damned sure try.

"We'll discuss it later," I state. "If you win."

Sasha laughs, her boobs jiggling to the point I'm afraid they'll fall right out of her sparkly blue cocktail dress. "Oh, sweetie, I always do."

Fucking wonderful.

I walk away, shaking off the unease that girl puts on me. Along the way to see Drew, I wave and stop to talk to a few teammates. I've been putting forth more of an effort to not be such a closed-off dick. The results are paying off. People don't seem so intimidated by me and are inviting me to shit. I don't necessarily want to go, but I at least don't shut them down.

Just wish Drew could go with me.

Wednesday was awesome. Getting to hang out with him in public. As a couple with no one giving us shit. I'm looking forward to the day we can do more of that.

Drew is in mid-conversation with several older men, Curtis included. He's in his element, looking hot as fuck and charismatic as hell. When he catches my stare, his blue eyes blaze and his dimple pops out.

Goddamn, he's good-looking.

"Damn, Brayden," Ashton's familiar voice rings out from behind me, his knuckle running down my spine. "Lookin' like a snack tonight. Those sorority bitches are gonna be throwing their daddy's checkbooks at you."

I swivel around, smirking, ready to toss a comeback his way, but I'm stunned speechless by the sight of them. Mia and Ashton. Ashton and Mia. Holy shit.

Mia is wearing a skintight, sparkly red gown that dips low in the front, showing off her delectable cleavage, and hugs every curve. Fuck her mom for ever insinuating she wasn't the hottest girl in every room. Her dark hair is twisted up into some fancy do and her makeup is flawless. Talk about looking like a movie star. Mia is a fucking starlet tonight.

And Ashton.

It's a good goddamn thing he doesn't dress like this every night.

Black suit. Silver tie. Dark hair mussed up into a just-fucked way. His hazel eyes scream bad boy, but he cleans up so well. You can tell he grew up with all this fancy shit because he wears it like a second skin, unlike myself, who tugs at the knot of his tie every two minutes.

"You guys…" I mutter. "Damn."

Mia laughs, stepping forward to hug me. "You look great, Bray. It's a good thing you're doing tonight."

"Sasha's mom was going to bid on me, but then Sasha shut that shit down quick," I say with a laugh.

"Just wait until Cougar Wendy gets here," Ashton deadpans. "She'll give her buddy Vanworth a run for her money. Literally. Rich bitches are vicious."

Just what I want. A bidding war between overly botoxed, rich, horny housewives.

I get dragged away from my friends by one of the fathers from the hockey team to congratulate me on all the wins we've had lately. I feel like a rubber ball bouncing between groups of people. But Drew says we need this in order to help raise money, so I do as I'm told. I'm thankful when it's finally time to eat.

Ashton has taken it upon himself to discreetly move name cards at the dramatically decorated tables until the four of us plus his parents are at one table. I'm thankful, because while schmoozing, I'd noticed my name on a card right next to Sasha's.

Drew sits beside Curtis and I take the seat beside him. Ashton sits next to his mom and Mia sits between us. While everyone chats, I lean over, stretching my arm around Mia, and hug her to me.

"You look gorgeous, woman," I say, giving her a peck to her neck. "Reminds me of that night in California."

She turns to look at me, our faces only inches apart, and chews on her bottom lip. "You don't think it's too tight?"

"Hey," I say, brushing my thumb along her bare shoulder. "Your mom's not here. We are. And I can guarantee every person at this table thinks you look amazing."

"Thank you," she murmurs. "You're so sweet."

"You're not just beautiful, but you're smart and funny, too. Your mom only wishes she were half of what you are, which is why she cuts you down. For her, she has to try really fucking hard to stay pretty and relevant. You just are. Effortlessly."

"Mom," Ashton complains, humor in his tone. "The hot hockey player is hitting on my girlfriend."

Wendy cackles and I chuckle. Drew places a possessive hand on my thigh under the table and squeezes. I throw him a wink that brings out his dimple again.

We spend the next hour chatting and enjoying each fancy course. This event is a little too pretentious for my liking, but having my people here helps.

"Oh shit," Ashton mutters over a mouthful of his chocolate dessert, glaring down at his phone. "Excuse me."

He stands up so fast, I'm afraid the chair will topple over. His face is a mixture of fury, confusion, and fear. I snag his wrist before he can walk away.

"You okay?" I demand, meeting his hazel eyes with mine.

"Yeah, I'll be right back," he assures me. He pulls from my grip and stalks out of the room like his ass is on fire.

"What the hell was that about?" I ask Mia.

"Not sure. If he doesn't come back in a few minutes, I'll go check on him."

Drew shoots me a questioning look and I shrug. Before we can figure out what Ashton's deal is, I hear Sasha's friend Courtney's annoying voice on the speaker.

"Thank you all for coming to the annual Atlantic Pointe athletic fund-raising event. Tonight, just by being here, you've raised thirty thousand dollars for the athletic department," Courtney says in a peppy voice, making everyone applaud. "A huge thank you to Mr. Vanworth and all the football alumni for making this annual event happen, each year more successful and attended than the years' previous." She waves a stack of cards in the air. "Now, it's the time where we give back to the community. The auction portion will be raising money for our Atlantic Pointe athletic scholarships. Those less fortunate rely on annual donations to be able to come and play at Atlantic Pointe University, while receiving a high quality education. Last year, we were able to provide full athletic scholarships to twenty students, who otherwise wouldn't have been able to attend Atlantic Pointe, thanks to this event!"

Everyone claps and whistles.

"I know with this year's auction, we'll be able to help many more students attend Atlantic Pointe without being worried about graduating in debt. We appreciate you all for showing up tonight and I am looking forward to tonight's main event." She grins. "I know my daddy has his heart set on the trip to Fiji, and my chapter president is looking forward to a date with a hockey player." Everyone chuckles. "The Delta Delta Delta sorority chapter is passing out auction paddles. Once they've been distributed, we'll get started. Thanks again and let's raise some money!"

Drew squeezes my thigh, drawing my gaze to his. His jaw clenches as he holds his paddle tightly in his fist. I see the intent written all over his face.

He's going to bid on me.

Curtis's hazel eyes bounce back and forth between Drew and me, reminding me why he can't bid on me. I cover his hand with mine and lean toward him. When he does the same, I whisper, "Don't."

An irritated snort can be heard from him, even over Courtney's loud voice over the intercom. She makes her way through all the lower ticket items, until she eventually makes it to the big ones. A bidding war ensues over a skiing trip for two to Aspen, Colorado. Even Drew gets in on that one and I can't help but think it's because he wants to take me with him. He loses to someone, but he's okay with it. Ashton comes back, an unreadable expression on his face.

"Before we get to the highest ticket item—the trip to Fiji—let's get to the fun part of the auction. Dates with the athletes!" Courtney bounces on her toes, making her boobs jiggle in an obscene way that probably has half the old men in here sporting chubs. "Let's get it started tonight with Xavier Paulson, our very own quarterback!"

Everyone cheers because that dude is pretty well-known around here. Football isn't as noteworthy as hockey at this university, but it's the second most popular sport.

"Xavier is twenty-two, enjoys hiking, and adores his momma," Courtney says, pausing to hold her palm to her chest. "Aww. I'm super bummed I can't bid on him. I'm a sucker for a momma's boy." Some of the football players razz Xavier from a table nearby. "Let's get the bid started at five hundred."

The guests of the event seem to enjoy bidding on actual people more than trips and basket items. Xavier has walked up to the stage and is strutting around like a rooster, catcalling the audience to raise more money. The highest bid—one of the Delta Delta Delta chicks—caps out at fifty-eight hundred dollars. I shake my head at the insanity of wanting to spend almost six grand on a date with a douchebag.

"Wow," Courtney says, laughing as she takes to the mic again. "Let's see if our next date can outdo our star football player." She points a long finger my way. Fuck. "Brayden Murphy, stand and let these ladies see what's up for grabs."

Drew's hand lingers on my thigh for a moment before he reluctantly pulls it away. I rise to my feet and half-ass wave to the room.

"Brayden is twenty-one, enjoys ice skating, and has dreams of joining the NHL one day! Who wants to start the bidding for a date with this hunky catch?"

"One thousand," Sasha says predictably, raising her paddle from one table over.

"One thousand," Courtney agrees, "anyone want to—"

"Fifteen hundred," someone calls out across the room.

"Two thousand," Mrs. Vanworth says. When her daughter glares at her, she shrugs. "It's for a good cause."

"Three thousand," Sasha bites back, snapping her paddle in the air.

"Bitches be crazy," Ashton comments. "You'd think by the way they're bidding on you, your dick is magical."

I smirk at him and Mia laughs.

"Four thousand." Another bid across the room.

"Five." This time Sasha.

"Six," Wendy hollers, waving her paddle and making Curtis's face burn bright red.

Ashton cackles. "Get 'em, Cougar Wendy."

"Ten thousand," Sasha states, a smug grin on her face.

I lean forward across Mia to whisper to Ashton. "I hope your mom wins. Sasha has grand ideas we're going to New York for our date."

Ashton looks past me and mutters an, "Oh fuck no."

"Twenty," Ashton says, raising his paddle.

Curtis chokes on his wine and Wendy snorts.

"You can't…" Sasha starts, horrified.

"We've got twenty thousand," Courtney exclaims, "from the dean's son! How's that for support? Can anyone beat that?"

Fucking Ashton.

"Thirty thousand dollars," Sasha states and then whispers something to her father. He nods. "Great, I win."

Ashton's apparently just getting started. I'm fucking entertained as hell, though.

"Fifty grand," Ashton says, standing. "Fifty grand for the hot hockey player. Going once, going twice…"

"Daddy," Sasha whines. He nods again. "Sixty!"

Everyone is cheering and laughing.

"A hundred grand," Ashton states, as though he's bored. "I could go all night."

Wendy grins. "He has it. Of course he does."

Spoiled rich shit.

"Daddy," Sasha begs. This time, he shakes his head.

"Date with a hockey player! Sold to the dean's son for a hundred thousand dollars! This is fantastic! Imagine how this will help our future athletes!" Courtney exclaims, ignoring the furious glare of her friend.

Ashton sits back in his seat as the auction moves to other items, none of which earned more money than my date. Drew and Mia seem relieved that Sasha didn't win. Wendy is getting drunk off wine and giggling at her son's antics. Curtis is annoyed, but keeps his lips pursed from saying anything.

Ashton reaches over, grabbing my tie and pulling me across Mia so he can grin at me. "For that kind of money, I expect a happy ending after that date." He waggles his brows at me, earning a groan from both Curtis and Drew.

Mia smacks him. "Ashton!"

"For that kind of money," I tease, "I'll give you a baby and a ring too."

This time, Mia smacks me.

# FOURTEEN

*Ashton*

"**A**shton!" Mia cries out, fisting the blankets on my bed as I plow into her from behind. "Holy fuuuuck!"

I smack her ass. "Quiet, woman. We have guests."

Her cunt clenches, making me groan. Goddamn this woman makes me crazy. I drive into her hard and relentless. Her cute little ass turns red from my handprint.

"Oh God!" she cries out, her body trembling with her sudden orgasm.

The way her body squeezes mine has me tipping over the edge. I yank out of her, rip the condom off, and then rub my bare dick along her ass crack, marking her skin with my seed. My veiny dick is red from fucking her and I crave to see it coated with her arousal. It looks good, though, sliding through the mess I've made on her. Gripping my cock, I tease at her asshole.

"I want in here one day, baby. You going to let me?"

She pushes back. "Does it hurt?"

"Fuck yeah, it hurts," I admit. "But once you get used to it, it's fucking insane."

I pull back, my dick flinging cum all over. Running my fingers through my release that's running between her pussy lips, I rub it against her clit until she's whimpering again. I bring her close to another orgasm, shoving my fingers inside her slick pussy, finding her G-spot, and making her cry out when I push on it just right. Her legs shake, but I'm not done with her. I slide my fingers out and tease her back entrance. She gasps when I breach the hole with the tip of my finger.

"Burns, yeah?"

"Yeah."

"Relax, baby."

"Ow."

"It's because you're so fucking tight." I knead her ass with my other hand as I ease my finger up to the knuckle inside her. "The more I play with your hole, the easier it'll get. Lube it up and practice later. Think of me while I'm on my date."

She groans and I pull my finger out.

"What?" I ask, feigning confusion.

"You. I can't believe you're actually going through with it." She shakes her head as she rises on shaky legs and starts for the shower.

"I won fair and square," I tease back, pinching her ass.

She starts the shower and once the steam billows from the water, we both step inside. I wash her like the queen she is and then she hugs me. Her mood has shifted and it makes my nerves tighten and spark.

"I'm just doing it to fuck with Sasha," I remind her. "If you don't want me to go, I won't. I'll just lie to Sasha and tell her it was amazing. I only bid on him to save him from that witch since Drew couldn't."

Her head tilts up. "I know. I'm just teasing. I want you to go have fun. Besides, Drew and I are going to binge watch *Riverdale*."

"I bet he's thrilled," I deadpan.

She smacks my chest. "He secretly likes it too." Her lips find mine.

"Brayden's your friend now. Things aren't like they were before. He's in love with Drew. I know it's just a date between friends."

Relief floods through me. "Good girl."

"Just don't kiss his devastatingly handsome mouth," she teases.

"Everywhere else is game, though?" I throw back. "His dick?"

"Asshole."

"His asshole?!" I gasp as though I'm scandalized. "You dirty girl."

"No, asshole," she groans. "You're an asshole."

"Your asshole," I remind her. "Love you, MiMi. Always."

"Same, Ashy C. Love you always."

"For a hundred grand, I expected roses," Brayden teases as we drive through town. "A teddy bear? Chocolate? Chivalry is dead. Dude, you didn't even open my door."

"You're more of a 'smack my ass and call me pretty' kind of guy," I tell him with a smirk. "You don't need me to romance you."

We both chuckle as I park a few blocks from the old-fashioned movie theater on Main Street since there's nowhere to park. It's not as up to date as the new theater up the road, but I prefer this one as I remember going to it a lot as a child.

"The look on your boyfriend's face was priceless when I asked if you brought enough condoms for our date," I say as I climb out. "Is it just me or is he hotter when he's mad?"

Brayden laughs, shaking his head. "It's not just you. A pissed off Drew is hot as fuck."

Even though it's snowing, the roads have been cleared. The sidewalks are another story. We slip and slide as we walk the few blocks until we make it to the outdoor ticket booth. I elbow Brayden out of the way when he tries to pull his wallet out, making him laugh. The cashier gives us a strange look but then hands us two tickets to the action flick we chose. Brayden is the gentlemanly one of us two and holds the door open for me. I make a beeline over to the concession stand.

"M&Ms, Whoppers, Skittles, a cherry Icee, a large popcorn with lots of butter," I say to the cashier. "Oh! Gummy bears. And some of those chocolate covered raisins." I run my knuckles down Brayden's spine. "And whatever he wants."

"An Icee and Twizzlers."

"Are you on a diet?" I ask, my brow lifted as I toss some bills down on the counter to pay.

He snorts. "Nah, just saving some snacks for the rest of the theater go-ers. Jesus, man. How do you look like that?" He waves a hand at me. "And eat like that?"

We both look at my mountain of snacks.

"I'm hungry," I complain. "MiMi depleted me of my energy."

As we collect our items, he chuckles. "It sounded like the other way around. She's so loud. I was pretty sure Drew was about to rub one out to the sound of you two earlier."

The thought of Drew jacking off on the couch is one I don't need to think about.

"So you two creeps just listened to us fuck? You dirty little shits," I say, cracking up laughing. "Don't worry. We've heard you two fucking like bunnies. It's kinda hot."

Brayden smiles, but it doesn't reach his eyes. He opens his mouth like he might say something, then shuts it. I'm curious, but don't press.

We make our way into the theater. I'm surprised to see that though they've kept the original architecture and style of the old theater, they've recently remodeled the seats to those cool ones the new theater has. I follow Brayden to the very middle at the very top and plop down beside him. As we wait for the movie to start, I inhale half my snacks.

It'd be way more fun if Mia and Drew were here.

Kinda lonely without them.

"What do you think they're up to?" Brayden asks, clearly on the same wavelength as me.

"Your boyfriend is probably cuddling my girl as we speak," I say with a laugh. "MiMi's a cuddler. It's not his fault."

"Yeah," Brayden agrees.

My heart does a twist inside my chest as I remember he's been with her in intimate ways and knows all about her cuddling.

"Sasha was so pissed," I say gleefully. "Nothing satisfies me more than the look on her face when her daddy told her no."

"I still can't believe you bid so much money," Brayden groans.

"It was either me or my mom. Trust me, you do not want to go on a date with Cougar Wendy. I'm still in therapy from the last time she went all horny housewife." My words are said in jest, but they cut with a bitter edge.

"How's therapy going?"

When Mia wasn't talking to me, I casually mentioned to Bray when he was over that I needed to see my therapist. Had he not encouraged me to go, I might not have. And, believe it or not, I think it helped me wrangle my brain some so I could get Mia back. I guess I owe the guy.

"We regularly rehash my childhood, my insecurities and fears, and my strained relationship with my parents. It's a delight."

He reaches over and squeezes my thigh. "Don't be like that."

"Like what?"

"Playing off something serious. I know it sucks to talk through that shit, but you're better for it, you know?"

His hand lingers on my thigh and my traitorous heart clenches painfully in my chest. It feels like a betrayal to MiMi because I like his hand there.

Friends can touch.

There's nothing sexual about my friend comforting me.

*Then why are you sporting a boner, Ashton?*

I rest my bucket of popcorn on my stupid dick and clear my throat. "Your mom excited to see me again?" I ask, turning to waggle my brows at him.

He chuckles, finally removing his hand to dig into the bucket for popcorn, which oddly enough does nothing to calm the state of my dick. "She's thrilled. Are you sure your parents aren't going to miss you for

Thanksgiving? I mean, Mia's parents are dicks and Drew's are gone, but you actually do have family."

"My parents don't do Thanksgiving," I say with a grumble. "Not in the traditional sense. We usually eat Cornish hens at some French restaurant my mom loves, meeting up with my grandparents. Pops interrogates Dad about his accomplishments, while Dad desperately tries to impress him. Mom and Grams get fucked up on wine while I count the minutes until I can leave."

"No pecan pie?"

"Fuck no."

"What a waste. You're in for a treat then. Mom goes all out."

I laugh. "Sweet Molly knows the way to my heart. Food."

"Are you sure it's cool if Drew and I tag along next weekend? I know it's your parents' cabin and all, but—"

"Dude," I cut him off. "The cabin is massive. Plenty of room. Plus, since we all cook for shit, the lodge up the hill from it offers five-star gourmet meals around the clock. The bar is pretty sweet, but I only know that because I go there to escape my parents. I don't want to escape you guys. The stocked bar in the cabin will be plenty."

I'm looking forward to the getaway weekend. When Mia mentioned Drew bid on the ski weekend at the auction, I was quick to suggest we use my parents' place. The ski resort our cabin is on is one of the top-rated resorts in the country. And free. Well, to us it's free. My parents paid a fuckton for that cabin—one they only go to once a year for their anniversary in January.

My phone buzzes and anxiety trickles through me. I dread the thought of it being another message like the one I got last night. A video from an unknown number.

Fucking Travis.

It's one thing to fuck with me, but that video was something that fucked with the ones I care about. He'd obviously recorded the four of us dancing at the Halloween party. The dancing was fucking hot, but what disturbed me was when Drew lifted his mask. Bray walked over to him and kissed him. It all happened so quickly, but each incriminating second was recorded. The text that followed after said, "Does your daddy know his hockey coach is a very naughty boy?"

It pissed me off so bad.

I sent a shit-ton of threatening texts back to Travis. I told him to stay the fuck away from my friends. He never responded back. As the movie starts, I pull my phone out to check the text. I'm thankful it's just a text from Mia. Sure enough, she's cuddled up with Drew and they took a smiling selfie. Fucking cute.

I'll be damned if I let Travis hurt Drew. Drew deserves to have friends and a fucking boyfriend. Travis threatening to tattle on him pisses me off.

"Our turn," I murmur to Bray. I hold my phone up. "Pretend you're sucking my dick."

He laughs. "Nice try."

We settle for just cheesing for the camera and then I send the pic. I shove the phone away, willing my nerves to settle. My leg bounces up and down. This time, when Brayden settles his palm on my thigh to calm me, I relax.

"You okay?" he asks, his breath hot and close to my ear.

All I can do is nod.

"Good." He presses a kiss to my neck and then settles back in his seat.

Stupid, hot, affectionate fucker.

I somehow manage to make it through the entire movie without losing my mind. By the time we're stepping outside, the assault of the icy wind has all the heat from his subtle, innocent touches pushed away. It's cold as fuck outside. I wish I'd worn my big coat and not just my leather jacket. I shove my hands in my pockets and complain the whole way back to my car.

As soon as we reach it, I screech to a halt. "What the fuck?"

"Someone slashed your tires," Brayden growls, his tone dripping with fury. "Who the fuck would do that?"

I grit my teeth as I squat to inspect the damage. "Fucking Travis."

"I'm going to kill him," Brayden seethes. "I hate that guy. Call your dad. Get that asshole kicked out of school!"

And risk Travis showing that video to him?

Fuck no.

"It's fine. It's just tires," I grumble.

"He vandalized your car, Ashton," he snaps. "He's already framed you for drug possession, tried to poison you with bleach, and put his fucking hands on you! I'll be damned if I let him hurt you anymore!"

I grab his coat, jerking him to me. "I can handle it."

His brown eyes flash with murderous intent. "Apparently not because you let this piece of shit walk all over you!"

I shove him away from me. "You don't understand."

"Then make me," he bellows.

Ignoring him, I lean my ass against the car and text Mia to let her know we need them to pick us up. I don't give her the details so she won't worry. Just a vague "car trouble" is all I wrote. I'm just pocketing my phone when snow slams into my chest.

"You can't ignore me," Brayden says, bending to ball up more snow.

He launches another snowball at me, nailing me in the forehead. Oh, it's on now, buddy. I start chucking snowballs at him as fast as I can make them. We go from pissed off to laughing as we chase each other between cars. I get stuck in a snow drift up against a storefront, slowing me down enough that Brayden's able to tackle me. We roll around on the snow until the brute fucker has me pinned. Our breathing is heavy and we're both grinning.

Reminders of that night in the locker room filter through my mind. The fight. The taunt. The kiss.

My self-destructive ass kissed him and sent my world exploding around me. I won't make that mistake again. But… something feels different about our proximity now. There's no anger or jealousy or confusion. Just two friends. Enjoying each other. My heart races in my chest, slowing to a stop when he pulls his beanie off his head.

"You're cold," he murmurs, shoving it down over my head. His eyes grow sad, making my chest tighten in response.

It's not the first time I've seen him do this.

"What's up with the beanies?" I ask, frowning at him.

His eyes slam closed. "You just looked cold."

"Brayden," I rumble. "Talk to me."

He lets out a heavy sigh before meeting my stare. "I don't know. I guess I just think that since I couldn't save him, I could save others. Maybe if he'd been dressed warmer…" He trails off, his eyes watering. "Maybe he would have lived."

When we were at Brayden's for dinner, where I met his parents, his dad let on that they'd lost their son when he was nine. Sad as fuck. I didn't realize how badly it eats up Brayden until now.

"You can't save everyone," I murmur.

"I should have saved him." He falls against me, his face against my neck. "I should have saved him."

I can't help but hug him because he feels like he's breaking apart. Maybe I can hold him together.

"You were probably a kid yourself, right?" I say, patting his back.

"It's no excuse."

"Despite what Drew calls you in bed, you're not God," I say, thankful when he chuckles.

His lips press to my neck. It's then I realize that his little kisses aren't sexual. They're thank-you kisses. I don't think he even realizes he does it.

I can't wait to jabber about what this means to my therapist.

"We leave them alone for two hours and they decide to have sex in the snow," Mia says, a teasing lilt to her voice.

Brayden lifts up and wipes at his eye with the palm of his hand. Drew zeroes in on the fact he's upset and tugs him to his feet. I climb to mine, dusting off the snow, and then hug Mia.

"Hey, girlfriend," I say, kissing the top of her head.

"Hey, boyfriend. Your car won't start?"

Brayden's sad moment melts away to fury once more. "Travis slashed his tires."

"He what?" Drew snarls, stomping over to my car. "What the fuck, Ashton?"

"It's fine," I snap back. "I'll call a tow truck and have tires put back on before the end of the week."

"It's not fine," Drew spits out. "This is so fucked-up!"

"Let it go," I warn.

He pulls out his phone and starts dialing. "Non-emergency. Thank you."

I grit my teeth, shooting Drew daggers with my eyes, but he ignores me.

"I'd like to report a vandalism," Drew says and then rattles off the address.

As soon as he hangs up, I flip him off. "I said I handled it, Daddy."

"Pretending it didn't happen isn't handling it," he throws back. "You better tell them it was Travis or I will."

All I can think about is the goddamn video.

Drew definitely doesn't need to be the one to tell them.

"Fine," I grit out. "I'll tell them I think it might be him. Happy?"

He nods, some of the tension melting away. "How did the date go?"

"It was fine until you two interrupted the happy ending." I smack Mia's ass. "Take us for ice cream after the cops show up, Daddy Drew. You owe us."

He flips me off.

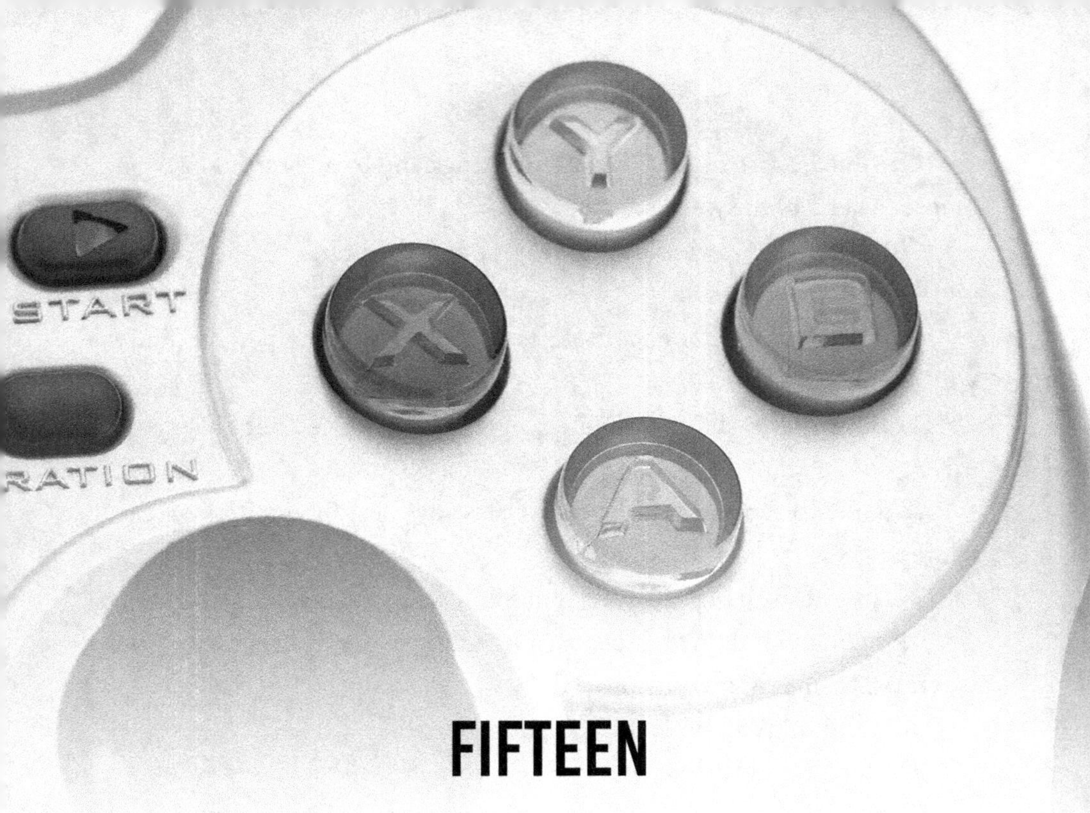

# FIFTEEN

*Mia*

"**H**oly shit," Brayden says, staring up at the front of Ashton's family's cabin. "If this is your vacation house, I'm afraid to see what your home looks like."

The authentic, three-story, log cabin with forest green shutters is situated on what appears to be several acres of land and looks like it's part of a movie set for a Christmas movie.

"It's as pretentious as this one," Ashton says, grabbing my luggage and his own out of the back of the SUV he rented since his car is out of commission. "This was my mom's anniversary present to my dad," he adds. "Nothing says 'Happy Anniversary, sorry for fucking my twenty-year-old trainer' like a vacation house at his favorite ski resort."

The bitterness dripping in his words has me reaching over and squeezing his bicep. Ashton's way of handling pain is by being sarcastic, but I know him well enough to know that he uses his smart-ass comments to push down the hurt and resentment he feels toward the way his parents behave. The funny thing is, they both love him, but he can't see past their imperfections to understand that.

Once we're inside, I glance around in awe. I've lived a life of luxury. My parents have a sky-rise condo in New York, a beach house in The Hamptons, and my childhood home was on a documentary about the most expensive homes of the rich and famous, but this cabin… Wow! I knew Ashton came from old money, but I had no idea just how wealthy he is. It makes my parents' beach house look like a shack. The walls are all real wood, the ceilings vaulted. I expected the inside to be gaudy, similarly to the way Wendy dresses, but it's actually beautiful. With rustic wood furniture, a massive floor-to-ceiling double-sided fireplace, and cozy looking plush, leather couches, it makes me want to cuddle up with Ashton by the fireplace and drink hot chocolate.

"Mia and I get the master bedroom," Ashton says. "There are eight other rooms, pick whichever one you guys want, but you might want to pick a different floor."

He smirks devilishly and I know something sexual is about to come from his mouth. I've given up on trying to stop him, and instead just embrace the fact my boyfriend wants me all the damn time and isn't afraid to show it. "You've heard how loud my girl is, and this weekend I plan to stay buried inside her as much as possible…" He pauses, tilting his head slightly in mock thought. "On second thought, feel free to room next to us. I know how much you like listening." He winks at Brayden, who groans, his face and neck slightly turning pink, and I stifle my laugh, not wanting to encourage Ashton.

"Let's go, MiMi. I only have three days to fuck you without the neighbors complaining." I don't remind him I *am* one of the neighbors, and I'm certainly not complaining. Ashton rolls our luggage down the expansive hallway and into the master bedroom. I groan, remembering the other night when he was deep inside me, making me come so hard, I was seeing stars behind my lids, and the neighbors started banging on the wall. Of course, that only made Ashton even more determined to make me scream, and then the next morning Curtis came over and told Ashton he needs to keep it down because he can't have his tenants complaining. He didn't mention why they were complaining, but he could barely look me in the eyes.

When we step inside, there's a huge four-poster king-sized bed in the center of the room. An armoire in the corner and a dresser and mirror facing the bed. It's all very rustic-chic and cozy.

"Don't worry," Ashton says, dropping the luggage and pulling me into his arms. "My parents haven't fucked in years, so the bed hasn't been jizzed on, but just in case, I had all the sheets changed and the place cleaned before we got here."

I laugh, threading my fingers through his hair and tugging him toward me for a quick kiss, before I pull back. "As much as I can't wait to break the bed in, I want to explore."

Ashton's face curls into a wide grin. "That's what I'm talking about. You want to start with the shower or on the balcony first. It's a little cold outside, but I bet I could keep you warm." He waggles his eyebrows.

"I meant explore the main resort. I looked it up on the way here and it's so adorable. They have these cute fireplaces and—"

Ashton's shakes his head. "There are seven here," he says, cutting me off. "And I can fuck you in front of each one."

"And they serve hot chocolate with marshmallows," I add, knowing he can't resist sweets. "Please." I hit him with my puppy dog eyes I've learned he can't resist.

"Fine," he says with a sigh. "But when we get back here, I'm fucking you on that balcony."

"Yay!" I clap then throw my arms around him. "Let's go drag Brayden and Drew along."

We go in search of the boys. We don't find them on the first floor, but when we get to the second floor, we come across a closed door, whereas all the other doors are open.

Ashton, like his typical self, barges in without knocking. "Let's go, lover boys. MiMi wants to have hot chocolate by the fireplace at the resort, and she wants you to go."

I peek around him and find Brayden and Drew lying on the queen-sized bed, both with their clothes still on, wrapped up in each other. They look up at the same time and their lips are red and puffy from kissing.

"We're a little busy." Brayden pouts like a little baby.

I almost feel bad for disrupting them, but they'll have plenty of alone time. I want to have some fun while we're here, and if I don't drag them out, they'll stay holed up in this house. Drew mentioned the other night when we were hanging out that it's been hard for them not being able to go in public together, but here, hours away from Hawk's Landing, they can go out and be together without having to hide.

"Get busy later," Ashton volleys. "If I have to be cockblocked, so do you. Let's go."

"Please," I say. "It'll be fun."

"Don't give us that look." Drew points his finger at me. "You know we can't say no to that look."

I bat my lashes playfully and they both groan but roll off the bed. "Thank you!" I give them each a hug, ignoring the hard bulge they're each sporting.

Since the cabin is a few miles from the main resort and it's snowing outside, we hop back into the SUV and drive over. The resort is even cuter than in the pictures on the website. Twinkling white lights are intricately strewn across the outside beams, and several wreaths are hanging in the center of each of the windows.

We step inside, shaking off the flutters of snow that landed on us during our walk from the vehicle to the resort, and I take a look around. It's like a Hallmark Christmas movie. At the entrance is a massive Christmas tree, decorated with colorful lights and large ornaments. I stop and take the place in. Families are sitting together, talking and laughing, enjoying the holiday. Couples are cuddled up by the fireplaces, drinking hot chocolate.

Tears of contentment prick my eyes at the beautiful sight in front of me. When I was younger I would watch all those Christmas movies and pretend it was my family in those movies, laughing and drinking hot chocolate. And when I got older and knew it would never happen, I would then hope that one day I'd have a family of my own so I could make those movies my reality.

"Mia, what's wrong?" Brayden asks, noticing that my eyes are glassy.

"Nothing," I tell him truthfully, because for once everything is perfect. "It's just… it looks like what a home is supposed to look like. What I always imagined…" I let my words trail off, but Brayden gets what I mean without me having to finish my thought. He saw the home I grew up in.

He pulls me into his side and kisses my temple. "You don't need them."

"That's right," Drew adds. "You have us."

"Damn right, she has us," Ashton says, taking my hand in his. He lowers his mouth to my ear. "You'll always have me, MiMi."

Their words plug each of the holes in my heart that my parents have made over the years. I never realized how much I was craving love and affection. Earlier today, when we spent Thanksgiving with Brayden's parents, was the first holiday I actually felt like I was part of a real family. Molly and I cooked and baked all day while the guys watched football. Then we sat together and ate, going around the table and telling everyone what we were thankful for. I'd seen scenes like that in movies, but never in real life, and it made me despise my mom that much more. Holidays for our family were spent on a movie set with catered food brought in, or if we were home, she'd have the chef make us some healthy meal. We would spend maybe ten minutes together at most before she and my dad would retreat back to their rooms. But today… today it felt like I was part of a real family.

After Ashton orders all of us Irish Bailey's hot chocolates, we find a cozy little corner with two couches in front of a fireplace and sit. Ashton hands me my drink and plops down next to me, while Bray and Drew take the couch diagonal from us. The cup is warm to the touch and feels good against my cold hands, and even better as it slides down my throat, instantly warming my insides.

"This is delicious." I take another sip. "So, what's on the agenda for tomorrow?" I curl my legs over Ashton's and he rubs his hand up and down my jean-clad thigh.

"Skiing for sure," Drew says.

"Hell yeah," Brayden agrees. "We need to hit the slopes first thing in the morning."

"Can you ski?" I ask Ashton when he doesn't say anything.

He scoffs. "I can do everything."

"Will you teach me how to?"

He side-eyes me. "I'd rather teach you something else… in bed, where it's warm and there isn't a chance of avalanches."

Brayden barks out a laugh. "In other words, you suck at skiing."

Drew snorts. "Finally, something Ashton isn't good at."

"Oh, I'm good," Ashton retorts. "Mom and Dad practically used that bunny camp as a babysitter every winter. I'll whip both your asses tomorrow morning, but then I'm spending the rest of the day with Mia warming me up."

"But I want to learn," I tell Ashton, who groans, already knowing he's going to give in.

"Fine, but you owe me," he murmurs, nipping at the corner of my jaw. "And I'm going to collect tonight."

"You're making me pay before you teach me?" I giggle as he nuzzles his face into my neck. "That hardly seems fair."

"I already told you I'm a spoiled brat, woman. Nothing is fair when it comes to me."

After we finish our drinks, we head back to the cabin, but not before I make the guys take pictures with me in front of the pretty Christmas tree. Since Ashton turned the heat on before we left, it's toasty warm when we get back. I kick off my boots and shrug out of my jacket, unraveling my scarf from around my neck.

"Can you give us a tour?" I ask Ashton, glancing around. So far, I've only seen the master bedroom.

"Are you punishing me for something?" he deadpans.

"What?" I say with a laugh.

"My mom always punished my dad by refusing him sex when he fucked up. All I want is to get between your legs and you're not letting me." He nips at my lips, grinning. "I mean, I'm into punishment, but I prefer the kinky kind, not the psychologically torturous ones."

"Oh my God. You're so dramatic." I encircle my arms around his neck. "It's just a little tour. I promise as soon as we're done, you can fuck me."

With Drew, Brayden, and me following him, he shows us all the different rooms: a huge state of the art gym, an indoor theater that rivals the actual ones, an indoor sauna, a massive kitchen, and several others.

"And this is the backyard," he says, opening a door that leads outside. I step out and my feet are instantly warmed.

When I glance down in confusion, Ashton laughs. "The deck is heated."

"Nice." I look up and find the coolest looking hot tub I've ever seen on the back porch. It's made of some sort of rock, making it look like a natural spring. There are several lounge chairs surrounding it, and when Ashton flicks a switch, it lights up turquoise. Tiny bubbles instantly start to form, and you can see the heat rising up in the frigid air.

"We should all go in!" Then I remember something… "Shoot, I didn't bring a swimsuit." I pout at Ashton. "You didn't tell me there was a hot tub here. Maybe we can find one somewhere—"

Before I can finish my sentence, I'm being lifted, caveman style, over Ashton's shoulder. He stalks us over to the hot tub and then drops me in, jeans and all.

"What the hell!" I shriek, thankful the water's warm.

Ashton is already removing his shirt and unzipping his pants while Brayden and Drew laugh at his antics.

"What are you laughing at?" I bark playfully at them. "Get in here!" I splash water at them and they only laugh harder. Then, since my shirt is sticking to me, I peel it off my body and throw it to the side, leaving me in my lacy bra and jeans.

Ashton steps into the water in only his boxers and wades over to me. His hazel eyes seem to glow in the turquoise reflection as he cuts through the water toward me like an alligator after his prey. I yelp when his arm circles around my waist while his other hand unbuttons my jeans.

"This okay, Mia?" he asks, his voice low enough so only I can hear.

"Yes. It's just Brayden and Drew."

His grin is wicked. "Then let's get you out of those jeans."

We laugh as he wrestles me out of my clothes that have stuck to my skin. When he finally flings them over and they splat on the deck, he pulls my back to his chest and kisses my temple.

"I think we scared them away," I say, motioning for the empty deck.

"Nah, those two can't pass up hot tub time with the hotties. Give them a second to get their dicks in order."

A few minutes later, two hockey gods dressed in black boxer briefs, carrying bottles of liquor, join us in the hot tub. Ashton reaches over and mashes a button that has bubbles rolling all over so it's too hard to see beneath the surface.

Drew hands us an unopened, icy cold bottle of vodka. I take it from him and unscrew the lid. It's cold but burns like fire all the way down my throat. I choke a little before passing it to Ashton.

"I'm going to fuck you in this hot tub." Ashton gulps the vodka before passing it back to me. "What do you think about that?"

"Sounds… *hot.*"

Brayden laughs. "Corny, Mia. Real cheesy."

I stick my tongue out at him, earning a chuckle from Drew.

"Children," Drew says, "behave."

"Sorry, MiMi," Ashton says, grabbing my boob. "Didn't mean to poke you with my dick. You know how I get when Drew goes all daddy on us."

Drew flips him off before slinging his arm over Brayden's shoulders, pulling him close. They're so cute together.

The next few drinks of the vodka go down smoother. My body feels weightless. One glance at Ashton tells me he's feeling pretty good himself.

"Oops," Ashton says a second before my bra loosens. "It fell off."

I giggle as he wrangles it off my body. He tosses it at Brayden and Drew, who've started to devour each other. It smacks them right in their heads.

Then it's on.

I scream when the boys attack, trying to get to Ashton, but he uses me like a human shield. I latch onto Brayden as Drew attempts to playfully drown Ashton. Brayden pulls me into his lap so we can watch them. His thumb lazily strokes my stomach, making me shiver.

"You're feeling good, pretty girl, mmm?" Bray asks, pecking the side of my neck.

"So good."

Bray laughs. "Me too. We needed a vacation."

Drew has Ashton trapped in a headlock, laughing his ass off while my boyfriend tries to escape.

"Let him go," I say, giggling. "You're hurting him."

Drew tugs at Ashton's nipple ring. "Ashton likes a little pain."

Red-faced from exertion and in a headlock, Ashton still manages to shrug.

"That thing you're poking me with is painful," Ashton chokes out. "I'll tough it out like a good boy, though, Daddy."

This sends them into another splashing chaotic moment where Drew tries to drown him while Brayden and I crack up laughing. Ashton eventually escapes and pounces on me, his hands moving my thighs to settle himself between them in front of me, poised for a kiss. It's strange to kiss him as I sit on Brayden with my legs spread, but I can't deny it's also hot.

Ashton kisses me hard, devouring me like he needs me to survive. I whimper when his hand pushes my underwear aside and his fingers slide inside me.

"My dick is huge, but you stay so tight for me, MiMi. You're a miracle."

I laugh, even as he bites my lip. Drew has moved to sit beside Brayden, both of them quiet as Ashton kisses me. He breaks the kiss and pulls away, bouncing his stare between each of us. His fingers curl up inside me, hitting me in just the right spot to have me gripping Brayden's thighs and arching my breasts out of the water.

"She likes that," Ashton says. "She also likes putting on a show. You like showing off your pretty tits, don't you?"

I shudder, thrumming with pleasure. Brayden's dick is hard as stone pressed against my ass. When Ashton rubs my G-spot again, I grind against Brayden, causing him to hiss. His hand flies out to grab Drew's neck and he pulls him in for a kiss. I can't help but steal a glance of them kissing since they're so close. Their tongues are starved as they duel with one another. It's hot. So hot.

Ashton pulls his fingers out of me and then rips my underwear like it's nothing. He fumbles with his boxers and then his hard cock is at my entrance.

This is wrong, right?

Doing this in front of the guys?

On them?

Ashton drives his hips up, his hazel eyes searing into me. I moan as he fucks me hard. Bray's arm wraps around me, as to keep me locked in place for his friend. The thought sends thrills of excitement pulsating through me.

Ashton's mouth is back on mine as he finds my clit. I'm dizzied with pleasure, overcome by the heat and buzzing from the liquor. There's a hand on my breast and I'm not sure it's Ashton's. I don't worry about it because it feels good, lazily stroking my nipple. When someone playfully nips my shoulder, I tear my mouth from Ashton's kiss to lock eyes with Drew's intense blue ones.

I must suck in a sharp breath because Ashton freezes.

Several silent beats fill the night.

And then Ashton is standing with me in his arms, carrying me away from the hot tub, through the cold, snowy night, and into the sanctuary of the master bedroom.

He fucks me like a madman, but something's off.

He's upset.

I hope I didn't fuck this up.

# SIXTEEN

## Drew

The minute the back door slams shut, Ashton and Mia disappearing inside, Brayden's mouth is back on mine. Our tongues thrash against each other. We don't stop to discuss what just happened. It's become the norm with us. Focus on the now, what's directly in front of us, and ignore the reality around us. I have no doubt this mindset is going to fuck us in the end, but for now, ignorance is bliss and all that shit.

As we kiss, I climb backward out of the warm water and onto the heated deck. We should probably take this to our room, but neither of us seems to be able to wait that long. We're both too worked up, too turned on. Too in the moment.

Brayden yanks my boxers down my thighs and throws them to the side, the sound of the wet material landing somewhere in the distance. He pushes me onto my back and the warmth of the ground heats my flesh. His wild brown eyes, filled with lust, meet mine as he removes his own, his rock-hard dick springing free. He's a man on a mission as he spreads my thighs and grips my ass, slightly lifting my lower half up. For a split second, I think he's going to fuck me, and my dick swells at the thought of him ramming his dick into my ass. Filling me with his cum. *The way Ashton rammed his dick into Mia's pussy a few minutes ago.* But Brayden doesn't fill my ass. Instead, he dips his face down between my legs and his wet tongue lands on the sensitive area between my ass and ballsac. He licks me there for several seconds and then takes one of my balls into his warm, wet mouth.

"Fuck," I grunt, feeling like I'm about to come. "Bray..."

"I've got you," he murmurs, taking my other ball into his mouth. His tongue licks and sucks, and I close my eyes, relishing in how good his mouth feels on me. He releases me and then his hand is stroking my dick, root to tip, up and down slowly, his tongue swirling around the swollen head. If he doesn't stop soon, I have no doubt I'm going to erupt in his mouth.

"Come here," I mutter, not wanting this to end yet. I sit up and grip the back of his neck so I can drag him up my body. Our dicks align as our mouths connect. It doesn't matter how many times I kiss him, touch him, feel him, it's never enough. I always want more. Call me selfish, but I just can't get enough of him.

"I want to fuck you so badly," he murmurs against my lips, as he reaches between us and fists our cocks. I kiss his mouth, suck on his neck, I lick each of his nipples as he rubs our dicks together, the mixture of water and precum creating the perfect friction to set us both off.

As we come together, our hot seed smearing across both our stomachs, I kiss him hard, not wanting our connection to end. Never wanting it to end.

When our dicks go soft, and we're completely spent, Brayden drops his head and kisses the side of my neck. Then his lips meet mine one more time, his tongue invading my mouth in the most delicious way before he retreats, falling back into the hot tub and pulling me along with him.

"I'm not sure Ashton would appreciate us cleaning our cum off in his hot tub," I joke, caging Brayden against the wall of the hot tub.

Brayden snorts. "On the contrary, he'd probably welcome it."

We both laugh, but it's forced because we know what we're doing—living in denial, ignoring the reality of our situation a little longer. The problem is, denying the truth doesn't change the facts, and the fact is… what happened tonight, while insignificant, changed everything.

"Fuck, my head is pounding," Brayden complains from somewhere in the room, as he rifles through the luggage. I'm too hungover to even respond, so I don't. After we got done in the hot tub last night, we came up here and spent the next few hours drinking and fucking around.

"Hey, are any of these pills for headaches?" he asks. It takes a second for his words to sink in, but once they do, I'm fully awake.

"No." I climb out of bed and take the daily pill organizer from him. "I'm sure there's some in a cabinet somewhere. I'll go look." I shove the container back into my luggage, ignoring the way Brayden is watching me with curiosity. I pull on a pair of clean boxers and pad out of the room to go find him some pain pills—as well as ignore more of that reality shit neither of us wants to deal with.

As I descend the stairs, I can hear Mia's moans. What the hell time is it? Do they ever come up for air? I swear the man lives inside of her.

I swing open each cabinet, until I find what I'm looking for. I pop two into my mouth and chase them down with some water, then pour Brayden a cup and bring them up to him.

"Thanks." He's dressed now in a pair of worn jeans and a long-sleeved Henley, a beanie on his head. "Are they up yet?" he asks, referring to Mia and Ashton.

"Yeah, they're fucking like rabbits."

Brayden snorts a laugh. "You want to take the golf cart over to the main resort and get breakfast? They can meet us over there later." During our tour last night, Ashton showed us the golf cart in the garage and said it's used to drive around when it's not snowing too badly.

"Yeah," I tell him, excited to spend the day out in public with my boyfriend. "That sounds perfect."

After I brush my teeth and get dressed, we head out. It's beautiful out here today. The sun is shining, helping to counter the chill in the air. When we arrive at the resort, we park and find the restaurant that serves breakfast.

"Two, please," Brayden tells the hostess. She smiles warmly and walks us back to our seats. There are four and I choose the one directly next to Brayden since I can. He grins at me and takes my hand in his, bringing it up to his lips to kiss. It's new, getting to kiss and touch in public, and I'm worried when we get home, we'll both miss it… crave it. We still have another six months before we can be seen in public together back home, and then, will Brayden want to? His plan is to join the NHL. Will he want to impact his career by coming out as gay before it even starts? I'd like to say the world is more open to gay players, but the truth is, humanity still has a long way to go.

"You okay?" Brayden asks, squeezing my hand.

"Yeah." I shake off my pessimistic thoughts and push them into that corner of reality we're refusing to acknowledge.

The waitress comes over and I order us each an eggs benedict meal with a side of home fries, two coffees, and waters. We spend breakfast talking about the slopes we plan to hit. Growing up, every winter my dad would take us skiing and snowboarding. That is until we stopped talking just before high school. I still went with my dad twice more before he died, but it wasn't the same without Bray.

"Do you think we should wait for them?" Brayden asks as we walk over to the pro shop to rent equipment.

"Nah, they'll catch up later. If Ashton has it his way, he and Mia will stay in bed all day." I'm also enjoying the one-on-one time with Bray, and I'm not quite ready to share him with anyone else yet.

After we're set up with our snow gear and equipment, we jump onto the lift and head to the first slope. We decided to start with a smaller, less intense one, since it's been a little bit for both of us.

We hop off the lift and take off down the mountain, both of us keeping up with each other the entire way down. The air whips around my face, my mask protecting my eyes as I soar to the bottom.

"Damn," Brayden says when we get to the bottom. "We rocked the hell out of that slope. I forgot how much fun that was. Want to hit the bigger one now?"

"Sure." I nod, ignoring the way my body is struggling to keep up.

We spend the next hour riding the slopes. When we get to the bottom of the red slope—a more challenging intermediate slope—we stop to take a small break.

"This is fun." Brayden beams, grinning from ear to ear. "I'm really glad we came out here." He pulls me close to him. "We needed this." He kisses the side of my neck, his lips lingering for a few seconds.

"Yeah, we did," I agree, my voice coming out breathy.

"Want to switch out our skis for snowboards?" he suggests, not even slightly out of breath.

I take in a large gulp of air, trying to catch my breath, as I nod in agreement, too winded to verbally answer. Brayden, attuned to me, notices. "You okay?" he asks, lifting his goggles up to his forehead so he can assess my features.

"Yeah." I wave him off. "Just out of shape." I laugh.

"Are you sure that's—" he begins, when each of our names are called.

We glance over and find Mia, dressed like a cute fucking little snow bunny, waving at us. She's fully dressed in a pink snowsuit, but the second I lay eyes on her, the image of her perfect, wet, naked tits jiggling as Ashton fucked her last night hits me hard, and I'm thankful as hell I'm wearing thick snow pants.

"Where's Ashton?" Brayden asks once we get over to her.

"Inside renting us some equipment," she says, giddy as fuck and not at all looking hungover.

"You sure you want to do this?" Ashton asks, walking out and handing Mia a snowboard. "It's not too late to turn around and go back to that warm bed." He palms her jaw and kisses along her neck.

"I want to snowboard." She pouts. "Please."

"I can show her," Brayden offers. "Drew over here has become an old man during his time off the rink and can barely keep up." He shoots me a teasing wink, and I force a smile.

"I've got this, man," Ashton says, his tone more serious than usual. "I don't mind showing my girl how to snowboard." He smiles softly at Mia, and something feels different… He's acting differently. Less playful. Less Ashton.

"All right." Brayden shrugs. "Then let's do this. We can all go to the blue slope. Drew needs a little break anyway." He nudges me playfully.

"I think I'm actually going to sit this one out. You guys go. My head is throbbing. I'm going to grab a coffee and some pain reliever and then I'll catch up."

"Then I'll go with you," Brayden says.

"No, don't do that," I insist. "Go snowboarding. I promise I'll catch up."

He eyes me curiously but in the end agrees. I watch as he, Mia, and Ashton take off to go grab Brayden a board, and then I take my skis off and place them against the equipment wall. I take the golf cart back to the house and run upstairs to our room. I swallow a couple pills and consider going back to the resort, but the bed looks comfy as hell, and I end up lying down. I close my eyes, telling myself I'm just going to rest for a few minutes, but I must end up falling into a deep sleep because the next thing I know, my name is being shouted as footsteps climb the stairs.

"There you are," Brayden says. "We were looking everywhere for you. Have you been sleeping this entire time?" He kicks his shoes off and climbs into bed next to me, pulling me into his arms.

I glance at my watch and see it's already late afternoon. "Yeah. Guess the fresh air knocked me out."

"You sure you're feeling okay?" he asks, concern etched in his features.

I suck in a large mouthful of air and exhale easily. "Yeah, I feel perfect."

There's a knock on the door and we both look up to find Mia standing in the doorway.

"We're going to go to dinner. You guys are coming, right?" Her eyes are wide and hopeful and even if we didn't want to go, I know damn well neither of us would be able to tell her no.

"Yeah," I tell her, sitting up. "I'm just going to shower to wake up and I'll be good to go."

Brayden grins at me. "I think I'll join you. I'm feeling a little dirty myself."

Needless to say, we're late for dinner.

# SEVENTEEN



**W**e find Ashton and Mia at a pub and grill at the lodge. Ashton has Mia's high-top barstool pulled close to him at the round table. They've already started in on an appetizer, but it doesn't look like they've eaten without us.

I wait for the jokes.

The taunts.

Usual Ashton shit.

Nothing.

Like earlier, he's clinging to Mia, barely looking at Drew and me.

"Glad you guys could finally join us," Mia says, smirking. "We were almost ready to eat without you."

I chuckle as I hop up on the barstool beside Ashton. Drew sits next to me and grabs a menu for us to look at.

"Hey, Ashton," I say, waiting for him to look at me.

"What's up?" he rumbles, a bored look on his face.

"You on your period or what, douchebag?" I kick his stool, making him jerk his attention my way.

Guilt flashes in his eyes and then he laughs, flipping me off. Still acting weird as fuck. I glance over at Mia and her brows are furled, clearly feeling the same way.

"What can I get you handsome fellas?" a blond chick chirps in greeting. "House special is a bison burger and a Moscow mule. We call it the Russian Redneck special. You game? I'll throw in some honeyed sweet potato fries for free."

"Yeah," Drew says. "We'll take two of those."

Ashton holds his fingers up. "Make it four."

"Great," the waitress says. "I'll be right back with your drinks."

Mia jabbers on about snowboarding until the waitress brings us back our Moscow mules. I sip on my drink, my attention bouncing back and forth between Drew and Ashton. They're both being weird as hell today.

"Listen," Mia says, straightening her spine, "I don't know if things are just quiet and weird because everyone is hungover or what, but I don't like it."

Silence.

"Are we going to talk about the big elephant in the room?" she asks, exasperated.

More silence.

"Boys are such brats," she groans. "Last night was fun. We were drunk. It happened. Can we get over being weird now? I, for one, thought it was kind of hot."

Drew laughs. "That makes two of us."

"Three," I agree, smirking.

All eyes land on Ashton. His lips quirk up. "Yeah, it was hot."

"There," Mia says, giggling. "Now stop being weird and go back to normal."

When Mia and Drew get locked into a conversation about a couple nearby, I lean forward, meeting Ashton's gaze.

"You really okay?" I ask.

He nods. "As long as Mia's happy, I'm happy. I don't ever want to make her unhappy."

It clicks into place.

Last night, by the four of us messing around, he thought he would lose her. Poor fucking guy. He clearly can't see how fucking crazy she is about him. I give his thigh a squeeze, letting him know I understand and that I'm here for him. His hazel eyes flash with gratitude as he brushes his thumb over the back of my hand.

"He's boning her sister," Mia says, earning Ashton's and my attention.

"Who? Sounds scandalous," Ashton chimes in.

"The blonde over there with that guy," Drew explains. "We've been watching them. There were three of them a bit ago, but the redhead left. He's clearly married or with the blonde, but he watched the redhead leave with puppy dog eyes."

"Oh," Mia hisses. "She's coming back. Watch his face."

The redhead smiles bashfully at him. He rubs at the back of his neck and licks his lips. The blonde doesn't notice the exchange since she's on her phone. The man winks at the redhead, making her turn bright red.

"That dirty bastard," Ashton says with a laugh.

We're distracted from our people watching when the waitress comes back with our bison burgers and sweet potato fries. It's good-ass food, but the Moscow mules are amazing. The ginger beer has a unique flavor and the vodka gives it a warm bite. Before long, we've made our way through too many Moscow mules and are tipsy.

Ashton leaves to head up to the bar and when he returns, he has a brown paper sack in his hands.

"Whatcha got there, Ashy C?" Mia asks, batting her lashes at him. "A present for me?"

"I bought us mules to go. Limes, beer, Grey Goose. Even the tin mugs. Let's take this party back home where we can sit by the fire." He nods toward the door. "As much as I'd love to watch ol' boy over there flirt with Red each time his wife is texting, I'd much rather feel Mia up without all these people as an audience."

I note that he waves at everyone but us.

"Wait," Drew says, "so your mom is a famous actress, whom you hate, but yet you want to follow in her footsteps? I don't get your line of thinking."

Mia drains her mule and sets it down on the coffee table, animated by the alcohol and her feelings toward her mother. "No. I have been shaped by her career, but I'm not following in her footsteps. I want to make the movies, not be in them."

"Like a director?" Drew asks.

"The writer." She blows a hair out of her flushed face. "I want to write the screenplays. To be the beginning of something that eventually turns into a movie. How cool would it be to watch a film, hearing them say dialogue you carefully labored over? To see the scenes take on visual life? To hear the songs and sounds you thought up?" She sighs. "I just think it would be one of the coolest things ever."

"You better invite us to your first movie," I tell her.

She grins. "Of course the three of you will be there. You're my people." She holds up her empty metal mug and shakes it. "Who wants another?"

I hand her mine, but Drew and Ashton are still working on theirs.

"What about you, Ash?" Drew asks. "Mia's our moviemaker and Bray's our future NHL player. What's the notorious Mr. Carter going to do?"

"I'm going to be a doctor." He shrugs.

Drew snorts. "For real. What do you really want to be?"

"A doctor. Not like an ER doctor or a surgeon or some shit," Ashton continues. "Psychiatrist."

"Dr. Carter then." Drew chuckles. "I like it."

Ashton's brow lifts. "You're not going to give me hell about it? Say I'm not focused enough or serious enough or smart enough?" There's a challenge in his tone. His knee is bouncing where he's sitting in an armchair and his hazel eyes are blazing.

"Nah, man. I think you'd be good at it. You read people well and make them feel better about themselves."

Ashton shoots his stare my way, confused by Drew's words. I nod in agreement. At first, Ashton can be a hard pill to swallow, but once you do, you're high off him. Addicted. You need him to feel complete.

My chest aches as I consider that. I'm not sure when he fell into the best friend category with Drew, but he did. He and Mia both did.

Mia bounces back into the room, her cute braided pigtails coming undone with flyaway hairs. She hands me a mule and then sits in Ashton's lap. He playfully nips at her tit through her sweatshirt. I find myself fixated on the way his lips curl away from his teeth—a wicked smile forming—as he bites her.

"So who fucked who first?" Ashton blurts out, cupping Mia's tit with his hand and grinning at us.

I laugh and shrug, looking down at my drink. Drew mumbles at him to mind his own business. The room grows quiet. I suck down my drink, needing to do something with myself.

"Wait…" Ashton says slowly. "You two haven't fucked."

Drew and I both snap our heads up to stare at him. Ashton's eyes are wide and so are Mia's. Like they're shocked.

"It's not that we haven't wanted to," I bite out, annoyed at their expressions.

"We just…" Drew utters.

"Don't know how?" Ashton offers, his brows furled together.

"I've seen gay porn." I lean forward and drop my empty mug on the table. "Just never did it before."

"But you want to," Ashton probes.

We both nod.

Mia's eyebrows are perked up, intrigued by our conversation.

"When?" Ashton asks. "Now?"

We all laugh, but then it grows quiet again.

"What if we fuck it up?" Drew mutters, voicing my own reservations. "What if I hurt him or he hurts me?" His hand covers mine and squeezes. "I don't want to mess this up."

Ashton darts his gaze back and forth between us. "It's sex, not rocket science. I've been fucking guys since I was fifteen. Been getting fucked by them just as long."

"It's fine," I grumble. "We'll figure it out."

"Maybe they need a coach," Mia offers.

Drew snorts. "Ashton as a sex coach. That ought to get interesting."

"I didn't hear a no," Ashton says, his lips kicking up into a devious grin. "Is that what you need, dude bro Bray? Someone to coach you on how to put your dick in?"

I laugh, flipping him off. "You're an asshole."

"The asshole who's going to teach you how to put it into *his* asshole," he deadpans.

Drew smirks, leaning back on the couch, shooting me a curious look. "So I'm getting fucked first, hmm?"

"Yes," Ashton answers like the bossy fucker he is. "Brayden's been wanting to fuck you since he first grew a pecker. Right, little buddy?"

I shoot him the bird again. "I revealed too much crap to you when these two weren't talking to us. I regret that shit now."

"Aww," Ashton teases. "Don't be a baby." Then, to Drew, he says, "Get naked and wait on the bed."

Drew nearly chokes. "W-What? You're serious?"

"I think you two need guidance," Mia agrees.

Ashton and Mia are double trouble sometimes.

"You can't do that shit," I say, shaking my head. "You're seriously going to walk us through fucking?"

Ashton ignores me, his attention on Drew. "Get naked and wait on the bed. Don't touch your dick, Coach. It belongs to Brayden."

Said dick hardens at his commanding words.

Drew fucking stands like he's going to obey.

Holy shit. He's going to obey. We're going to do this.

"Hands and knees on the bed. Keep that ass up because Brayden is going to lick your tight hole," Ashton says, his lust-filled eyes searing into me. "Aren't you?"

"Y-Yes," I choke out.

Mia grins, wearing the same naughty expression as Ashton.

Drew walks off and I scrub my palm down my face. Panic threatens to take over, but then I realize I'm not alone. Ashton won't let us fuck this up. He won't let me hurt Drew.

I trust Ashton.

He fucks around with us a lot, but he's serious about this.

He wants to help.

"How long do we wait?" I croak out.

Ashton laughs. "Five bucks says he's already naked and his dick's dripping with precum."

Mia licks her lips and fuck if that doesn't make me even harder. I stand on shaky legs and clear my throat again. Ashton and Mia both stand. He takes her hand and surprises me by taking mine. Mia and I follow after Ashton, exchanging mutual looks of excitement.

The moment we walk into the room and my eyes zero in on Drew's muscular, naked body, I freeze. Holy fuck he's hot. This is hot. The whole goddamn thing. I'm terrified of screwing shit up, but I want to try. So damn bad.

"MiMi and I are going to sit in the armchair over there," Ashton says, peeling off his shirt and tossing it. "Pretend we're not there, but listen to what I have to say."

Ashton sits in the chair and then motions for Mia to come sit in his lap with her back to his chest. He looks like a king all sprawled out, smug and powerful. His queen sits in his lap, eager to be involved in whatever shenanigans he's pulling this time.

"Brayden," Drew rumbles, his voice tight with need. "Don't just stand there."

I yank off my shirt and fumble with my jeans. Once I kick out of them, I peel off my socks and then shove down my boxers. I glance over at Ashton, who has both his hands beneath Mia's sweater, kneading her breasts. His eyes peruse down my front and when he settles them on my dick, he smirks, clearly enjoying the view.

"I need… I need a condom, and uh, lube," I mutter.

"No," Ashton rumbles. "You need to give his hole some attention. Don't be selfish, Bray. Lick it and get it nice and wet."

I approach Drew's muscular ass, gripping each cheek, appreciating the fact I'm about to have him in an intimate way. "God, you're beautiful," I murmur.

"Aww," Mia whispers.

I can't help but flash her a grin and a wink before bending to bring my mouth to Drew's crack. He hisses when I tentatively lick the puckered hole. I'm pretty sure he liked the sensation, so I grab his cheeks, pulling them so I have better access, and lick him really good. He curses, making Ashton chuckle.

It doesn't take long until I'm lost to the obsession of his asshole. I lick it and tease it and tongue it. He groans when I press into him with my tongue, obliterated by the unusual sensation.

This is fucking amazing.

"Don't touch it, Coach," Ashton warns. "Not your dick to touch."

"It's driving me crazy," Drew complains. "I need to come."

"Patience." Then, to me, Ashton says, "Suck on your finger. Get it nice and wet."

I slide my finger into my mouth, stealing a glance Ashton's way. Mia's sweater is gone and so are her jeans. She's a fucking vision in a black bra and matching panties. Ashton's jeans are shoved down his thighs. She's sitting on his lap, facing us, riding his hard dick through his boxers. I'm transfixed by the sight, but manage to pull away to focus on Drew's pleasure.

"Tell me if it hurts," I murmur. "I'll stop."

Drew groans when I press my finger into him. He's so goddamn tight. I won't last a second inside him. I'm going to damn well try to last at least three.

Slowly, I fuck Drew's ass with my finger, loving the way he shudders and moans.

"MiMi," Ashton rumbles. "Can you go get the boys some lube and a condom?"

"I'll be right back," she squeaks out.

When she returns, she sets them on the bed for me.

"Put some lube on your fingers," Ashton instructs. "This time, use two fingers. And hook your fingers toward his front so you can feel his prostate."

I slip out of him and then squirt the lube all over my fingers, making a mess. Because it seems like a good idea, I rub it all over his hole, too. Drew presses against my fingers, needy for more. He groans when I slide two fingers into him, careful to stretch him slowly. I make sure he's good and lubed up before I curl my fingers like Ashton suggested.

"Fuck, Bray!" Drew cries out, his ass clenching around my fingers.

"Did I hurt you?" I bark out.

"Hell no. Do it again. Holy shit, do that again."

He whimpers—fucking whimpers—when I press against the spongy place inside of him that seems to be the hot button of pleasure. I jerk my gaze over to Ashton to flash him a thankful smile when I get caught staring at something I probably shouldn't.

Mia's tits.

Bare and jiggling, pulled out over the top of her bra. Her panties are gone and Ashton's fingers are inside of her. Both their eyes are fixated on us. I manage to pull my stare away to peek at Drew, who's watching them watch us.

Holy fuck.

I focus on rubbing him in just the right way, bringing him close to the edge of pleasure only to pull back at the last second. Drew is practically begging for more. I ease another slippery finger inside of him, amazed at how he accommodates the intrusion. Soon, it'll be my dick.

"Fuck!" Drew curses. "I'm fucking coming!"

I'm shocked he's able to come without ever touching his dick. It's fucking fascinating. When he's done trembling, I slide my fingers out and grab for the condom.

"Scoot up the bed," Ashton instructs, his voice breathy.

One glance and I know why. His dick is between Mia's pussy lips as she rubs herself up and down along his length. He pinches her nipples, making her cry out. Fuck, they're hot.

I grab the condom, opening it with my teeth. Then, I roll the rubber down over my aching dick. I lube it up and then prowl over to Drew, who's still on all fours. Slowly, I tease at his hole with the tip of my cock. As gently as I can, I press into him.

He curses, and so does Mia. Drew's head snaps her way. He keeps his eyes trained on them as I push inside his hot, tight body. I ease out and then drive deeper inside of him. Over and over, I inch my way in until I bottom out inside of him.

My best friend.

My Drew.

My soul mate.

I slide out and slam into him a little harder than probably necessary. He lets loose a guttural growl. I think he likes it. Wrapping my arm around his front, I pull him up so his back is against my chest. He cranes his neck, seeking my mouth with his. We groan as we kiss messily, my hips thrusting greedily into him. I slide my hand down to touch his dick, and sure enough, he's hard again. I fist his dick, jacking him off in tandem with each buck of my hips.

It feels too fucking good, which means I don't last long. All too soon, my balls are seizing up and I'm coming deep inside him. It must set him off, too, because his dick twitches as heat gushes over my fist.

Holy shit.

So fucking hot.

I'm afraid to move, unable to let him go in this moment. We break our kiss, our eyes drawn to the other couple in the room. It's now I can hear their sounds.

Ashton's feral grunts.

Mia's needy whimpers.

Her tits are fucking divine, bouncing prettily as he fucks her. I'm fixated on how red her pussy is as it stretches to take his girth. His dick is slick with her arousal. Strong hands bite into her thighs as he pulls her up and down along his length like she's his own personal fuck toy.

No condom.

Jesus.

My own dick has softened some now that I've come and I'm not in a rush to pull it out of Drew's perfect ass.

"Come, Mia," Ashton growls, smacking her pussy. "Come all over my dick."

Drew's ass clenches, making me suck in a sharp breath because it feels too good. I need to get rid of this condom and hunt down another one. And yet, I need to see this through.

"Ashton!" she cries out, her entire body tensing in his arms.

He bites into her shoulder and then his dick is pulsating as his nuts tighten. I watch in fascination as he drains his release into this girl.

Unprotected.

I fucking hope she's on the pill.

But I also don't hate the idea of imagining her pregnant either, which is a strange fucking thing to think about with your dick in someone's ass.

While they try to catch their breath, I ease out of Drew. I kiss the side of his neck. "I'm going to get another condom. Can you handle me again?"

He collapses on the bed, breathing heavily. "Give me five minutes to catch my breath."

I give his ass a playful smack. "I'm counting down."

"You're welcome," Ashton says, earning our attention.

He pulls Mia off his dick and it bounces out of her, still fucking hard. Cum runs out of her abused pussy, dripping all over his groin.

"Thank you," both Drew and I say at once.

By the time I locate another condom, Mia and Ashton have disappeared, but my hot boyfriend is ready for round two.

# EIGHTEEN

*Ashton*

Impulsive. Inconsiderate. Selfish. Thoughtless. Rash.

All the words my parents, teachers, and therapists have used to describe me come flooding back, bouncing around inside my head like popcorn.

Destructive.

To myself and others.

Drew and Brayden didn't need me to interfere last night. I wanted to. And that makes me a horrible person.

I have Mia.

For how long?

She'll grow tired of my shit eventually.

Fuck.

As soon as we get back from dinner, I leave the kitchen where everyone is laughing and make a beeline for the bedroom. Drew and Brayden spent the day on the slopes again, but I couldn't do it, couldn't be around them, so I lied and said I had a migraine. Of course Mia, the good person she is, insisted on staying in with me. We watched a few movies, but for the most part, I slept. Because at least when I was asleep, I could escape the guilt I feel.

When the guys returned, Mia insisted I needed to get out and eat something, and dragged us all to dinner. Nobody asked if I was okay, but I could see the concerned looks they were shooting me. I don't deserve their concern, though.

I strip out of my clothes down to my boxers and crawl into bed beneath the covers. Dragging the pillow over my face, I try to keep down the bitter pill of regret I keep swallowing over and over again.

It's like acid.

A painful reminder.

I'll never be the right man for her. I'm too fucked up. Too jaded. Shattered by the people who were supposed to be a good influence. They ruined me when they ruined themselves. I'm hardened in all the wrong spots and I don't know if I can ever be soft where Mia needs me to be.

I will ruin her like Mom ruined Dad.

And because she's Mia, she'll stick around, unhappy but taking it like a fucking champ because she feels like something is better than nothing.

I don't want to give her something—a quarter of what she needs.

I want to give her everything.

My chest aches painfully. Tears of anger and devastation burn at my eyes, threatening to build but never do because I'm broken. Unable to feel normal. Half sane and the other half of me guided by my motherfucking dick.

Hate.

All I feel is hate for myself.

I should break up with her before she falls too hard. Before we're in too deep. Before marriage and fucking kids. If not, they'll turn out to be little fuckups like me.

Christ.

I can't do this.

The blankets pull back and the angel in my dark world slides beneath the covers, seeking me out. I can't fucking look at her.

"Ashton, what's wrong?" Her voice cracks, sad and confused. "Is it me?"

I fling the pillow away, glowering at her pretty face. "Fuck you, Mia, for even considering that."

Hurt fills her brown eyes and then she hardens them. "Stop."

"Stop what?"

"This bullshit you're doing," she snaps. "Blaming yourself. Carrying the burden all alone. I'm tired of it, Ashton."

*I'm tired of it, Ashton.*

*I'm tired of you.*

I squeeze my eyes shut as my heart cracks down the middle. "I can't do this to you."

Her fingers are like silk, gently stroking my cheek. "Look at me, baby."

Because I can't deny her a thing, I open my eyes.

"I love you, Ashton Carter," she tells me so fiercely, I feel it in my marrow. "But I don't love the way you hate yourself."

"MiMi…"

"Shh. I'm speaking now and you're going to hear me out." Her fingers run through my hair. "You and I are special. Wouldn't you agree?"

I nod because fucking duh.

"And Drew and Brayden are too."

Guilt swarms up inside me. Last night had been like a fantasy come to life. I'd been so turned on and I hate myself for it.

"We connect with them," she murmurs. "It doesn't feel bad when we're around them. It feels right." She kisses my mouth. "I don't feel like you're leaving me to play with them. I feel like it's something we're doing together. As a team."

"I don't play team sports," I joke, and then wince because joking now is fucked-up.

"I love your strange sense of humor," she reveals. "How you can crack a joke when we're trying to be serious. That's you, baby. I love how you're a big flirt, not just to me, but to those other two special guys in there. You're fiercely loyal to us."

To us.

My heart twists in a strange way inside my chest.

"Guys," Mia calls out. "Ashton's pouting and he needs a group hug."

I roll my eyes at her. "I don't need a group hug." I kinda want one, though.

Drew is sturdy and reliable. He's just there. Strong and brave. Fuck, I didn't realize how much I leaned on his steady strength, but I do. I need it. All daddy jokes aside, he provides something to me that I desperately crave.

And Brayden? He's like the dude bro best friend I never had. He's fierce and loyal and an asshole who can be gentle when he needs to be. He's loving and caring. A fuckin' momma's boy if I ever saw one. Kind and there. He's just always there.

My Mia.

Sweet, darling, precious Mia.

The light in my dark world. The yin to my motherfucking yang. Cutest damn thing to walk the earth. She's blunt and forward and courageous. Full of laughs and sweet as hell. I could run off a cliff and my girl would be fucking skydiving behind me, ready to grab hold of me and open her parachute before I splatter into nothingness.

I don't deserve their friendship.

Their closeness.

Their goddamn love.

And yet…

The bed dips down as a big, strong hockey boy wraps around me, kissing my neck as he playfully tickles me. A growly coach cuddles my girl and searches my eyes to make sure I'm okay. Somehow, it doesn't feel so horrible and wrong with them all here in this moment.

Like maybe… they get me.

A scary thought because I've been drifting through this world for so long misunderstood.

Three people out of seven billion seem to see inside me like no one ever has.

"MiMi," I mutter, touching her red, pouty lips. I want to tell her I'm sorry for being so weak. No words come.

I watch the way Drew strokes her hair as he watches me with intense blue eyes. He teases his finger down her bare shoulder, dragging the blanket down.

"Where's your shirt, sweetheart?" Drew asks, teasing the strap of her bra.

She smiles. "It's Ashton's fault."

Bray laughs, his hot breath tickling my neck.

"How is it my fault?" I ask, arching a brow.

"You were practically naked first." She shrugs. "I thought it was a naked slumber party."

"I didn't get the memo," Drew says as he sits up to remove his shirt. "Did you, Bray?"

"Nope. They always leave us out of the good stuff," Brayden says from behind me. The bed moves and then he's crawling under the covers behind me.

My eyes close when his hard dick presses against my ass. We're just in boxers. Too little between us. I'm too weak for this shit.

Needing my girl to ground me, I lean forward and capture her mouth with mine. She moans, sending curls of desire straight to my dick. A masculine hand rubs down my pectoral muscle and then Brayden pulls on my nipple ring. I groan in pleasure. His hand travels south and I don't stop him. I can't.

My breath hitches when his hand dips into my boxers, wrapping around my hard cock. I thrust against his grip, moaning into Mia's mouth. The bed moves again as Drew walks off, but then he's back, sliding under the covers with her. I'm trying desperately to focus on her lips, but Brayden is so fucking skilled with his hand. I don't even fight him when he lets me go to pull my boxers off. When he curls back around me, he's bare, his dick sandwiched between us.

Fuck.

"Feel this," Mia moans, drawing my hand to her thighs. "Doesn't it feel good?"

There's a hand already there. Drew's. His fingers are sliding through the lips of her pussy, making her mewl. I slide my finger inside of her with his, a partner with him as he fingers my girl. I'm so fucking hot over the fact we're both fingering her that I nearly come from the sudden, slippery intrusion into my ass.

Brayden.

A slick finger probes my ass that hasn't seen action since long before Mia and I hooked up for good. Precum leaks from my tip. I'm over-fucking-whelmed by these people. I pull my hand from Mia's pussy, offering it to Brayden. His growl is ravenous as he sucks her from my finger.

Holy fuck.

"Oh God," Mia cries out. "That feels good, Drew."

She says his name, and rather than feel like a punch to the gut, it's like a stroke down my spine. I turn my head, desperately needing to see Brayden's face. His dark eyes are homed in on me, burning with desire. For me. For us.

Drew kicks the covers away. My girl is now fully naked and coming. It turns me the fuck on watching him bring her to orgasm with just his fingers.

"I'm going to fuck Mia," Drew says, his eyes searing into mine and then darting to Brayden's. "And you're both going to watch."

Fuck him and his hot, sexy mouth.

"Your boyfriend's about to take my ass because yours is too wrecked to take it again," I taunt, unable to help myself.

Brayden laughs and then bites my neck. "After I wreck you, Mia will be the only one left."

His finger slips out of me and then he's pushing in two. Fuck it hurts, but I've missed the feeling of something inside my ass. I hate to admit that, but it's true. Before Mia, I lived for this shit.

"Ride him so we can watch," I command, my voice husky and raw. "Please."

Mia grins at me. "Since you asked so sweetly."

Drew flops onto his back and grabs a couple of condoms from the nightstand. He hands one to Bray and then he tears open his. I watch eagerly as he rolls it on his dick that I know from experience is fucking perfect.

"Get on that big dick, baby. Make your tits bounce. I fucking love watching your tits bounce," I rumble. I stroke my cock, watching as she gets on her knees.

"Mine," Bray growls, biting me hard enough I release my dick.

"Mean ass," I grumble.

He removes his fingers from my ass, leaving me empty and aching, and then he tears the foil with his teeth. I can hear him lubing himself up behind me, but I'm focused on the way Mia straddles Drew's waist. Her small hand grips his dick and then she's sliding down over him.

I hold my breath.

Waiting for my world to explode.

To want to die inside.

But all I feel is love and warmth and need.

Mia bounces like a good girl, Drew's hands tugging at her nipples hard enough to make her yelp.

"I want to look at you when I fuck you," Bray says, kissing my neck again. Fuck, I love when he does that. "Do it before I make you."

"Bossy fucker," I complain, though not too hard.

I scoot onto my back, enjoying the better view of my girl as she fucks my hot roommate. Bray prowls over me like a fucking starving lion. I'm drawn to the Adam's apple that's so goddamn lickable in his throat. He's rough—just how I like it—as he jerks my knees apart. Then, he dips down, licking his way up my dick from root to tip. Holy shit.

"All that abstinence with your boyfriend makes you a dicksucking pro, dude bro Bray," I rasp. My fingers dive into his hair, urging him to suck me. His lips wrap around my cock, his tongue lashing eagerly at me.

"So hot, oh my God," Mia whimpers.

"Fuck yeah," Drew groans, his voice strained.

I want to look at them, but Bray has me captive with his hungry stare. He sucks me as though I can nourish his goddamn soul. And, like the generous fucker I am, I give it to him. My nuts tighten and then I'm coming in his perfect mouth without warning. The little pro gulps it down like he needs it. He pops off my dick, saliva running a stream from my dick to my navel, and he crawls up my body.

"You're so fucking hot, Ashton," Brayden murmurs against my mouth. "So hot."

I moan against his mouth, accepting his deep kiss as his dick probes at my asshole. We both groan when he enters me swiftly. He doesn't have the gentleness and care he had with Drew. It's more feral. Needy. Desperate.

I love it.

I love him.

I nip at his bottom lip, digging my fingers into his shoulders. He bucks into me hard and claiming. When Mia makes a sound, we both pull from our kiss, unable to keep from looking at them. Drew's hand is tangled in her hair as he devours her mouth with his. She's fucking him like she's crazed with need.

That's my dirty girl.

Mine.

Fucking my sexy roommate.

Also mine.

Brayden drives into me hard, drawing my gaze back to him. Burning brown eyes. Knowing smirk. Sharp jawline. Hot-ass hockey boy who drives me fucking wild.

"Mine," I murmur to him, kissing him hard.

Mia cries out, signaling her orgasm. Drew makes a grunt as he follows her. I'm overwhelmed by the sensations of the three people in this bed with me.

Brayden's dick—fucking huge, stretching me as his mouth devours mine.

Mia's hand curling around mine and squeezing.

Drew's fingers toying with my hair.

I just came, but my dick is weeping to come again. As though he understands, Brayden grips my cock, driving into me in tandem with the way he fists my cock. It's ragged and savage. I fucking love it. Brayden has fucking stamina because he brings me to orgasm before he reaches his peak. When he finally does, his cock swelling in size, he collapses on my sweaty, messy chest. His lips find my neck for a kiss and then he chuckles.

No one says anything for a long time. Even after Brayden climbs off me to fetch something to clean us up with. Even when Mia slips to the bathroom for a moment. Even when Drew disappears to turn off lights in the cabin.

They all return to me, and I feel fucking overjoyed that they do.

As soon as the bedroom goes completely dark, I pull Mia to my chest, hugging her tight. I need to know she's still with me. She cuddles her sweet, sexy body against mine, kissing my lips.

"Good night, Bray," Mia says, amusement in her voice.

"Night, Mia."

"Good night, Drew," she sings.

"Night, beautiful."

"Good night, Ashy C."

"Night, MiMi."

I drift off with Brayden wrapped around me like a goddamn koala bear, Mia nuzzled against my neck, and Drew's hand in mine.

If this is a dream, I don't want to wake up.

# NINETEEN

*Mia*

"Let me in, MiMi," Ashton begs lazily. We're lying in his bed, and I need to get up for school, but being wrapped in his warm arms is keeping me in bed. He was supposed to get up early for swim practice, but he skipped it this morning.

"No way." I shake my head. "These gates are locked for the next four days." When I woke up yesterday morning, tangled up with my three favorite men, I realized I started my period—which is both a good and a bad thing. Good because Ashton and I have been careless, so at least I know I'm not pregnant. Bad because my boyfriend is insatiable and apparently a little blood doesn't scare him away. It's probably because he's never seen a woman during her time of the month. I should give in, just so he won't keep bugging me, but it might scar him for life.

"What about through the back?" he asks, gliding his hand up my thigh and cupping my ass. "Will you let me in the back door, MiMi?" he taunts, his warm breath hitting my ear and sending chills up my spine. My body buzzes at the thought of Ashton fucking me the way Brayden fucked him. The way Ashton has fucked everyone, besides me, all his life.

"Yeah," I breathe. "The back door is open."

Ashton stills at my words, as if he wasn't expecting me to agree, so I rub my ass against the bulge in his boxers, emphasizing my answer. I saw the way he walked Brayden through being with Drew, making sure he was gentle and didn't hurt him, and I have no doubt Ashton will do the same for me.

"You sure?"

I turn my head and pull him down to me for a kiss. "More than sure."

He pulls my panties down my legs and then reaches into the drawer for his bottle of lube, squirting some onto his fingers. He's fingered me in my ass several times now, so when his finger glides right in, it feels good.

"Fuck, you're so tight. I don't want to hurt you," Ashton says, sounding very un-Ashton-like. He's confident and sure of himself in everything he does… except when it comes to me.

"You could never hurt me," I assure him, reaching back and connecting our mouths. He adds another finger and then another and soon I'm grinding against his hand, fucking his fingers. I feel full in such a different way.

"Put your dick in me," I beg, wanting to feel connected to Ashton in this way.

He tears open a condom, but I pull it from his mouth and drop it. "We don't need that," I murmur. "I want to feel you… all of you." We haven't used a condom several times now. There's no reason to use one now. I make a mental note to go by the doctor and get on birth control.

He spreads my cheeks apart and I feel the tip poking at my ass. "Tell me if it hurts," he warns as he pushes himself slowly into me from behind. Even with all the times he's fingered me, it still burns, but I don't complain, not wanting him to stop.

I lift my leg slightly, setting my foot on his thigh to give him better access. "Jesus," he groans. "I'm never going to last in your perfect ass." He keeps pushing into me, little by little, until he announces that he's all the way in.

"Fuck me," I demand, wiggling my ass.

"You're too perfect," he whispers. "It's like you were made just for me." He reaches around and finds my clit.

"No, I'm on my period," I remind him.

He smacks my hand away. "I'm not an expert in pussy, but I took Sex Ed in school, and I know your clit isn't out of commission."

While fucking me, he massages gentle circles along the sensitive nub, and all too soon my orgasm overtakes me. My entire body shakes, and I'm so lost in my pleasure, I don't even realize it when Ashton pulls out of me and rolls me onto my back. My eyes open just in time to see him fist his dick, pumping several times before ropes of cum shoot out all over my belly.

He leans over me and crushes his mouth to mine. "I love you, MiMi. So goddamn much."

"I've been thinking," I tell him. We've showered, and since I was already late to my morning class, we decided to play hooky and spend the day together in bed. We're lying in said bed with my head on Ashton's chest, while he plays with my hair. We're watching reruns of an old show, but I'm not really paying attention. I have too much on my mind.

"Oh, yeah," he says, "about what?"

"This weekend…" Ashton's fingers still. "I really liked what we did."

He releases a harsh breath, but doesn't say anything.

"Did you"—I glance up at him—"like what we did?"

I know he did, but I need him to admit it out loud.

"I like anything we do," he says. "You know that. I'll take you any way I can get you." He dips down and kisses my forehead.

"But did you enjoy being with Brayden… and Drew?" Technically he wasn't with Drew—I was—but for me, we were all together.

"I enjoyed watching Drew fuck you," he says, ignoring the part about Brayden fucking him.

I sit up so I can face him. "Why can't you admit you liked what happened?"

He sits up straighter, a pained expression marring his features. "I told you I like anything that happens with you." His hands grip the curves of my hips and he tugs me onto his lap.

"What if I wanted the four of us to be together again?" I ask, throwing it out there.

His eyes widen slightly. "I'll do whatever you want. As long as it makes you happy."

I sigh and wrap my arms around his neck, hating how insecure he is about us. I know it's because he hurt me in the past and he's afraid of doing it again, but I have faith in him, and I wish he would too.

"Would it make *you* happy being with them again?" I push. "And don't give me another bullshit answer about me being happy."

He swallows thickly. "Why are you doing this, MiMi?" He tightens his grip on my hips. "I'm happy just being with you."

"Because I love you," I tell him. "Enough to admit that you need more than just me… I saw the look on your face when Brayden was fucking you. You missed that…"

"So, we'll get a dildo and you can ram it into my ass," he bites out.

"That wouldn't be the same and you know it. The connection wouldn't be the same." I frame his face with my hands. "What the four of us share is different. It doesn't lessen or cheapen what you and I have. It adds to it. If you tell me you honestly don't want to be with Drew and Brayden ever again, then I'll drop it, but I think you know what I'm talking about. I think you feel what I feel."

Ashton's Adam's apple bobs in his throat. "How would this work?"

"I was actually looking it up online," I admit sheepishly. "On the way home yesterday while you were sleeping. There's a name for when multiple people are in a relationship… Polyamorous. The four of us could be together, in a relationship."

Ashton stares at me for several seconds before he speaks. "I'll do whatever you want, MiMi. Always. On one condition… No matter what happens, I never lose you."

"You're never going to lose me," I promise him.

"A poly-what?" Brayden asks from the couch next to Drew.

"Polyamorous," I repeat. When Drew and Brayden got home from their afternoon practice, I asked if we could all talk. I explained my thoughts about the four of us being together and I think I shocked them stupid.

"And not just sexual?" Drew asks. "But together… in a relationship?"

"That's right," Ashton says, tightening his hold on me. Once I showed him all the blogs where people are happily in polyamorous relationships, he seemed to ease into the idea more. "The four of us would be together in every way."

"And you're on board with this?" Drew eyes Ashton, knowing how protective he is of me. "You're okay with me coming home and fucking your girl."

"She would be our girl," Ashton says. "Just like you would be mine, and I would be Bray's." The guys both nod in thought.

"Growing up, I always felt like something was missing," I tell the three of them. "I didn't know it at the time, but I was craving love and affection… attention." This is something I haven't even admitted to Ashton. I needed to know how he felt first and I didn't want to guilt him into it. "All the things my parents didn't have the desire to give me."

Drew's jaw ticks in anger, and Brayden's hands form fists. "I'm not telling you this for you to feel sorry for me or be mad on my behalf. I'm telling you so you understand where I'm coming from. Each of you, in your own way, fills the voids my parents left behind. When I'm with you guys, I feel so full of love… I feel wanted and desired."

I move off Ashton's lap so I can look at all of them. "Ashton and I talked and we would like for the four of us to be together in a relationship. I know it's not conventional, but since when do any of us follow the rules of society?"

Brayden chuckles, looking at Drew. "I told you I wasn't the only one thinking about it."

"You guys talked about this too?" I ask.

"This morning," Drew says. "While you guys were in your room… fucking." He clears his throat. "We got home from practice and heard you. Brayden wanted to go in and join."

Ashton grins. "Aww, dude bro Bray is addicted to my dick."

Drew shakes his head but laughs. "So, how would we do this?"

"We would be together… as a unit," I explain. "The four of us. Together, separately. Obviously we've never done this before so we would have to see how it goes."

"I can't even be with Bray in public," Drew comments.

"Only until the end of the semester," Brayden tells him, threading his fingers through his own.

"But Brayden could be with us in public," Ashton says. "Mia and I don't give a fuck who knows what. And everyone would think the three of us are together."

"We could just take it one day at a time, explore the possibility and see how it goes," I tell them. "If it doesn't work out, just like in any relationship, we would break up… go our separate ways." Even if the thought makes me feel sick.

"I'm not going anywhere," Ashton murmurs. "I don't give a fuck how it goes. You're mine."

"If you guys need time to think and discuss, I understand," I tell Drew and Brayden. "And if you decide it's not something you're interested in, I will completely understand and respect that. I don't want to lose your friendship. The three of you have come to mean so much to me and if nothing else, I hope we can be friends."

"Get over here," Drew says.

I glance at Ashton, seeking his approval, and with a soft kiss to my lips, he releases me. I pad over to Drew and Brayden, stopping in front of them.

"I meant both of you," Drew says, looking around me at Ashton.

Ashton gets up and saunters over, dropping onto the couch next to Drew. Brayden tugs me down into his lap, so I'm lying across him, and Drew pulls my legs across his own.

"For this to work, we have to always be honest with each other," Drew says. "No jealousy, no hiding what we're feeling."

"Agree," I say at the same time Ashton and Brayden both nod.

"How would *this* work with all of us?" Brayden asks, palming my breast over my hoodie. I glance over at Ashton, who has his gaze trained on Brayden's hand, his eyes filled with lust.

"We've all been intimate with each other," I point out. "And prior to this, we were close individually. I read that some people are only together, all of them, and others are together individually." Brayden pinches my nipple through the material, and I gasp, the feeling shooting straight to my core. "I think if I'm tutoring and you guys want to get frisky, I'm cool as long as you give me cuddles when I get back." The guys laugh.

"Fuck, so we're really doing this, huh?" Drew asks, his eyes landing on Brayden.

"Yeah," Brayden says, kissing the side of my neck. "We are."

# TWENTY

## Drew

"Are you off the rag yet?" Ashton asks Mia, his hand already sliding up her thigh and into her pajama shorts. She's currently spread out across the couch, her head in my lap and her legs in Ashton's.

"Nope," she says, popping the P. "And as much as I would love for you to take my ass, I need to get to the tutoring center." She jumps off the couch and blows us each a kiss, then disappears into the bathroom.

"Maybe I should join her," Ashton muses, adjusting himself. "I bet she'd let me take her in the shower." He waggles his brows. "Wanna join us? We can tag team her."

I laugh, glancing at the clock on the wall. I have time... But this would be the first time we're together without one of us, since Brayden is in class. I came home to grab a quick lunch and ended up getting sucked into the show Mia and Ashton were watching.

I consider it for a moment. It's one thing to talk about all of us being in a relationship, but it's another to actually cross that line. If I go in there, it feels like it will solidify things, make it real. At the cabin, what happened could be considered a one-time thing, but if we do it again, and without Bray, it will change everything.

As I'm getting up the courage to stand, Mia comes out in only her towel. "I thought one of you would've joined me in the shower." She pouts playfully, and Ashton jumps up from the couch.

Her brown eyes meet mine and I stand as well. The look of want in her eyes is all I need to see to know that despite how fucking crazy this all is, I want this. I want them. All of them.

When I get into the bathroom, Ashton is already stripping out of his clothes and Mia is dropping her towel. "I call dibs on her ass," he says, dropping his pants and boxers onto the ground and then joining her in the shower.

Once I'm done removing my clothes, I open the door to the large, double-head shower. Mia and Ashton are already kissing, and his fingers are playing with her pussy. I step in and under the rainfall, enjoying the warm water and the show.

With Mia's back to me, I step up behind her and kiss her wet, naked shoulder.

"Finger her ass," Ashton says, handing me the bottle of lube. "Get her ready to take my big dick."

I squirt some lube onto my fingers and then push one between Mia's ass cheeks. She groans, kissing Ashton while he fingers her. I pull my finger out, then insert two, pumping them in and out of her tight-ringed hole.

"That's it, MiMi," Ashton croons. "Come all over our fingers, baby." At his words, Mia detonates. Her ass clenches around my fingers and her entire body shakes as she climaxes. Ashton pulls her face to him, kissing her hard. When he pulls back, he says, "Turn around and face Drew."

She turns toward me, moving her hair out of her face, and I take a moment to appreciate her. Her lips are slightly puffy from kissing Ashton and her rose-dusted nipples are pointed. I can't decide if I want to kiss her or suck on her tits.

As if she can read my thoughts, she smirks. "My nipples get really sensitive during my period. Be gentle."

I nod once then take her tits into my hands. I massage one, while my lips wrap around other. She groans in pleasure, jutting out her chest, silently demanding more.

"Stroke his dick, MiMi," Ashton tells her. "Make our boy come hard." He squirts more lube onto her ass and then pushes into her from behind. She moans loudly, grabbing my dick with one hand and my shoulder to hold herself up with the other. I let go of her breast and my mouth locks onto her neck, sucking and licking her wet flesh.

The harder Ashton fucks her, the harder she strokes my dick, and all too soon, my orgasm is rocketing through me at the same time Ashton roars out his own.

When he pulls out of her, she finds her footing and glances up at me. "Next time I want you both," she says. "Ashton in my ass and you in my pussy."

Ashton laughs. "No more watching porn for you, MiMi."

Mia giggles but doesn't correct him. She's so fucking cute.

"Shit," she says, as if remembering something. "I have to get to the tutoring center. I'm going to be late." She quickly shampoos her hair and washes her body and then hops out, leaving Ashton and me in the shower.

"Be ready to take lots of showers with that dirty girl," Ashton says to me, loud enough she can hear. "She's been researching positions that make *me* blush."

She laughs at his words as she exits the bathroom.

"Do you think Brayden could fit in here with us?" I ask as I soap down my front, my eyes skimming over Ashton's lean, but still muscular frame.

"We'll make him fit." He smirks. "Just like we all fit in that bed."

His mouth is twisted into a devious grin that I crave to taste. Leaning forward, I kiss his naughty lips. It's a sweet kiss, nothing more. We've come and are sated, but I just wanted to taste him.

Because I can.

Because we've agreed this is okay.

And it feels pretty fucking right.

He nips at my lips as he soaps me down. I'll be down to fuck the moment my dick is ready to play again. The idea of being with Ashton that way excites me. Just like I felt with Mia. This whole thing feels pretty damn good. Weird as fuck, but fantastic.

"Feed me before you fuck me, Coach," Ashton says, nipping at my bottom lip, a move that does wake my dick back up. "Pretty please."

"You're fucking spoiled," I playfully tease.

"You like spoiling me, Daddy." He can't even say that shit with a straight face before he loses it to hysterical laughing.

I turn the water off and step out of the shower, chuckling at his words as I grab a towel and throw one to Ashton. After we've both dried off, we wrap our towels around our torsos and head out to get dressed. I hear a door slam shut and assume it's Mia leaving, so I'm shocked when I step out of the bathroom and find Curtis standing in the doorway of Ashton's bedroom.

Fuck.

I freeze, unable to move or speak. Ashton squeezes past me, giving my ass a smack before he also screeches to a halt.

"What the hell did you do?" Curtis growls at his son.

It guts me that it's automatically Ashton's fault. It's not. This was us, not him. A group effort, not Ashton being the villain and dragging us all to the dark side with him.

"Curtis, let me explain—" I start, choking out my words.

"I came on to him," Ashton snaps, cutting me off. "That's what I do, Pops. I swing my dick around, hoping it lures in all your friends and colleagues just to fuck with your mind."

Curtis's face turns crimson and his hazel eyes harden. "I told you not to mess with him. He's a coach and you're the fucking dean's son, for crying out loud! You know how bad this looks on me?"

Ashton, God love him, doesn't even flinch, though I know it hurts that his father sees him as anything but the perfect, hilarious, kind man he is.

"Don't worry, Dad, I didn't fuck him and he didn't fuck me. Looks like you stepped in just in time to intervene."

I scrub my palm over my face. "We—"

"I don't want to hear about what sort of shit my son has roped you into. I get it. He can be persistent when he wants something, but don't worry about your reputation here. My son is probably already thinking about his next conquest, one that I'm sure will embarrass me even more than this." Curtis turns on his heel, storming out of the room.

Snagging up my discarded jeans, I throw them on and chase him to the door. "Curtis, wait."

He flings open the door but turns his angry gaze on me.

"I'm sorry," I choke out. "I didn't mean for you to find out that way." Or at all.

"Keep your dick in your pants, Thompson, or we're going to have big problems. Consider it a warning. I may not want to report this shit because it'll bring severe shame down on me and this university, but it doesn't mean someone else won't notice and do it anyway." Curtis scowls. "For your sake, I hope it was a one-time thing and my son has already moved on to the next shiny toy."

I open my mouth to defend Ashton, but Curtis storms away. I shut the door and stalk back to the bedroom to find Ashton pacing, his face twisted in fury.

"Ashton," I growl, gripping his jaw, forcing him to look at me. "I'm sorry."

He frowns, looking just like his father. "Why? It's my fault."

"None of this is your fault," I rumble. "It's unfortunate he saw what he did, but it doesn't change anything about us. Only that we need to change the fucking locks."

Ashton laughs. "I do feel a little bit happy that I ruined his day. Sorry you were a casualty."

"He doesn't know you like I do—like *we* do. You're fucking amazing, Ash. Hilarious and hot and affectionate." I give him a kiss. "And loyal. Fuck your dad for not seeing it."

And in a very vulnerable, un-Ashton like move, he hugs me tight, like he's afraid if he lets me go, I'll disappear forever.

It does something to me.

Wraps tentacles of protection around the place he's carved inside my heart.

I may be royally screwed as far as the dean's concerned, but I won't let it take the driver's seat in my mind. No, my concern lies with Ashton. He doesn't need to be made to feel like he's a cyclone that wrecks through everyone's worlds with no regard to the consequences.

"Ready for me to feed you, boyfriend?"

He laughs. "If it includes ice cream, I'm so in."

"Whatever you want," I say, nipping at his ear.

And I mean it.

It feels really good to make someone like Ashton Carter happy.

Really good.

# TWENTY-ONE

*Brayden*

I shake my head as I walk out of class reading Ashton's text.

**Ashton: Is your dick ready?**

**Me: Depends. For what?**

**Ashton: My mouth.**

Fucking Ashton. It's thrilling to know that he's serious and I'm allowed to do this with him because we're doing this. We're really doing this. My parents will probably shit bricks when they discover I'm dating three people all at once, but I can't find it in me to worry too much over that now.

Because I have them all.

Mia, Drew, and Ashton.

**Me: What sane man ever said no to a blowjob? Of course I'm fucking ready.**

**Ashton: My blowjobs are the best. Mia just got home and we're discussing with Drew who gives the best head. You're the only one who can answer this question. After I blow your mind.**

**Me: Awfully confident. Have you seen Mia's lips? Fucking swollen and perfect. And Drew's tongue? The bar is high, man.**

**Ashton: Tongue, lips… yeah, yeah, yeah. I can guarantee neither of them will suck you down their throat the way I can. Oh, Mia says hi and that this is awfully graphic for text.**

**Me: It's hot. Hey, beautiful.**

**Ashton: Hey yourself.**

**Me: That was for Mia.**

**Ashton: Sorry, she's too busy kissing Drew now. I guess it'll have to be for me instead.**

**Me: Fine, it's for you too. See you in a few.**

I shove the phone into my pocket, grinning. The thought of Ashton blowing me while Drew and Mia watch is almost too much to take. I'm looking forward to a blowjob competition. I'll be the true winner in the end.

"Brayden!" a high-pitched voice calls out.

Groaning, I turn to face the person. Sasha. Lovely. "Oh, hey."

"How've you been?" Sasha asks, touching my forearm. "I've been meaning to talk to you since the auction, but the sorority keeps me so busy."

"I'm good. Just headed home." Well, not mine…

"I could walk you," she offers.

"It's fine. What's up?"

Her pink lips purse, clearly annoyed at being turned down. "I just wanted to apologize."

"For?"

"For what happened at the auction." Her brows knit together. "I'm sure that was embarrassing in front of everyone. Your team. Coach. The dean. I know how private you are about certain *aspects* of your dating life."

"What was embarrassing?" Jesus. Did someone see Drew and me holding hands at the auction under the table? "And what aspects are you talking about?"

Her nose scrunches up. "Ashton bidding on you, silly. Everyone knows he's gay." She studies me for a moment. "People might wonder about you too."

I open my mouth to speak, but she continues.

"No one is going to hold it against you if you don't go on the date. He probably just wanted to humiliate me and his father. Ashton's like that. I've known him since I was a teenager. He's just rotten."

"Sasha," I growl, my voice laced with warning. "You can stop worrying because it was fine. Ashton and I had a great date."

Her eyes widen comically. "Ew, you poor thing. He actually made you go through with it? If he put his hands on you, we can report this—"

"Stop," I snap. "Leave him alone."

My harsh words have her recoiling. "Brayden…"

I'm about to bail, annoyed with the way she talks about Ashton, when I see him.

Not Ashton.

Travis.

Rage builds up inside me hot and quick. I take off running in his direction, dumb Sasha long forgotten. Travis sees me coming and sprints down the corridor. He skids to a halt and darts down a hall. I run after him, turning the corner just in time to see him slip into the restroom. I rush toward it and fling open the door. My chest heaves from exertion as I seek him out. A stall door starts to close, but I stop it with my arm.

"What the fuck, man?" he snarls.

I shove my way into the stall, crowding him against the partition wall. He groans when I press my forearm against his windpipe, leaning in to glower at him.

"You think it's okay to fucking slash Ashton's tires? To frame him for drugs? To threaten and try to poison him?" I press harder, making him wheeze. "I should beat your fucking ass for that shit!"

"For Ashton? He doesn't deserve your loyalty," he hisses.

"Fuck you. You don't get to say what Ashton deserves."

"If you're going to beat me up, defending your boy's honor, then do it." He laughs cruelly. "That's right. You can't. That would get you kicked off the hockey team and probably out of this school."

This little bitch.

"Don't text Ashton. Don't look at Ashton. Don't fucking touch Ashton." I snarl at him. "I'd give that shit up just to watch you piss your pants as I kicked your goddamn teeth in." I release him and smack his cheek. "I'm not fucking playing with you. Fuck with Ashton and it's guaranteed, I will fuck with you."

I push out of the bathroom stall, eager to get the hell away from that snake before I lose control. As much as I want to kill him, I can't. I'll get in trouble. He doesn't need to know that, though. I want him to have felt my wrath and the seriousness of my words. As soon as I exit the bathroom, I nearly knock Sasha over.

"Brayden, we're not through discussing this," she whines.

"Later," I grind out.

I'm pissed the entire way home. Practically fuming by the time I reach Ashton and Drew's. When the key Drew gave me doesn't fit in the lock, I have a moment of panic.

What's happening?

For a brief moment, my insecurities swell up inside me. They don't want me anymore. Then, as fast as those thoughts appear, they vanish.

Ashton promised a blowjob.

And if there's anything I know about Ashton, it's he never jokes about a sexual promise.

I bang on the door. Mia answers with a smile. Pulling her to me, I kiss her supple lips, needing to feel like I matter and belong here. She returns the kiss with urgency, calming the storm that was brewing inside of me.

When we pull apart, I let out a heavy sigh. "I thought you guys locked me out."

"Silly boy," she says, swatting at my chest. "You're one of us."

"We're locking Dad out," Ashton says as I walk in with Mia, shutting the door behind me.

"Oh boy," I groan.

Drew exits the kitchen, looking fucking hot in sweatpants and no shirt. "He saw something he shouldn't have."

"Fuck," I hiss. "What happened?"

Drew stops to kiss me. "He walked into the bedroom as Ashton and I were leaving the bathroom in nothing but our towels."

"We were still horny as fuck because Mia is insatiable," Ashton tattles, "and were discussing how next time we're going to cram the four of us in there when that cockblocking asshole waltzed in."

I drop my bag on the floor, grabbing Ashton's hand. He threads his fingers with mine. "What did he say?" I demand, searching Ashton's eyes. "What did he do?"

"Blamed me, of course," Ashton says, a dry laugh barking from him.

Hurt. Pained. Sad.

I pull him to me, hugging him tight. "Fuck that asshole."

"That's what I said," Drew grunts.

"Me too," Mia chimes in.

"So you changed the locks?" I ask, unable to break free of the hold I have on Ashton. Sometimes he's so broken, I just want to keep him held together.

"Can't have him trying to get peep shows when we have our bj wars," Ashton says, meeting my stare with a shit-eating grin.

I kiss his stupidly hot mouth. "You're so damned confident you're going to win."

"I know my worth in this world," he jokes.

His comment rubs me the wrong way. Ashton is a fuck more than a good lay. I cup his jaw, leaning my forehead against his. "You're worth a whole lot to us."

Mia and Drew both agree.

"Come on," Ashton says. "I'm tired of whipping their asses at NHL 20. Play with me. I'll suck you off later."

I leave them to take a quick shower in Drew's bathroom and then change into some basketball shorts, bypassing my shirt altogether. When I return to the living room, Drew and Mia are stretched out on the sofa, cuddled up. His fingers stroke the bare skin on her thigh just below her shorts. Ashton already has the game started and is sitting on the coffee table. His eyes skim down my bare torso and he licks his lips.

"Not fair for you to distract me," he complains.

I chuckle as I sit next to him, our thighs touching, and pick up the controller. "If I want my dick sucked, I have to woo you."

He palms me over my shorts. "If you want your dick sucked before the game instead of after, all you have to do is ask."

"If you keep touching me like that, I won't be asking," I growl, leaning in to kiss his neck. "I'll be taking."

He sets the controller down and slides to the floor, coming between my thighs. "You keep talking to me like you're going to destroy my throat with your dick and I'll give you whatever you goddamn please."

I lift my hips as he draws my shorts off my ass and down my thighs. My heavy erection bobs out, leaking precum already. His devilish, starved grin does me in as he flicks his tongue across the tip.

Because I can't help myself, I roughly fist his hair. With Drew, he's always so hungry for my dick. When Mia sucked me off, she was so sweet and innocent about it.

Ashton, though…

I can tell he's going to try and rule me from his knees.

He grips my cock, stroking it lazily. "Ready to die by dick sucking overload?"

"I mean, are there better ways to go because I'm not sure there are." I grin at him until he wraps his mouth around my cock.

A guttural groan escapes me as his tongue lashes with purpose against my shaft. He pulls all the way off, licks the tip, and then slides down for more. Way more. I nearly come off the coffee table when my dick pushes down his throat.

So fucking tight.

So hot.

Holy shit.

Before I can embarrass the hell out of myself, he pulls all the way off, gives me a flirty wink, and then dives back down. My grip tightens in his hair. This time, when he starts to pull back in that teasing way of his, I yank him back down, groaning at the way his nose tickles the hairs at the base of my cock.

"You want to fucking win," I grit out, pulling his hair up and down to dictate the pleasure I want from him, "you gotta earn it."

He makes a gagging sound that feels really fucking good on my dick. I ease up on my grip, allowing him to come up for air, and then I buck my hips up, eager for more. His mouth works its magic again, taking me deep in his throat. It's fucking hot to see slobber run down his chin each time I allow him to breathe.

"Swallow me down, baby," I murmur. "It feels good."

He hums around my dick just as his hand rubs my balls that are slick from his saliva. I curse at the abrupt way I come. Cum jets down his throat and it's the most divine feeling. With each pulse of my dick, his throat constricts. Once I'm spent, he slides off my dick. I take a moment to admire this handsome guy. His lips are wet and swollen, hazel eyes half-lidded. Dark hair is mussed from my mishandling and his chin is wet. Super fucking hot.

A smug grin curls his lips up. "Who won?"

He knows he did.

Just wait until Drew learns to deep throat like that. I know my best friend. He'll compete until he's the fucking champion. Rather than giving Ashton what he wants, I shrug.

"It's a tie," I say with a smirk, dipping to kiss his mouth. "Guess you guys will have to continue to battle it out."

"Sonofabitch," Ashton states. "You play dirty, man. It's a good thing I play dirtier."

Mia flips through every damn Netflix show she can find before settling on something that's in fucking subtitles. Ashton groans and Drew chuckles.

"We need a bigger couch," I say, twirling a long strand of Mia's hair.

She's curled up in my lap with her feet in Ashton's lap as he gives them a massage. Drew's on the other end of the couch, his arm around Ashton. We barely fucking fit.

Mia's phone buzzes and she reads the text, groaning. Since I can see, I read it too.

**Mom: A reminder that the California Actors' League Winter Soiree is in two weeks. I expect you to be there. I've ordered a stunning ice-blue Vera Wang ball gown in your size. That is, if that's still your size. If not, call Dayna about some weight loss supplements. I can't make a change this close to the event.**

"What a bitch," I grumble.

Ashton grabs Mia's phone to read the text. "Tell her you're in great shape from fucking all your boyfriends." He tosses it at Drew.

"Delusional-ass woman," Drew complains after he reads the text, handing it back to Mia. "Ignore her."

The phone buzzes in Mia's hands.

**Mom: Will you bring the same young man again? I'll need to accurately RSVP if you intend to bring a plus one.**

"Tell her you're bringing a plus three," Ashton gripes when she shows him the text.

She sits up. "You want to go?"

"To fuck with your mom and support you? Hell yeah," Ashton states. "They'll come too."

"Of course I'll be there," I tell her, pressing a kiss to her neck. "Just like last time. I've got your back."

She turns her attention to Drew. He frowns, a sad as fuck look on his face.

"Mia," he mutters. "I'll come too, but…"

"You can't be seen at such a public event because of your position," she says, reaching for his hand. "But you'll still come? We can stay at a hotel together. The four of us."

He pulls her hand to his mouth and kisses the back of it. "I can do that. The event itself, I can't, though. I hate that. I want to be there to help protect you from your wicked witch mother."

"As long as you're waiting for us when the dumb thing is over, I'll be happy." She beams at him and then texts her mother back.

**Mia: Plus two.**

**Mom: Two? Whatever. Make sure they know it's a black-tie affair. Don't embarrass me.**

"I can't wait to meet Mommy Dearest," Ashton says in a sinister tone. "Cannot fucking wait."

"Are you going to be good?" Mia asks, poking him with her foot.

"MiMi, I think we both know the answer to that question." He playfully bites her toe and then we go back to watching the dumb show we have to pay extra close attention to so we know what the fuck is going on.

Everyone goes quiet and the mood is content.

I could get used to this.

Every damn day.

# TWENTY-TWO

*Ashton*

*Two Weeks Later*

I want to bite her ass.

It's delectable as fuck. The light blue, sparkling evening gown she was supposed to wear was waiting in concierge when we arrived at the hotel. Shoes. Accessories. A goddamn stylist. I'd been pissed to watch Mia transform into this doll for dressing up, but when they finished, my dick wasn't pissed at all.

Mia is the hottest goddamn woman to walk the face of the earth.

Even now, as I follow behind her and Brayden into the fancy-ass hotel this event is at, I only have eyes for her. The other women—celebrities I recognize well—don't hold a candle to my girl. Our girl. Brayden is proud as fuck to have her on his arm. I'd be on the other side, but she seemed nervous and I didn't want to make a scene. Besides, I'm enjoying the view of her perfect ass.

"Cristal?" a man asks, holding a tray filled with champagne flutes.

"Thank you," she says. She takes one and then Brayden and I each take one.

I've had Cristal plenty because Mom is a fancy bitch like Mia's. It's okay. I prefer the cheap vodka that makes me puke and hate my soul when I've had too much. I'm not a fancy guy.

Brayden sets his down on a table as we pass.

He sure as fuck isn't a fancy guy either.

I pull out my phone, texting Drew.

**Me: Cristal. Y or N.**

**Drew: Is this a trick question?**

**Me: Are you a fancy fucker, boyfriend?**

**Drew: My dick is fancy.**

**Me: Send me a pic.**

He sends me the middle finger emoji instead.

**Me: SOS.**

**Drew: Really need a savior?**

Imagining Drew blazing in here all hot as fuck in his sweatpants—since that's all he was wearing when we left—makes my dick hard.

**Me: I'll keep you advised.**

**Drew: The answer to your question is no. I prefer beer.**

**Me: I love you.**

It's meant as a joke, but I suddenly don't feel as though it's a joke. For the past couple of weeks, we've all grown closer. I thought we'd split off maybe, but those big-ass hockey players join Mia in my bed every damn night. My bed is an oversized king, so we all fit, but I wouldn't complain if we got a bigger one.

**Drew: Love you too, Ash. Love all of you.**

My heart squeezes in my chest. It feels right with the three of them. So right. At first, I was worried I would fuck things up with Mia, but I've never seen her so happy. She really rocked my world when she said how deprived of love she was growing up, and that she craves extra love because of it. It shaped the way I viewed this new group dynamic we have.

Mia deserves more.

We can all give it to her if we work together as a team.

She deserves it.

As much as I want to live in this happy as hell moment with them, I can't help but have this niggling feeling of the other shoe waiting to drop. I don't trust Travis with that video he has. And after Dad busting us, it's especially worrying. Considering he hasn't used it, he probably only intends to threaten me with it, but I still worry.

"Hello, darling," a woman purrs. "Are you an actor or a model?"

I lift my gaze where I was staring at my phone and am confused to find my lovers are gone and I'm stuck with a botoxed woman who looks like she may have been on one of Mom's soaps she used to watch when I was a kid.

"What?" I ask, scanning the room for my people.

"I'm Barbara Lyndell from A World Apart." She preens. "And you are…"

"Ashton. Just Ashton. Have you seen a drop-dead gorgeous brunette in a pale blue dress walking with a sexy-ass dude in a suit who looks like he could bench her?"

"Claire's daughter?" she asks, frowning, though her forehead doesn't wrinkle at all—totally juiced up on the good stuff. "They're probably over there." She points a long red fingernail to a crowd of people laughing. "Are you friends with the girl?"

"She's my girlfriend," I state. "If you'll excuse me…"

She bites her claws into my tuxedo jacket. "What a lucky girl. Claire wants her to go into the biz. It's lovely she's dating an actor now. Her mother will be pleased. Last I heard, little Mia was dating a poor college boy. Claire was devastated. Had to seek therapy and everything."

I gape at this woman. "Are you tight with Claire?"

"Everyone in this biz is tight. Keep your enemies close, your enemies closer."

"That's not how the saying goes—"

"In Hollywood, we're all enemies. We're just really good at acting. Send Claire my love."

I pull away from the dinosaur and stalk through the crowd, needing to be near my girl. These people are vultures. Sick assholes who get off on the perverseness of seeing others suffer.

My girl needs rescuing.

We're getting the fuck out of here and soon.

I'll text Drew after I find her and Bray and get him to grab an Uber to pick us up.

Pushing past someone I know I've seen in at least ten movies, I make my way into the inner circle of the crowd. A woman who looks like an older version of Mia smiles at her group of starving vultures just waiting for her to slip up so they can feast on her. They laugh because they're good at acting as Dino-Barbara says. I hate them all.

Mia is stiff, clutching Brayden's hand tight. I don't know what's being said, but I can tell Mia is the butt of the joke based on the veins popping in Brayden's neck. The man beside Claire also resembles Mia, but he's missing her fire and flare and strength. He's a spineless pussy.

"Hey, baby," I say, slinging my arm over Mia's shoulders. "Your ass is looking fantastic in this dress. You ready to bail on this lame-ass old people show and get back to the hotel?" I nip at her neck, loving the breathy laugh that escapes her.

Claire isn't laughing now.

Her icy glare is fixated on me.

"Darling," Claire hisses. "I'm confused. Do you know this young man or should I have security show him out?"

"He's with me," Mia bites out.

Claire glowers at her. "Your decisions regarding your life lately are concerning. First, you've developed this eating disorder where you consume everything in sight and now, you're acting out sexually. You're an embarrassment to me and your father."

I turn my glare on Claire, slowly inspecting all her flaws and letting it show on my face. Wrinkles she tries to hide. She and Ancient Barb must see the same skin doc. Skin that's no longer smooth and perfect like her daughter's. Thinner hair than her daughter's. Saggier tits. Pursed, wrinkly lips. It's the sneer on her face that makes her so horrible to look at.

She's ugly inside and out.

Everyone knows it, especially her.

"Mia, is this old witchy woman bothering you?" I ask, ignoring the bitch.

"Mother," Mia says, straightening her spine. "My decisions are mine to make, not yours. This is my other boyfriend, Ashton."

The group around us gasps and her father's face pales. He says nothing. Does nothing.

Her mother, though, is furious.

Red slowly turns to purple on Claire's face like a pimple ready to burst. She raises her hand, but I preempt her move, releasing Mia to stand in front of her. The vile woman smacks me hard against the cheek, her eyes flickering with hatred.

Several cameras flash.

I step forward, sneering at Mia's horrible mother. "Your friend Barbie Lyndell thinks it's time for you to see your therapist again. This time, why don't you seek help for the emotional and mental abuse you've spent eighteen years inflicting on your daughter?"

"How dare you," Claire seethes. "She is my daughter and our relationship is none of your business."

"The hell it isn't," I snap. "She's my goddamn girlfriend and I'll be damned if I let you belittle her like she's a piece of shit. Apologize."

"Mia," Claire shrieks. "Are you going to let him speak to me this way?"

"He's right." Mia steps up beside me and takes my hand. "You're horrible to me."

"People are watching," her mother hisses.

"I'm sure they've all witnessed your cruelty firsthand, especially Dad," Mia says, lifting her chin. "These two men are my boyfriends and I won't be ashamed of that. I'm tired of not being enough for you—for either of you."

"Mia," her father murmurs weakly but gets shut down with an icy glare from Claire.

"You don't want to do this," Claire warns.

"I already have," Mia says as Brayden takes her other hand. "We're leaving. I think we've overstayed our welcome."

"You walk out that door with them and I will disown you! You can kiss your spoiled life goodbye!" Claire shrieks. "I will cut you off before you take your first breath outside that door!"

"Goodbye, Mother." Then to her dad, she says, "Thanks for sticking up for me, Dad."

I flip the bitch off and then drag my girl away from the horde of ravenous onlookers. As we pass the osteoporosis Barbara, she cackles.

"Lovely show, young man. I knew I liked you." She winks like I did her a goddamn favor.

I flip her off too. "Go home, old lady. You're a decrepit antique in a room full of shiny trophies. I'm embarrassed for you."

She gapes at me, but I don't give a fuck. I'm so over these monsters. All I care about is getting my girl the fuck out of here. We make it outside and Brayden bulldozes a path for us to the parking garage. His phone is pressed to his ear as he urgently speaks to someone. By the time we make it away from the curious people, a limo screeches to a halt in front of us.

The window rolls down, revealing our motherfucking prince charming. Thank fuck.

We climb in with Drew. Mia gets pulled into his arms while I settle in the seat across from them with Brayden. I'm quaking with fury. How fucking dare that bitch say those things to our girl?

"You okay?" Drew asks, stroking her hair.

"I am now." She smiles my way. "Thank you guys for being here."

"I'm sorry," I grumble. "I know she's your mom, but she infuriated me with how she spoke to you."

"I'm glad it happened," Mia admits. "It was inevitable."

"I shouldn't have exploded in front of all those people." I pinch the bridge of my nose. "Fuck."

Brayden's hand rubs at the back of my neck. "You spoke seconds before me, man. I wasn't going to take any more of the shitty remarks about our girl. If Drew were there, he would've done the same thing."

"My heroes," Mia says, laughing. "Ashy C, look at me."

I drop my hand to stare at the most beautiful girl in the world.

"I love you," she assures me. "And as much as I dread the fallout of what my mother will do, I don't regret it. It gives me pure joy you put her in her place in front of all her friends."

They chatter lightly the entire way back to the hotel while I stew. It's not until we've showered and I have Mia's naked body beneath me that I finally feel okay with what I did.

We'll protect her.

From everyone.

Especially toxic bitches like her mother.

I go to sleep, confident in the fact we always will.

# TWENTY-THREE

*Mia*

"Is this really necessary?" Brayden asks, yanking my chair over to his. "We could've done this at your place… at Ashton and Drew's…" He throws his arm around me and nuzzles his face into my neck, and for the millionth time in the last hour, I shake my head and move my chair away from him.

"Yes, it's necessary." I hit him with a pointed look I hope comes across as stern. "You can't keep your hands off me *here*. Do you really think we'd get any studying done in private?"

Brayden shrugs. "Maybe not English or History, but I bet we could get other studying done." He waggles his brows and I pull the front of his hat down to cover his eyes.

"How're you feeling about your finals?" I ask, changing the subject.

"Good. It's crazy to think after this, I'll only have one semester left and then I'll be a college graduate."

"You've got this." I reach over and squeeze his hand.

A couple walking by glances over at us, intrigued. The rumor mill is running on overdrive. I've heard the whispers. Seen the looks. We haven't confirmed anything because it's nobody's damn business, but since returning from the disastrous event in California, Brayden, Ashton, and I have been spending time together publicly. Sometimes Ashton walks me to class holding my hand, or Brayden kisses me in the tutoring center. I'm not ashamed to love three men and I refuse to hide it—with the exception of Drew. I hate that we have to keep him a secret, but it's not about being ashamed. He would lose his job if anyone found out that he's dating a student—or three.

"I'm studied out," Brayden says, standing. "Why don't we go grab a coffee before I head to practice?"

"Fine," I agree, since I could use a caffeinated pick-me-up.

When we get to Starbucks, which is located on campus in the quad, I order on my app like I always do so we don't have to wait in line, but when I click to place my order, it comes back denied. Weird. I click to purchase using a different card, but it does the same thing.

"Did you order?" Brayden asks.

"I think my app is messed up."

When we get to the front of the line, finally, I give the barista our order and hand her my credit card.

"I'm sorry, but your card has been declined," she says, flinching.

I hand her another card, but she shakes her head. "I'm sorry, it was declined too."

"I got it," Brayden says, shooting me a sympathetic look. He hands her his card and it goes through without issue.

"Thanks. I'm going to see what's going on with my cards."

"I'll meet you at the table," he says, leaning over and kissing me softly.

I walk over to an empty table and pull up my bank app first. My hands shake as I wait for the home screen to pop up, and when it does, I nearly hyperventilate. Zero. There are zero dollars in my bank account. How is this even possible? Was my account hacked? But then I remember my credit card was declined too.

I open up my contacts and pull up my mom's number… Then scroll up to my dad.

Before I hit call, Brayden comes over with our coffees and sits down. "Everything okay?"

"I'm sure it's just a mix-up," I murmur, taking a sip of my coffee. My peppermint mocha latte is usually sweet, but today it tastes like cardboard, and I know it's because I'm freaking out. Mom warned me… I thought because I haven't heard from her in a couple weeks, she forgot about me. But I should've known better.

"My parents want to have us all over for dinner," Brayden says, taking a sip of his own coffee.

"That'll be fun." I force a smile. I love Brayden's parents. They're so sweet and nurturing. "Maybe Molly can show me how to make a new dish." She's been sending me easy recipes to try out and so far they've been a success. The boys have not only eaten them, but none of them have died from food poisoning.

"I want to tell them about us." He gnaws on his bottom lip. "I'm a little worried they'll flip, but I want them to know." He doesn't say it, but I know he's thinking that he has enough secrets he's keeping from them.

"I think initially they'll be shocked, but I don't believe they'll disown you or anything." Not like my parents have…

"I don't think so either," he says, staring out the window. I follow his line of vision and see Drew walking across the quad. I want so badly to call him over to join us, but we can't.

"I can't wait to get the hell out of here," Brayden says, anger dripping in his words. I know he's thinking about finally being free to be with Drew out in public but…

"I have three more years." If I can even afford to continue here. If I'm right and my parents did cut me off, there's no way they're going to keep paying for my apartment, or my utilities, or my food.

Brayden frowns as if just realizing that when he leaves, I'll still be here. And I have no clue where Ashton will be… And if Drew is still the coach here, we'll be in the same position we're in now.

"Yo, Brayden," a guy calls out. "Practice in ten!"

"Shit, I gotta get going." He jumps up and then dips down, kissing me goodbye. "I'll see you at home later." Home… It's technically neither of our homes, yet it feels like more of a home than the one I grew up in.

When he's gone, I take my coffee outside and call Dad. He answers on the first ring.

"Mia." The single word is laced with sympathy, and I immediately know there wasn't a mix-up.

"So, it's true," I say in greeting, not even bothering to ask the question.

"Your mother felt it was best—"

"To cut me off financially while I'm in college?"

"To go with tough love," he finishes.

"What the hell is tough love?" I hiss. "Neither of you has shown me any kind of love in years. Now you want to try and parent?" Angry tears leak from the corners of my eyes.

"Your mother feels you're making bad choices, sweetheart. Come home and we'll help you get back on track. You can enroll in college here, live at home…"

I swallow the lump in my throat, knowing this is probably the last conversation we'll ever have because I can't be part of a family who doesn't love and accept me. Ashton, Brayden, and Drew are my family. They love me and accept me. They support me…

"I'm not coming back," I tell him. "This is my home." And I'll do everything in my power to make sure of it.

He sighs. "I understand, but if you change your mind…"

"I won't." Nothing can make me change my mind about my boys. They're mine and I'm theirs and anyone who doesn't understand can go kick rocks.

Without bothering to say goodbye, I hang up and head over to the financial aid office.

"How can I help you?" a cheery, gray-haired woman asks.

"I'm interested in applying for a loan." Because I'm under twenty-five and my parents make too much money, I'm not eligible to receive any grants.

"Here's the website." She slides a paper over to me. "This tells you everything you'll need on hand when you apply. Applications must be received on or before April thirtieth to be eligible for the summer."

"Oh, no, I need to apply for… now."

"I'm sorry, but all financial aid is closed for the spring semester. The earliest you would be approved, if you're approved, is for summer."

My heart plummets into my stomach. "Okay, thank you." I take the paper from her and walk out of the office. My mind is numb and my body is on autopilot the entire walk back to my apartment. Normally, I would go straight to Ashton's, but I need a few minutes to myself and I haven't been home in several days.

When I step up to my door and unlock it, an envelope falls to the ground. I pick it up and, seeing it's from the leasing management office, nearly throw up my coffee. I rip it open and read it twice before it sinks in. It's a letter of non-renewal of my lease. I'm being evicted by my parents.

Slamming my door closed, I rush down the hallway and fly down the stairs. I have to fix this. They can't kick me out of my apartment. I'll be homeless.

When I enter the office, I walk over to the first person I see. "I received this letter. It says I need to be out in two weeks. This can't be right."

The woman's brows furrow as she reads over the letter. "I'm afraid this is correct. Your lease is up at the end of the month and we received your denial to renew."

"That was my parents," I explain, trying to remain calm. "I would like to renew."

She types away on her keyword and then frowns. "I'm sorry, but when we received the letter, we signed a contract with someone else. There's a waitlist and—"

"So, that's it? You're kicking me out of my apartment without anywhere to go." Hot tears spill down my cheeks and I almost feel sorry for the woman, who looks extremely uncomfortable. This isn't her fault. It's my parents', and it's mine. Theirs for pulling this shit, and mine for not staying two steps ahead.

Snagging the letter off the desk, I run out of the office, needing to get myself under control. My chest is tightening and my body is shaking. My hands are trembling so badly, I can barely hold the letter between my fingers. I wander mindlessly around campus, unsure where to go from here. I have no job, no money, and soon I'll have no place to live.

Then there's the issue of school. I'm going to have to take at least a semester off, so I can come up with the money to rent another apartment. But if I do that, will I lose my scholarship? I'll have to look into that.

And by the time I'm back in school, Ashton and Brayden will have graduated. That reality damn near knocks the wind out of me. In less than six months Brayden will be on his way to whatever city drafts him, and Ashton… he's mentioned more than once that he has no desire to stay here past graduation. Drew will still be here, but it's not as if we can live together. We can't even be seen together in public without him risking his job.

I wrap my arms around my waist, cold and heartbroken at the thought of losing school, my apartment, and my guys.

"Mia," a masculine voice calls out, cutting through the fog of my thoughts. When I glance over I find Drew walking down the sidewalk. He's dressed in his suit, having come from practice and probably a meeting.

The second he sees me, his lips turn down in a frown. "What happened?" he asks, ignoring that we're in public and pulling me into his arms. He wipes the falling tears and I close my eyes, breathing in his comforting scent. For several minutes, we just stand here. Me in his arms, my head against his chest. Drew, holding me tightly, running his fingers up and down my back.

"Talk to me, baby," he murmurs after a while.

"My parents cut me off," I choke out, wrapping my arms around him tighter. "My money, my apartment… They took it all away."

Drew's grip on me tightens. "Are you fucking serious?"

"They drained my accounts, canceled my credit cards… They even made sure to let the leasing company know they won't be renewing my lease. I have two weeks to move out."

"Fuck," he hisses. Then he pulls back so he can look at me. "We'll figure this out. I promise." I nod slightly, wanting to believe him, but I don't know how we're going to figure it out.

Drew walks with me through campus, never letting go of me. When we get inside his and Ashton's apartment, both guys are already there. They're playing a video game and when they hear the door open and close they glance back.

Ashton is the first to speak. "What the fuck happened?" He springs to his feet and stalks over to me.

"Her parents cut her off," Drew says since I'm now crying too hard to speak. "And your fucking dad evicted her."

Ashton tenses. "He what?"

"How?" Brayden barks out.

"It's his building," Drew grumbles. "I thought he was better than that."

"It's okay, Mia," Brayden says, rubbing his hand along my back. "We'll figure it out."

"Goddamn right we will," Ashton growls. "I'm going to figure it out right now."

Brayden pulls me to him and I watch as Ashton dials his dad, putting him on speaker. Drew remains scowling nearby with his arms crossed over his chest while Ashton paces, thrumming with rage.

"Hello?" Curtis greets.

"You kicked Mia out? What kind of asshole are you?" Ashton berates. "You can be mad at me and the shit I pull, but do not ever think you can punish me by hurting her. Fuck you, man!"

"Hold the hell on, Son. What's going on?" Curtis snaps back, annoyed. "I don't know what you're running your head about."

"Give me a fucking break, Dad. It's your goddamn building!" Ashton fires back. "Don't play stupid."

Drew walks over to Ashton and speaks. "Mia's been evicted."

"There must be some misunderstanding. She wouldn't just get

evicted," Curtis states, confusion in his tone. "Let me take a look at my email. All evictions have to be sent to me."

We wait quietly, a thread of hope keeping us on edge, as Curtis taps away on his keyboard. After a few minutes, he groans.

"I was afraid of that," Curtis mumbles to himself. "It's not an eviction. There was a signed non-renewal of the lease by her parents."

"Same fucking thing!" Ashton yells. "You let it happen. Fix it!"

"I can't just fix it, Ashton," Curtis grinds out. "There's already a new lease that's been signed. The new tenant will take possession in two weeks."

"Undo it," Ashton orders.

"I can't," Curtis mutters, exasperated. "It's a matter of legality. I can put her on the waitlist—"

"Thanks for all the help, Dad," Ashton sneers. "Mia's homeless now."

He ends the call, tossing his phone onto the couch before he yanks me into his arms. I cling to him, overwhelmed by the sudden changes in my life.

I'm sobbing so hard, I'm hyperventilating now. Ashton strokes his fingers through my hair.

"Shh, MiMi," he murmurs. "We'll take care of you. You'll move in here. Sleep in my bed. Everything's going to be fine."

I nod, because I want to believe it will all be okay. With my guys touching me and whispering assurances, I think it might be.

"They took all my money," I tell Ashton. "I won't be able to help pay—"

"You're not paying for shit," Ashton growls. "Don't you dare worry about money or housing or anyfuckingthing. Between Drew, Brayden, and me, we'll make sure you're all taken care of. You trust us?"

I pull away so I can give him a watery smile. "Yes." And that's the truth. I trust all three of them completely. I should've known my guys would have my back. Instead of wandering around aimlessly for hours, I should've come straight here. We're a unit. A family. When one of us needs the others, we're there for each other. They're not my parents. They love me and would never let anything happen to me.

Ashton kisses my forehead. "Good. Now go find an ugly sweater. We're going Christmas tree shopping to celebrate."

"To celebrate my financial ruin?" I say with a weak laugh.

"To celebrate you officially becoming ours. And picking out a family Christmas tree for our living room seems like a fucking fantastic way to do it."

Officially becoming theirs…

That's something to celebrate for sure.

# TWENTY-FOUR



"**D**on't start something you can't finish," I say, arching a brow at Mia, who's standing in the middle of Ashton's room with just a towel on.

"What?" She chews on her bottom lip. "I'm just getting ready to go visit your parents."

"No, MiMi," Ashton says, not looking up from his video game. "You're prancing around asking to get dicks in every one of your holes."

Drew snorts out a laugh as he enters the bedroom. "Every hole, hmm?"

She puts her hands on her hips over her towel and scowls. "I am not. It's not my fault you three are horny asses who can't let a girl walk through a room without a fuss."

"Not just any girl," Ashton pipes up. "Our girl."

"I guess we could make time," I tease, grinning at her. "Seeing as you're hinting about wanting three dicks."

"You guys are assholes," she grumbles, unable to hide her laugh. "I hate you all."

Mia's a big liar.

She doesn't hate us.

And she's totally fucking prancing.

When she passes by the bed, Ashton tosses the controller away so he can grab her towel. It falls away, exposing her perfectly curvaceous body. She sighs as though she's annoyed, making a great show of bending over to open one of the drawers on Ashton's dresser that he emptied for her to store some clothes in. My dick hardens just thinking about being inside our girl.

We've done lots of stuff.

The one thing I haven't done, though, is fuck Mia.

Not that we haven't wanted to. It's just, when we all get together, it gets a little crazy. Each time, it just hasn't worked out that way. Today, though, I'm going to make sure it happens.

On the same wavelength, Ashton starts stripping as Drew kicks his shoes off. I whip off my hoodie and shirt, eager for this little detour before we have to leave to go have dinner at my parents' house. By the time Mia turns around, having slowly settled on the skimpiest pair of red panties she has in her drawer, we're all naked and stroking our hard dicks.

"We'll be late," she whines.

Ashton stretches out on the middle of the bed, curling his finger to beckon her over. "You shouldn't have strutted in here, swaying that ass, MiMi. You know we can't resist you."

She smirks. "Fine, you caught me. I've never lived with boys before, though. I'm not sure I know how to act."

After Christmas tree shopping a few days ago, the three of us helped her pack up her stuff. Since her parents were being such dicks and cut her off, and she insisted she didn't want to completely depend on us, we helped her sell the furniture on CampusList to give her some cash. Then, we moved all her stuff into Ashton's place. She's officially ours.

"Get the lube," I tell Drew. "We gotta get Mia's ass nice and slick to take Ashton's big dick."

He grins like a loon from the bed. "Damn right."

"And I'm going to sink inside this pretty pussy I've been dreaming about since the day I met you," I say to her, dipping to kiss her lips.

"Both?" she asks, a nervous edge to her voice.

"Or one at a time," I offer. "Whatever you want, Mia. I just need to be inside you. I'm starting to feel neglected."

She laughs. "Poor Brayden."

Drew approaches, the lube in his hand. "What's it going to be, sweetheart? You going to let us tag team you or are you going to be a good girl and take all three of us like you were born to do?"

Her eyes flutter closed and she gasps as he pushes his finger inside her ass. I grip her jaw and kiss her hard, in a claiming way. She's ours and I want her to know it.

"Fucking hot," Ashton growls. "I could whack off to the three of you all damn day until my dick fell off."

Mia and I smile through our kiss at his words. I pinch her nipple and then slide my hand down to her pussy. She whimpers when I rub her clit.

"You like that, baby?" I murmur.

"Yes," she breathes. "So much."

"I'm going to fuck your throat," Drew growls. "While these two guys fuck you senseless, I'm going to let you put those pretty lips around my dick."

She moans in pleasure. It's easy to bring her to orgasm. Mia gets incredibly turned on by dirty talk. Add in a little ass play while you touch her pussy and she goes off like fireworks on the Fourth of July.

Her cries of ecstasy are garbled and incoherent, making the three of us guys chuckle. Once she's come down from her high, Drew removes his fingers from her ass. He grips her hair, tugging her head backward, and then plants a hot kiss on her lips.

After their sexy-ass kiss, I guide her over to the bed and help her on it. Ashton smacks her thigh when she tries to straddle him.

"Other way, cowgirl." He takes the lube Drew hands him and then rubs it all over his dick. "Get on it and ride."

Mia glances my way, her brown eyes darkening with lust. "Tell me what to do."

"Put Ashton's dick in your ass and lie back so he can hold you," I instruct. "I want that pussy open and waiting for me."

She nods, straddling him but facing me. Then, she eases down over his dick, making both her and Ashton groan. Once she's impaled on his cock, he pulls her back against his chest. With her tits jiggling and him inside her in a fuck-hot way, I'm so turned on.

"Straddle her face, Drew," I instruct as I pull pillows on either side of her to give him something to kneel on. "Put your thick cock in her mouth. Hold on to the headboard."

He flashes me a deviant grin before he climbs into position. I love that his ass is on display for me. I give it a bite that has him growling.

I take extra care to lube up my dick and her pussy. With my fingers inside her, I can tell this is going to be a tight fit with Ashton's dick sharing space behind a thin wall of tissue. They both groan from the simple intrusion of two fingers. I straddle Ashton's thighs as I place each of Mia's legs over my shoulders. She's exposed and spread apart, waiting to be filled by a third dick. The sounds coming from her mouth are sloppy where I know Drew is fucking her mouth. Each time his ass flexes, more precum dribbles from my dick.

"Relax, baby," I murmur. "I'll go slow, but I think this is going to feel really fucking good for all of us."

Gripping my dick, I tease her opening and push against her hole. There's resistance because she's so tight and Ashton has already filled her back end with him. But, with a little maneuvering and a lot of whimpering on her part, I manage to squeeze the fat head of my cock inside her. Ashton curses when I inch in slowly. It feels like my dick is being strangled in the best possible way. I can feel the firmness of Ashton inside her ass through her pussy wall. It's fucking insane.

"Holy shit," I hiss out. "Fuck, you're tight, Mia."

She gags on Drew's dick, clenching her pussy. I grip onto Drew's hip for leverage as I buck slowly into Mia. It's maddening how good it feels. Like every movement might lead to an embarrassingly quick orgasm on my part. I have to go at a snail's pace so I don't hurt her, but also so I don't come like a chump.

Ashton is trapped beneath everyone, but it doesn't stop him from bucking upward. It reminds me of the way his body moves when he's in the water. So fucking strong.

Everyone is moaning and grunting, each of us finding great pleasure in each other. I rub on Mia's clit, hoping to give her another orgasm before I find mine. She hums around Drew's dick, making him hiss. His movements become more erratic, causing her to gag. When she comes with a howl like a fucking banshee, all the while squeezing the fuck out of my dick with her tight-ass pussy, I release her clit to help Drew over the edge. He groans when I slide a finger into his ass, seeking out his prostate.

"Jesus!" Drew snarls. "Fuck!"

His ass cheeks clench just as Ashton curses. I can feel Ashton's dick swelling up, pressing against mine, and I lose it. I'm no longer able to hold on. Cum floods out of me as Ashton's does the same based on the throbbing his is doing. All the sensations must be too much because Mia screams in pleasure.

My heart is pounding right out of my chest by the time I come down from my high. I ease out of her, watching in awe as cum runs out of her abused pussy.

It's then I panic.

"Shit, Mia," I bark out. "I didn't use a condom."

"I'm good now," she assures me. "No babies anytime soon."

Drew climbs off her and flops down onto the bed, breathing heavily and unusually pale. Ashton slides Mia off his dick, sending more rivers of cum running out of her.

"I'm clean," I assure her. "So you don't have to worry. I got checked out when I started getting intimate with Drew. We both did."

"I'm clean too, Mia," Ashton says. "When I had to get tested for marijuana, I made them check me for STDs as well, so I could throw that in my dad's face too." He shrugs. "I've always been careful… until you."

"I guess that's settled," Mia says, giggling as she wiggles between Ashton and Drew. "I was a virgin, so I'm good too."

I prowl over her, covering her body with mine, loving that we're all always smashed together and it feels right. "You look good with cum in your ass and in your pussy." I kiss her mouth hard. "And you taste good with cum in your mouth."

She grins at me. "I'm going to be sore for a while, but I can't wait to do that again."

"Dirty, dirty girl," Ashton says. "How does after dinner sound?"

Her laugh is adorable. "Ha. Ha."

Drew is quiet, but he's smiling. I reach over and stroke his blond hair out of his eyes. "You okay?"

"Just worn out. You people exhaust me," he complains.

"Aww, Daddy needs a nap," Ashton jokes.

"Fuck off, brat," Drew throws back, laughing. "Let's get cleaned up and over to Molly and Tim's. I'm starving."

As I climb off the bed, I can't help but let nerves overcome me.

I'm going to tell them.

Not about Ben. I'll never be able to tell them that.

This.

I'm going to tell them about this. Us. My relationship.

I hope like hell I'm not exchanging one family for another one. I need both. I need all the love and support I can get.

*Ben, if you're looking down on us, put in a good word that Mom and Dad don't hate me for having two boyfriends and a girlfriend. Better yet, probably best not mention that to the big guy upstairs.*

The house is bustling with life.

Laughter.

Love.

My heart swells, ready to burst. Ashton and Drew have Dad locked in conversation while Mia listens intently as Mom explains how she manages to get the chicken fried to perfection every time. I'm happy as hell seeing them fit in so well with my family.

Ashton is cheerful and relaxed.

Drew is content and all smiles.

Mia is eating and her eyes twinkle with delight.

I should probably wait until after we finish our meal, but I can't. I need to tell them. It's eating me up inside. After I wolf down my food, I set my fork down and clear my throat.

"Mom, Dad," I say, earning their attention. "There's something I need to tell you both."

Everyone goes quiet, even big-mouth Ashton, as I work up the nerve to say the words. It's as though Ashton, Mia, and Drew all want this too. Acceptance and love. I hope like hell I'm not about to ruin this happy moment for them. This is one secret I can't keep from my parents, no matter the outcome. They need to know.

"You know how Drew's my boyfriend now," I say, easing into the conversation.

Dad nods and Mom smiles.

"We, uh, we were sort of invited to be in a relationship with Mia and Ashton," I rush out, unable to meet their eyes now. "I know it's not conventional and you won't understand, but we're happy. I know, deep down, that's all you guys want. Drew, Mia, and Ashton all make me happy. I love them."

I finally lift my gaze. Dad's brows are furrowed in confusion, but not anger. Mom's eyes are welling with tears, but I know they're happy ones.

"Drew's the daddy," Ashton blurts out, making my mom snort out a laugh. "In case you were wondering the dynamics. Brayden's the muscle. He beats up all the dicks trying to hit on us. Mia's the cook and the maid."

"Asshole," Mia gripes, swatting at him. "Don't listen to him."

"The four of you," Dad says slowly. "Together? How does that work?"

Mia and Drew both burn bright red while Ashton cackles.

"You really want to know how it works?" Ashton taunts.

Dad blanches. "No, er, not like that. I meant… do you get jealous? I don't understand."

"We're all open and honest," I explain. "There's no jealousy because we all really enjoy being around each other. This thing is built on friendship and trust. The romantic love is just bricks stacked on top of that."

Dad's shoulders relax. "I can see you've discussed the dynamics then."

"At great lengths," Drew assures him. "Everyone is happy."

"Does anyone give you a hard time at school about it?" Mom inquires. "Bray, honey, I hope you set them straight if they do."

I roll my eyes at Ashton for planting the seed in my mom's head that I'm the relationship bodyguard. "Yeah, Mom, I make sure no one messes with us. Well, the three of us. Drew can't be seen in public with us."

Mom frowns, saddened by my words. "It won't be forever."

"How did your parents take it?" Dad asks both Ashton and Mia. "Assuming you told them."

"Dad will just think I'm sabotaging everyone's lives and reputations, so I haven't told him." The bitterness in Ashton's tone has Dad clasping his shoulder and squeezing.

"He'll come around because he loves you," Dad assures Ashton. "What about you, hon?"

Mia's lip wobbles and her eyes water. "They, uh, my parents…" A tear streaks down her cheek. "They disowned me."

"Oh, honey, no," Mom cries out, standing to rush over to Mia. She hugs our girl, kissing the top of her head. "They're rotten parents if that's the case. You're a sweet girl and deserve all the love, even if it comes from three people all at once. Screw them for being assholes!"

Drew and I laugh at Mom's cursing. Dad shakes his head while Ashton smirks.

"You're not mad?" I ask Dad.

He studies me for a moment. "You're a grown man, Brayden. I trust you know what you're doing. You've never been one to make bad decisions." He smiles. "For the first time in years, I feel like I have my son back. You just needed to find the right relationship to bring your heart some peace."

I shoot Drew a relieved look. "Thanks, Dad. It means a lot to me. To us."

Mom pulls away from Mia, stroking her fingers through her hair. "I, for one, am thrilled you have these lovely people as your partners. Having a houseful of you wonderful kids makes this old woman very happy."

"Old?" Ashton scoffs. "Please, Molly. People like my mother pay thousands of dollars a year to look like you. You're a young hottie. If we're not careful, people are going to think you're a part of our harem."

Dad grumbles. "Don't call it a harem. And don't invite my wife to it."

"We could always use another daddy in the group," Ashton jokes, ribbing my dad. "There can never be enough daddies."

Mia smacks him and then everyone is laughing again.

Fuck, it feels good.

It feels really, really good.

"Brayden!"

I stop texting Mia to greet some guy from my English class named Eric. "What's up, bro?"

His face is red and pinched. "Man, I hate to be the bearer of bad news, but someone just sent me this. I don't know why, maybe because

I'm your friend, but I thought you'd want to see. I hope it was just me because it looks really bad."

My blood runs cold as I stare at the video playing on his phone. It's the night of the Halloween party. The four of us dancing. It's hot and erotic. Touching and rubbing and grinding. Everything is fine until Drew lifts his mask up. His face is as clear as day. And then my stupid ass walks over to him, boldly planting a kiss on his lips before pulling his mask back into place.

No.

Fucking no.

My phone buzzes.

I blink out of my daze to see a text from an unknown number. I click on it and see the same fucking video Eric just showed me. Shit. Fuck. There's no way only the two of us received the video.

Then my phone goes off again. This time it's Finn, asking why I was kissing Coach.

Another text comes through from another teammate. Then another and another…

Shit.

It's been sent to a lot more people than Eric.

"Thanks, man," I choke out. "Just, uh, delete it, please."

"No problem," he says. "Good luck."

I take off in a sprint, rushing to Drew's office to talk to him. Earlier he'd said he was working on some stuff. While I'm making the trek across campus, my phone buzzes again.

**Mia: I just got a video text. OMG!!! Where is Drew?**

I type as I head toward the athletic building.

**Me: If I had to guess, with Curtis.**

**Mia: Oh no.**

**Me: Where's Ashton?**

**Mia: Swimming. He's going to freak.**

**Me: I'll find Drew. Get ahold of Ashton.**

**Mia: Everything's going to be okay. Love you.**

**Me: Love you too.**

I sure as fuck hope so.

I'm winded by the time I enter the locker room. I head straight for Drew's office. His secretary greets me with a smile.

"May I help you?"

"Is, uh, Coach Thompson in there?"

"He is," she says. "He's in an unscheduled meeting with Dean Carter, but I don't anticipate it being much longer."

I pace the locker room for twenty minutes, ignoring more texts from friends and teammates about the video that was seemingly sent to everyfuckingone. Eventually, the office door opens and Drew steps out.

Crushed.

Heartbroken.

Shamed.

This is bad.

This is so fucking bad.

# TWENTY-FIVE

## *Drew*

I step out of the office with Curtis trailing behind me and come face to face with an ashen-looking Brayden. Our eyes meet and I can see the myriad of emotions flashing through his features. Anger. Hurt. Pity. He's seen the video. I imagine everyone on campus has at this point. It was the reason for Curtis's and my emergency meeting. The reason I've made the hardest decision I've ever had to make.

"Drew," Curtis says, extending his hand. "I'm truly sorry it's come to this. If you ever need anything…"

I nod, shaking his hand back. "Thank you, sir. I'm sorry too." I can hear the wateriness in my voice, so I take a deep breath. I can't let Brayden see me upset. I can't let him know how badly my heart is breaking. If he does, he'll use it against me.

Curtis nods toward Brayden then disappears, I'm sure to give us some privacy. Not wanting anyone to overhear our conversation, I motion for him to enter my office. I swallow thickly. Correction: *Old office.*

Fuck, I'm going to miss this office.

This team.

This school.

It was my last link to hockey.

But more than anything, I'm going to miss the three people who quickly dug beneath the surface of my chest and buried themselves into my heart.

"I'll tell everyone it's my fault," Bray blurts out the second I close the door behind me. "I asked you to the party and then I kissed—"

"Stop." I hold up my hand, unable to listen to his pleas. I need to end this quick. Rip it off like a Band-Aid. Otherwise, I'll lose my resolve. And I can't do that. Not if I want to protect the three most important people in my life. "It's over with. I already handled it."

Brayden sighs, misunderstanding my words. "Okay, good. So Ashton's dad said he'd take care of it? That's good. Yeah…"

"No." I shake my head. "His hands were tied. I'm the coach, and the video not only showed you kissing me, but I was dancing with Mia, another student here. Even Ashton was in the video."

Brayden's jaw clenches. "What do you mean his hands were tied?"

"I had three options," I tell him robotically. "Deny it and let them investigate, admit guilt and let them decide my fate, or… quit." I scrub my palm down my scruff, remembering the disappointment that bled from Curtis when I admitted to him that I was intimate with all three of them. I could've lied, but I'm not ashamed of the love I found, and I wasn't about to lie to the man who took a chance on me and gave me this job. He deserved to know the truth. At first he tried to blame Ashton, but I made it clear his son was not to blame. I also told him Ashton is one of the best people I've ever met and if he's smart he'll try to get to know the man his son is instead of trying to mold him into something he'll never be.

"What did you decide?" Brayden asks slowly.

"I chose to quit."

"The fuck?" Bray hisses. "We can fight this. Explain we were friends before any of this happened…"

"And drag you through the mud? Fuck that. This is a small school, pretty much in the middle of nowhere, and most likely, that video won't leave here, but if I fight this, there's a chance it can spread, and I will not let it fuck up your career before it even begins."

"My career?" Brayden spits. "Fuck my career! If you're not coaching, I'm not playing!"

"Yes, you are." I step toward him, needing to be close to him one last time. "You worked too damn hard to let a scandal ruin your shot at playing in the NHL. I already had my opportunity and…" I choke up, the tears in my eyes burning behind my lids. "I will not let this shit follow you. Owners don't like drama, and we both know if you keep playing the way you are, you're a shoe-in as a first round draft pick."

"Fuck this!" he barks, swiping his hand across the papers on my desk. They go flying in the air and scatter everywhere. I want to pull him in for a hug and kiss him, tell him we'll figure this out. But I can't do that because there's nothing to figure out. I'm the coach and I've had sex with three students, one of which is my player. The public won't care that I'm their same age, or that I'm in love with them. They'll see it as a scandal and come after all of us.

"Why are you doing this?" He gets in my face. "You ran when we were younger. Then, for whatever bullshit reason, you quit the NHL, and now you're just going to quit coaching here without even putting up a fight."

I open my mouth to argue, but he continues. "And don't you dare say you're doing it for me! You always, *always* take the easy way out. Shit got hard with us and you bailed! Shit went down in the NHL and you bailed! And now, shit gets a little tough, and surprise, fucking surprise, you bail."

"I'm doing it for all three of you," I tell him calmly, needing him to understand, while on the inside, I'm about one step away from losing my shit. "Mia's dream is to one day write screenplays in Hollywood, and Ashton wants to become a doctor. And you… You've worked your entire life to one day be able to play in the NHL." This shit will follow them everywhere they go and I can't let that happen. I'm in a position where I can protect them and that's what I'm going to do.

"And what about you?" he hisses.

"Bray." I frame his face with my palms, hoping it will calm him down. I don't want the last time I see him, for God knows how long, to be like this. "I love you for caring about me, but I always knew my time with hockey was limited." I flinch, realizing what I just admitted, and quickly continue. "I chose to leave the NHL, and coming to coach here was the only way to have a piece of hockey with me, while getting to be close to you."

Brayden's face softens. "So, what happens now? Maybe… maybe you can get a job coaching somewhere else."

Knowing what I say next is going to destroy us both, I lean in and press my mouth to his. I take a moment to try and memorize everything about the kiss, hoping when I'm alone, I'll be able to close my eyes and remember how he felt—strong yet soft lips, how he tasted—like peppermint and something uniquely Brayden, how he smelled—like pine trees and snow. My heart sinks, remembering Christmas is right around the corner. It would've been our first one together, and now I won't be there with them.

"Drew," he says, forcing me from my thoughts. "What happens now?"

"Now, I leave," I tell him. His eyes widen in disbelief. "You have four months left of your hockey season and a semester left of college, and then soon after, you'll be drafted. I can't stay here, on campus, muddying up your reputation. As long as I'm here, people will talk, and if you have any chance of entering the draft without this hanging over you, I have to stay out of the equation."

"No." He jerks his head out of my hands. "No. You're not leaving. Ashton's apartment isn't technically on campus…"

"It's not, but this is a small school in a small town. It's best I leave so people can find the next scandal to gossip about. If I stay, they'll put the pieces together, that we're all together. It's bad enough you're publicly dating Ashton and Mia. We can't risk adding your coach, a former NHL player, to the mix."

"No," he says again. "No. You're not leaving."

"Yes, I am." I step away from him. "And I'm leaving today. While in my meeting with Curtis, I got a flight scheduled for a couple hours from now." I didn't plan to see any of them before I left. I had hoped to grab my stuff from the apartment and leave before they could get to me and try to convince me to stay. I know it sounds selfish as fuck, but I couldn't chance the three of them cornering me, just like Brayden's doing now.

Brayden's features morph into anger. "Are you fucking serious right now? Just like that? You were going to pack up and leave without saying a word to any of us! We were supposed to be in this together," he spits. "I come out of class and find out about the video and meanwhile you're already planning your getaway." His palm hits the center of my chest and I stumble back. "Fuck this and fuck you!" he roars. "We were never in this together."

He stalks out of the office, slamming the door behind him, and I take several breaths, trying to calm my breathing. I know what I'm doing is the right thing, and one day Brayden, Ashton, and Mia will understand that, but right now, it fucking hurts.

In the time Curtis learned of the video from the person who brought it to his attention, to his meeting with me, it had been sent to virtually everyone. Curtis assured me he would do everything in his power to work with the IT department to get the video shut down and to find out who's responsible for spreading it. In return, I told him I would walk away, so the school isn't caught up in a scandal. I don't give a fuck about the school, but I do care about Brayden, and if the NHL thinks he's a risk before he gets drafted, they will blacklist his ass so fast, and I won't let that happen to him. He deserves to get drafted, to play in the NHL. He deserves to know how amazing it is to play your heart out in front of thousands of hockey fans and to win a ring. To have people wearing your number and asking for autographs. And I won't be the reason he loses it all before he gets it.

Maybe one day, when the dust clears, we can somehow try to make this work… Fuck! I can't think about this right now. I need to get my shit and leave. I need to protect them. That's my priority.

I grab the couple items of mine from the office and leave the key on the desk, then head home. Fuck, home. Soon it won't be my home anymore. I'll be back to being on my own. The thought makes my heart clench in my chest. Those few years on the road, I missed having a real home. Growing up, my dad was always gone, but Brayden's family welcomed me into their home, and after my dad passed away, my grandma did the best she could, providing me with a place to lay my head. But nothing felt as much like a home as the apartment I share with Ashton, Mia, and Brayden—might as well say he lives there since most of his shit is in my room and he hasn't slept in the dorms since we got together.

Body numb, I make the quick walk to the apartment so I can pack my shit. I didn't come here with much, since I wasn't sure if I was going to stay, so there isn't much to pack. When I get home, the apartment is thankfully empty. Brayden's right, I'm taking the coward's way out by running, but it's the only way.

I stalk through the living room, trying not to focus on the little things, like the plates in the sink from breakfast this morning, where Ashton made us all pancakes and then proceeded to lick the syrup off our bodies. My dick—and heart—swells at the memory. I'll never be able to look at syrup the same way again.

I step into my room and glance around, my stomach bottoming out when I notice all of Brayden's stuff mixed in with mine. His Ice Hawk's hoodie hanging over my desk chair. His beanies tossed haphazardly on the bedside table and dresser. His schoolbooks splayed out across my desk.

I get choked up as I remember the way he lay across my bed last night studying with Mia for their finals while I worked on plays for our upcoming game. My eyes go to the floor where Ashton's Xbox rests. Since I have the desk and told them I needed to work, they all piled in here. I only got a little bit of work done before they lured me to bed and we made love.

Raw emotion claws at my throat, knowing there's a chance I may never lie in bed with them again. If I had known this morning would be the last time the four of us would be together, I would've kissed them harder, held them tighter. I would've made sure to tell them how much I love them.

I grab my duffle bag and make quick work of stuffing my clothes inside. Adrenaline is coursing through my veins, making it hard to breathe. Every second in here with my memories is making me weak. I throw my toiletries inside and figure anything else I might need I can buy once I get to where I'm going.

*Hopefully this is just temporary…*

As I'm zipping up my bag, my breathing becomes labored. I take several gulps of air, but I can't catch my breath. Fuck, my heart hurts.

I reach for my phone to try to call… someone.

"Drew!" Ashton barks, the door slamming closed. "I know you're here and Brayden told me the shit you're trying to pull." He steps into view as my vision goes blurry. "Sorry, man, but we're not letting you… Drew." He eyes me with concern. "What the hell is wrong with you?"

"My…" I stumble forward, dropping my phone. "I can't…" I gasp for air. "My heart."

# TWENTY-SIX

*Ashton*



*Twenty Minutes Ago*

Pointing. Laughing. Pitying looks. Whispering.

I reach the end of the pool, launch myself out of the water, and stalk over to Travis, who sits on the bleachers wearing a shit-eating grin.

"What the fuck did you do?" I growl, flinging off my goggles and yanking off my swim cap.

He sneers at me. "When you point at someone, you have four fingers pointing back."

"Three, you fucking moron," I growl.

"It's a figure of speech, not literally—"

"I don't give a fuck. Tell me what you did."

He smirks, shrugging. "I don't know what you're talking about."

As some kid passes, I grab his phone out of his hand. Just like I suspected. The video that was sent to me has now apparently been sent everywhere based on the looks I'm getting.

I toss the phone back at the kid. "Delete that shit."

"Sure, man," he grumbles.

Swiveling around, my hands fisted, I snarl at Travis. But he's gone. Took off like a fucking pussy. I'm going to destroy him. I stalk over to my bag and throw my hoodie and sweats on over my soaked body. By the time I locate my phone, I have a million missed texts and calls from Mia, Brayden, and Dad.

Nothing from Drew.

Fuck.

Travis, that little bitch, is going down.

I throw on my shoes and stuff everything in my bag. Once I've slung it over my shoulder, I hurry out of the building toward my car. I dial back Brayden, who answers on the first ring.

"What happened?" I grind out.

I know what happened.

Travis threw us all under the fucking bus and now Drew is going to be the one who gets in trouble.

"Drew…" His voice cracks. "He's leaving."

Over my dead body.

"Drew's not going anywhere," I growl. "Let me fix this. I'll talk to Dad—"

"He quit, Ash. He's leaving. Flying the fuck out of here. Away from this—away from us."

My stomach hollows out at his words. He can't bail. We'll figure it all out. Drew just needs to give me a goddamn minute to sort it out.

"I'll call you back," I tell him. "I'll fix this."

"I don't think you can."

We hang up and I dial Dad.

"Hello?" Dad answers, his voice tight.

"How could you?" I spit out.

"It's beyond my control, Son. That video has my employee kissing his player and dancing with his hands all over another student. The four of you…" He huffs and then rushes his words out, as though he's mortified to have to even say them. "Everyone knows the four of you are together. It's unethical for Drew to be in a relationship with one student, much less three. It'll cause a huge storm if I don't do my part."

I knew, eventually, he would figure it out, and now he has proof. But, rather than being cool as shit like Tim and Molly, Dad is the king of morality and hell-bent on doing the right thing. In this case, running Drew off.

"You didn't even try," I accuse. "You fired him because you're embarrassed!"

"I didn't fire him. He quit. I didn't do this for me, Ashton. It's for the best it's come out, though. He's a coach and—"

"You can't handle the fact that we're all together!" I belt out. "Admit that's what this is about. Now that people know your own goddamn son is in a relationship with three people, it'll destroy your reputation. Admit it, Dad, you were just waiting for something like this to happen so you could shut it down."

Dad sighs. "I honestly don't know what you expected from me. Do I condone the fact you're sleeping with three people? No. If it were three students, though, I wouldn't get involved. This is between me and my employee. I'm the dean, for crying out loud. I can't let this go, especially since the video was sent to everyone. All I can do is damage control, and Drew leaving his position is a step in the right direction."

I throw my bag into my car and climb in, trying not to mow down anyone in my haste to get home.

"We can't lose him, Dad," I rumble, my fear bleeding into my anger. "Brayden says he's leaving."

"I'm sorry," Dad states. "Maybe it's for the best."

Fire burns hot inside me. "And Travis gets off without a smack on the hand? Dad, you know he did this. The weed. The bleach in my water bottle. The threats. The slashed tires. He hates me and wants to fuck up my world. You can't do shit about him?"

"Bleach? Slashed tires? What are you talking about?"

"He's a monster trying to destroy my life!" I bellow, slamming my hand on the steering wheel. "And you let him. Because your job is more fucking important than your own goddamn son. But that's how it's always been for you, huh? Doing grand gestures to show the community what a fine, upstanding citizen you are, at the stake of your family."

"Ashton—"

"If you don't deal with him, I will," I warn. "I'm tired of letting him get away with all this shit. He crossed the line sending that video to everyone, because now he's beyond hurting me. He's hurting them too."

"Ashton, I don't know about the other stuff with Travis, but I'll look into it. But the video?" He sighs heavily. "He didn't send it to me."

I pull into a parking space in front of my building, snag my bag, and climb out of my car. "Of course he did."

"It was brought to my attention by another... concerned student."

"Who the hell is concerned about my goddamn love life?" I snap, flinging open the door to the building. "This is such bullshit and you know it!"

"Sasha. You know her dad is—"

"What?" I bark out.

"She only showed me the video. I doubt she was the one to spread it. If you're worried about Travis being the culprit, I'll have the IT department investigate him first. Just come by my office and we'll discuss this like adults."

I take the stairs two at a time. "Sorry, Dad, but I have to take a raincheck. I need to go convince my boyfriend he can't fucking leave us or our hearts are going to break. Great talk."

"Ashton—"

I mash the end button and then push inside my apartment. "Drew!" I yell, slamming the door closed behind me and dropping my bag to the floor. "I know you're here and Brayden told me the shit you're trying to pull."

I stride into his bedroom and find him at the counter in his bathroom, a bag in one hand and his phone in the other.

Pale.

So fucking pale.

"Sorry, man, but we're not letting you…" I trail off when his knees buckle, alarm surging through me. "Drew. What the hell is wrong with you?"

"My…" He stumbles, his phone slipping to the tile with a loud clatter. "I can't…" He gasps. "My heart."

I rush him as he clutches his chest, his body seizing. I grab onto him as he falls, landing hard on my ass, the big guy crushing me beneath him. Rolling him over to his back, I quickly realize something's wrong. Really fucking wrong.

His lips are bluish in color.

I don't think he's breathing.

"Drew, babe, you can't do this. What the fuck is happening?" I choke out, panicking. "Wake up, man. Wake the fuck up." I dial 911 and put it on speaker when they answer. "My b-boyfriend isn't b-breathing. Holy fuck. Holy fuck."

"Calm down," the operator says. "What is the address of your location?"

I rattle it off, my eyes never leaving Drew.

"Do you know how to perform CPR?" the operator asks next.

"Y-Yes," I stammer, my training kicking in from all the years of swimming.

"Good, we have a responder on the way. They're only a couple of minutes out. Stay calm and listen to what I need for you to do."

As the woman walks me through the steps I'm rusty on, I begin chest compressions. My heart is in my chest as tears blur my eyes.

Check pulse.

Tilt his head back.

Pinch his nose.

Breathe air into his lungs.

Chest compressions.

Repeat.

I go through the steps over and over, growing sicker and sicker to my stomach the bluer his skin turns. I'm choking on a sob when the operator tells me they're entering the apartment. Two EMTs rush into the bathroom, ushering me out of the way and taking over.

"He's in cardiac arrest," one of the EMTs says.

They pull out the defibrillator and cut his shirt open. All I can do is watch as they press the paddles to his chest, ready to try and jump-start his heart.

"Clear."

His body jolts as they shoot the voltage into him. The machine doesn't beep and continues to show no heart activity.

No.

This can't fucking happen.

I'm frozen in fear, unable to do anything but pray like fuck he'll start breathing again.

"Clear."

He jolts again as they hit him with the defibrillator once more.

Nothing.

"Come on, Drew," I beg. "Please."

"Clear."

*Beep.*

The professionals are moving with trained ease, working their hardest to get Drew's heart to pump again. All I can do is watch, fucking useless to help.

"Clear."

*Beep. Beep.*

My heart is galloping enough for the both of us. If only it were that easy.

"Clear."

"We've got a pulse," one of the men says, reading the machine. Then, to confirm, the other EMT checks his carotid.

"Low, but there," the other guy confirms.

I sob in relief, finally allowing myself to breathe.

"He's stable," one of them says. "Let's get him into the ambulance."

While they strap him down to the gurney, I gape at how horrible he looks. The mask they've attached to his face pumps air into his chest. His skin is still tinged blue and he's not moving or speaking, but he's getting oxygen and his heart is beating, even if only barely.

I rush after them, my entire body trembling. People peek their heads out of their doors in the hallway, checking to see what the commotion is about. I realize I don't have my phone or anything. I'm certainly not turning back for it. We make it outside, and as they load him into the ambulance, Dad shows up.

"What's going on?" he asks, clutching my shoulder. "I came to talk to you and… is that Drew?"

Nodding, I swipe at the tears that won't quit fucking falling. "I lost my phone. Mia… Brayden."

He hugs me. "Go with him. I'll find them."

The EMT allows me to climb inside with Drew while the other one drives. I clutch onto Drew's cool hand, silently begging for him to be okay.

He has to be okay.

We can't lose him.

We just can't.

My hands won't quit fucking shaking. I don't know what time it is or how much time has passed since we arrived at the hospital. Not long since no one has gotten here yet. Dad is the first to show, a worried frown on his face. I hate how much I need him right now. He walks right up to me and pulls me to his chest.

I'm so pissed at him.

And yet… I sob against his shoulder.

"He can't die, Dad. He can't."

"He's not going to die," he promises, though he doesn't sound certain. "He'll pull through."

I cling to my father because I need his strength. I'm unravelling so fast, I don't know which way is up. A few minutes later, two of my favorite people rush us.

"What happened?" Brayden growls. "Is he okay?"

I step away from Dad to pull Mia to me. She's crying and it's then I realize Brayden's lashes are wet too. Swiping at my eye with my palm, I let out a ragged sigh.

"He, uh, he was standing in his bathroom packing his bag it looked like. He was just so pale. Clutched his chest and mentioned his heart. I thought he meant his heart was hurt from having to leave us at first, but he fucking meant literally." I squeeze my eyes shut, more hot tears rolling out. "I, uh…"

Brayden hugs the both of us, leaning his forehead against mine. "What, Ash?"

"I was so f-fucking scared. I didn't know what to do. I c-called nine-one-one. They told me to do CPR." My body trembles with a sob. "They… The paramedics took over and… fuck."

"What?" Mia whimpers.

"He, uh, he didn't have a pulse. C-Cardiac arrest they said. He was so fucking blue." Brayden squeezes me, urging me to continue. "They used the defib and it took like five shocks before they got his pulse going again. That's all I know."

We cling to each other, crying for what seems like forever, all of us worried as hell. Then, we hear voices speaking with Dad. A sob. And then Molly is hugging us.

"It's okay, kids," she coos. "Everything's going to be okay. Our Andrew is a fighter."

I want to believe her.

I really do.

"He's only twenty-two. How could he have a heart attack?" I ask, my voice a whisper. "I don't understand."

Brayden pulls away and our eyes meet. "His dad…" His bottom lip trembles. "I should have known."

"What?" both Mia and I ask.

"His dad died from a heart condition. I think… I think maybe it's genetic."

I jerk my gaze to Dad. "The thing written into his contract that he didn't want to discuss…"

Dad's lips purse and he nods. "I'm sorry, Son. He didn't think it'd be a problem since he's been medicated for it."

Brayden curses. "He was taking medication. I saw it Thanksgiving weekend. I should have pushed and asked what it was for."

A heart condition.

Medication.

Why would he keep this from us?

"The important thing is," Molly says, "he's here and they can take care of him."

But they didn't see him.

His pale face that turned blue with each passing second. His dark blue lips. No sounds. No movement. He was dead. They jump-started his heart, but he was dead.

I think I'm going to be sick.

I barely make it to the trash can before I puke my guts up.

He has to live.

I'm not going to be able to live without him.

# TWENTY-SEVEN

*Mia*

Heart condition.

Stroke.

Lack of oxygen to the brain.

Coma.

Those four pieces of information keep running through my head on repeat as I stare at Drew's lifeless body. After the doctors got him stabilized and ran extensive tests, that's what we were told. He has a heart condition. For some reason he had a stroke. The lack of oxygen to his brain caused him to slip into a coma, and they don't know if or when he'll wake up.

I've been sitting by his bed, holding his hand for what feels like days, listening to his heart beat on the monitors. The doctors have no answers. He should've woken up by now, but he hasn't. My phone vibrates in my back pocket, but I continue to ignore it, not giving a shit who it is. Everyone I need is in this room with me. Ashton and Brayden finally fell asleep on the couch. I should probably get some sleep as well, but I can't bring my-self to let go of his hand.

I had just finished taking my last final for the semester and was walk-ing over to the tutoring center, when I received the video of the four of us dancing at the Halloween party. Not too long after, while I was in the middle of trying to help a student study for his final—completely distracted and unable to focus—I got the call that Drew was being taken to the hospital.

After hours of waiting for news, we learned that Brayden was listed as Drew's emergency contact. He was in shock. They hadn't talked in years, yet he listed him. That says a lot about how much Drew loves Brayden—even when they weren't talking.

My phone buzzes again and I pull it out to turn it off, when I see the word Dad flash across my screen. Without thought, I press answer.

"Mia," he says, his voice sounding pained over the line.

"Yeah," I croak out. I should be mad at him—hell, I am—shouldn't want to talk to him, but for some reason I need to hear his voice. I can't explain why.

"I've been trying to get ahold of you. I need to talk to you. Your mom—"

"I need you, Daddy," I blurt out, fresh tears filling my lids. Up until now, I've kept it all bottled up inside, not wanting to upset Ashton or Brayden. They're always here for me, and I wanted to be strong for them.

"What's wrong?" he asks.

"I'm at North Michigan General."

"Are you hurt?"

"No." I shake my head even though he can't see me. "My boyfriend Drew is. He…" I choke out, trying to talk softly so I don't wake the boys up. The last thing they need is to feel like they have to comfort me. "He had a stroke. I need you, please."

I don't care how mad I am at him.

I don't care how much he's hurt me.

My father is one of the best heart doctors in the United States and if anyone can fix a heart, it's him. And that's what I need him to do. Fix Drew's heart. Make him better so he'll come back to us. Because we can't lose him.

"I'm on my way," he says. "I'll be there as soon as I can."

We hang up and a throat clears behind me, startling me. I swivel around and Ashton is staring at me, his eyes bloodshot from lack of sleep.

"Is he coming?" he asks, running his fingers through his messy hair.

I nod. "I know he's not—"

"Stop," he says, getting up and walking over to me. He kneels in front of me and presses his hand to my cheek. "You don't have to explain. He's your dad, and if it means he can help Drew…"

A sob bubbles out of me. I've been trying so hard to hold it together. "What if he doesn't wake up?"

"He will," Ashton says, his eyes glassy. "He's just resting for a bit. But once he's ready, he'll wake up."

I nod in agreement, wanting to believe him.

A little while later, Brayden wakes up. He's quiet, refusing to even look at Drew, and I know at some point I need to ask him what's going on in his head, but right now we're all barely hanging on.

We spend the morning in Drew's room, quiet and lost in ourselves. The nurses come in and out, checking on Drew, but nobody has any news. Brayden's mom brings us lunch, demanding we eat. Afterward, she and Tim go home to shower, telling us they'll be back soon.

When the door opens a couple hours later, I expect it to be them or the nurse, so I'm shocked to see my dad walk in. He's dressed in a suit, like the one he wears to work every day, and with him is the doctor who's in charge of Drew's case. His eyes lock with mine and suddenly it's all just too much. The waiting. The not knowing.

I throw myself into my dad's arms as tears well up from deep inside and course down my cheeks. He wraps his arms around me and tells me he loves me while I breathe in his comforting scent. Memories from when I was a little girl surface. Him putting a Band-Aid on my skinned knee when I fell off my bike. Being the one to stitch me up when I tripped and hit my head on the table. Taking care of me when I had the flu and my mother refused to go near me. He's always put her first over the years, let her call the shots, but when I needed him, *really* needed him, he's always been there, and now I need him to make Drew better.

When I finally pull back, he smiles softly down at me. "We need to talk, but right now, let's focus on your boyfriend's condition."

It warms my heart that he referred to Drew as my boyfriend. Then I wonder if maybe he thinks I've replaced Ashton and Brayden. Drew wasn't with us the night I told my parents about them.

My dad's eyes glance over my shoulder and a small smile tugs at his lips. "I feel like we didn't get to properly meet last time." He extends his hand out to Ashton. "I'm Harold Lexington, Mia's father."

Ashton glares at his hand for a long moment, and I hold my breath, waiting to see how he'll handle it. He's protective of me, all of my guys are, and they know how badly Dad's choice to go along with Mom's decision to disown me and cut me off hurt me. Ashton's gaze meets mine, and I nod slightly, silently asking him to let it go for now. It's like he said earlier, if he can help Drew...

"I'm Ashton, Mia's other boyfriend." He shakes my dad's hand.

"Nice to meet you, Son."

Ashton's jaw ticks, but he doesn't correct him.

"Dad, you remember Brayden?"

"I do," he says, stepping over to him and shaking his hand as well. "Good to see you again. I'm sorry it's under these circumstances."

Brayden doesn't say a word, just nods and shakes my dad's hand.

Dad clears his throat, then walks back over to me and the doctor, who is standing patiently in the corner, waiting for him.

"I've taken a look at the tests Dr. Palmer has run. Drew has what we call an 'athlete's heart.' His heart muscles are thicker than they should be. Because of this, blood flow leaving the heart is restricted. You might've seen him struggling to catch his breath when he's overly active."

Brayden curses under his breath then finally speaks. "Yeah, I have. When we went skiing. When we were messing around in the rink. I chalked it up to him being out of shape and gave him shit for it."

Guilt shines in Brayden's eyes. "Don't go there," I tell him, cutting across the room and hugging him. "You couldn't have known. None of us knew besides Drew."

"But I should've," he argues. "I should've known he wouldn't just leave the NHL. I knew he was hiding something and I didn't push him to find out what."

"Can you fix him?" Ashton asks my dad.

My eyes swing over to Dad, but it's Dr. Palmer who speaks. "Right now, our main concern is him waking up."

"He *will* wake up," Ashton hisses. "And when he does, I want to know if you can fix him."

"Hockey is his life," Brayden adds.

"Unfortunately, his condition can't be fixed," Dad explains. "Most people don't even know they have it. They lead a normal life. But those, like Drew, who play an active sport, find out because they put strain on their heart for long periods of time. It can be treated, which, according to his medical records, he's taking medication for, but there's no cure. There's no surgery to fix him."

"Then how the hell did this happen?" Ashton asks. "He wasn't playing hockey when he collapsed. He was…" He swallows audibly. "He was packing his shit."

"The heart attack could've been brought on due to several different reasons. Looking at his chart, his medication is too low. If he's active, it should've been reevaluated. He also might not have been taking it. If he was stressed, it could've put strain on his heart…"

Brayden curses and walks over to the corner, tugging at the ends of his hair. I want to comfort him, but I also want to hear what my dad is saying.

"So, he'll never be able to play hockey again?" Ashton asks.

"Not at a professional level," Dad explains. "The medication slows down his heart, preventing him from going at full speed, which will keep him from playing at his best. And even if he were fine with that, no professional team will let him play in his condition. The risk of heart failure is too high. He could have a heart attack while playing. No team will take on that risk."

We all go quiet at his words. Heart failure. Drew had a stroke. He could've died.

Fresh tears fill my lids and Ashton pulls me into his side. "Don't go there, MiMi," he says, knowing my thoughts without me having to verbalize them. "We aren't going to lose him."

"You getting him here when you did saved his life," Dad says to Ashton.

"During cardiac arrest, immediate chest compressions are key," Dr. Palmer adds. "Because of your quick thinking, he's still here. I'm certain of that."

Had he been alone… I can't even imagine it.

"When will he wake up?" I ask, even though the doctor has said he doesn't know.

"Unfortunately, now it's a waiting game. It could be hours… days…" His sad eyes meet mine, silently telling me what I don't want to hear. He might never wake up.

"Fuck this!" Brayden barks, stalking out of the room.

"Should we…" I begin, as Ashton says, "I'll go."

The doctor excuses himself, letting Dad know to inform him if he needs anything before leaving Dad and me.

"I know now isn't the best time," Dad says once we're alone—well, alone with Drew sleeping next to us. "But I thought you should know I've left your mother."

I gasp in shock, never expecting him to say that. "What?"

"It's why I've been calling you. I've hired a lawyer and filed for divorce."

"Why?" is all I can come up with.

"Because she's not the person I married. I don't know when she changed, or why I refused to see it, and I wish I could go back and fix what I allowed her to destroy, but when Drew called me—"

"He called you?" I glance over at the beautiful man sleeping. "When? Why?" He never mentioned this.

"Shortly after your mom signed the non-renewal for the lease and drained your bank account. We had a long talk and he made me see the mistakes I've made, putting my wife above my daughter over and over again. I've been a coward for far too long. I didn't want to see what was happening right under my nose. But he made me see it, and I'm so sorry, Mia." He goes to touch me, but I back up.

"You're sorry?" I scoff. "She spent years putting me down, locking me in a metaphorical cage to keep me under her thumb. I was so desperate to make her love me, I starved myself, trying to be perfect for her, but no matter what I did, I was never good enough. And the entire time you watched, you saw what she was doing. When I asked to go to Michigan, you knew it was so I could start over, get away from her. You said you supported me, but the second I did something you didn't approve of, you allowed her to cut me off. You told me it was tough love."

"I know. And I can't take back what I said, or the choices I made, but I'm hoping one day you'll forgive me and give me a chance to make things right."

"I have three boyfriends," I point out.

"I know." He nods. "And it's obvious they all love you deeply and take care of you. The way your mother and I should've loved and taken care of you."

"We take care of each other." I look at Drew, loving him that much more for reaching out to my dad. For trying to fix the broken so I would be happy. "I appreciate you coming here," I tell him. "It means a lot to me that you would drop what you were doing and get on a plane to come here, but I don't think I can forgive you. Too much has happened. I love you and you're my dad, but…"

"I understand," he says, his face contorted as if he's in physical pain. "I know it won't happen overnight, but maybe over time…"

"Maybe," I agree noncommittedly. "Right now I just need to focus on Drew and Ashton and Brayden." They come first. They'll *always* come first.

"If you need me, I'm only a phone call away," Dad says, stepping forward. I allow him to hug me for several heartbeats before I move out of his hold.

"Thank you."

Just after Dad leaves, Ashton enters, sans Brayden. "Where is he?"

"I don't know. I was hoping he came back here." He glances around the room. "Did your dad leave?"

"Yeah."

He gives me a questioning look, but I shake my head, not wanting to get into all that now. "I'll go look for Brayden. Stay with Drew." I need a moment to catch my breath.

The hospital isn't big, but he could be anywhere. I check the outside waiting area, the cafeteria… I briefly wonder if maybe he left.

I'm pulling out my phone to call him, when I notice the hospital chapel. I step inside and find him sitting in the front pew, his head down and his shoulders shaking.

I sit next to him and take his hand in mine. When he looks up at me, his eyes are red-rimmed and his face is slightly puffy from crying.

"Ben was brought here," he mutters. "Died here. In the pediatric wing."

My heart fissures, and I pull him into my arms. "I'm so sorry, Bray." I hold him as tight as I can, wishing my love could physically transfer from me to him.

"We fought," he says after a minute.

"You and your brother?" I ask, confused.

"No, me and Drew. He said he was leaving to protect us and I went off on him."

Oh no. His quietness, the look of guilt, all makes sense now. "You didn't cause his heart attack," I say carefully, knowing full well he isn't going to accept my words.

"I cursed at him, got in his face," he says, his voice resigned. "I was so upset…"

"You didn't know about his heart, and even if you did, people argue all the time."

"You heard your dad. Stress to the heart—"

"Stop it," I demand. "You aren't the reason your brother died, and you aren't the reason Drew is in the hospital. You need to stop blaming yourself for everything."

Brayden is quiet for a long time, while I hold him, wishing there were a way to lift some of the weight he's carrying off his shoulders. He refuses to speak to his parents about his brother. He believes he's the reason Drew had a stroke. If Drew doesn't wake up, I don't think Brayden will survive it. He's already barely hanging on. One more pound and I'm afraid it'll be too much for him to handle.

"I'm going to go check on him," he says, his voice barely a whisper.

"Okay, I'll go with you."

We walk, hand in hand, down the hall back toward Drew's room. Just before we get there, I see his parents coming down the hall. "Go ahead," I tell him. "I'll be inside in a moment."

He nods, not noticing his parents, and goes inside.

As I walk toward them, contemplating if I'm making the right decision, his mom smiles sweetly at me, and I know what I need to do. In the short time I've known her, she's done nothing but be loving and accepting. If she knew what Brayden's been telling himself for years, she would set him straight. She would never let him believe he killed his brother.

"Can I talk to you guys for a minute?" There's a chance Brayden's going to be mad at me for what I'm about to do, but I have to do it—for him.

Molly and Tim both nod.

"Of course," Molly says. "Is it Drew?"

"No. It's about Ben."

# TWENTY-EIGHT

*Brayden*

I can't take this.

Again.

The guilt. The self-hatred. The agony.

Ben. Now Drew. Maybe it'll be Ashton or Mia next.

Why is it my actions always hurt those around me?

Ashton reaches over, threading his fingers with mine, momentarily silencing my awful thoughts that are on repeat inside my head. "You think loud. It hurts my ears."

I let out a small laugh, devoid of humor. "You should hear it from the inside."

"You could tell me," he offers, his hazel eyes searching mine.

Gritting my teeth, I break my stare from him to look at Drew. Strong, fierce, powerful Drew who's lifeless and hooked to machines. Because of me. "Some shit is better left unsaid."

He squeezes my hand but doesn't say anything else. I glance at the clock, wondering what's taking Mia so long. She's so brave. I can tell she wants to burst into tears every three seconds, but she holds it together like she's doing it for us. I love that girl.

Speaking of that girl…

She slips into the room, a guilty expression on her face. My parents follow in after. As soon as I see my parents' faces, my gut hollows out.

Mia wouldn't.

I tense up, clinging to Ashton like he's my lifeline and I'm about to get sucked into a black void I'll never escape from. Panic claws up my throat and my eyes burn.

No.

Please, no.

I can't lose them too.

Mia's eyes water as she nears. "Please don't be mad at me. I couldn't let you hurt yourself any longer, Bray."

I gape at her, my throat aching with emotion. Anger flashes hot inside me, but it's doused in despair. Fear of the unknown threatens to consume me.

Ashton starts to pull away as my parents approach, both of them horror-stricken, but I tighten my grip on his hand. I can't do this. Not alone. I can't do this.

Mom sits beside me, taking my other hand as Dad kneels in front of me. Tears of dread pool in my eyes, leaking without my permission.

"Oh, honey," Mom says, her voice shaking. "Oh, my sweet, sweet boy."

"I'm s-sorry," I choke out. "I d-didn't mean t-to."

Dad ruffles my hair, pressing his forehead to mine. "Brayden, Ben's death was not your fault."

A sob tears its way out of me. I can hear it echoed in both my mother and Mia. I can't look at them. I'm ensnared in my father's fierce glare.

"It was my fault," I whisper, admitting to him what I've wanted to say for years. "It was all my fault."

"No," Mom hisses. "It was not your fault. I will not have you drowning in this guilt, thinking you're responsible."

"But I was!" I cry out, my heart aching. "You told us to stay inside while you went Christmas shopping. It was too cold to play outside, but I took him anyway." I squeeze my eyes shut. "He got pneumonia because I took him in that cold weather. It was me. I did this to him. Your son is dead because of me."

"Nonsense," Dad barks out. "What happened to Ben was an accident. An unfortunate one. He'd been suffering from chronic colds for years."

"But I took him outside," I argue. "He wouldn't have gotten sick if it weren't for me!"

"I refuse to believe that," Dad states. "He'd already had two bouts of bronchitis at Halloween and then Thanksgiving. His lungs were failing him. The pneumonia was a sad inevitability. It's not your fault his little body was too weak. Not your fault."

"But—" I start, but Mom shushes me and squeezes my hand.

"Not your fault," she says. "Your brother adored you. Worshipped you, Brayden. Why do you think he never played sports himself? He wasn't cut out for it because he was too sickly. Maybe you don't remember this about Ben, but it's the truth. He loved that his brother was strong and athletic and played hockey like a champ. The fact you gave him one last chance to play and be a kid was the best gift he's ever gotten. We love you, Brayden, but we won't allow you to take the blame anymore. Ben died loving you and thinking the world of you, as he should. It's time to live up to those big brother expectations."

Mom pulls me to her and I release Ashton's hand to cling to her. I think back to all the times in our childhood. How I never got sick, but Ben caught everything. The flu, fevers, respiratory infections. He missed school a lot, whereas I always had perfect attendance. Maybe he really was sick and I never realized just how much.

"It hurts," I whimper. "It's hurt for so long."

"No more hurting alone, baby," Mom murmurs. "You have your daddy and me. You always have. And now you have Mia, Ashton, and Drew. No one wants to watch you suffer. We want you to let go of that guilt and be happy. Had Daddy and I realized it was this that has been eating you up all these years, we would've had this conversation a long time ago. It's time to heal, sweetheart. We're here to help you."

The weight that always crushes down on me feels lighter.

"I'm sorry," Mia says, leaning her head against my shoulder. "Please don't hate me. I just couldn't watch you kill yourself over this any longer."

It's then I realize Ashton has pulled her into his lap and her hand now covers my hand he's holding.

"I could never hate you," I tell her. "Ever. I love you."

She smiles and presses a kiss to my lips. "I love you too, Bray."

"For the record, I love you too," Ashton says. "I think I fell in love with your ass before your heart, but all that matters now is I love both."

We all laugh.

I lean forward and capture his mouth with mine. "I love you, Ashton."

It's bittersweet to share this moment without Drew. More guilt flings my way, but without the burden of thinking Ben's death is all my fault and that my parents would hate me, it's a little easier to bear. Drew's condition is out of my control, just like Ben's was. All I can do is pray to God Drew will make it out of this alive.

"You kids look exhausted," Mom says. "Why don't you go home and nap? Daddy will stay here with Drew while I cook up some supper. I think after some rest and a good home-cooked meal, you all will feel better. Okay?"

I give my mom a quick kiss on her tearstained cheek. "Okay. I'll take these crybabies home and put them to bed."

Ashton laughs. "Says the guy with snot running down his nose."

Smirking at him, I swipe at my nose with my middle finger.

We all laugh again, and fuck if it doesn't feel good.

I wake to a boner against my ass. It's dark out, but a quick glance at the clock tells me it won't be for long. I'm physically and emotionally drained. While my secret about Ben had been revealed to my parents and we were able to work through those emotions, it did nothing for the state Drew is in. He's still not here with us where he belongs.

I can't believe he was going to leave us.

And now he might leave us for good.

Imagining a life without Drew makes my stomach churn. He's always been a part of my life, and recently he's been a vital part. Like an artery that runs through my body. Without him, I'll bleed out, suffering without his love and life running through me. I know Mia and Ashton feel just as connected. The three of us are suffering without Drew. We need him. And *when* he wakes up, we'll remind him that he needs us too.

School.

Hockey.

NHL.

Careers.

Nothing matters in the grand scheme. I'd give up everything to keep Drew right here with us. We're a foursome and we can't function missing a quarter of us. Every piece is necessary for our happiness.

*When* he wakes up, I'll do everything in my damn power to convince him. I know Ashton and Mia will be right there with me. We'll kidnap him if we have to. Ashton would probably be into it, the little freak.

"Thoughts. Loud. You forget I can practically hear inside your head," Ashton says, flexing his hips so I'll feel his morning wood. "You okay?"

"Just thinking," I murmur, not wanting to wake Mia.

"We're going to get him back," he says, caressing my abs and kissing my shoulder. "You know that, right?"

If he'll ever wake up, I'm certain we'll persuade him.

"Yeah, I know." I turn my head to meet him for a kiss. "And then we're going to get a bigger bed because your boner is not a good alarm clock."

"I beg to differ," he argues, rubbing against me again. "Feels pretty good to me."

A girlish giggle has me smiling.

"I think boner alarm clocks are the best alarm clocks," our girl says, scooting close to me. She presses a kiss to my lips.

I hold her to me, enjoying the way Ashton clings to me from behind. All we're missing is Drew. I'd thought, at one time, that it might be strange or crowded seeing three people at the same time, but it turns out that when one of us is missing, it's cold and empty.

I need all three of them.

"As much as I want to strip Bray down and take his sexy little ass while he makes you squeal, Mia, we better get up and showered. Molly promised us breakfast, too. I need her food more than I need sex." Ashton gives my ass a squeeze and then he climbs out of the bed. "Let's go."

It's more than that.

He feels it too.

So does Mia.

It's why we haven't touched each other sexually since Drew was rushed to the hospital. We don't feel right without him. Like if we hold out for him, eventually he'll come back to us.

"Better get up before he hogs all the hot water," I say, kissing Mia's forehead.

We join Ashton in the shower, and despite the hot bodies in there with me, we don't do anything other than bathe. When we get Drew back, we'll take a million hot, filthy showers. That's a promise.

I'm more relaxed as we walk through the snowy parking lot toward the hospital. The flakes are fat and fluttering all around. At one time, I hated the snow, but today, I find beauty in the scene before me. The way the air puffs out white each time we breathe. The fact that Mia and Ashton are wearing matching Ice Hawks beanies—beanies I gave them. Seeing them in my beanies makes my heart swell in my chest. Mom fed us a huge breakfast and fussed over us like we were toddlers. It means a lot to me that she treats Mia and Ashton like they're her kids too. I know it means a hell of a lot to them too.

"What do you guys want for Christmas?" Ashton asks. "I haven't even done any shopping."

"Me neither," I admit.

"And I've been too poor," Mia says with a laugh. "Though Dad must be trying to make amends because I noticed my account had several more zeros this morning."

Relief floods through me. I wasn't keen on her father, but I was glad he left his bitch wife and seems to be attempting to bridge the gap between them.

"Oh great," Ashton complains, looking down at his phone.

"What?" I peek at the screen. It's a text from his dad asking him to call him. That it's urgent.

"Just call him," Mia urges. "We'll wait for you."

He groans but dials his dad, putting him on speaker. Curtis answers on the first ring.

"Ashton," Curtis states in greeting. "How are you?"

"My boyfriend's in a coma. What do you think?" he throws back.

Curtis sighs. "I'm sorry. I just worry about you is all. Your mother and I both do."

"Funny," Ashton deadpans. "What do you want?"

"I wanted to let you know that we started the investigation on the video that was leaked. After interviewing Sasha, she admitted that she took the video and sent it to Travis, but she didn't forward it to everyone else. To escape academic probation for being a catalyst for what happened, she spilled everything she knew. Corroborated what you'd said about the bleach and the threats made to you. Apparently, Travis saw her as an ally since she was angry at you for outbidding her for the date with Brayden. He admitted to her that he also planted the marijuana in your bag and slashed your tires." Curtis sighs, making the sound rattle through the phone. "I'm sorry, Ashton. I thought I was doing my job right, but you nailed the hammer on the head when you said I chose my position over you. I was trying to do the right thing, and in return, it hurt you."

"What happens now?" I ask, unable to keep quiet. "Will that asshole be held responsible for hurting all of us?"

"His grades were suffering, so he was going to be put on academic probation for the upcoming semester, so this newest stunt he pulled has forced the university's hand. He's been suspended until he can prove he wasn't the one who sent the video. If he fights it, I'll have to involve the police, and I made sure he knew this. Last I checked, he was packing up his dorm and going back to Ohio."

"At least we won't have to deal with that asshole hurting you anymore," Mia says to Ashton.

"I don't think he'll be a problem from here on out," Curtis agrees.

"Thanks," Ashton mutters. "If that's all, we better get inside."

"Actually," Curtis says, his voice tight. "I was wondering if you'd have dinner with me and your mother. It's been a while and with Christmas around the corner, I thought—"

"No," Ashton barks out. "Not unless the people I love can come with me."

I smile at him, proud of his bravery to stand up to his father.

"Of course," Curtis tells him. "I may not exactly agree with the things you do, but I can tell when my son is happy. Despite what you may think, it's all we've ever wanted for you. I know I come down hard on you a lot, but it's because I know your potential, not because I'm trying to change who you are."

"This isn't a phase," Ashton says. "I want you to know that. I know I'm a lot of things—reckless, careless, wild—but not when it comes to them. They're the smartest, most right thing I've done in my life. I love them. All three of them. And if you can accept that about me, then maybe we can find better footing with our relationship, Dad."

"I can respect that," Curtis agrees. "Plus, you know I like all three of them. It doesn't change anything with Drew as far as the university is concerned, but as your father, I can accept that he's your boyfriend. Drew is a good man. Brayden and Mia are great people too. So what do you say? Dinner one day soon?"

Both Mia and I nod at him.

"Yeah," Ashton grunts. "I guess so."

"Good," Curtis says, relief in his tone. "We'll talk soon and figure out a day. Bye, kids."

We all say bye to him and Ashton pockets his phone. He holds one of my hands and Mia holds the other as we walk in. After being here for several days, the staff is used to seeing the three of us together. At first, we got a few sour looks, but then, the nurses took a liking to us, especially Ashton because he's a nut, and they started babying us, bringing us snacks, extra pillows, and generally looking out for us. People are a lot more accepting than you'd think. Especially the ones who love you.

"Elaine," Ashton calls out to one of the nurses when he sees her exiting Drew's room. "Any donuts you can steal us today from the break room?"

"You literally just ate," I state, chuckling. "Like fifteen minutes ago."

He shrugs. "I'm always hungry."

Mia giggles, swatting at Ashton.

It's then I notice the look on Elaine's face.

Teary. Smiling.

"I was hoping you three would show up soon," she says, her grin widening as she opens the door.

My heart seizes inside my chest. Ashton is the first to snap into action, dragging me and Mia along. It isn't until he pulls us into the room that my entire world spins around me.

Drew.

Our fucking Drew.

Awake. No longer attached to machines making him breathe. Sitting up in bed, looking tired as hell but alive.

"Dr. Palmer just stepped out a bit ago," Elaine says. "But Drew's doing great. Aren't you, honey?"

Drew's eyes slowly roam over Ashton, Mia, and then settle on me. "I am now."

I'm the first to launch myself at him.

I hold on to him, and I'll be damned if I ever let him go.

# TWENTY-NINE

## *Drew*

Brayden wraps his arms around me and I feel like I can finally breathe again. When I woke up early this morning, alone, my stomach bottomed out. Not because I was attached to tubes and in a hospital room, but because I thought Brayden, Ashton, and Mia were done with me. And I wouldn't blame them. I pushed them away, was attempting to run when Ashton found me. I don't remember anything after that, but I imagine Brayden told them I was leaving. Rather than fearing for my condition, I was regretful of what I'd done to them.

Once Brayden releases me, he drops into a chair by my bed. Mia sits down in the chair next to him and trails her fingers up and down my arm while Brayden holds my hand. Ashton plops into a chair on the other side and grabs my other hand. My heart swells as I glance at each of them. Ashton has dark circles under his eyes. Mia's are puffy. And Brayden looks pale, his own eyes a bit bloodshot. They've been worried about me. Because they love me. And I was going to leave them.

"Well, hello again," Dr. Palmer says, walking in. "Still feeling okay?"

"Better than earlier," I croak, my voice incredibly hoarse. How could I not be with the three most important people surrounding me?

"As I told you this morning, you had a stroke," he explains. "I want to ask you some questions now that you can talk. Have you been taking your medication as prescribed?"

When I first woke up and sort of panicked, they took me off the machines and checked my vitals. After a few tests, they gave me some water for my throat since it was scratched from being intubated.

"Yes." I would never risk my life like that. I saw what it did to my dad.

He nods. "Were you stressed leading up to the time of the stroke?"

Before I can answer, Brayden speaks up. "Yes, he was. We got into a fight."

I sigh, hating that he's blaming himself for this. "An argument isn't going to cause a heart attack," I tell Brayden, locking eyes with him. "This was not your fault."

I look at the doctor. "I was under some stress because of personal stuff going on, but the truth is, I felt like something was wrong for a while. I just ignored it, not wanting to deal with it."

Ashton's hand squeezes mine at the same time Brayden's does.

Mia gasps. "Drew! This is your heart. You can't ignore it when something is wrong. We could've lost you."

My gaze swings over at her glassy eyes. "I'm sorry."

"In that case, we're going to up the dosage. Our initial thought was that you were undermedicated, which can happen. We're going to keep you here one more night and run some tests, but as long as everything looks okay, you can go home tomorrow. Make sure you follow up with your cardiologist and try to avoid stress as much as possible."

"Thanks, Doc. Will do."

With a smile and a nod, he excuses himself, leaving the four of us alone. I'm not sure what the hell to say, but I can't stand the silence, so I speak up.

"Did I miss anything important while I was out?"

Ashton snorts. Brayden growls. Mia giggles.

"I called my dad," Mia says. "I was hoping he could fix you." She frowns and I move my hand out of Brayden's to cup her cheek.

"I know how hard that must've been for you."

"He showed up. Told me he's divorcing my mom." She shrugs. "Apologized." Her eyes meet mine. "Told me you called him."

Fuck, I should've told her. I did it out of anger one night after she cried herself to sleep, not understanding why she's not enough.

"Thank you," she says, smiling. "I've never had anyone stand up for me until you three."

"Are you guys okay now?" As much as I despise the man for choosing his bitchy wife over his daughter, I know Mia would love to have a relationship with him.

"No, but I think maybe one day we will be."

I lean over and kiss her forehead. "I'm glad."

"Mom and Dad know about Ben," Brayden says, shocking the hell out of me.

"They know… everything?"

"Yeah, they said he was sick for years. Refused to let me take the blame."

I breathe a sigh of relief. "You were a damn good brother and he died knowing that."

Brayden nods in agreement.

"My dad kicked Travis's conniving, psycho ass back to Ohio," Ashton remarks. "Sasha the sorority bitch is the one who videoed us the night of the Halloween party, then she gave it to Travis, who shared it with the entire campus."

Ashton clears his throat. "I knew about the video, but I thought I could handle it. I'm sorry." He drops his gaze, and I squeeze his hand.

"The entire situation sucks," I tell him. "Don't blame yourself for that shit. What's done is done."

"I've brought breakfast," the nurse announces, walking in with a tray of food. She sets it down. "I'll be back later to run some tests the doctor ordered. Until then, eat and rest." She winks at the four of us, and I laugh that she knows about us and seems okay with it.

The rest of the day is spent with us talking about nothing of consequence. I know it's because none of them want to address the elephant in the room—me leaving—or risk stressing me out. Occasionally I'm wheeled out for tests, and when I return, they're still there waiting for me.

Molly and Tim stop by to check on me, and so do Curtis and Wendy. When nighttime rolls around, I insist the three of them go home and sleep in an actual bed, but they refuse, Ashton and Mia taking the couch and Brayden crashing on the pull-out reclining chair.

Maybe it's because I've technically been sleeping for days, but hours after they fall asleep, I'm still awake, wondering how the hell I'm going to leave them.

"Home sweet home," Ashton says as we walk into the apartment. The doctor came by this morning, and after giving me my new prescription, discharged me. Since the three of them all came in Ashton's car, we piled into it to go home.

Fuck, home. I need to make a new flight reservation. When I asked the doctor if it was okay to fly, and he said yes, I could feel all three of their glares on me, but I ignored them, thanking him.

The first thing I notice when we get inside is the Christmas tree we decorated. Then I remember tomorrow is Christmas Eve. Our first Christmas. Mia walks over and turns it on and it comes to life. Beautiful multicolored lights with big colorful ornaments. She was never allowed to decorate her own tree growing up, so she insisted we pick everything out. My eyes land on the snow angel ornament. The one Brayden picked out in memory of Ben. The snowman, to symbolize our weekend away at the snow resort. The book for Mia. The hockey puck for Bray and me. The M&M for Ashton. Every ornament means something. My heart clenches in my chest. We've only been together for a short period of time, but we've already created so many memories. Can I do this? Leave all of the memories—and the people I've created them with—behind?

*It's to protect them*, I remind myself.

I step into my room, with the three of them on my heels, and see my duffle bag on the bed. I pick it up and set it on the dresser, knowing we're going to have to have this conversation sooner rather than later.

"I'm leaving," I tell them, turning around and leaning against the dresser.

"Cool," Ashton says. "Where are we going?"

"What?" I splutter in confusion. "No. *I'm* leaving." My gaze bounces between the three of them. "My stroke and heart attack don't change what happened. A video circulated around campus of the four of us dancing… of Brayden kissing me."

"You're right," Brayden says. "Your stroke and heart attack don't change what happened, but the four of us being together changes *everything*. If you leave, so do we. It will suck leaving with only one semester left of college, but…"

"But we don't give a fuck," Ashton finishes, "because this relationship is more important than anything else."

"I'm only a semester in." Mia shrugs nonchalantly. "I can transfer anywhere. Where are we going? I hear Colorado is nice this time of year. Oh! Or we could go to Florida, enjoy the sunshine. I'm not really sure about this whole snow shit."

Ashton snorts and Brayden chuckles.

"You guys…" I'm at a loss for words. These three have become my entire world, but I can't let them do this. I can't allow them to fuck up their futures for me. "Maybe after you graduate." I look at Ashton. "And you get drafted." My eyes go to Brayden.

"Nope," they both say in unison.

"We don't care who knows we're all together," Brayden says, stepping over to me. "You're ours and we're yours and anyone who gives a shit can go fuck themselves." He kisses my lips and my heart soars. I've missed his touch so much.

"Agreed," Mia says, walking over to me. "I've seen way more scandalous shit in Hollywood." She kisses my cheek, but when her lips linger,

I turn my face, connecting our mouths for a few too short moments. She tastes so good. Like sweetness and comfort.

"So, what'll it be?" Ashton asks, joining the three of us. "Are we staying or leaving?" Like them, he kisses me as well. On my neck, his tongue darting out and quickly licking my flesh. My dick stirs, and I let out a low groan.

For a long minute, I look between them, all willing to face the fire with me. Because of their love for me. They're right. Our love is the most important thing and if they're willing to put everything on the line to be together then I need to fight with them, not against them.

"Leaving," I tell them. "In six months when we find out where Brayden's getting drafted."

"If I get drafted," Brayden points out.

"You will," I assure him. "You're too talented not to."

"I'm down," Ashton says. "I can continue school anywhere. It'll be nice to have a fresh start out of this town."

"Me too," Mia adds. "I don't care where I am as long as I'm with you three."

"Then it's settled," Ashton says. "In six months we're the fuck out of here." He glances over at Brayden. "Try to get picked up somewhere fun, like Miami or New York."

Brayden rolls his eyes. "If I get picked up, I won't have a choice."

"Whatever." Ashton shrugs. "Let's go watch one of those cheesy Christmas movies Mia loves so much. I'll make us all some hot chocolate, extra marshmallows."

"You love those movies too!" Mia slaps Ashton on the arm as he walks out of the room. "I saw you shed a tear when we watched the one with Santa's daughter."

"Bullshit," Ashton argues. "I had something in my eye."

Brayden, Mia, and I sit close to each other on the couch. Brayden takes my hand in his and brings it up to his lips to kiss it, while Mia drops her head against my shoulder, surfing the channels to find a movie. A few minutes later, Ashton comes over carrying mugs of hot chocolate.

He drops onto the couch next to Mia and throws her feet over his legs. I look around and know there's no way I ever could've left these three. Even if I had run the other day, I wouldn't have lasted without them. They're my lifelines, a part of me, and I'm the same to them.

I couldn't survive without them by my side.

I almost didn't.

# THIRTY

*Brayden*

*Seven Months Later*

"Do I season both sides?" I ask Dad, my phone trapped between my ear and my shoulder. "Not gonna lie. It looks like shit. I'm probably going to poison everyone."

Dad laughs. "It's raw meat. Of course it looks like shit. Season both sides and let it sit in the marinade for an hour or so. Make sure your grill is nice and hot. You've got this."

When you live with three other people who also don't know how to cook very well, you have to step up your lessons and fast. Ashton and Drew make a pretty damn good breakfast. Mia and I usually handle dinners using Mom and Dad as our emergency help hotline. Somehow, we're adulting when it comes to cooking meals.

"Okay," I say after I season the other sides of the steaks. "We're good to go. Tell Mom I love her."

"She sends her love. We both do. Take care of the kids for us."

I laugh and we both say bye as two strong arms wrap around me from behind.

Drew.

Warm. Strong. Intense.

I never take his embraces for granted. Not anymore. Each one feels like a gift. Now that he's doing great, having adjusted to a higher dosage of medication, he's the same ol' Drew we know and love.

"Can you grab my phone so I can wash my hands?" I ask, trying not to get distracted by the dick pressed against the back of my swim trunks.

He kisses the back of my neck and then sets the phone down on the counter. While I wash my hands, Drew puts the meat back in the fridge.

"It's boring out there without you. Ashton's being Ashton and Mia's sunbathing," Drew tells me, grabbing my hand and tugging me to him. "At least you'll play with me."

I smirk at him, loving the lust glimmering in his gaze. "We'll convince them to play with us."

We walk to the back door, hand in hand. Our new house is fucking amazing. Drew technically bought it, but we all pitched in in some way. Because I got drafted to the Minnesota Arctic Lions, I had a nice chunk of cash to buy us some furniture to fill this big-ass house. Ashton poured his money into gaming consoles and televisions, naturally. And Mia? That girl custom ordered us a monster of a bed for our bedroom.

It's home.

Our home.

And we're all here. No one left behind.

As we step out into the backyard, I find Ashton and Mia doing as Drew said. She's in a tiny yellow bikini that barely covers her and he's flying through our pool like the dolphin he is, swimming laps. Drew lets go of my hand to grab us a couple of beers from the outdoor fridge. After he pops the tabs, he hands one to me.

"I like it here," I tell him, tipping my beer at him. "What about you?"

"Hell yeah."

We drink our beers, enjoying the hot June weather in our backyard. Since it's summer, we get to enjoy ourselves a bit. I have my obligations for summer training and press meets for the Arctic Lions, but my schedule won't get intense for a few more months. Mia enrolled in the local university to finish her undergraduate degree, already taking some summer classes. Ashton says he's not doing shit until the fall, but he's also enrolled, for his master's. Drew easily got picked up as the head hockey coach at the high school one town over. Everything just fell into place when I got drafted. And, like they vowed, they each picked up their lives to come with me.

"She looks hot, yeah?" I say, setting my beer down.

"Very hot. What kind of boyfriends would we be if we didn't cool her off?"

We share a mischievous look as we abandon our beers to sneak up on our girl. Her giant sunglasses take up half her face and she has a serene smile on her face. Not for long. Drew prowls up behind her while I head for her feet. Like we've practiced it a thousand times, he grabs her hands while I grab her feet.

"Ashton!" she shrieks. "Help!

Laughing, Drew and I pick her up from her lawn chair, carrying her out to the edge of the pool.

"Do not throw me in, assholes!" she bellows. "I just dried my hair like thirty minutes ago!"

"Looks like you're gonna have to dry it again, MiMi," Ashton says to her, cracking up. "Toss my girl here!"

"Don't encourage them!" Her words are drowned out by a scream when we toss her into the pool. She sinks and then comes up thrashing, her dark hair plastered to her face. "Assholes!"

Drew dives in and I cannonball right next to her to splash her again. She tries to kick me under the water to no avail. I wrap my arms around her waist, popping out of the water to grin up at her.

"Love you, babe," I say, flashing her my most innocent smile. "I was trying to cool you off."

She rolls her eyes but threads her fingers in my hair to press a kiss to my lips. "Love you too."

Her legs wrap around my waist as I carry her into the deep end where Drew is playfully grinding into Ashton from behind. They're both laughing and then it ends with them trying to drown each other.

"Why does Drew even try when we're in the water?" Mia asks. "It's like a rubber duck trying to play chicken with a shark. Ashton can hold his breath longer than the three of us combined."

Sure enough, it ends with Drew giving up, sputtering out water. Once they're done horsing around, Mia swims over to Drew to baby him. I grab the front of Ashton's swim trunks, hauling him to me for a kiss. We're in a heated battle of tongues when a basketball lands in the water beside us with a splash.

Ashton pulls away from our kiss to grab the ball. "I already told you two," he hollers at our neighbor Eric. "It's a foursome, not a sixsome. Sixsomes don't exist."

Eric climbs over the fence, shaking his head. "Just because I'm gay doesn't mean I'm trying to get my husband to join your orgy shit."

Ashton laughs and throws the ball at him. "Tell Byron that. I see the way he checks out my boyfriend's ass." He shrugs. "Both of them, in fact."

"You're a dick. And here I thought the bigoted assholes who lived here before were a problem."

"Where is Byron anyway?" Mia asks. "We bought enough steaks for you guys to come to dinner."

"He's still at the office, but he'll be home soon." Eric sits down on one of the loungers. "I pulled out some ground turkey for spaghetti, but Byron isn't as sold on the diet as I am. He'll probably race me over here for steak. I need to grab a shower. When are you cooking?"

"We'll start the grill in about an hour. Seven?" I say, pulling Ashton to me and kissing the side of his neck. "You know we're shit when it comes to cooking. Maybe bring a salad or something."

Eric laughs. "I can do that."

"Any more problems out of your other neighbor?" Drew asks, his tone growing serious.

"Nah, she's outnumbered now." He chuckles. "At least we were a normal gay couple 'bringing down the value of the neighborhood.' The four of you showed up a couple of weeks ago and really stirred shit up."

"I told Ms. Greenwood if she has a problem with gays, she should move to… oh, that's right. Everywhere she goes, there will be gay people." Ashton shrugs. "She didn't like that."

"At least she's leaving us alone," Eric says. "The only bright side of your riff-raff assess moving in next door."

"You love us," Mia teases. "Your dog does at least."

"Cinnamon loves anyone who feeds her scraps. Thanks to you, little girl, she shit all over Byron's laptop bag." He shakes his head, but he's smiling. "You guys are all right, I guess. I just use you for a distraction to get Ms. Greenwood off my nutsack and Byron uses you for the steak. We're hardly friends, definitely not love, and we'll never be an addition to your fucked-up orgy situation."

We all laugh. Eric is gruff, but he's funny. And as much as he likes to give us shit, he's a cool guy who really is thankful we moved in next door. The neighborhood we got our house in is full of older people who aren't as welcoming to what they don't consider traditional relationships. But, since we're us, we moved right in, not hiding a damn thing. When Eric and Byron walked over, we were tense and ready for battle, but they seemed relieved to finally have potential friends in the neighborhood.

"We only put up with you because Byron is cool as hell," Ashton taunts. "You're just the eye candy."

Eric flips him off before tossing his basketball back over the fence. "See you assholes at seven."

Once he climbs over the fence, we go back to horsing around. Mia tries to escape, but we never let her. Living with three guys must be hard. She doesn't complain too much.

"You're tipsy," I tease, smacking Mia's ass as I carry her down the hall to our bedroom. "When you're tipsy you always want anal. You just weren't supposed to announce that over dinner."

She cackles. "Shouldn't have kept making me margaritas. It's all your fault."

I carry her into our bathroom that has a massive shower. Our needs for a house were different than most homebuyers. We needed a huge master bedroom and bath. The guest rooms could be small for our offices, but we all wanted to share a bedroom. Once I get the water started, I strip Mia down for a quick shower since she practically made out with Cinnamon all night. I was glad when they finally left and took that yapping dog home.

"You always offer to babysit drunk me to get out of cleaning the kitchen," she tattles as I set her down under the hot spray of the water.

"And you always get drunk so you don't have to do the dishes," I tease back.

Her lips curl into a wicked grin that has me kissing her pretty mouth. We manage to get little washing done, but get hot and bothered. I turn off the water and towel us down before guiding her to our giant bed.

Admittedly, it's my favorite thing about our house.

It's huge.

I toss her onto it and give her thigh a little smack. "Let me kiss your pussy while we wait on our boys."

Her eyes are hooded and she shamelessly spreads her thighs apart. I prowl onto the bed, hungry for my girl. She moans when I lick at her slit. Now that we've been together so long, I have Mia's body memorized. I know exactly what to do to make her toes curl. All it takes is a few teasing nips and ravishing her clit with my tongue before she's crying out my name.

"Naughty," Ashton says from behind me. "Started without us." He smacks my ass. "Get on your hands and knees, hockey boy."

At first, taking it up the ass kind of fucking hurt. But Ashton and

Drew both taught me to enjoy it. The thought of having Ashton inside me has my dick leaking with precum.

"MiMi," Ashton instructs as he strips down to nothing. "Your drunk ass is gonna suck some dick."

"Yummy," she says, sitting up on her knees.

He laughs. "Drunk ass."

"Lube," Drew says, tossing a bottle on the bed. He sheds his clothes in record speed.

I climb on all fours like Ashton instructed, waiting for him to prep my ass. His touch is reverent as he caresses my ass. Ashton likes calling the shots in bed, and we often fall into the role of letting him. He's always trying new positions and swapping shit up. It only gets weird when Mia's been looking at porn. Then, we end up in some strange predicaments that usually have us laughing by the end.

"Come here," Ashton tells Mia as his slick finger penetrates my asshole. "Crawl under Brayden so you can suck his dick."

She squirms her way beneath me, so that we're in a sixty-nine position. I playfully smack at her pussy that's within reach.

"Drew, prop MiMi up with some pillows so she can reach his dick," Ashton instructs.

Once Mia has been lifted up, she starts teasing my dick with her tongue. I groan when Ashton pushes a second finger inside me.

"Let Brayden suck on your dick to get it nice and wet so you can fuck our girl," Ashton tells Drew. "Do your parts so I can focus on tearing up this tight ass."

I groan when he pulls his fingers out and then kneels behind me. Drew stands on the bed, his feet on either side of Mia, offering me his dick like a snack. My mouth parts, watering for a taste.

Mia takes my dick deep in her mouth as Ashton pushes the head of his cock inside of me. I groan, overcome with pleasure. Drew chooses that moment to roughly shove his dick past my lips. I'm overwhelmed by sensations. They're everywhere all at once.

Mine.

They're all mine.

I start to gag, as does Mia, when Drew pulls away. Ashton slides partway out of my ass before driving into me hard. Drew and Ashton seem to be taking turns slamming into me, each of them owning different holes. Mia sucks dick like it's her goddamn job.

I love these people.

Drew pulls out, smacking my mouth with his dick. I know from experience, he's close to coming. I should suck on him to tease him some more, but I know our girl needs to be stuffed by his big cock. Ashton knows too.

"I can smell MiMi's arousal from here," Ashton says. "She's craving dick, Drew."

Drew kneels down between her legs, easily lifting her ass with his hands, and then slides into her slick entrance. She moans around my dick, making me see stars.

The harder Drew slams into her, the harder Ashton slams into me. Mia comes first, and the way she gags on my dick when she does has me spurting out my release with no warning. Drew makes a groaning sound and then his hips are flexing slower, with purpose, as he comes. Ashton is last, and I know the second he's losing control, because he digs his fingers painfully into my hips, as a small groan escapes him.

We finally detangle ourselves from one another and Drew cleans everyone up.

"Thanks, Daddy," Ashton teases.

Drew curls himself around Ashton, pinching his pierced nipple. "I hate that shit."

"Nah, you like it," Ashton argues.

Mia is content pressed between Ashton and me. I kiss her mouth and then Ashton's. Then, I lean across him to grab Drew's mouth too.

I love these people so fucking much.

"Good night, Daddy Drew," Mia sings.

"Night, Mia."

And then to me she says, "Good night, boyfriend Bray."

"Night, baby."

"Good night, Ashy C."

"Night, MiMi."

And we fall asleep like we do every night—bound together by friendship, fierce loyalty, and unimaginable love.

Always together.

Never apart.

# EPILOGUE

*Ashton*

*Five Years Later*

"Congratulations, Dr. Carter," Dr. Anderson says, smiling with pride. "I knew you could do it."

This. Fucking. Guy.

As my doctoral advisor, he spent more time trying to talk me out of going after my PhD than actually advising me. In hindsight, that asshole probably threw out some reverse psychology on me. Instead of walking away, I worked harder, pissed that this guy didn't think I was smart enough.

Now he's looking at me with a knowing expression that has me re-thinking everything.

"Thank you, Dr. Anderson," I state back, shaking his hand.

I leave the stage, my chin held high. Years ago, this felt like a pipe dream. Something I wanted to do, but wasn't sure I was capable of. Now, it's mine.

Dr. Ashton Nathaniel Carter.

Surprisingly, school became much more enjoyable when I didn't have Dad dictating my every move. Also, once it was in my specialized field of study, I liked it a helluva lot more. And, when you have the sexiest little tutor in the whole world, it's a breeze.

I scan the auditorium, looking for my family, but there are too many people. I make my way to sit beside my buddy Reese. He and I are the only two graduates with a PhD in psychology this semester. The rest are in different fields of study. Reese is a total fucking nerd who sucks ass at video games, but he's cool as hell and Peyton loves him.

"Anderson act like he's now your number one fan or am I just trippin'?" he asks, his black brow arched high.

"Dude, he was seconds from sucking my dick he was so proud." I shake my head. "He was a total douchebag before I went in to defend my dissertation, telling me it wasn't too late to quit. Fucking asshole."

He shakes his head. "Someone gave him a degree that allowed him to fuck with heads, and he sure as hell fucked with ours."

"Not anymore," I say, grinning.

We bump fists.

After this, we're on to bigger and better things. This move to Chicago—because of Brayden's trade to be with the Chicago Freezes a few years ago—was the best one yet. Drew took a position at the University of Chicago, coaching their hockey team. He's a hot commodity wherever we go, but at least this city has been really good to us. Even Mia has had better opportunities regarding her scripts. Just last month, she sold her first screenplay to an indie production studio based here in Chicago. Our girl will have her first movie one day in the near future.

As for me, I already have a job lined up at Chicago Mental Health Hospital in the LGBQT division. Reese will also join me there, but he's going to be dealing with substance abuse patients. My patients will all be ones I not only can relate to, but ones I'm confident I can help.

Before long, the ceremony is over and I'm hugging Reese before heading off to find my family. I find Drew first in the crowd. He shoulders his big ass through the swarm of people, nearly knocking me off my feet with a bear hug.

"So fucking proud of you." He pulls away to plant a kiss on my lips. "And you look hot, Doc."

My dick twitches. "We can play doctor later. These people don't want to watch me give you a rectal exam."

"Poppa!"

I see Peyton over everyone's head as she sits on her dadda's shoulders. Her blue eyes twinkle and her grin is just like her mother's. As soon as Brayden is close enough, she launches herself at me. I catch our little girl, snuggling her to me. Drew takes my diploma from me so I can take our kid.

"Hey, squirt. Miss me?" I ask, tickling her.

"Ganny and Peepaw said we can get ice cream!" she shrieks. "Let's go!"

My dad shrugs as he walks up, a guilty look on his face. "How was I supposed to say no?"

"He didn't even try," Mom tattles.

They're both wearing matching grins, proud of this day and me. It's amazing how far we've come as a family. There was a time I thought they hated me and I was pretty sure I hated them. But with Drew's, Mia's, and Brayden's guidance, I worked on my relationship with my parents. Mom's been sober for a few years now and it's amazing what a difference it's made in my parents' marriage.

"Congrats, babe," Brayden says, leaning in for a kiss.

"That's Dr. Hottie to you," I tell him, smirking.

He laughs. Peyton pets my face. She's a super affectionate kid like that.

"Where's Momma?" I ask her.

"Mom and Dad went with her and Harold outside for some fresh air," Brayden says.

Worry niggles at me. "She okay?"

"Nine months pregnant and wearing heels?" Drew asks. "What do you think?"

"We better bail," I say. "Where are we going for dinner?"

"Your mother had reservations at La Bastille on the river, but…" Dad trails off. "They don't have ice cream."

Weak.

That motherfucker is so weak for his grandkid.

"Looks like we're headed to Holiday Pizza. They have self-serve ice cream and skee-ball machines," I say with a triumphant grin, holding my fist up for Peyton.

She giggles, bumping it, and then squeezes my neck. We all make our way through the crowd. I smile seeing Brayden and Drew holding hands. Because of Brayden's popularity with the NHL, our relationship—that people tried exploiting early on in his career—is no longer a surprise to most people. In fact, we have quite a bit of support. Brayden's been a huge supporter for the LGBTQ community, encouraging his teams to put focus on those non-profit organizations that sometimes get overlooked. Turns out, we're also not the only polyamorous relationship out there, either. We've made friends, here in Chicago, who are like us.

I find Mia sitting on a bench between Harold and Molly. Tim paces, a worried expression on his face.

"What's wrong?" I demand, passing Peyton to Drew so I can squat down in front of my woman. "Go to Daddy, angel." At least now I can get away with calling him Daddy.

"Look at my ankles," Mia whines, kicking off her heel.

I take her foot in my hand and massage the swollen flesh. "Cutest foot I've ever seen."

"Suck-up," she teases, rubbing her large belly that's about to burst with our son. "You did it, Dr. Carter. Seeing you up on that stage was worth putting heels on for."

I pluck her other shoe off, tossing them both in the grass behind her. "I prefer you barefoot and pregnant. Come on. Fried mushrooms are calling your name, Momma. I'll carry you to the car."

"My hero," she croons, her brown eyes twinkling.

I scoop her up and carry her along the sidewalk toward the parking lot. She buries her face against my neck, sighing happily.

"Did you ever think, when I forced you to be my pretend boyfriend at that party and rescued you from that boy you were going to go home with, that we'd get here?"

"You being carted off by a hot doctor?" I ask, laughing.

"No," she groans. "That you'd have two husbands and a wife."

Not legally of course, but we still did the ceremony and in our hearts, we're one.

"I tried to snag us a couple more husbands," I tease. "Eric and Byron said no, though. Dream killers."

We didn't really invite them into our relationship, but we still like to joke about it. Every now and again, the Millers come to Chicago to spend a weekend catching up with us. They've been good friends to us.

"Ha. Ha," she deadpans. "Hey, Ashy C?"

"Yeah, MiMi?"

"I'm glad I kissed you that night on the couch. When you only liked boys and I hoped like hell you'd like me too."

I squeeze her, pressing a kiss to her head. "Me too, beautiful, me too." I set her to her feet beside Brayden's Denali. "Even though girls have cooties, I made an exception for you."

"I don't have cooties," she sasses.

"How do you explain this?" I ask, poking at her giant stomach.

"Super sperm."

With Peyton, we were trying. Maxton, though, was an oops baby. Mia was on birth control and we still knocked her ass up.

"Whose sperm is the super-est?" I waggle my brows at her.

"And to think they gave this guy his PhD," Drew grumbles, pinching my ass as he passes.

Drew buckles Peyton into her seat. I wink at Mia and help her into the vehicle to sit beside Peyton. Drew sits beside her, his hand settling on her belly. Fucking adorable. I climb up front with Brayden. Once the car starts, he reaches across the console, his fingers threading with mine.

As we sit in traffic, all of our parents trailing in cars behind us, I can't help but pause to enjoy the moment.

My family.

Mine.

Turns out, if you can dream it, you can have it.

And my dreams have always been big.

What can I say?

I'm spoiled. I get what I want.

Now I have everything.

*The End*

*If you enjoyed this duet, make sure you check out the other books by K Webster and Nikki Ash!*

Co-written books by Nikki Ash and K Webster:
authornikkiash.com/co-written-books-by-k-webster-and-nikki-ash

Other books by K Webster and Nikki Ash

K Webster's books:
authorkwebster.com

Nikki Ash's books
www.authornikkiash.com

# K WEBSTER'S ACKNOWLEDGMENTS

A super thank you to Nikki Ash. Thank you for being such a great, caring friend. I've enjoyed writing with you! Love you bunches!

Thank you to my husband. You're my hero. Love you, boo.

A huge thank you to my Krazy for K Webster's Books reader group. You all are insanely supportive, and I can't thank you enough.

A gigantic thank you to those who always help me out behind the scenes. Elizabeth Clinton, Ella Stewart, Misty Walker, Holly Sparks, Jillian Ruize, Gina Behrends, Wendy Rinebold, Ker Dukey, J.D. Hollyfield, Nicole Blanchard, and Nikki Ash—you ladies are my rock!

Misty, thank you for always being there for me no matter what! Love you!

A big thank you to my author friends who have given me your friendship and your support. You have no idea how much that means to me.

Thank you to all of my blogger friends both big and small that go above and beyond to always share my stuff. You all rock! #AllBlogsMatter

Emily A. Lawrence, thank you so much for editing our book. We love ya!!

Thank you, Stacey Blake, for always making my books so pretty! You're an angel and I love you!

Lastly but certainly not least of all, thank you to all of the wonderful readers out there who are willing to hear my story and enjoy my characters like I do. It means the world to me!

# NIKKI ASH'S ACKNOWLEDGEMENTS

Kristi, my favorite part of writing with you is the way you make me feel safe to push the limits and boundaries. Knowing you have my back. Every book we write together stems from our love of books. I'm so thankful for our friendship and for what you teach me as a writer. To Bret and my children, thank you for being my biggest supporters. I couldn't do this without you guys. To the ladies who help make this book amazing: Emily, thank you for taking our words and making sure they're perfect. Stacey, thank you for making them pretty. Andrea, thank you for treating our books like they're your own. And to the readers and bloggers, and especially my Fighters, thank you for reading and reviewing and sharing my books. There are so many books out there, so it means the world to me that you choose to read mine.

# ABOUT K WEBSTER

K Webster is a *USA Today* Bestselling author.  Her titles have claimed many bestseller tags in numerous categories, are translated in multiple languages, and have been adapted into audiobooks.  She lives in "Tornado Alley" with her husband, two children, and her baby dog named Blue. When she's not writing, she's reading, drinking copious amounts of coffee, and researching aliens.

Keep up with K Webster

Facebook: www.facebook.com/authorkwebster

Blog: authorkwebster.wordpress.com

Twitter: twitter.com/KristiWebster

Email: kristi@authorkwebster.com

Goodreads: www.goodreads.com/user/show/10439773-k-webster

Instagram: instagram.com/kristiwebster

# ABOUT NIKKI ASH

Nikki Ash resides in South Florida where she is an English teacher by day and a writer by night. When she's not writing, you can find her with a book in her hand. From the Boxcar Children, to Wuthering Heights, to the latest single parent romance, she has lived and breathed every type of book. While reading and writing are her passions, her two children are her entire world. You can probably find them at a Disney park before you would find them at home on the weekends!

Reading is like breathing in, writing is like breathing out.– Pam Allyn

Contact Nikki Ash

Facebook: facebook.com/authornikkiash

Twitter: twitter.com/authornikkiash

Instagram: instagram.com/authornikkiash

Amazon: amazon.com/author/nikkiash

Website: www.authornikkiash.com

Nikki Ash's reader group:
www.facebook.com/groups/booksbynikkiash

Subscribe to Nikki Ash's newsletter:
bit.ly/NikkiAshNewsletter

www.ingramcontent.com/pod-product-compliance
Lightning Source LLC
Chambersburg PA
CBHW070301310726
48976CB00005B/1513